Mitch hauled c [illegible] again, worked it back and forth in the hope t [illegible] whatever was jamming the contr [illegible] l car, he was pretty sure of tha [illegible] e tail, maybe in the rudder ge [illegible] ter unless he could actually fi [illegible] 450 feet now, and he could se [illegible] g light, along with the first shadow of the coast. [illegible] t the problem, or wasn't the worst problem. The wind had been rising with the dawn, steady out of the southeast, and the airship wanted to turn with it, turn north and west and away from the land. He risked letting go of the elevator again, used both hands on the rudder, and thought it gave a little before the nose dropped too far and he had to grab the elevator wheel again.

"Jerry!" Mitch looked over his shoulder. "I need your help here."

"OK." Jerry stumbled toward him, bracing himself on the chart table and the back of the captain's chair. He looked like hell, Mitch thought, gray-faced and unshaven and determined, and guessed he himself didn't look any better.

"Take the elevator wheel," Mitch said. "Hold it just like this."

"OK," Jerry said again, and braced his hip against the pilot's chair. He took the wheel gingerly, blinked as he assessed the resistance, and then nodded. "OK, I—I think I've got it."

"Keep the bubble in the center," Mitch said. "See there? Just like a level."

Jerry nodded, and Mitch slid out of the chair, took the rudder in both hands. He planted his feet, turned the wheel as hard as he could left and right and left again. It barely moved, maybe an inch or two of play, but he thought as he tried it again that it was moving just a little more. Yes, he was sure of it, it was moving further—if there was something in the gears, maybe this was chewing it up, giving him a little more control. There was a warning twinge in his groin, the old scars pulling, but he ignored it, tried a few short hard turns to the right. Pain blossomed, but he thought the wheel gave just a little more. Yes, this time he was sure it moved, and he turned it back and forth again. There was maybe a twenty-degree arc of movement, and he turned it hard again.

"Mitch, I'm losing it," Jerry said.

Cover illustration by Bob Eggleton and David Niall Wilson
Design by Aaron Rosenberg
ISBN 978-1-951510-52-7
 For information address Crossroad Press at 141 Brayden Dr., Hertford, NC 27944
www.crossroadpress.com

First edition

LOST THINGS

by Melissa Scott & Jo Graham

CROSSROAD PRESS

OTHER BOOKS BY MELISSA SCOTT

The Silence Trilogy

Five-Twelfths

Silence In Solitude

Empress of Earth

Burning Bright

Dreamships

Trouble And Her Friends

Shadow Man

OTHER BOOKS BY JO GRAHAM

Black Ships

Hand of Isis

Stealing Fire

The Ravens of Falkenau

The General's Mistress (upcoming)

DEDICATIONS

For my grandparents
Elma Shoffner Wyrick Edwards (1900-1988)
Lt. Granville Glenn Wyrick Sr. (1895-1940)
Col. Raymond F. Edwards (1890-1982)
with love from Jo, your "angel"

For Great-great-aunt Marion (Lt. Marion L. MacNab)
&
Great-great-uncle Alex (Col. Alexander J. MacNab)
Veterans of both World Wars
With thanks for the books, the sword, and the inspiration
Melissa

The world is full of lost treasures. Some of them are better off not found.

In 1929 archaeologists began draining Lake Nemi looking for a fabulous treasure. What they awakened had been buried for two thousand years. For a very good reason.

Prologue–May, 1929

The bowl of the lake reflected nothing. On bright nights the full moon seemed magnified by the water, as though it had come to rest in the dark pool. That was why the Romans had called Lake Nemi Diana's Mirror.

The sounds of the massive pumps covered any noise it might make, working night and day to drain the lake. It was the most significant archaeological site in a generation – two Roman ships from the reign of Caligula, resting beneath the waters of Lake Nemi in almost pristine condition. But then It knew all about the ships. It had known them for a very long time.

They were ruins in the mud, a few beams exposed as the lake drained. They were gone like the Sanctuary of Diana that had once graced the shore. But She was still here. Far away in the woods the man heard it and stiffened – the faint baying of hounds.

It inhabited this man. It wore him, frail thing though he was, already weakening in Its grasp. They were running, he and the man, his sedentary feet made fleet by fear. They were running through the woods while briars grabbed at them, while moonlight mistook their path before them. The hounds were louder. They were coming. The hunters were behind. They could see the flashes of their strange torches, incandescent in the darkness, silver against the trees. A white hound led the pack, sharp nosed and keen, the others following her. It was She who led.

The man's breathing was harsh. They were being driven. Out of the trees, out of the wild wood. Now there were shouts behind, calls from one hunter to another in strange, bastard Latin. The hunters had seen them. The ground was muddy and they slipped. This man was no hunter, no soldier, and he had been run hard. He slipped and slid down the bank, one leg catching beneath him, knee twisting. He was down. The white hound crested the bank, beautiful and implacable.

And then She was not there. It was two brown ones, bloodhounds, the man thought, and they stopped and set up a cry. It was only a moment before the hunters came up. Silver lights played over their face, and they cringed, It and this man, hiding from the brightness.

"Poor soul," one of the hunters said, sliding down the bank. "It's Signore Gadda all right."

They wore blue uniforms, all the hunters. A second one climbed down, lifted this man's hands from his face. "Signore Gadda? Can you understand me, sir? Do you know what has happened?"

This man would reply, but It would not let him. It could see the white hound behind the hunter, and It screamed.

The first hunter spoke again. "I thought we'd never find him. His wife is frantic. God help him." He moved his hand across his chest, as though making some sign of warding.

Another man climbed down, a tall man in middle age, wearing black rather than the blue uniforms, and the second hunter spoke to him. "Signore Davenport, it is definitely your man. But I do not think he understands a word."

"It is a terrible tragedy," Davenport said, and he leaned over them. This man knew him. This was his leader, his patron. He was afraid he would lose his job. But he could not speak. "Vittorio? Can you hear me?"

It screamed. There was the smell of incense on this one. He reeked of Her.

"We should take him to the hospital in Rome," one of the hunters said. "I will send a man to tell his wife that we have found him but that he is very ill."

"Yes, definitely the hospital," Davenport said. "Vittorio...."

The hunters hauled them to their feet, dragging them from the wood, from the ships, from the wild, but It did not resist. To Rome. That had potential.

One of the hunters shook his head to the other. "What makes a man do this? Suddenly go mad and dash into the woods to live like an animal?"

“Perhaps they can help him at the hospital,” Davenport said. “Some kind of seizure or stroke, I do not know.” He looked at this man again, his face a study in concern. “Perhaps he will know his wife when she comes.”

“To Rome,” they whispered. “To Rome.”

Chapter One

Five thousand miles away, Lewis Segura jerked awake. Not a dream of barbed wire and trenches this time, or even the sickening lurch a plane makes when it stalls, the nose beginning to dip down. It had been worse than that, weirder than that. There had been a lake, and things like snakes, like giant eels, moving through the depths, screams underwater that wakened echoes where there couldn't be any; a dark wood, and shapes within it, and at the last a white hound appeared between trees, waiting for him, her head raised, her eyes as blue as the summer sky. His heart rang with familiar certainty: this was coming, this was true.

He sat up, craning his neck to see the clock on the table. Not even midnight. Alma slept next to him, burrowed into her nest of blankets, the pale sheen of her blond hair against the darkness. Her breathing was even and steady. Whatever had wakened him hadn't bothered her, and heaven knew Alma had her own ghosts.

He hugged his knees to his chest, hoping Alma would wake. He'd always dreamed like this, even before the war, but since then—since then there had been more nightmares, tinged with smoke and the sound of guns, but the true dreams had remained, clear and distinct. If this was one of them—well, it was a warning, surely?

He closed his eyes, trying to make sense of the sequence of images, of the struggle under the water, the serpent twining around a drowning man, rings of flesh and scale like a hundred clutching hands. And then there had been the screams, silent and mindless and horrible, bubbling with icy water. He'd run toward the woods like a man pursued until he'd checked, seeing the white dog. And behind her.... Behind her stood three women, caught in moonlight, one with a bow strung and ready in her hand, another with a poppy as scarlet as fresh blood, the thin petals resting gently against her white-robed shoulder. Between them stood a third woman, hands upturned, a veil covering her hair. They were all the same, he realized, the same fine-boned face, serene and stern at the same time; their eyes were blue, implacable. In the water behind him something roiled beneath the surface, and the dog bared teeth in a silent snarl.

He crossed himself like a child, but the images were still vivid, the silent women, the snarling dog, the thing beneath the water and the thrashing terror.

Lewis took a deep breath, trying to put the emotion behind him. If it was a true dream, a warning, what did it actually mean? Stay away from water? The closest lake was a good five miles away, and he didn't swim anyway. Beware a white dog? No, the dog had been hunting the thing in the water, the same as the women. They hadn't been interested in him, just the lake and its secret. Bow and poppy and veil, three identical women, or one woman seen three times.... He couldn't make sense of it, and the fear was still heavy in his gut.

Alma was still asleep, her back to him, curled around her pillow. He thought for a second about nudging her awake and pretending he'd done it by mistake, but she'd had a busy day, taking a charter to Grand Junction and back. It wasn't a long flight, but it meant threading the passes, and for a guy who didn't like letting a woman fly him even when she did own the company. Lewis didn't want to wake her.

Instead he turned over carefully, listening to the faint strains of the radio coming up from downstairs. Jerry was awake, or maybe it was Mitch. Jerry had lived there for years, maybe since the operation that had taken part of his right leg after the war, and Mitch lived over the garage until he could get a place of his own, which Lewis figured would happen about the same time that Jerry went back to teaching, which was to say never. But his bosses' living arrangements were none of his business, especially since Mitch was part owner in Gilchrist Aviation and he was just a hired pilot. Even if he shared Alma's bed.

Lewis turned over. Alma's soft breathing was slow and soothing. Sometimes the dreams were all right, like the one that had led him to Alma. It had been a good dream, too: a plane that he'd never flown, shaped like one of the Stahltaubes he'd seen before the War, but every bit as maneuverable as the bird it mimicked, so that he had swirled and spun, not in defense but in sheer joy of flight. Below him stretched Long Beach, the airfield and its lines of planes, the crowd with their heads tipped back to see him dance.

The flare had gone up to call him in, and he'd taken the plane up toward the cloud deck, which made no sense in retrospect, but at the time had seemed the most reasonable thing in the world. He'd risen through the clouds into sunlight and blue sky and a sweet green runway stretching straight and clear before him, the windsock barely twitching on its stake beside a hangar like a young cathedral. He'd brought the bird-plane down, felt wheels kiss the sod, brought it gently to a stop beside the hangar, and a fair woman in a blue dress turned away from a scarlet biplane. It was for him, he thought, his plane, his freedom, and the woman smiled. Our Lady, the Queen of Heaven, and he'd awakened with the joy still sounding in his bones.

At the time he'd been out of work three weeks and was starting to think he knew how a dope fiend felt when he couldn't get his fix. He still might not have gone to the airshow except that at the Legion meeting Frankie Onslow had said that he'd heard that a guy named Peters, who belonged to a Post up-state, had a crop-dusting service and might be looking for a pilot. The combination of the news and the dream seemed to be telling him something, so he'd taken a couple of dollars from his last pay packet and ridden the trolley out to the show.

Of course, Peters hadn't been hiring, but he'd mentioned a man named Stalkey who'd taken Lewis's name and the phone number of the boarding house, and mentioned another guy named Wiggins. Wiggins was equally non-committal, but said he'd heard that Jeff Forrest had a new mail contract, and wrote the name and hangar number on a scrap of paper.

"But he's got a couple of planes in the stunt show," Wiggins said. "I wouldn't go over there till after."

That made good sense, and anyway Lewis was hungry by

then, and his feet were getting sore, so he found himself a spot in the grandstand to unwrap his sandwiches. Bologna wasn't his favorite, but it was cheap and ok with a lot of mustard. He ate both of them and folded the waxed paper into a triangle, watching the stunt plane swirl and dive. With the right plane he could do pretty much everything he was seeing. He could do better than most of the pilots—if it were a combat situation, he could take them all.

That way lay danger. He fished in his pocket for a nickel instead, bought a Coke, and climbed out of the stands to watch the rest of the show. The white Jenny just finishing its loop was Forrest's, and if that was his best pilot, Lewis figured he stood a chance at any jobs that were going.

He wouldn't go over there yet, though, would wait until the crowds cleared out a little. He shaded his eyes, squinting, found the next plane as it dropped down out of the high blue, lining up on the runway. The loudspeaker crackled, the whine of the plane's engine already swallowing the words.

"—Al Gilchrist—Cherry—"

Weird name for a plane, Lewis thought. A girlfriend, maybe? It dropped lower, another Jenny, coming in low and tight. It was cherry red, red as lipstick, red as the plane in his dream—it was the plane in his dream, every detail just as he'd seen it, down to the blue and white roundel on its tail. As it passed the first pylon, it rolled, wings tipping up and over, kept rolling, maintaining height, maintaining a perfect line as it rotated around its own center, around the pilot himself in his cockpit. Lewis's muscles tensed, feeling in imagination the aileron hard over, the world spinning around him: not the hardest maneuver in the world, but hard to do well. And this was done well. Gilchrist finished the last roll just before the end of the course, snapped level to flash upright past the pylon. The crowd cheered—at least some of them knew what they were seeing—and a stranger in a shabby jacket leaned close to shout something.

"Nice," Lewis shouted back. "Real nice."

The red Jenny was circling back to land, coming in almost sedately. She bounced once, twice, then settled and slowed, trundling toward the hangars. He should follow, he knew. That was what the dream had meant, he was sure of it—maybe Gilchrist needed another pilot, maybe he was hiring—but that was too good to be true. He couldn't rely on dreams when he had real leads to follow up. He pulled the slip of paper out of his pocket instead, checked Forrest's hangar number.

He should have known when he got there that it was a bad idea. Forrest's planes were all white, decked with red and blue stripes like bunting, and the Legion flag hung from the rafters, limp in the heat. A couple of boys in what looked like old uniforms were sitting just inside the door; they pointed him to Forrest, a big man who'd put on his khakis for the occasion.

"Mr. Forrest?" Lewis put on his best smile. "Ham Wiggins said you might be looking for a pilot with military experience."

The big man turned, pushing his doughboy's hat onto the back of his head. "I might be," he said.

"I put in four years regular Army, three of that with the Air Service," Lewis said. "And I've been flying as a civilian ever since I got out."

"Barnstorming," Forrest said.

"Some. I worked a couple of years for a guy who had a mail contract. Then I did some charter work. I've dusted crops, and I've given lessons."

Forrest was starting to look interested in spite of himself. "Huh. What's your name, son?"

"Lewis Segura. Lieutenant—"

But the interest had died. Forrest shook his head. "Sorry. I only hire American."

I am American, damn it. Lewis had been down this road often enough to know there was no point in arguing. "Suit yourself," he said, and turned away. He could feel the boys smirking as he left the hangar, wished he'd kept the Coke bottle so that he could smash it. It wouldn't take much, they'd been too young to have served, despite the cocky uniform—wouldn't even take a gun to kill them – even a broken bottle would do, the jagged edge sharp as any blade. There was no good thinking like that. Lewis kept walking, dust in his mouth and the odor of gasoline and oil filling his lungs. It smelled like France, or like the France he'd known best, the hangars and the rickety houses where the squadrons lived. Where he'd learned to fly, where a dozen friends had died—

He shoved that thought back into the box where it belonged, jammed his hands into his pockets. There would be work, somewhere, even if the barnstorming tours seemed to be dying away. A flash of red caught his eye—Gilchrist's red Jenny, half out of its hangar, the paint seeming even brighter in the sunset light. It was unmistakably the plane he'd dreamed about, and in spite of himself he drew a little closer. It was just to check the design on the tail, he told himself, but the dream-memory had him in its clutches: this plane was for him, was going to take him back to the skies.

The design was exactly what it had been in the dream, too, a circle and cross that looked military, but when you got up close was probably meant to be a stylized compass. There was writing underneath it, too, Ps. 22:16-17, and as he frowned, trying to remember, a woman stepped out of the hangar. She had been in the dream, too, tall, tanned, with bobbed blonde hair held back in a blue kerchief that matched her eyes, and the joy he had felt then crashed over him like a wave. He controlled it sharply, knowing she'd only find it unnerving, blurted out the first thing that came to his lips.

"Are you the mechanic?" He blushed as red as the Jenny.

She smiled, amused and friendly and not at all a dream. "And the pilot, too." She held out her hand. "I'm Al Gilchrist."

She'd needed someone to ferry a new plane back to Gilchrist's base in Colorado, and he'd jumped at the chance. She'd had a run of work then, joking he'd brought her good luck, and after it slacked off she'd offered him a job on salary. And a room in her house until he found someplace permanent, but by then she'd also welcomed him to her bed. That was worth remembering, a dream that had brought him something good. He couldn't convince himself that this latest one would end the same way.

Alma rolled over and propped up on one elbow, her eyes wide open. "Can't sleep?"

Lewis shrugged. "Just edgy. It feels like a Santa Ana, but we don't get those here. Like a change in the wind."

"I know what you mean," Al said. She turned on her side

and drew him in, his head against her shoulder, against the soft warm skin of her upper arm, her hand curling around his back. The music curled up from downstairs, teasing at him, not quite clear enough to hear all the notes but never going away. "Jerry's got that up awful loud," Alma said. "I guess he can't sleep either."

"I don't mind," Lewis said. The music was almost like another touch. It was a strange magic, how radio could reach out across the miles, connecting people who had never seen each other, connecting people listening at the same time, swing and dip, on the wings of sound.

"Ok," Al said. She bent her face to his brow, lips brushing sleepily across his hair. "I don't either."

There was something he'd meant to say, something he'd meant to ask her or maybe tell her about the dream, but it was fading now. He'd tell her about it in the morning, Lewis thought, but the music twined around him like Alma's arms, drawing him down into silence.

Chapter Two

Lewis rinsed out the shaving brush under cold water, and ran his hand over his newly smooth chin. Some guys could do two days between shaves, but not him. By the middle of the afternoon he'd look like he hadn't bothered, something that used to be a point of contention in the Air Corps. "Somebody get that Segura to shave," the CO would say, six hours after he had. Fortunately, most of the time they'd had more things to worry about than the state of his chin. Or maybe that was unfortunately.

He'd managed to get more sleep than he'd expected, and actually felt almost human as he headed down the hall toward the kitchen. He could hear the coffee perking, smelled it and the hot grease in the frying pan. He was kind of hoping it would be Alma at the stove, even if that meant grounds in the coffee and taking over the eggs so nothing burned too badly, but instead it was Jerry, leaning hard on his cane, spatula in the other hand as he stared at the pan: Lewis took a breath and a step, the floorboards creaking underfoot, and Jerry pivoted on the cane and his good leg.

"Oh. Good morning."

"Morning," Lewis said. Jerry's hair was damp, and he had the pinched look that meant he'd been putting up with being handled. Mitch had probably helped him get into the bath before Lewis was awake, which was always kind of a sore subject, even though Jerry and Mitch were old friends.

"Coffee's ready, I think," he said.

Lewis nodded, and went to the cabinet to fetch a cup for each of them. He was careful not to touch the blue-banded lusterware that stood in neat forlorn stacks next to the chipped everyday plates. That had been Gil and Alma's, a wedding present, if he'd put the clues together right, and like the big armchair in the living room, it hadn't been used since Gil died. It was mustard gas that killed him, gas and TB: a bad way to die, and from the few things Al had said, she hadn't been spared any of it.

Jerry had turned the gas under the coffee down to a bare simmer. For a second, Lewis thought he was going to insist on pouring, but then he gave a wry smile, and turned his attention back to the frying pan. The bacon was smoking, Lewis saw without surprise—unlike Alma, Jerry could actually cook, but could rarely be brought to give it his full attention—and Jerry swore and snatched it off the fire.

Lewis controlled the desire to help, and the back door swung open. Mitchell Sorley was tall, good-looking, built like an athlete, the sort who made all-State and maybe all-American; he'd been a junior lieutenant at the start of the war, made Captain by the end, and walked away from the Army anyway. It would have been easy to be jealous, Lewis thought, except the man was basically such a good guy. A good guy with seven confirmed kills....

"So," Mitch said, coming in and putting the newspaper on the table. "What the hell was so important that you got me up early?"

Jerry leaned his cane against the stove and scraped burnt eggs and bacon onto a plate. "You said you were going to be back. I didn't think it would be a problem."

"I was," Mitch said. "And it wasn't. What are you up to, Jerry?"

"I'm not up to anything."

"The hell," Mitch began, and Alma spoke from the hall door.

"Jerry."

"I...." Jerry made a face. "There might be a phone call for me. That's all."

And if that was all, he wouldn't be making a fuss about it. "I'll cook," he said, and Alma gave him a quick smile. It was thanks enough, and he busied himself with the eggs and the slab of bacon, got the pan filled again while Jerry limped back to the table.

"It may not come to anything—he may not even call. I just don't know."

"Is this about Henry's translation?" Alma asked, and Jerry sighed.

"Yes."

"I thought you said you weren't going to take the job," Mitch said.

"He offered me two hundred and fifty dollars," Jerry said.

"Well, Henry's got it," Alma said. "But I thought you said he didn't need you."

"Well, he oughtn't. Not from what he said in his first letter. But—" Jerry added sugar to his coffee, avoiding her eyes. "I told him I had to see the original to do it."

"Oh, for Christ's sake," Mitch began, and the telephone's bell cut him short.

For a second, everyone stood frozen, and then Alma moved, caught the phone out of its niche and lifted the receiver to her ear. "Hillcrest 6-2912. Hi, Maggie. Yes, he's here."

Lewis looked up from the stove, caught a glimpse of an unexpected eagerness on Jerry's face. It was gone in an instant, ruthlessly controlled, and Mitch shook his head.

"This is Henry we're talking about—"

"It's for you," Alma said, and set the telephone in front of Jerry, who shoved his plate out of the way to make room. The cord was stretched tight, so that he had to lean forward a little to reach the stick. "Long distance from Los Angeles."

"Thanks," Jerry said. "This is Ballard."

There was a moment of stillness, the bacon loud in the pan. Jerry had the receiver cupped to his ear, the other hand curled around the candlestick base. His long face was suddenly alive, intent, as though he were listening with his entire being. Behind him, Mitch's face was set in stone, and Lewis wondered what ever made him think the man was easy-going. He looked at Alma, trying to read what was going on, and was startled by her worried frown.

"I need to see the original," Jerry said. "You know that. The difference between a chip in the tablet and a worn letter—it's all in how you look at the object. Well, the original or a good set of photographs—and I mean good photographs, you'll need to get someone who's used to photographing artifacts."

Mitch breathed a curse, and Lewis glanced hastily back at the pan, swung it away just in time to keep the bacon from turning black.

"Then, really, I have to work from the original," Jerry said again. "And if you can't get photos, I'll have to come there."

"Oh, goddammit," Mitch said. Alma waved a hand at him, made shushing noises.

"Yes," Jerry said. "All right. I'll be there tomorrow—noon? Good. Thank you." He set the receiver back on its hook, looked around the kitchen. "So. Would one of you be willing to fly me to Los Angeles today?"

"God damn," Mitch said, more in disbelief than anger. "You're kidding, right?"

"Not at all," Jerry said.

"Jerry," Alma said, but he wouldn't look at her, and added another spoonful of sugar to his already treacle-sweet coffee.

Lewis looked from her to Mitch and back again, and decided to keep his mouth shut.

"What exactly does Henry want?" Alma asked, and this time Jerry darted a glance at her.

"I told you. He wants me to translate the inscription on what sounds like a curse tablet. He doesn't want to give me a transcription, why I don't know—though, really, I do need to see the tablet, you can't be sure of a transcription unless you've done it yourself or you know the person—"

"What's wrong with it?" Alma said.

Jerry grimaced. "I don't know. Maybe nothing."

"Jerry…."

"It may, and I stress may, have some issues of provenance," Jerry said stiffly.

Mitch laughed. "Of course it does."

"Look," Jerry said, and shoved his glasses further up onto his nose. "This is what I do, damn it. All I want is to be in Los Angeles tomorrow for this meeting. I'm willing to pay—"

"Don't you dare say that," Alma said. For the first time, she sounded angry. "We'll fly you there. You've agreed to it, so we're committed. Fine. But don't you dare offer to pay me."

Jerry ducked his head a little. "It's a lot of money, Al. Two hundred fifty."

"Too much," Mitch muttered. He shook his head. "Joey's already said he'd handle the Allen job, and I think that's the only thing on the books. I'll get the Terrier checked out for you, Al, and if I can clear the books, I'll come along. If you don't mind."

"Thanks," Alma said. "If you can't, Lewis can take it."

Mitch looked sideways at him. "Are you sure?"

Lewis scowled, and Alma shook her head. "It'll be fine, Mitch."

"All right." Mitch paused, staring at Jerry as though he wanted to say something else, but then he shrugged, and pushed his way out the back door again.

"We need to pack," Jerry said, and shoved himself to his feet. The kitchen door swung closed behind him.

It didn't take long to pull together underwear and some clean shirts and, after a moment's thought, his one good suit. Lewis was knotting his tie in front of the dresser mirror when he saw Alma appear in the doorway behind him. She'd changed for the flight, slacks and a white shirt buttoned like a man's, her bobbed blonde hair sleek and smooth. She gave him a tentative smile, and, when he smiled back, came to stand behind him. "So," she said. "Are you up for Los Angeles in the Terrier?"

"You checked me out on her yourself," Lewis said. "But if you'd rather Mitch took the job—well, you're the boss."

"It's a long flight, and I'd rather have both of you along," Alma answered. "Mitch—"

She paused, groping for words, and Lewis made himself smile in turn. "Mitch doesn't want me on the flight. And I don't want to be a problem."

"It's nothing to do with you," Alma said. "Not you personally. It's this job of Jerry's he doesn't like."

"You don't sound real happy either."

"I'm not. I've known Henry Kershaw for years, and if he's found something he needs Jerry to look at, when he can afford any expert at the University in Los Angeles—there's probably something fishy somewhere."

"You mean like art theft?" Lewis asked.

"We should be so lucky," Alma said. "Henry—Henry's a big man, and he likes to play around with big things, and sometimes they're even too big for him. I don't want to get involved with any of his schemes. I sincerely hope this is nothing more than a stolen artifact that Henry doesn't think he can get translated through more official channels. It could be. He buys antiquities on the black market sometimes."

"Expensive hobby," Lewis began, and then the name hit him. "Henry Kershaw? The owner of Republic?"

"Yes. That Henry Kershaw." Alma smiled thinly. "Henry knew Gil before the war, and right after the war Gil did some test piloting for him." Before he was too sick. The words hung in the air between them.

"He's a big fish," Lewis said. Republic was one of the largest aviation companies in the country; they had a dozen mail routes and a regular passenger service. Republic also built planes—the Terrier was a Kershaw design—and just this month they were supposed to launch a zeppelin-style airship built for the New York to Paris route. Henry Kershaw was smart and lucky and rich, one of the few men who'd managed to make millions off airplanes.

"I hope it's just that he's got something stolen from the Vatican Museum or something," Alma said. "I hope." She pursed her lips.

"Ok," Lewis said. There was something wrong here, something more than met the eye. After all, they didn't know the thing was stolen, and even if it was, it was hardly their fault. Lewis met her eyes in the mirror. "What's going on around here? Something's not normal."

Alma smiled ruefully. "Does it have to be?"

"No." To his own surprise, he meant that. "What's normal, anyway?"

"That depends on where you're standing."

"I'm trying to stand with you," Lewis said. That was a little too honest, and he winced. He hadn't meant to be. They hadn't said things like that, not even in passion. Too soon for both of them, he thought. Gil had only been dead two years, and Victoria.... Victoria was another story.

Alma lifted her head, her expression oddly naked. "Lewis."

"I'm sorry," he said in turn. "This isn't the time."

"It's just that it's complicated," Alma said. "And I'm not sure you'll believe me. Or that you won't be frightened."

"I'm not that easy to scare," he said, and managed a smile.

"You know, I did survive the Western Front."

To his relief, she smiled back. "I know. And I promise I'll tell you. But it's a long story, and we have to take Jerry to Los Angeles. That's going to take all day."

He nodded, turned his attention to finishing his tie. Alma came closer, rested her chin on his shoulder. It was different being with a woman tall enough to do that, but Lewis had decided he liked it. Lewis tucked the ends of his tie between the buttons of his shirt and turned to face her, his hands going to her waist. "Everything feels wrong today. I had a really weird dream last night."

Alma waited, warm and solid under his touch, and the words spilled out of him, the water and the creature and the dog in the woods, and the women who waited with it. "Three of her. Three identical women, or the same one three times, all in white. One was carrying a bow, and one had a poppy, and the third one had a long scarf over her hair." Alma was frowning, and he shook his head. "In Flanders' fields the poppies grow.... I don't know."

"All the same age?" Alma asked, and he blinked. "Not different ages?"

"All the same age," Lewis said. "Like in a three-way mirror at a tailor's shop, you know, the ones so you can see how the suit looks from the back, but if you stand right in front you see yourself three times? Like that. Only one had a bow, and one had a poppy, and the third one a veil—"

"The middle one?"

"Yes." Lewis frowned. There was something about Alma in that moment that reminded him of the dream-women, for all that they had been a decade younger, and more beautiful than she had ever been, a keenness, an intensity in her gaze. "Why?"

"Let me show you something." Alma pulled away, crossing the hall to her bedroom, and he trailed behind.

Her room was cool and quiet, the bed neatly made, or at least the covers were pulled up decently to the pillows. Her suitcase stood ready, closed and latched at the foot of the bed. Alma opened the top drawer of the chest, releasing a whiff of verbena. Two pairs of rolled silk stockings, a couple of big men's handkerchiefs that must have been Gil's, and an old striped blue tie.

Some boxes, one of them the blue velvet box that assuredly had held Alma's wedding ring. But that was the one she picked up, and turned to face him.

"Like this?" She lifted the lid.

Propped up on the oyster satin was a gold coin about the size of a silver dollar, but there the resemblance stopped. Instead of walking Liberty there were three figures, three young women together, the lines of their dresses blurred but still present, the craftsmanship true over the centuries. The surface was worn, but nothing could hide its beauty, or the symbols in the women's hands. One held a bow, another a poppy, and the third looked straight ahead, her hair covered by a veil.

"Like that," Lewis said, swallowing. He reached a tentative finger toward it. "May I?"

"Of course."

He lifted it out, feeling its heft. Solid gold. It was old. Very, very old. And magnificent still. "What is it? Where did you get it?" And why did I dream about it, about them? But that was a question he couldn't ask, not even of Alma. It required too many explanations, begged too many more questions that he couldn't answer.

"It's a denarius minted in Rome in 43 BC," Alma said. She kept her eyes fixed on the coin. "Gil found it during the war and brought it home. The image is a commemoration of the shrine at Aricia to Diana Nemorensis."

Lewis touched the woman on the left, the one with the bow, trying to remember the stories. "Diana. That's the huntress."

"That's one of her aspects," Alma said. She took the coin, replaced it in its box, then, after a moment's hesitation, slipped the box into her pocket. "We'll talk more, I promise. But—"

Lewis nodded. "Los Angeles."

He rode down to the field in the back of Alma's Ford, crammed in with the suitcases, their corners jabbing him on the turns, and he was glad when they pulled to a stop beside the Gilchrist hangar. The big doors were already open, the Terrier drawn out into the sun, Mitch on a ladder under the port wing fiddling with one of the cylinders of the radial engines.

"Everything Ok?" Alma called, pulling past him into the hangar. Mitch lifted a hand in answer, and she hauled up on the parking brake and shut off the engine.

"Just checking the magneto." Mitch brought the ladder back into the hangar, leaned it against the wall. "I talked to Joey, and he said he'd take care of the Allens and anything else that comes up while we're gone."

Lewis turned his attention to the luggage. Out of the corner of his eye, he could see Jerry hauling himself out of the front seat, the wooden leg slipping on the grass, but he knew better than to offer to help. Instead, he carried the bags out to the plane, Alma's pretty blue case and his own battered satchel, Mitch's plain brown suitcase with his initials in brass beside the handle and patches where he'd scraped the stickers off after each trip. Jerry's suitcase had the faded remains of a dozen steamer tags, and frayed stitching in one corner. It was as heavy as if he'd stuffed it with rocks, and Lewis gave him an annoyed glance.

"What's in here, cement?"

"Books." Jerry was carefully, even elegantly dressed, his neat blue suit perfectly pressed, scarlet tie in an impeccable Windsor knot, his hat brushed, the brim curled just so. Lewis's smart answer died unspoken. Alma heard, though, and glanced over.

"Jerry, are you sure you need all of that?"

"Of course I'm sure," Jerry said. "There are references I'm going to want that I know Henry won't have."

"I heard there were some pretty good libraries in California," Mitch said, dropping down off the ladder.

"Apparently Henry's not talking to the DeChance people these days," Jerry said.

Lewis tugged open the Terrier's rear hatch. It was a compromise of a machine, designed to carry mail or passengers or both, but as compromises went, it was pretty elegant. The rear bulkhead could be moved, offering seating for six at its furthest extent, or it could be shifted forward, and the space filled with mail bags or other cargo. Or a spare fuel tank, he remembered, but there was no need for that on this run. Nets and straps lay ready; he secured the suitcases, Jerry's in the center, along the plane's midline, and backed out of the tail, latching the hatch behind him. The others were standing at the base of the Terrier's stairs, but as he approached, Jerry tucked his cane under his arm and began dragging himself up the metal steps.

"The weather's supposed to be good all the way," Alma said briskly. "We'll have high clouds to start, then clearing toward the coast."

"Ok." Lewis couldn't help looking at Mitch. He'd thought the Terrier was Mitch's baby. The other man shrugged. "I thought you might like to ride shotgun, at least the first leg."

"Yeah," Lewis said. "Thanks."

Alma smiled, and in spite of all the weirdness and undercurrents, Lewis felt his spirits lift. "I figure we'll refuel at Gray and then Las Vegas, and that should get us into Grand Central around seven-thirty or so. It shouldn't quite be dark, and they're set up for night landings anyway."

"Ok," Lewis said again. He glanced automatically at the sky, the thin high clouds, and the pale blue between. "We might get a bit of a headwind there at the end."

Alma nodded. "That's why I thought we'd stop in Las Vegas, which should give us a decent cushion."

"Be a good time for those supplemental tanks Gil was talking about," Mitch said. "Did Jerry tell you where Henry's put him?"

Alma gave him a wary look. "No."

"The Roosevelt," Mitch said. "Henry's paying for him, mind you, but not us."

"That's Henry all over," Alma said. "Well, we'll just have to hope there are some cheap rooms—"

"I've stayed there," Mitch said. "We can pretty much afford one room. And one of us ought to share with Jerry anyway."

"Well," Alma said. For the first time since he'd known her, Lewis thought she looked a little flustered.

"Look," Mitch said, with a fair assumption of man-of-the-world insouciance. "It's Mrs. Ballard or Mrs. Segura, Al. I know which one I'd rather be."

"Thanks a lot," Lewis said.

Alma smiled at that, her expression lightening. "Of the choices, I'd rather be Mrs. Segura. But, Lewis, this is a company expense—"

"No, no, I'll pay—" Lewis stopped, embarrassed. Alma's cheeks were pink, but she managed to breathe a laugh.

"You pay, and I'll pay you back half. It's only fair."

"And I get to be Mrs. Ballard," Mitch said, with a grin that didn't quite reach his eyes. "Ready, Al?"

"Whenever you are," Alma said, and swung herself aboard.

Chapter Three

Mitch had left the cabin set for four, two pairs of wicker basket seats screwed to the decking facing each other, and a reasonably generous aisle between them leading to the cockpit. Jerry had already settled himself into a back seat so he could face forward, and he'd pulled up the varnished folding table, too, sat with his leg outstretched and book in hand, a cigarette tucked in the corner of his mouth. Mitch grabbed the cushions from an empty chair and dropped them into the seat across the aisle from Jerry. There was a picnic basket and a thermos in the seat facing him, and Alma gave him a nod.

"Good thinking."

"There's not much at Gray," Mitch answered. "And it's a long way to Las Vegas."

"Yep," Alma said, and tugged open the cockpit door. She folded it back, latching it open, and took her place in the pilot's seat. Lewis joined her, fastening his belts, and followed her instructions to get the engines started. There was no tower here, and not much traffic, and Alma advanced the throttle, easing the big plane out onto the grassy strip.

"Clear," Lewis said, raising his voice to be heard over the engines, and Alma nodded. The windsock at the end of the field was nearly motionless; she kicked the rudder, adjusting their line, and opened the throttle. The Terrier rumbled forward, tail popping up almost at once, the three engines howling, and even as Lewis felt the plane go light, Alma hauled back on the yoke, lifting the Terrier into the air. It rose smoothly, delicate for such a big bird, and Lewis could feel his own fingers tingling just a little, anticipating the plane's motion.

She leveled out at 8500 feet, and put the plane into a gentle turn, straightening once the sun was at their backs. Mitch had filled in a flight plan, Lewis saw, even though he and Al had made this trip a hundred times. He collected the clipboard, glancing at the flimsy with the weather report, and folded it back to check the landmarks. A long day, he thought, but not a bad one, as long as the weather held. And there was a lot to learn about the Terrier.

They'd been flying for just over two hours when Alma leaned across, raising her voice to be heard over the engines. "Want to take her for a bit?"

"Sure," Lewis shouted back, and there was the usual shuffle while they swapped control. He concentrated on getting the feel of yoke and rudder, keeping everything steady, making sure he had a sense of how the machine would react before he tried a couple of smooth, gentle turns. He'd only flown a trimotor a handful of times before, and most of that had been in Fords. The Terrier was smaller, lighter, with what felt like just as much power at his fingertips. That made it tricksy, for a big plane, the same barely-leashed feeling he'd had with the rotary engine fighters, the sense that one wrong move would flip the machine out of his control.

"She's not as touchy as you think," Alma shouted, and he gave her a wry smile. He supposed he should resent that he was learning from her and not from Mitch—that he was working for her even while he shared her bed—but the time for that had passed a long time ago. Victoria would have hated teaching him anything, needed him to be all-knowing, always in charge, and at the same time she'd seemed angry when he did try to manage things for her. Splitting with her was probably the smartest thing he'd ever done.

Alma took the controls back for the descent into Gray, and he watched the way she handled the landing, impressed once again by her strength. The Terrier pulled like a bigger plane, but she kept it neatly in line, and brought it to an easy stop on the edge of the tarmac. They all climbed out to stretch and grab a smoke, even Jerry, while Mitch paid for the gas and supervised the lanky kid who drove the fuel truck. There wasn't much at the field, just hangars and an office and the fuel trucks, but Alma walked across to check the latest weather reports, and came back with a shrug and a smile.

"No change. Want to take this leg, Lewis?"

He hesitated, wanting to say yes. It wasn't just that she was beautiful—and she wasn't, really, not like a movie star, anyway. She was certainly pretty, even in the mannish slacks and the camp shirt that showed the sweat under her armpits, but it wasn't just her looks that made him want to show off. It was the competence, the strength and the strong common sense, too, and that was what made him shake his head. Screwing up was not going to impress her. "I'm not ready to land her, not in Vegas," he said.

Alma smiled then, tapped his shoulder lightly, as much affection as she ever showed in public. "Fair enough. How about you get us mostly there, and Mitch or I will take the landing?"

"I'd like that," Lewis said. The fuel truck pulled slowly away, gears grinding, and Mitch came around the tail to join them.

"You want me to take this leg, Al?"

"Lewis'll do it," Alma answered. "And you can take us into Grand Central."

Mitch's nod was absurdly gratifying. "Ok. Want a sandwich before we take off?"

Alma glanced at her watch. "I'll eat in the cockpit. We'll be cutting it a little close at the end anyway."

Lewis ground out the last of his cigarette, and climbed into the plane. Alma had already taken the co-pilot's seat, was fastening her belts. Lewis settled himself into the pilot's seat, and began running down the checklists again. Mitch appeared in the cockpit door, handed a pair of sandwiches over Alma's shoulder, and disappeared again. Lewis thumbed the ignition switches one after the other, and the engines rumbled to life, propellers blurring to invisibility. He taxied slowly onto the runway, scanning the sky for traffic, then checked the windsock a final time and opened the throttle. The Terrier lurched forward, not as smoothly as under Alma's hands, but then he felt the tail lift, the plane steadying under his touch. The airspeed was good; he tugged the yoke back, and the Terrier rose sluggishly, then faster, rising into the wind. Lewis grinned—there was nothing in the world like flying—and banked to settle the Terrier on course before beginning the climb to cruising altitude.

The weather was still good, the few wisps of cloud below him barely thick enough to obscure the ground. There was nothing to do but hold the Terrier steady, learn the feel of her in his hands and feet. After a while, Alma poked him, held out a sandwich wrapped in waxed paper.

"I'll take her for a bit, if you're hungry."

He was, he realized, and nodded. "Thanks."

He wolfed the ham and cheese, feeling how Alma's touch differed on the controls, then took over again. The landmarks unreeled below them: highways, a river, a big white building in the middle of a green field. Mitch came forward with the thermos, and they shared a cup of the coffee, thick and sweet, before Alma took the controls back and began the descent to Las Vegas. It was an impressive sight, Lewis thought, an unexpected splotch of green in the middle of the desert. The field was well on the outskirts, though, and Alma brought them down in a swirl of dust, bouncing across the concrete in the sudden crosswind. The controller waved his flags, signaling them to get off the runway, and Alma brought the Terrier to a gentle stop between two hangars. She'd left plenty of room for the fuel truck, Lewis saw, peeling himself out of the pilot's chair.

The heat was like a blow. Lewis checked in the doorway, and Mitch squinted up at him from the shade of the wing. "Lovely, huh? Let's hope we can get fueled up quick and get out of here."

He had to raise his voice to be heard over the sound of a biplane revving its engine, and another plane was circling the field, waiting for the controller to wave it down. Lewis made a face. At this rate, they'd be on the ground at least an hour, and the cabin was going to be an oven.

Alma handled the refueling this time, and somehow charmed the fuel truck operator into servicing them first, but even so it was almost forty minutes before they could get the engines started again. Being a passenger was something to be endured, even when he trusted the other pilot. He stretched out in the wicker seat, trying not to pay attention to every shift and jostle as the Terrier made its way onto the runway. He could see the flagman as Mitch turned for take-off, the go-flag held up and out, and then the engines picked up speed and the Terrier rumbled forward. He felt the tail lift, and then the ride evened out as the plane left the ground. He glanced out the window, watching the ground drop away, then made himself slump further in his chair and close his eyes. Might as well try to rest, he told himself, and didn't expect to manage it.

He drifted off to sleep after a bit, an uneasy doze that broke every time the Terrier dropped a few feet. The air was choppier now, probably because they were over the Sierras, but he refused to look. He hadn't been a passenger since—well, since right after the War, and he'd realized right away that it was a bad idea. That was the end of 1918, or maybe the beginning of 1919, and the details were a blur, just the panic remaining. He turned his mind firmly away, shifted to a more comfortable position against the thin cushions. He must remember to tell Alma to replace them before they carried passengers, he thought, and drifted off again.

He dreamed he was back in France, back in the air, crouched in the back cockpit of the Salmson 2 as they circled over the German lines. He knew what was coming, and he pounded on the fuselage behind Robbie's cockpit, trying to get his attention, banging and pointing to the gun the size of a house that was slowly, inexorably lining up on them. They were so low he could see the Germans frantically turning their aiming wheels, could see the blue-striped shell that they were manhandling into the breech. Machine gunners had seen them, too, were standing up in their holes to fire at them. He tried to return fire, but he couldn't depress the Lewis gun far enough, and wasted ammunition firing at nothing. And still Robbie flew slowly on, while the giant gun tracked them, mouth open to swallow them—

He jerked awake, aware in an instant of his surroundings, and that the Terrier was steady in flight. The light had changed: they were chasing the sun now, flying into evening, and he glanced surreptitiously at Jerry, hoping he hadn't noticed. The other man seemed to be drowsing, too, his book face down on the fold-out table, and Lewis leaned back again. The sound of the engines was like a drug, dragging him back into sleep.

This time, he was back in the shattered wood behind the German lines. It was probably the only scrap of unshelled land for miles, barely enough to land in, surrounded by trees that had been blasted in some earlier offensive. A few of them were starting to send up green shoots, and a part of him knew that was wrong, just as it was wrong for it to be night, without moon or stars to light his way.

There was something out there, he knew suddenly, something hungry, and he rummaged in the cockpit until he found a signal flare. He lit it, and the stark light cast a sputtering circle around the damaged plane. Robbie was unconscious in the forward cockpit, and he knew he needed to get him out, drag him into the back so that he could fly them home, but the thing that circled outside the light was just waiting for its chance. He drew his revolver with the other hand, put his back against the fuselage, but the thing came around again, so that he turned, gasping, only to see empty air. Something moved at the edge of his vision, a shadow crawling like gas; he flung himself around, revolver ready, but the thing had moved, was behind him again.

And then a dog barked, high and distant, and then another and another, baying now like hounds in a pack. The moon broke through the clouds, and he snapped awake, gasping for breath.

Jerry looked at him, one hand in his pocket. "You all right?"

"Yeah." Lewis shook himself, shaking away the residue of the dream. It was just a nightmare, nothing to do with the other dreams. It was just a lesson: never fall asleep while flying. "Yeah, I'm fine."

Mitch brought the Terrier into Grand Central in the thickening dusk, just before the moment where the tower might have waved them off while they got the field lighted up. They taxied up to the brand new terminal, stucco so white it almost seemed to glow, tower jutting against the purple sky, and Mitch insisted on unloading them before he took the plane to the rented hangar space. Alma wasn't sorry to have the chance to freshen up—a movie star could arrive at the Roosevelt grubby and sweating, but not an ordinary mortal—and she wasn't surprised to find that the Ladies' Lounge had a dressing room. She left Jerry and Lewis at the coffee shop and lugged her suitcase up to the second floor. The attendant didn't seem surprised to see her, just shuffled off and came back with a damp washcloth and a towel that actually looked as though it would do some good. Alma washed her face and hands gratefully, and ran her wrists under the cold water until she felt almost human again.

The attendant pointed her to a changing room, and she dug her blue frock out of the suitcase and stripped out of shirt and pants. She stood for a moment in her bare feet and combinations, savoring the cooling air, then hastily pulled on stockings and pumps and slid the dress over her head. The matching cloche was dented; she pressed it out, and settled it to hide her untidy hair. Powder was pointless, with her complexion. Instead, she craned to see that her seams were straight, then clicked the suitcase closed, left a nickel in the attendant's dish, and headed back down to the main lobby.

The men were waiting for her under one of the arches that gave onto the field, where the lights were strongest. Jerry tipped his hat at her approach, and Lewis put his hand to his cap in something like a salute, his glance appreciative. Mitch lifted his hat as well, set it onto the back of his head. He had his jacket over his arm

"We got lucky, Al. Nomie Jones is still running the rentals here."

That was good news on all counts—Nomie had served with Gil, gave them a break on the hangar fee—and Alma nodded. "That's good news." There was an orchestra tuning somewhere, she realized, looked up the stairs to see lights and movement, and shook her head as she realized there was a restaurant there, apparently with a dance floor.

Lewis grinned. "Feels too much like work, doesn't it?"

Alma nodded, and Jerry laughed. "Oh, come now, don't you know this is where you go to see the stars? The ones who fly, anyway."

"It's still too much like work," Alma answered.

Chapter Four

Mitch leaned back against the pillows and closed his eyes, while Jerry hunted around. He'd long since learned to tune out things that didn't concern him, and Jerry's search through his reference books was out of his league. Mitch was pretty cheerful about that. He'd never had any pretensions to academic brilliance.

Yes, he had a degree, and he'd earned it, but it was more the result of concerted effort than natural talent, a lot like some other things in his life. Mitch had learned a long time ago that everybody gets one good, golden talent if they're lucky, to make of what they can. All the rest of life is hard work.

His talent was airplanes. The first day he'd been up he'd understood what to do, felt it all suddenly make sense in a way that nothing else before ever had. This was it. This was the thing, the beautiful thing that Mitchell Sorley was born to do. No more kind of sort of getting it, trudging along in the middle of the pack laboring to do what others did with rare grace. In the air he was reborn.

Gil had seen it. Lt. Colonel Gilchrist had given him the chance to shine.

Gil was pretty much the epitome of everything he was supposed to be, cool, laconic, and remorseless, meaning without remorse. You got the feeling there wasn't anything that could throw him, anything that could possibly be bad enough to ruffle his feathers, much less break him. Nerves of steel, some guys said, but Mitch thought it was more like no nerves. It was less like a guy who reaches into a fire out of courage and more like the wounded with nerve damage who'll touch something burning and never know it.

They'd just been transferred to Aviano in Northern Italy, the 24 planes in the squadron, to back up the ground war against the Austrian offensive around Venice, when he'd seen the picture, a slightly crumpled formal portrait of a woman with long dark hair, a secret smile and the high collared shirtwaist of a decade ago. He'd asked the exec, Browning, if she was Gil's wife. Browning had been there from the beginning, since they were back in the States, and he gave Mitch a hard look. "She's dead," he said shortly. "Her and the baby both. Leave it alone."

He had, of course. He'd never said a word to Gil about it. But he filed it away, the thing that made Gil cold in the air, taking the kind of chances man and machine couldn't bear. The French called it sang froid. Mitch thought it was more like not caring. Gil had picked Mitch up when he'd had to ditch, and Mitch had his tail the first time things went pear-shaped over the Piave River.

And then there was Alma. She was an ambulance driver with the corps, an Army brat who'd grown up at various posts all over the west, the motherless daughter of an Army Sergeant whose benign neglect had translated into remarkably checkered experiences. She spoke a little Navajo and a great deal of Spanish, knew how to break a horse and set a leg, could find her way with nothing but a compass and the stars, and was utterly and completely confounded by the niceties of behavior expected of civilized women. Mitch thought her father had done her no favors, not that he would have said it. There wasn't much a decent young woman could do that she was fit for.

His own mother would have been dumbfounded and then felt terribly sorry for her. But then his mother was used to getting food on the table three times a day for ten people, baking two pies a day for dinner and breakfast, curing cheese and pickling a hundred quarts of vegetables every summer. She'd sent four boys off to college to better themselves, and all of them had. Mitchell was the oldest, Trinity College class of 1915. Well, he supposed it was called Duke University now, but it had still been Trinity when he'd graduated. He'd gone straight into service, charging off to France as soon as he had the sheepskin in his hand. Frank was class of '18, and he was a surgeon now. Charles was class of '19, and he was a minister. Howard was the baby, class of '24, and he'd just finished law school and gone home to Winston-Salem to set out his shingle. And Grace and Evelyn were both married. There were ten grandchildren between them all, and Mitchell the only one not settled down.

The bed gave as Jerry manhandled the case of books onto it, and Mitch opened one eye. Nope. Didn't need help. Just that abstracted look Jerry got when he was thinking hard, his gold framed glasses creeping down his nose.

Jerry had been an artillery officer, a Classicist who never got tired of walking the footsteps of the Caesars, and certainly never shut up about it, not for ten minutes. He'd been with the artillery defending Venice, a rotten job actually. Much more so than providing air cover, though it hadn't been until Vittorio Veneto in October that he'd been wounded, in the same battle as Gil, less than a month before the Armistice. Alma'd probably saved his life, stopping the bleeding, though ultimately she hadn't saved his foot. It had to come off a year later anyhow.

By that time Alma and Gil were married, and so Jerry had come to stay with them. Easier all around for everybody that way.

Jerry plopped himself on the side of the bed. "What do you think of Segura?" he asked.

Mitch opened his eyes. "He's a good pilot," he said cautiously.

"I mean in other senses."

Mitch blew out a long breath. So many minefields there. "I don't really know yet," he said cautiously. "He's strong. I couldn't tell you what kind of mix he has, but he's got some pretty serious power behind it. He's air, which is a good thing. I had a look at his discharge papers. May 25th is his birthday."

Jerry snorted. "You know the solar position isn't definitive."

"Well, unless you want to ask him what time he was born and where, it's what we've got." Mitch looked at him seriously. "You know Alma wants him in."

"I'm reserving judgment," Jerry said. He raised a placating hand. "I'm not saying no."

"I didn't say you were," Mitch said. He hesitated, but it had to be said. "It's not like replacing Gil."

"In any sense?" Jerry's mouth was tight.

"That's Al's business, not ours."

"I'm just saying it will be a problem," Jerry said. "If it turns out that he's not good material. Or if he spooks."

Mitch nodded. There was nothing he could say that wasn't too stark, too cruel.

"Besides," Jerry said, "It's not like it was back during the war and right after. We haven't pushed ourselves in years."

Since Gil stopped pushing, Mitch thought. Since Gil was too sick. Maybe he should push, maybe he should try harder to get Jerry and Al going, to work the boundaries again. It had been dispiriting, a cart with three wheels teetering along out of balance, the absence of Gil a continual wrong note. But there had to be structural things that would fix that, even if Jerry insisted it wasn't proper form. A tripod has three legs and stands.

"Well," Mitch said, "Let's see what Henry's got for us. And hope it doesn't bite."

"It won't," Jerry said grimly. "Not me at any rate."

Lewis lay in the dark of their seventh-floor room, listening to Alma's slow breathing beside him, wondering if she was really asleep, or if she just couldn't bring herself to talk right now. He'd wanted to ask questions, to make love, to celebrate this unexpected holiday, a fancy hotel in Los Angeles and no real obligations. But it had been too awkward, signing the register at the desk downstairs while Alma tried not to look at him. Mr. and Mrs. Lewis Segura, Colorado Springs, Colorado, USA. While Alma tried not to look like she was afraid someone she knew would suddenly pop out of nowhere in the lobby of the Roosevelt Hotel in Los Angeles and say, "My goodness, Alma! When did you and Lewis get married?"

"Just now," she'd have to say, "in Las Vegas." And then they'd really have to. It was easy to get married in Las Vegas. They didn't even require a blood test. Just walk in, say who you were, and nobody would even ask for proof of anything, much less the proof of his divorce from Victoria which wouldn't hold water in half of these United States and put him wrong in the eyes of God forever and ever. It wasn't like he could really marry Alma anyhow, not in the Church.

Maybe that didn't matter to her anyway. He'd asked her once

what she was and she'd laughed and said, "Contrarian." Probably some kind of Protestant, at least on paper. She and Gil had been married by an Army chaplain, a strictly civil service in the army hospital in Venice two days after the Armistice. He'd seen the certificate. Mitch had been one of the witnesses and someone with the unlikely name Iskinder Yonas Negasi had been the other.

But nobody would ask any questions in Vegas. Not that he and Alma were in a marrying place. It was just that saying they were married was much too close, treading too near the edge.

It was awkward. Which was probably why as soon as they'd gotten to their room, Alma had proclaimed she needed a bath. Not that she didn't, it had been a long hot layover in Las Vegas, and the dress shields she'd unpinned from her flying blouse had been nothing but damp little wads. But then there had been a late dinner, hurrying before the dining room closed, and then she'd told him to go ahead and bathe, which he also needed, and by the time he'd come to bed, she'd been curled under the sheets, apparently sound asleep. He listened for a moment longer to her breathing, soft and steady in the dark, settling himself to sleep. It would be better in the morning.

He dreamed he stood in a wood in starlight, a light wind blowing across him, touching his face like cooling breath. He stood beneath trees, but it only took a moment to walk to the edge of the forest and look out, down a long hillside to a lake that whispered opaque like a blackened mirror in the starlight. It should have been frightening, and yet it wasn't.

A white hound paced him, her long nose held high, looking up at him with blue eyes as bright as Alma's. She snuffled at his hand and he bent to pet her, kneeling before her on the thick mat of pine needles, caressing her soft ears. "There, good girl," he said. "There." Her fur was like silk, warm beneath his hand.

She butted his hand, then got up and walked a few paces. She stopped, looking back at him expectantly.

"You want me to follow you?" Lewis asked bemusedly. "Ok. I can do that."

He followed her under the eaves of the woods, through paths cast into deep shadow. Lewis couldn't have said how long he walked or how far, the white hound glimmering like a star ever before him.

There was the sound of chanting, and he was in a room. It was no place he'd ever been before, but it was modern. Though candles were lit, illuminating precious little, there were electric lamps turned off, a chandelier with electric bulbs hanging dark from the ceiling. Four men and four women were there, standing in a circle around empty space, their identical white robes veiling their forms, their bare feet soundless on the thick oriental carpet.

He heard a growl and looked down. The white hound stood beside him, fur standing up on the back of her neck, and her teeth were bared. He looked where she did, at one who drew the eye. He was fifty, perhaps, tall and handsome, with the kind of rugged physique that aged well. He had dark hair threaded with gray, a square jaw, and his movements were purposeful and sharp, gesturing to thin air and speaking words that ought to be familiar but weren't. He almost caught the sense of them, but not quite.

The hound butted his hand again, and her meaning was as clear as if she'd spoken. Look. Look at that one. Know him.

Unerringly, as though Lewis' gaze had touched him, he looked across the circle and met Lewis' eyes, his hand moving in a gesture that was far from random. It hurt. It burned. It was like taking a sudden blow to the chest that shoved him backwards, away from the room, away from the light….

Lewis jerked awake, sitting up before he was even aware what he was doing, the sound of his own breath harsh in his ears. He could still almost feel it, like a blow to the solar plexus….

Alma rolled over and sat up. She was sleeping in her combinations, and a silk teddy in a pale pink that was probably supposed to match her skin, but the deep v at her neck was tanned a lot darker, while beneath the fragile lace trimmed edge her nipples showed through the cloth. "Lewis?"

He didn't trust himself to speak yet, just sat breathing, bending forward over his knees.

Alma leaned against his back, her arm across him. "It's just a bad dream," she said quietly. "Just breathe and let it go."

"Not just a dream," Lewis muttered, scrubbing his hands across his face. "Not this time. It'll happen." He was too thrown to lie. "Sometimes I dream about things that come true."

He felt her stiffen almost imperceptibly against him, but her hand was gentle on his shoulder, kneading the stiff muscle. "Like what?"

"I dreamed about you before I met you. Well, not about you, exactly. About the plane and about the airshow. I knew that if I went something good would happen." Lewis rubbed the heels of his hands against his eyes. "I do it a lot."

Alma took a deep breath, controlled, like she was taking off. "And this was a dream about something bad? Happening to you?"

"I don't know," he said, and told her the dream, his heart slowing to normal as they talked, the quiet dark of the hotel room safe and anonymous around them. "I don't know who that man was," he said. "I've never seen him before in my life. But I will see him, I know that. And he'll try to kill someone." He looked at her sideways, her face pale in the reflected light from the street. "It's ok if you don't believe me, Al."

"I believe you," Alma said slowly. "I believe you completely."

"You don't think I'm crazy?"

"I think you have an untrained clairvoyant gift." Alma squared her shoulders as Lewis blinked. "That's unusual, but not unheard of. I've known a number of clairvoyants. They're more uncommon than more typical energy projection mixes, and for some reason it's less common in men than in women, but some of the best known clairvoyants in history have been men. I wouldn't say you're unique."

"What?" Lewis sat up straight, the sheet pooling around his lap. She looked so awkward, sitting there in her thin teddy, biting down on her lower lip. He couldn't snap at her. Lewis took a deep breath. "Are you some kind of Spiritualist?"

"I tried to tell you," Alma said. "I was trying to. But it's complicated. At first I didn't know you well enough and then...."

"Then you were afraid I wouldn't understand?"

Alma nodded.

Lewis reached for her hands, folded her strong fingers in his. He'd wanted answers, and he couldn't complain now that he was getting them. "Ok. How about you start from the beginning?'

"When I met Gil he was already a member of a lodge, the Aedificatorii Templi. It wasn't an old lodge, but it had a pedigree." Alma looked at him as though wondering if she should continue. "Technically it's an offshoot of the Golden Dawn, founded by people who left the Golden Dawn when there was a horrible schism about twenty five years ago."

"We're talking about a bunch of magicians here," Lewis said slowly. "About black magic."

"No!" Alma looked indignant. "I should hope you know me well enough to know that I'd never be involved in something like that, never! Magic isn't black or white, Lewis. Not any more than a machine gun is, or an airplane. It's a tool that serves its user, just like any other. And what it does, whether that's good or bad, depends on what someone is using it for."

Lewis nodded slowly. "My grandmother could find lost things," he said. "It was a thing she did for people. She said it was a gift from God."

"Exactly like that," Alma said. "There are some people who have these gifts, and it's their responsibility to use them for the good of the world, for the good of humanity. To serve God in whatever form one prefers by serving His creation."

"In whatever form one prefers?"

Alma bit her lip again. "The world is a really big and complicated place, Lewis. Lots of different peoples have tried to find the divine, and have made names for it based on what worked for them in their culture and time. You're Catholic, but do you, personally, really believe that all Presbyterians are going to hell?"

Lewis took a deep breath but didn't look away. "No," he said quietly. "I've known some good people who weren't Catholic. Some really good people. I don't believe they're going to hell."

"My dad used to say that you should judge people by their actions, not by how loud they prayed," Alma said. "I bet you've known some churchgoing people who weren't so good."

Lewis snorted. "Oh yeah."

Alma shifted, the light through the window making a stripe across her shoulder. "So that's all I'm asking, Lewis. Wait and judge us by what we do."

"We." He didn't need to ask. "You and Mitch and Jerry."

"Me and Mitch and Jerry." Alma nodded. "We're what's left of the lodge, of the Aedificatorii Templi. Some of them were killed in the war and some of them moved on. It's just us now."

"Just you." It made sense. Lewis was absolutely certain she wasn't making this up. It fit with the strangeness he'd seen, the odd sense that something was just a little off. He turned her hand over in his gently. "So what do you do?"

Alma let out a long shaking breath. "Not much, lately. So very little. Since Gil died…." She closed her hand around his. "Not much," she said, "in terms of saving the world."

Lewis looked at their linked fingers in the stripe of light across the bed. "Saving the world," he said softly. It was absurd. Kings and dictators and presidents, demagogues and revolutionaries and anarchists with their guns, all lined up around the globe trying to tear humanity apart and against them what? This insignificant woman in her silk teddy? Mitch and his beloved passenger plane? Or Jerry with his missing leg and a doctorate in archeology?

"If we don't," Alma asked softly, "Who will?"

Lewis blinked. It was as though some enormous piece slid into place in silence, echoes deeper than his hearing could bear.

"It's being part of something," Alma said. "Something a lot bigger than we are, vaster than all our lives. We are builders of the Temple, guardians of the world, just like uncounted ones before us and yet to come. It may be that the battles we fight are small in the grand scheme of things, but you know that there's no such thing as an insignificant battle. There's no such thing as a fight that we can afford to lose. You learned that in the war, right? There's no unimportant village."

"Not when it's yours," Lewis said. The picture was there in his head, a cottage on the western front long since evacuated, long since abandoned to war. They'd sheltered there two days once, waiting for the weather to clear enough to get back to the aerodrome. Robbie had laughed because he'd carefully washed all the dishes they'd used, put them away in the cabinet. They'll just get blown up when there's shelling, Robbie said, but Lewis did it anyway. They might not. And someday maybe the people would come home. He was a guest in their house, an ally, maybe a friend. Guests don't leave a mess behind them.

Alma saw the change in his face, even if she didn't know the reason for it. "You do know," she said quietly.

He nodded.

"It would be great to be part of a big movement," she said. "I'd love to have all the bells and whistles, the pomp and circumstance and the beautiful things and everybody's approbation. But we don't have that. It's just us. We do the little things, we mend what we can, shore up the walls. We do what needs doing."

"Like being detached," Lewis said. "When you're sent on a mission with just a few men, and maybe nobody will ever know if you got through or not." His eyes met hers. "But you do it right anyway."

"For honor," Alma said evenly, her eyes on his.

"For God."

"That too." She closed her eyes and squeezed his hand. "I've been worried about telling you this. But I knew I'd have to sooner or later."

Sooner or later if they were serious. Sooner or later if he were someone she could love, not just a way of filling up the empty place in her heart with a hired man who didn't matter. The thought made a tiny trickle of joy swell up inside him.

Lewis swallowed. "So what do you…do? Are you a clairvoyant?"

Alma smiled, and the light in her eyes could have powered Los Angeles. "Me? No. I can't do any of the oracular stuff. I'm a strong ground. I'm not a half bad Hermeticist, but mostly I handle energy. Picking it up, putting it down, and anything that's specifically geophysical." Alma shrugged. "I'm a Taurus. May 17th. Pretty damn typical." Her eyes flicked over his face. "You're a lot more interesting."

"Thanks." He supposed that was a compliment. "And Mitch and Jerry?"

"Mitch is an Aries. He's fire with a lot of earth in his chart. He's a strong foil, a real powerhouse. Jerry's a Cancer, July 5th. Cardinal water. He's got a very fine touch, very good perceptions, a good hand with manipulation. He's our scholar, but I imagine you've guessed that." Alma smiled again.

"Yeah, I could have gotten there," Lewis said. He didn't want to ask it, but he did. "And Gil?"

Her smile faded. "Gil was a Libra. Balance and moderation in all things, or perhaps just being caught between. Stronger than Jerry but more finely focused than Mitch. He was our Magister, our leader."

"And now who is?"

"Nobody." Alma looked down at her lap. "We haven't decided. We haven't needed to."

"Because you weren't doing anything." Lewis nodded. He could see how it shook out. And so it was time to change course. "So what about this translation Jerry's doing? What does it have to do with all this?"

"Henry Kershaw was in the lodge with Gil before the war," she said. "It was a lot bigger then, and a whole bunch of Air Corps types were involved. He moved on to a different lodge later, a richer one that was neutrally focused – interested in exploring magic for its own sake, to expand humanity's knowledge rather than to channel the Work into specific positive directions. Scientific magic in its purest form. Try some things and see what works." Alma snorted. "The problem with that is that sometimes the things you discover aren't always put to good use. It's like chemistry. There are an awful lot of good things that can be done. And then there's the guy who invented mustard gas." Her jaw tightened. "Right now Henry's in a huge lodge here in LA. A lot of dabblers and movie types, people who want to be told they've got a lot of talent or who want to be involved with something forbidden and exciting." She shrugged. "Not that it's bad, but it's not exactly a serious working group. They have beautiful costumes and do reenactments of ancient festivals, Bacchic revels with bathtub gin. I don't have any objection to a few Bacchic revels," she said, a mischievous expression crossing her face, "but a lot of what they're up to is just overpriced parties. It doesn't do any harm, but it's not exactly the Great Work either."

Hollywood swimming pools and Bacchic revels were adding up to something in his head, something that looked a lot like Theda Bara dressed as Cleopatra with all the parts of the movie in that nobody could actually film. Lewis felt a slow blush rising in his face. "Like...what? Public gamahuching?"

Alma turned bright red. "I've never done anything like that in my life. Truly."

"I never thought you did," Lewis said quickly. Though the idea of Alma.... He ripped his head away from that train of thought. "So what does Kershaw need Jerry for?"

"He says he has a curse tablet, a Roman artifact, and he wants Jerry to translate it." Alma shrugged. "Don't ask me why. Latin's not exactly an obscure dead language. It's not like Demotic or something really exotic that Jerry reads. He could find plenty of other people. Which is what makes me nervous. He's willing to pay Jerry an awful lot of money and put him up like this." She gestured to the ceiling of the Roosevelt Hotel.

"For something that isn't worth that much money." Lewis nodded. "That would make me nervous too."

"I don't want to say this to Jerry, but maybe Henry's just doing him a good turn. Giving him work because he thinks he's hard up because of his leg." Alma shook her head. "Henry might do something like that. He was a nice guy, a good friend of Gil's. Otherwise, I don't see what the angle is."

"Unless this thing is stolen," Lewis pointed out.

"True." Alma brightened. "Which would make sense. Jerry won't go to the police and Henry knows it. But I don't like to see Jerry get involved in something like that."

"I don't see how you can stop him," Lewis said.

"I don't either. But I can sure as hell guard him and make sure he doesn't get in over his head." Alma stretched out her legs, kicking them free of the sheet, bare and lovely and entirely distracting. "That's why I said I'd come with him."

"Because you're in a lodge together." Lewis was trying to put it together. Like being a strike team, like being wingmen.

"Because we're family," Alma said.

Chapter Five

Jerry paused in the lobby, bracing himself on his cane. There were too many stairs in the Roosevelt for his taste, two steps here up to the restaurant, three steps down to the sunken seating area, four steps to the ballroom's foyer, never mind the elegant staircase that led to the mezzanine. He fished his watch out of his pocket, checking the time and getting breath and balance back. Three minutes till noon, and sure enough, a young Mexican in dark blue livery was making his way through the lobby. Jerry knew he wasn't hard to spot, saw the moment the chauffeur spotted the cane, saw the flicker of his eyes as he confirmed the artificial leg. After that one glance, though, the young man met his eyes, pulling off his cap politely.

"Dr. Ballard?"

"Yes?"

"Mr. Kershaw sent me, sir. The car's out front."

Jerry followed him through the lobby, aware that the younger man was holding back to match his pace, and let himself be handed into the back seat of a Packard sedan exactly the same shade of midnight blue as the chauffeur's uniform.

"I expected a Pierce Arrow," he said, and the chauffeur's mouth twitched once before he had it under control.

"I believe Mr. Kershaw prefers a quieter ride, sir."

Touché, Jerry thought. The chauffeur put the car into gear, and eased it, purring, into the traffic. Jerry set his cane between his feet and leaned back against the cushions, trying to relax.

It wasn't just that he didn't like Henry. He'd spent long enough in both academia and the Army to have learned how to deal—well, perhaps not comfortably, but efficiently—with people he didn't care for. And it wasn't just that Henry worked in a tradition that he considered unsound. That was Henry's problem, and Henry's lodge's, and if they wanted to waste their time with amateur theatrics, that didn't concern him. It wasn't even a matter of trust, ultimately. Gil had trusted him in mundane matters, and for the rest, that didn't matter unless he was going to share the work, and that was never going to happen. He'd told Henry that ten years ago, and he meant it still. And it wasn't the money, Henry'd earned that—well, maybe he did envy what the money could buy, the freedom to travel, but he knew the business kept Henry from doing much more than buying up stray pieces that made it to the States. No, what was eating him was that Gil had always liked Henry, in spite of everything, in spite of his helping to break up the lodge the first time around, and these days he resented anyone Gil had known who was still alive when Gil was dead.

And that was unsupportable: trite, sentimental, and exhaustingly pointless. Gil would have laughed in his face at the very idea, and Alma—No, better not to pursue that train of thought. Better not to pursue any of this, in fact, and keep his mind on the business at hand.

If Henry said it was a curse tablet, that's probably what it was. He'd also said it was Roman, but Jerry rather doubted that. Even if Henry's Latin wasn't up to the job, there must be half a dozen people in this fancy new lodge who could translate it. He was willing to bet that, along with the movie stars and the thrill-seekers who were there for the costumed naughtiness, there was an inner circle who knew what they were doing. If the tablet was Roman, and Henry wasn't asking them about it, then there was something wrong about the tablet. If it wasn't Roman—probably Henry didn't recognize the source, and didn't want to admit it to the others. He'd always been sensitive about having had to cut short his education.

The Packard turned off the main boulevard onto a tree-lined street that wound up into the base of the hills. The houses were bigger here, with stone walls and iron gates—expensive houses, and getting more expensive the higher they went. Typical of Henry, he thought. But it was a hell of a place for a temple.

They turned in at an open gate, between pillars topped conventionally with eagles. The drive curved sharply to the house, three stories of gleaming white stone with bright red tiles on the roof. The door was set back beneath a triple arch, and the chauffeur brought the car to a gentle stop and hopped out quickly to open the car door. Jerry swung himself out—he'd almost mastered the art of getting out of a car without a struggle, even if it meant moving in segments, like a camel—and as he got his cane braced under him, he saw Henry in the doorway. He hadn't changed much, though perhaps the suit was even more carefully cut. He still had the beard he'd grown at the end of the War, trimmed now to a neat line that made him look like a Montenegrin diplomat, and the thick wavy hair was subdued by a ruthless barber.

"Welcome," Henry said, and they clasped hands under the central arch. His hand was hard, callused: still working in the machine shop, Jerry thought, and managed a tight smile. Behind them, the Packard pulled away, and Henry waved toward the shadowed interior. "I appreciate your willingness to help."

"I was curious," Jerry said frankly. "I still am. You never did explain what was so odd about this tablet that you couldn't read it—"

"All in good time," Henry said, with a quick, wry smile that negated some of the pomposity.

Jerry followed him down the hall, the knob of his artificial leg skittish on the tile floors. It was time Alma added another layer of rubber—past time, really, but they'd been in a hurry leaving Colorado. To either side, wide doors revealed expensive furniture, sunlight hanging in the still air; the sound of water was suddenly louder, and the hall opened onto a wide terrace that overlooked a semi-enclosed patio. A fountain played in the center, and outside a swimming pool glittered in the sun, and beyond it was a low-roofed pool house faced with a pillared loggia. Jerry tipped his head to one side, abruptly aware of a change in energy, and looked at Henry.

"That's your temple?"

The other man shrugged. "It seemed—suitable."

"Oh, very." Now that he looked more closely, Jerry could make out the symbols worked into the pool's mosaic borders, could just sense the larger rosette of stones at the bottom of the pool itself. There were statues, too, set in the niches of the wall that defined the area. Most of them were copies, not unskillful, but one or two, the ones closest to the pool house itself, were true antiquities. "You didn't."

"Let's not argue," Henry said. "My office is this way."

Jerry swallowed his objection, and followed. The office was at least half a library, two walls covered with floor to ceiling shelves, a third wall draped with heavy curtains. As he crossed the threshold, he felt the ghost of wards, but didn't bother looking for the symbols.

Henry drew the curtains, letting in the sun, and Jerry realized they were overlooking the pool again. Which meant Henry probably used this space for his workings as well, which might explain the odd sensation teasing at the back of his mind….

"Have a seat," Henry said, and reluctantly Jerry lowered himself into the chair that stood waiting at the edge of Henry's massive desk. Henry turned toward the bookcases—oh, not a secret compartment, Jerry thought, and then saw the locked cabinet set in among the shelves. The doors were glass and the key was in the lock: apparently it was just to keep idle hands away from the old books, or at least that was what one was meant to think. Henry murmured something, and turned the key. The door swung open, and he produced a small package wrapped in burlap, and set it on the desk in front of Jerry.

"Go ahead, open it," he said, and turned to re-lock the cabinet.

The wrappings were tied with string, none too clean. Jerry plucked it free, and unwrapped the coarse fabric to reveal a bright silk scarf.

"It was what I had," Henry said, and leaned his hip against the desktop.

Jerry lifted an eyebrow, but folded back the first layer of silk. Power warmed his fingertips, trembled in his hands, old and strong and not unfriendly. He took a sharp breath, peeling back the rest of the layers. The tablet lay revealed in the sunlight, the dull lead stamped with seals that he knew he should recognize. Letters had been dug deep into the surface, familiar Latin ritual phrases mixed with ones he didn't know, and words, whole lines, in an alphabet he recognized all too well. No, Henry wouldn't recognize Etruscan, and probably neither would anyone else in his lodge, unless Davenport was still a member. He touched the first seal gently, and the power nipped his finger like a spark.

"What the hell have you got here?" he said, half to himself, and Henry sighed.

"I was hoping you could tell me."

Jerry lifted the tablet, careful to keep the silk between his fingers and the metal surface, and turned it over to check the reverse. As he had more than half expected, there were symbols there as well, and another ritual phrase calling down punishment on anyone who disturbed the work—no, on anyone who disturbed the binding. And that was not what he had expected at all. He turned the tablet upright again, frowning, and Henry said, "Well?"

"Where was this found?" Jerry tilted the tablet. The surface was blurred, worn, almost as though it had been exposed to wind or water. Or to something that rubbed constantly against it, trying slowly and without patience but with infinite time to wear away its bonds. The image made him shiver, and he scowled at Henry. "You're going to have to tell me sometime, you know. If you want me to make a decent job of it."

Henry made a face. "What I know is what I was told."

"Yes, all right." Jerry tilted the tablet again, the power in it strong and cold even through the protecting silk. Its weight seemed to shift with the movement, as though there were a blob of mercury trapped within it, pouring along hidden channels. There were no signs of a plug, or seams; the corner seals were discolored at the center, as though—maybe—something had been pressed into or through the lead, but that would be a visible symbol of the binding, *defixio* made literal. He checked the back again, but the discoloration didn't go all the way through. Perhaps not, then, he thought, and became aware that Henry was still silent.

"So what did—he? she? this person—tell you?"

"I was told," Henry said, carefully, "that it was found in conjunction with the excavations at Lake Nemi."

Nemi. The Sanctuary of Diana at Aricia, by the lake that had been known to the Romans as Diana's Mirror. Where fisherman had for centuries dredged up fragments of mysterious ships from the bottom of the lake. Where just last year the Italian government had opened an extremely well-financed and internationally staffed expedition that was not only excavating the sanctuary and sections of the surrounding grove, but actually draining the lake itself. The last report he had seen said that the superstructure of the first ship was now above water, and that it was far larger than any Roman ship previously discovered, and would rewrite half a dozen well-worn assumptions....

"Why aren't you asking Davenport?" he said aloud. "Or isn't he part of your lodge anymore?"

Henry's eyes flickered, and for a second Jerry thought he was going to agree, but then he made another face. "Bill is—he's not interested in this piece."

"That makes no sense at all," Jerry said. Even at first glance, he could tell this tablet was something special, especially to anyone who knew anything at all about occult history. "Doesn't he know you have it?"

"He knows," Henry said. "He—well, that's not important. He's got other things he's handling right now, including a donation of bronzes to the University—"

He stopped, and Jerry looked at him over the rim of his glasses. "Davenport is here? In Los Angeles?"

"He arrived on Tuesday," Henry said, after a moment. "Leave it, will you?"

"It doesn't make sense," Jerry said again. "He must see—feel, anyway—he must know what he has here—"

"There's a story that goes with it," Henry said. "Not a very nice one."

"They usually aren't," Jerry began, stopped as the expression on Henry's face really registered. "Go on."

"One of the Italian archeologists working on the dig had a brainstorm and disappeared for a month. Just up and vanished one night, and a week later some guy hunting mushrooms spotted him up in the hills above the lake. It took the cops a good month to track him down, but they finally managed to catch him.

He was stark staring crazy by then. Couldn't talk, didn't recognize anybody, not even his own wife. They took him to a hospital in Rome, but he was in pretty bad shape from being on the run so long—malnourished, feet cut to hell, you get the picture."

Jerry nodded.

"There wasn't much they could do for him," Henry said. "Bill said the doctors thought he might have had some kind of stroke, maybe. The sad part is, he was starting to get better—he'd calmed down some, actually seemed to know his wife—and then he had another stroke, and that one killed him."

"Not nice," Jerry said, after a moment. "But what does that have to do with the tablet?"

"I think Bill got the tablet from Gadda," Henry said. "The Italian guy. And I think he can't figure out how to explain having it, so he's trying to pretend it doesn't exist, at least until he can think of a way to bring it back to light. But I want to know what it says."

Jerry nodded again, thoughtfully this time. It mostly made sense. Oh, there were plenty of things that Henry wasn't saying, but he was willing to bet most of those had to do with lodge politics. Davenport had been pretty scathing about Henry's talents, or lack of them, back in Italy; he'd been willing to use Henry, and Henry's money, when the lodge split, but he probably hadn't had any reason to change his opinion since then. And, knowing Davenport, he wasn't going to go out of his way to be polite about it.

"All right," he said. "Fine. Not Davenport. What about Geoffrey Bullfinch? This is right up his alley, and he's just down in San Valencez, which is a hell of a lot closer than me. Not to mention that he'll work for free if it interests him."

Henry looked away again. "There's been some—call it tension—between the lodge and Bullfinch lately."

"He and Davenport fought about—what?" Jerry asked.

"You name it," Henry said, his expression sour. "Archeology. Provenance of certain relics. Proper procedures."

"And you went along with it."

"Our Magister took Bill's part, yes," Henry said. "As he should."

"Right," Jerry said. He'd never thought it was the Magister's place to support his people unreservedly, but this wasn't his kind of lodge. "So not Bullfinch, either. Fine, I'll see what I can do. Do you know anything more about where this was found? Or if there were any more of them?"

Henry shook his head. "You know everything I know. Why?"

I doubt that, Jerry thought, but looked back at the tablet. "This—" He pointed to the concluding lines, careful not to touch the surface. "This implies that there are more tablets. See? It's all plurals here."

Henry nodded. "Can you read it? I recognized the Latin, but that...." He pointed in turn. "It looks like runes."

"It's visually similar," Jerry said. "It's Etruscan, actually, and that's unusual. The Romans used it as a ritual language, of course, very much the way we use Greek and Latin, but you don't often see it written out. It's mostly found on tombstones. And of course the real problem is that Etruscan is a lost language."

"Which means?"

"Nobody knows how to read it," Jerry said. "There's been some progress recently, a few people who've managed to pick out—they think—Indo-European roots to some words, but it's not at the point where you can know what it says."

"Damn," Henry said, half under his breath. "So you're saying this is pointless?"

"Not entirely," Jerry answered. "I can give you the Latin, of course, and I think I can figure out some of the Etruscan by context. We've got a date here, consuls' names, and I'm guessing this is going to be the reign of Claudius. You've got something I can look that up in?"

"Maybe," Henry said.

Jerry went on as though he hadn't spoken. "So it's not like this is going to be Etruscan as it was spoken by the Etruscans, it's going to be more like ritual Latin, and that means I ought to be able to guess at some of it. Especially since there's a fair amount of information in the other sections."

"All right," Henry said. He pushed himself up off the desk. "Let me ring for some sandwiches, and we can get on with it."

Jerry nodded absently, not really listening. The tablet began with a fairly standard invocation to Diana, a recitation of her titles and attributes as Diana Nemorensis, and then the usual language apologizing for any imperfection in the rites—no, it was a more particular apology, for some ritual fault well known to everyone, apparently. And then the first Etruscan section, and a more specific confession of fault, this one having to do with the profanation of the priesthood of the shrine, and then…. He stopped abruptly, pushing his glasses up onto his nose as though that would clarify the translation.

Diana in all your aspects, heal the wounds and strengthen the bonds that here imprison this spirit of the underworld.

Oh, Henry, he thought. What have you gotten yourself into?

Alma put her hands on her hips. "You told Henry what?"

"I told Henry I needed more time with it." Jerry carefully sat down on the edge of the neatly made bed. He'd returned to the hotel at mid-afternoon, just before Mitch and Alma had decided to go look for him. They'd given it until three for him to show up or call, and Jerry had showed at ten of. "It's Latin and Etruscan both, some of it quite intriguing. From what I can determine based on context…."

Mitch interrupted him in a calm, strong voice, not bothering to get up from the chair by the window. "Jerry, you can translate Latin in your sleep. Hell, I could probably have read the damn thing in three hours. And nobody can read Etruscan, so it doesn't matter how much time you have with it. What gives?"

Lewis thought that Jerry looked a little embarrassed. "There's a lot that can be worked out by context. The Etruscan sections aren't that long, actually. They seem to be the form of the actual invocations, which all follows since Etruscan was an ancient and obscure language when the tablet was made."

"Which was when?" Alma asked, her hands still on her hips, though her voice held more interest than irritation.

"The first year of the reign of the Emperor Claudius, or 794 Ab Urbe Condita." He glanced at Lewis apologetically. "That's 41 AD to you."

Lewis shrugged as if to say he didn't have a horse in this race.

"So you're fascinated by it, and you told Henry you needed another day." Alma shook her head. "Ok, Jerry. What's so interesting?"

"It starts off in a very conventional invocational form, asking the goddess Diana to attend upon the speaker and to grant him her good will. Then it apologizes for any displeasure he might have incurred. It takes up pretty standard expiationary language – *expiare*, to atone or make reparations – though it doesn't indicate exactly what crimes the speaker is making amends for. Then there's a section of Etruscan, and another round of apologies. Then the speaker states that he is presenting appropriate sacrifices to Diana and asks for her help. This is where it really gets interesting." Jerry's long face was animated, and Lewis couldn't help feeling a stir of curiosity. "He asks for her help in imprisoning *animus infernus* – a spirit of the lower regions."

Mitch uncrossed his arms. "So this is a very early form of a banishing ritual? That's interesting in a historical sense. There's always been a gap, hasn't there? Between the pure Hermetic models and the Early Byzantine."

"It is fascinating for that reason," Jerry said, twisting around to look at him, his tie akimbo. "And I can't stress enough that this tablet is an important find for that reason alone. But there's more. Not only is this a complete invocation dating from the Early Empire, but it was also found in situ at the Temple of Diana at Lake Nemi."

Alma's eyebrows rose. "Ok, that is interesting. I know you said they started excavating there last year."

"Oh, they've started excavating, all right," Jerry said regretfully, and Lewis couldn't help but wonder if Jerry wished he were on the dig. "They've been excavating at the sanctuary, and now they've started draining the lake to raise the Nemi ships, the Roman barges that were sunk at some point. It's a colossal archaeological expedition, well funded by the government, with all the latest equipment and the best experts. They've exposed the beams of the first ship, last I heard. It's going extremely well and it's certainly a notable find."

"Let me guess," Alma said. "William Davenport."

"Yes." Jerry smiled grimly. "Of course."

Lewis felt he was missing something important somewhere. "Wait," he said. "Who's William Davenport?"

Jerry didn't answer, just looked at Alma, who shrugged. "Dr. William Davenport is a well known archaeologist and excavator.

He and Jerry don't see eye to eye on a lot of things. Well, on a lot of things that wouldn't make a bit of difference to you or me."

"The interpretation of syncreticism in Hellenistic material is of vital importance," Jerry said. "Whether you want to interpret the Lochias Kouros as indicative of Indian iconography of Krishna or not...."

"We get it," Mitch said, sitting up on the edge of his chair. "So the bottom line is that Davenport filched this thing from his own dig and sold it to Henry under the table."

"Henry didn't say that in so many words," Jerry replied.

"Yes, but he's got it. And Henry doesn't look like the Italian government to me," Alma said. "Surely they expect to keep the finds for their museums if they're paying for the dig, not have the pieces sold off to private collectors."

"I expect so." Jerry had the good grace to look embarrassed. "I think there's some kind of issue about Davenport, from everything Henry wasn't saying."

Mitch shrugged and reached for the glass of ice that was slowly melting on the side table. "You know Henry. He's all poise and charm, but he wouldn't know genuinely occult if it bit him in the ass. And Davenport's the real deal. Henry may be satisfied with putting on a good show to Hollywood types, but Davenport wouldn't be. He never was. So there's some tension in their lodge. Not our problem."

"I think you're underestimating Henry," Jerry said, and there was a spark in his eye. "Gil thought...."

"Gil thought Henry was all wind and you know it," Mitch said. "A nice guy, but full of wind."

"It doesn't matter what Gil thought," Alma said steadily. "And it doesn't matter what's going on between Henry and Davenport. Jerry will finish up the translation Henry's paying him for, and then we'll all go home. We're not in any position to get into a bunch of infighting in somebody else's lodge." She gave Jerry a stern look, and to Lewis' surprise he didn't argue.

"I think you're right," he said. "We can't get into that. And there's something wrong, no question about it." He looked up at Alma, pushing his gold glasses up on his nose. "Because not only could Henry have called in Geoffrey Bullfinch if he'd been willing to eat a little humble pie, but Davenport is here, in LA. There's no reason to get me to translate this. Why doesn't he just ask Davenport?"

Mitch's brow furrowed. "Davenport is here? And Henry's paying you $250 to do this? What the hell?"

"That's what I'm wondering," Jerry said mildly. "That's why I told Henry we'd be back tonight."

"Tonight?" Alma said incredulously.

"Henry invited us to come back tonight. They're celebrating the Ploiaphesia."

"The hell they are," Mitch said. "That was back in March."

"You know Henry," Alma said, throwing up her hands. "Why keep to the ancient calendar if it suits everybody's schedules better to do it any old time they want?"

"What's the....whatever?" Lewis asked. If it was something dangerous he was hardly going to let Alma just walk into it, but he could bet she'd insist on going if Jerry and Mitch were.

"It's a navigation festival," Alma said. "It's supposed to be around March 5th. It marked the beginning of the sailing season in the ancient world, when ships were blessed by Isis." She looked at Mitch. "Don't ask me. I have no idea how Henry intends to bless ships twenty miles inland at his house. It is at his house, right, Jerry? Not at a marina somewhere?"

"No, it's at his house," Jerry said. "He has a swimming pool."

Alma's eyebrows rose at that, and Jerry went on. "He said they have a lot of people coming, that it was a semi-open ritual since it's a festival not a working, and that we'd be more than welcome. I can have another look at the tablet during the party, and you guys are welcome to join them for dinner. It's buffet."

"After the ritual or before?" Alma asked.

Jerry spread his hands. "After, I should hope. But you know...."

"The bar will be open anyway," Mitch said, twitching an eyebrow at Lewis. "I'm up for Henry's liquor even if it does come with dinner theater."

"That's not entirely fair," Jerry began.

Alma pinned him with her eyes. "I take it you told Henry we didn't have anything suitable to wear? And of course he said he'd take care of it?"

"Um, yes," Jerry said sheepishly. "But I'm sure…."

"And he's sending a car?"

"At six thirty," Jerry said. "They're not supposed to start until eight. Until it's getting dark."

"And until everyone has a chance to get off work and go home and change." Mitch shrugged. "Ok. I'm in. Let's see what old Henry's up to."

"I'll come," Alma said, her eyes steady on Jerry. "But this is the last time you accept an invitation for me without asking me. Understood?"

Jerry nodded. "I am sorry, Alma. But I didn't think this was a conversation we wanted to have over Henry's telephone."

"I'll come," Lewis said, and everybody looked around at him. He put his hands in his pockets awkwardly. "I mean, unless I wasn't invited."

"Of course you were invited," Alma said with a glance at Jerry as if daring him to say otherwise. "And we'd be glad for you to come."

"Sure," Jerry said insouciantly. "The more the merrier. It's a festival after all."

Chapter Six

Lewis hung behind the others going in, trying to look like he paid calls on Hollywood millionaires every day. They were obviously expected. A pretty young woman with hair a shade of platinum blonde rarely found in nature had greeted them at the door, her navy blue dress just a shade more fashionably cut than Alma's and her heels just a little bit higher. It wasn't that she looked like a tart. Just like a woman who had a good deal more money to spend on her looks than most.

She greeted Alma warmly, a handshake that was ladylike and proper both. "Mrs. Gilchrist! I'm Mary Patterson, Mr. Kershaw's personal assistant. It's a very great pleasure to meet you. He's spoken of you on so many occasions."

Alma looked flustered, which only pointed up the difference between them, not just a decade and a half in age, but Mary Patterson's cool charm contrasting with Alma's obvious discomfort. "It's nice to meet you too," she said.

Jerry, on the other hand, brushed past her with barely concealed haste. "Mr. Kershaw said that I could work in his office."

"Yes, Dr. Ballard. Mr. Kershaw is waiting for you there. I can show you or if you…."

"I know the way," Jerry said, and stumped off rapidly down the hall.

Mary Patterson affixed a smile to her ruby lips. "Well. Then I will show you to guest rooms where you can change. Mr. Kershaw said that he hoped you would find everything you need. If you'll come upstairs?"

Alma frowned after Jerry, but short of dashing after him there wasn't much she could do.

"We appreciate it so much, Miss Patterson," Mitch said, his hat in his hand like a gentleman. "Thank you for your trouble."

"It's no trouble at all, Mr...." Her pretty face brightened. Mitch was handsome, in a broad shouldered, rugged kind of way, and when he put on his best Southern manners women did tend to melt.

"Mitchell Sorley," he said, putting out his hand. "And the pleasure is mine."

"Mr. Sorley," she said. "Thank you."

Alma cleared her throat, and Lewis realized Mitch had just covered Alma's uncomfortable moment with perfect smoothness. Oh yes. There was a reason Mitch was an ace.

Mary Patterson led them upstairs. Evening was falling, and the house seemed dim and cool after the bright heat of a Los Angeles day. "The guest rooms are right here," she said, her hand on the dark carved wood of a Spanish style door. "This one is for Mrs. Gilchrist, and you gentlemen are two doors down. The door between is a bath if you'd like to freshen up."

"Thank you," Alma said, pushing open the door.

"Please call if you need anything," Mary Patterson said. She gave Mitch an especially bright smile and walked away, her heels silent on the tapestry floor runner.

"Right," Mitch said. "Lewis?"

"Here," Lewis said, and followed him into the other guest room.

It was large, though probably not one of the house's grandest, and the windows looked out over the drive. Lewis twitched the sheer under curtain aside to look down at three cars lined up below, waiting for someone to take them around to park. As he watched, an elegantly dressed woman got out of one, her lowered face entirely obscured by the brim of her hat.

He turned to see Mitch watching him, his jacket over his arm. "Don't let it bug you," Mitch said. "Henry made a lot of money in the last few years. That's all. He's a good mechanic but only a fair pilot. He wasn't born with a silver spoon in his mouth."

"It wasn't bothering me," Lewis said, letting the curtain fall back into place. "It's just that this stuff...." His gesture included the two neatly folded mounds of white clothes on the bed.

"Is kind of spooky?" Mitch grinned reassuringly. "I was nervous as hell the first time Gil took me to something. But there's nothing to worry about with this. It's a festival. It's like watching a play. Nobody's going to expect you to do anything." He grinned again. "That's when you should be nervous."

Lewis nodded seriously. "I don't know if I can do this."

"If you can or if you want to?" Mitch's eyes were uncharacteristically keen.

"Either one," Lewis said.

Mitch clapped him on the shoulder. "I don't know either. If you can, or if you will. But don't let Alma bully you into doing something you're not comfortable with. She can be a force of nature."

"Alma doesn't bully me," Lewis said.

"Then you're the only man in all creation she doesn't," Mitch said. "You'd think Gil would have been able to stand his ground with her, but he didn't. It's a good thing, really. Alma has more sense than most people." Mitch loosened his tie and picked up one of the two bundles of clothes on the bed. "I'm a pilot. I could care less about the business end of things. If Alma didn't keep the accounts and manage the bookings, I'd be working for Henry, saying 'Yes, Mr. Kershaw' and 'No, Mr. Kershaw' instead of being part owner." He picked up the second bundle and tossed it to Lewis. "I think we're about the same size, so it probably doesn't matter who gets which one."

Lewis unfolded the bundle, which turned out to be a long white robe like the one he'd worn back in boys choir, stiff satin smelling just like that, faintly redolent of incense. The front fastened with half a dozen buttons hidden behind a placket. Mitch had taken off his tie and draped it neatly across the bed, then pulled the robe on over his head over pants and shirtsleeves.

Lewis shrugged and started unknotting his own.

"Technically we're not supposed to wear anything under them," Mitch said, smoothing out the folds of his sleeves. "But since we're not doing energy work it doesn't really matter. And it gets a little drafty." He grinned at Lewis' expression. "I expect these are actually choir robes," Mitch said. "Ordered from a church supply company. Easiest way to fit out a big group, if not as good as sewing your own to specs."

Lewis digested that for a moment. There was something obscurely comforting about the choir robes. How much scary black magic could you do in a choir robe? “Ok,” he said. “I’m ready.”

Mitch looked him over. “It’s like wearing a uniform,” he said quietly. “It puts everybody on the same footing, emphasizes the similarities. This is our uniform, just like the ones you and I wear in the Reserves.”

“I get that,” Lewis said, and he did. The robe’s weight on his shoulders felt right.

“Good man.” Mitch gave his arm a swift squeeze. “Now let’s go find Al.”

The upstairs hall was dark and quiet, lit by a dim lamp on a console table. Downstairs they could hear the sound of a few voices in the entrance hall. “I’m going to make a pit stop,” Mitch said, putting his hand to the bathroom door. “I’ll catch up to you in a few minutes.”

There wasn’t much Lewis could say to that, and hanging around in the hall seemed awkward. He knocked on the other guest room door. “Alma?”

There was no answer, so he turned the knob carefully and went in. The lamp had been turned off, and a quick glance convinced him she wasn’t here. She must have already finished dressing and gone down. Lewis pulled the door shut and headed for the stairs.

The sun had set, and only the light in the foyer had been turned on. The hall was dim. There might be voices further back in the house, or maybe in the backyard, but here it was quiet. At the far end of the hall that Jerry had hurried off down earlier there was a spill of light through an open door, and cautiously Lewis went toward it. He hadn’t even met the master of the house, and it seemed rude to just wander around like this, like he was rubbernecking or maybe casing the joint. There were voices. Maybe he should go back.... No, it was Jerry’s voice.

“I don’t know what you expect,” Jerry said, and Lewis thought he sounded tired and resigned. “Sometime we have to take some risks. Otherwise we might as well not call ourselves a lodge. What are we? The lodge of ostriches that stick our head in the ground? If we’re not actually going to do anything we might as well pack up."

Lewis took a few steps closer, his feet silent on the carpet.

Jerry sat in a chair at the massive wooden desk, a Tiffany lamp casting a warm light over the books and papers before him. Alma stood facing him, her back to the door. She wasn't wearing a choir robe. It was a gown of cream colored silk, pleated and caught in many folds that dropped elegantly from a high waistband, and she wasn't wearing anything beneath it except her combinations and maybe not that. The folds showed off her height and the curves of her breasts when she raised her arm, silhouetted against the light.

"It's dangerous, Jerry."

"Of course it's dangerous," Jerry said. "And fascinating and imperative." She stirred and he forestalled her, his voice low. "Al, this is what I do. This is what I am. You can't ask me to ignore this. I have to have something left, if this is the only one of my passions I can pursue."

She took a breath, and Lewis heard the soft regret in her voice. "Oh, Jerry."

His face froze as he looked past her, seeing Lewis standing there. "Lewis," he said evenly.

"Hello," Lewis said, stepping forward into the light, his face flaming. "I was just coming down."

Alma turned around, and Lewis heartily wished he were anywhere else. That conversation was not meant for his ears. Bad enough that Alma had chosen him over her old friend without him hearing Jerry's humiliation. He'd thought maybe she didn't know that Jerry had it bad for her, but clearly this was something that had hung between them for a long time, Jerry playing the gentleman and stepping back for Lewis. Hell, maybe he'd stepped back for Gil too. Lewis felt a wave of sympathy wash over him. It couldn't be easy, being the one without a whole healthy body and without Alma too. It was understandable if Jerry's good sportsmanship wore a little thin at times.

"So what are we doing tonight?" Lewis asked, his eyes on Jerry, not Alma, just as if he hadn't heard a word.

"We're going to join Henry out by the pool," Alma said. She didn't look away from Jerry, and there was a tiny frown between her eyebrows. "And Jerry's going to work on this tablet for a while longer."

Jerry nodded. "Just a while, Al. I'll come out when it starts."

"Ok." Alma took Lewis' arm like he was going to take her in to dinner. "We'll see you in a few minutes."

"Sure," Jerry said, but he was already turning back to the work before him.

Alma stood in the doorway from the conservatory to the loggia that overlooked the pool, her arm in Lewis'. Henry hadn't been kidding that it was a big crowd. There must have been twenty-five people milling around the area near the swimming pool, dressed in various kinds of robes and pseudo-Egyptian finery. Most of them had congregated by the open bar, where a white-jacketed bartender was serving, oblivious to any strangeness. It had been a long time since she'd been to anything this big, and never something quite this fancy. There had been some big ones right after the war, before the lodge split. It felt like a million years ago, on the other side of a dark divide, back when she'd been almost entirely sure that everything would work out.

Of course it hadn't. The wages of sin, some might say. Piss poor luck, Gil would have said, and she could almost hear him say it in imagination. Talking with the dead had always been beyond her, and while she could do a better job of finding a competent medium than almost anyone, so far she'd resisted the temptation. It would be like smelling food but being unable to taste.

"Ok?" Lewis asked.

Alma gave him a sideways smile. "Absolutely," she said.

Henry had spotted her and was coming around the pool, leaning in to kiss her on both cheeks in a very European way. "Alma! You can't guess how delighted I am that you decided to come tonight. You look exquisite."

"This is a beautiful robe," Alma said, leaning in to his gesture. "And you look good yourself, Henry."

"Thanks." Henry took a step back, looking Lewis up and down like a stereotypical movie dad. "So who's this?"

"Henry, I'd like you to meet Lewis Segura. He's been working with us." At Gilchrist Aviation, Alma added silently, knowing that Henry would take it for something else. "I don't believe you met during the war since he was on the Western Front, not in Italy."

"Mr. Segura," Henry said, offering his hand.

"Mr. Kershaw." Lewis took it without hesitation. "I've heard you're a pilot."

"Well, you've heard right," Henry laughed. "You too? Alma does run to a type."

"I fly," Lewis said modestly, and Alma knew better than to give him a testimonial. It would just make him sound like an amateur, and make her sound enamored.

"He has the DSC," Mitch said, joining them, his white robe smooth over the collar beneath it. "So yeah, Henry. He's pretty fair."

Henry laughed. "Says the ace with seven kills! Ok, I'll take that as the last word!"

Lewis tried to look humble, something Mitch had down to an art.

"It's good to meet you, Mr. Segura," Henry said. "I hope you'll have a drink and relax."

"Thank you," Lewis said.

Alma steered him away from Henry toward the bar, leaving Mitch in conversation. She lifted her head in response to the faint breeze blowing across the pool, feeling it cool against her cheeks. "Let's get a drink."

"Ok," Lewis said. He seemed perfectly comfortable, and she was glad.

"Thank you for coming with us," she said.

"It's no trouble." Lewis gave her his lopsided smile. "How often do I get a chance to go to a Hollywood party?"

"I don't either," Alma said. She glanced at the bartender. "A gin fizz, please."

"Same," Lewis said.

It was a little surreal, watching the stars come out dimly over the hills, faded to nothing by the lights of the city. In Colorado the air was clear and the stars bright, bright as they were in the air, navigating by them like some wayward explorer. A clear night, with the moonlight to cast the ground in sharp relief, and the stars to guide by....

"You look really beautiful," Lewis said, and she looked around. His hazel eyes were warm, lingering on her face like his hand against her cheek.

"Oh," she said.

"I'm glad you told me about this," Lewis said. "I really am." He glanced around the pool, the milling people, Mitch still talking to Henry. Jerry had come out and joined them, leaning on his cane. He hadn't changed, and his suit was a dark spot amid the white.

"I was afraid to," Alma said frankly. She supposed Gil had been, when he'd told her things that would have sent any sane woman running for the hills.

Somewhere at the other end of the terrace unseen musicians struck up the opening chords of something Stravinsky. They were probably behind the white canvas marquee tent that hid proceedings around the pool from the neighbors. Rite of Spring, Alma thought. Of course. Suitable background music. From the tent emerged a slow procession, four young women in white gowns walking decorously, sistrums shaking in their hands, followed by four robed men carrying what looked like a gilt covered canoe laden with fruit. Well, as sacred barges went it probably wasn't too far off, Alma thought. It did the job.

Gracefully, they carried the barge toward the pool's edge, toward the broad steps that gleamed pale beneath the water. For a moment Alma wondered if the girls were going to wade in. The water would surely render their thin white silk entirely transparent. But no. They stopped at the top of the steps, theatrically arranged two by two, while the priests carried the barge down between them until they were knee deep and the barge rested on the smooth surface of the water.

The unseen musicians stopped and the girls began a pretty a cappella number, something Alma was entirely missing since she didn't speak the language.

Lewis frowned and leaned in. "What's that?"

"Greek," Alma whispered back. And probably inappropriate, but Hellenistic syncreticism was very forgiving, as traditions went. You could mangle it in a lot of directions and still have the core hold firm.

As they finished, a fifth priest stepped forward, a tall, saturnine older man with a green bough in his hand to use as an aspergillum. He lifted it toward the barge, beginning a long invocation of Isis' titles. "Hear us, oh Lady of the Living and the Dead, Mistress of Magic…."

Beside her Lewis stiffened suddenly, his face paling beneath his deep tan. "That's him."

Alma put her hand on his arm and felt it shake. "Who?

"The man in my dream," Lewis said. His eyes didn't leave the rite before them. "That's him. The one who tried to kill me."

Alma swallowed, a chill running up her spine. Around them all went on as it should, the ritual flowing beautifully and smoothly. The girls took up another song, more up tempo this time, sistrums raised, and the priest stepped back, letting the barge go so that it floated freely on the surface of the pool.

"Do you know him?" Lewis' voice was deliberate.

Alma nodded. "That's William Davenport."

She saw him look up suddenly, his back rigid, and her eyes flew to Lewis, but Lewis seemed fine, watching him intently but with no distress. And Davenport wasn't looking in their direction. He was facing across the pool, his chin rising, power snapping in the air around him like an unseen wind.

Across the pool one person stood out amid the white robed dancers preparing to begin, dark suit and gold rimmed glasses. Jerry looked straight back. They looked like duelists caught in the moment before the passage of blades, and Alma felt the deep tremor, like subsonics or the faintest rumble of a barely perceivable earthquake. She felt it rush outward, flying at Jerry like a punch. No, like a speeding automobile careening into a man standing unwittingly in the middle of the street, transfixed by the onrushing headlights.

She had no finesse, no care. But what she had was power. Power lay in the ground beneath her, in the earth beneath her feet, through marble and concrete to dirt and sandstone, to the bones of the hills. She ripped it up, feeling it pour through her, rushing upward from her feet, through her body and down her arms, fire from earth, fire from the deep wells beneath California. It burned in the palms of her hands, flowing through her like a spark through a circuit, and she flung it outward.

Aegis, she thought. One word. Athena's shield, bronze and unbearably bright, the snakes on the gorgon's head twisting viciously, glittering before Jerry, sheltering him behind its solidity. Nothing might pass the aegis, not while power remained to hold it. And she had all the power of earth at her command, deep and inexorable. The power would hold far longer than she would.

In some other place, where people moved slowly as a film at half speed, a few heads were turning, the truly sensitive looking around like those who have felt the earthquake when others have not. Mitch raised his head unerringly, seeking. Henry jerked around at his side, searching for the source of the thunder.

Behind the aegis, Jerry spoke a word. It broke in dazzling shards of invisible light, attack and shield and all, shimmering into nothing at the word of banishment.

And then all was silent. Davenport turned, following the other priests back toward the tent, and Jerry stood shaking, his hand trembling on his cane in the middle of the crowd. Alma saw Mitch hurrying toward him purposefully, Henry at his side.

"What the hell was that?" Lewis said quietly.

Her hands cramped. She was a little lightheaded, momentarily drained, the current cut too fast. But Lewis' arm was steady. "Magic," she said.

Chapter Seven

Lewis waited until they were back at the hotel, waited through the end of the party with its explanations and awkwardness, through Mitch taking charge and calling them a cab, through the long ride back to the Roosevelt. Lewis waited until they'd let themselves into Alma's room, all four of them crowding into the circle of light cast by the lamp. Lewis looked around at the three of them, suddenly seeming like strangers rather than people he'd known for five months. "What just happened?" he said.

Mitch sat down in the chair, his hat in his hand, looking suddenly old and tired. "Davenport attacked Jerry. He was using some kind of projection of elemental force, and if Alma hadn't countered it…." He glanced up at Jerry. "It would have been bad."

"A stroke, a heart attack…" Jerry smiled thinly. "The strain, you know. Not good for someone in poor health."

Alma stalked around the bed and sat down, unbuckling her shoes. "Well, it didn't happen that way," she began.

"I still don't understand," Lewis interrupted. "You're saying that these things, this magic, can kill somebody and make it look natural! That's…." He scrambled for words. Wrong? Impossible?

"It would be natural," Jerry said quietly. "I would die from a heart attack. It's the most natural thing in the world. The question is what precipitated it."

"I think killing somebody with a curse is pretty much supernatural," Lewis said.

"There isn't anything supernatural about it," Mitch said from the chair. "Magic obeys natural laws. Look, everybody knows that being shocked with an electrical current can make your heart stop. All this is doing is delivering the shock without the wires." He shrugged. "Current moves through air all the time by ionizing the atmosphere. That's what lightning is."

"You're saying this man can control lightning." Lewis twisted his hat brim in his hands.

"Not as much current as lightning," Alma said, dropping her shoe on the floor. "A much smaller amount of energy, but one that can still do harm. I couldn't have grounded it if it had been much more current."

"Grounded it."

Alma nodded. "That's what I did. I ran the current to ground, absorbing it back into the earth so it wouldn't hurt anybody, the same thing that happens when lightning hits a lightning rod. It grounds."

Lewis frowned. "How?"

Alma opened her mouth and shut it again. "I don't know," she said. "I just know it works."

"That's what our tradition is about," Jerry said ponderously. "Hermetics is about the experiential discovery of effective esoterica through empirical study. Based upon the philosophy of the Hellenistic sage Hermes Trismegistus…."

Mitch got to his feet. "Come on, Jerry."

"What?"

"Let Alma explain."

For a moment Lewis thought Jerry would protest, but instead he shrugged, his eyes on Alma, a look passing between them that Lewis couldn't interpret.

"It's her place," Mitch said, and Lewis wondered if he meant because they were sharing a bed, or because of something else.

"Goodnight, then," Jerry said. He opened the door and waited for Mitch to precede him out. "See you in the morning."

"Goodnight, Jerry," Alma said. "Mitch." She twisted around on the bed, crossing her stockinged feet beneath her. Mitch gave her a two fingered salute and pulled the door closed.

Lewis came around and sat down in the chair, still hunting for words. "I don't understand how these things can be real," he said quietly. "It flies in the face of science."

Alma shook her head. "No, it doesn't." She took a deep breath, as if considering. "Do you understand how an aircraft works?"

Lewis nodded. "Yes. I mean, I understand about lift and

thrust, about airspeed and wind direction and all of that. That's science."

"And it's new," Alma said. "People forty years ago didn't understand it, much less people five hundred years ago. The principles of flight were always there, but we didn't understand how to use them yet." She sat up straighter, her bare feet in their silk casings tucked under her legs. "But people could observe birds. Probably people have done that since the dawn of time! They could see how birds flew and they could imagine flying. They could observe how baby birds learn to fly, how they glide first and how they tilt their wings to provide lift. Leonardo da Vinci designed a glider that works. He just didn't have an engine to give him sufficient airspeed to actually build a plane." Alma smiled. "He didn't understand the principles, but he knew what he saw and he could experiment based on what worked."

"Ok," Lewis said slowly. "So what does that have to do with magic?"

"To Leonardo, flying was magic. If somebody from the fifteenth century saw one of our planes they would think it was supernatural. But it isn't. It's just that we know more than they did." Alma reached for his hand. "But we don't know everything. We know a tiny little fraction of everything there is to understand about the universe. And a lot of the things we don't understand seem supernatural to us. Like Leonardo, we can observe and we can theorize and we can use to a limited extent the things our observations teach us, but we can't explain it all. Not yet. Hermetics is sometimes called scientific magic, and that's why. We use the empirical knowledge accumulated by different generations and different cultures and we try to understand why it works. Sometimes we can reproduce results and sometimes we can't. Sometimes we can see why a formula has power, and sometimes we don't know anything except that it does. And every century, every decade, we understand better. We understand more about the 'supernatural,' about the way the world works beyond what science can currently explain. Does that make sense?"

"I suppose," Lewis said slowly. "But I don't understand.... How can a person influence electrical energy?"

"We are energy," Alma said. "We all have electrical energy in our bodies." She looked down at their interlaced hands, turned hers in his so that their palms were together. "Hold still." She let go of his hand and moved hers back, three inches between their palms. "Now tell me what you feel." Slowly she moved her hand closer, quarter inch by quarter inch, until only three quarters of an inch remained between. She looked up at Lewis with a smile that was pure trouble. "What do you feel?"

He stared at their hands, ordinary, not quite touching. "It feels warm," he said. The warmth was growing between their palms even though they didn't touch. "Really warm."

"That's what happens when your electrical field interacts with mine," she said. "You can feel it. That's what energy feels like. That's the thing we're manipulating."

Warm, and stronger than he'd expected, right there against the heart of his palm.... And then stronger, like pressure, like she'd pressed her palm to his, though she hadn't moved. He looked at Alma, at the faint pleased expression of concentration on her face, the same one she wore when she flew. "What are you doing?"

"Pushing a little," she said. "That's all. Just manipulating it a little bit, like pushing with my hand."

"That's...." Lewis didn't have the words for it. His eyes met hers, blue and delighted, as though it were fun. "That's real."

"I told you it was," Alma said.

Jerry hung his suit coat in the room's narrow closet, pulled off his tie and loosened his collar. Mitch had tossed his jacket onto the back of the chair, and pulled out the bottle of bourbon. He poured himself two fingers, and held up the bottle in silent question, but Jerry shook his head. He went into the bathroom, rolling up his sleeves as he went, and turned on the tap, waiting until the water ran as cold as it was going to get. He washed his face and his hands, ran a damp cloth over the back of his neck and held his wrists under the stream. He hadn't been that close to dying in a long time, not since the war—well, not since they'd had to amputate his foot, but he wasn't going to count that—and he didn't like it.

"You Ok?" Mitch called, and Jerry shut off the water and dried his hands.

"I'm fine," he said, and limped back into the main room. Mitch had taken the one comfortable chair, so Jerry sat on the bed, stretching his bad leg carefully on the spread. "I hope to hell she doesn't spook him."

"I thought you didn't want to work with him," Mitch said.

"I never said that." Jerry dragged the pillow into a more comfortable position. "I said I wasn't sure. Anyway, it doesn't look as though we have much choice."

"It's her right," Mitch said again.

"She's not Magister," Jerry said. He hadn't meant to say it so bluntly, hadn't meant to say it at all, but the words hung in the air between them. Mitch fixed him with a stare.

"Gil's dead."

"Yes, I *know* that."

"We need a leader," Mitch said.

"We've been fine—"

"We have not been fine without one," Mitch said. "We've barely done anything since he died, and what we've done—it's been going through the motions, Jer, you know that. Alma's the logical choice. I don't want it, and you—"

"What makes you think I don't want it?" Jerry asked. He was perversely glad of the argument, anything to take his mind off the moment when he met Davenport's eyes and knew there was nothing he could do to stop the rush of power.

"You've never showed the slightest interest," Mitch said.

"That was before Gil died," Jerry said.

"Are you saying you don't trust Alma? Because after tonight, that would be pretty damned ungrateful." Mitch glared at him.

"Yes, it would be," Jerry snapped, "and of course I trust her. She's damn good, and before you say it, no, it's not the first time she's saved my life. Why is it so hard to imagine that I might want to be Magister myself?"

There was a little silence, and Jerry saw Mitch take a breath. "Do you?" he said. "Do you really?"

And this was how lodges broke, Jerry thought, statements made in anger that men were too proud to take back, in anger that was a mask for fear. He ran a hand through his hair. "No," he said. "Not— no."

"Then it has to be Al."

"Yes." Jerry closed his eyes.

Mitch reached for the bottle, topped up his own glass. He held it out again, and this time Jerry nodded. Mitch poured a second glass and carried it across.

Jerry took a sip of the bourbon, letting it scorch its way down his throat. "That wasn't Davenport," he said quietly, and Mitch gave him a sharp look.

"What do you mean?"

"It wasn't just Davenport," Jerry said again. "I mean, he doesn't exactly like me, any more than I like him, but it's not his style to randomly try to kill his academic rivals. There was something else there."

"Are you saying he was possessed?" Mitch asked.

"It's a good guess," Jerry said, "and an even better guess that Henry knows something he wasn't saying. I think I need to have words with him in the morning."

Jerry got out of the taxi stiffly and climbed the steps to Henry's house. The light of morning wasn't kind. Miss Patterson had dark circles under her eyes that even Hollywood powder couldn't conceal, but her lipstick and mascara were defiantly perfect. It could not have been an easy evening for her, Jerry thought, cleaning up after the ritual had gone rather obviously wrong—not the physical clean up, of course, she'd have staff of her own for that, but she'd have been the one smoothing ruffled feathers and providing explanations. He gave her a smile of sympathy, but she wouldn't meet his eyes.

She led him down the hall to Henry's office, past rooms where a few glasses still stood on side tables, and the rugs were rumpled. Jerry was willing to bet there were still a few people sleeping off hangovers, from drink or otherwise, in the bedrooms upstairs. She tapped on the door, and opened it without waiting for a response.

Henry looked up from the papers spread across his desk, and gave a nod of greeting. "Thanks, Pat," he said. "Tell Mrs. Russo to send up some more coffee, if you would, and then you can take the rest of the day off."

"I'll tell her," she answered, "but I need to stick around. There's still a lot to be done, Mr. Kershaw."

"Can it wait?"

She hesitated. "Some of it...."

"Then do whatever can't wait, and take off. You did a hell of a job last night."

She smiled then, tired but game. "Thank you. I'm just sorry—"

"What happened was not your fault," Henry said. "There's nothing you could have done to prevent it."

She gave Jerry a swift, dubious look, but nodded. "Thank you, Mr. Kershaw. I'll have Rosa send up more coffee."

The door closed softly behind her, and Henry waved vaguely toward the waiting chairs. Jerry lowered himself carefully, propping his cane to hand against the edge of the desk, and lifted an eyebrow. "Nice to have good help."

"She's very good," Henry answered. "Used to work for one of the studios, assistant director. It comes in very handy when we're trying to do a nice ritual."

Jerry supposed it would, which raised several questions, but, interesting as it would be to pursue the matter, it wasn't relevant. "You've got a problem here, Henry."

"No kidding." Henry twirled a fountain pen between his fingers. "I had no idea he'd try something like that—I don't even know why—"

"Don't you?" Jerry fixed him with the stare he'd used on ungrateful undergraduates, and Henry looked away.

"I didn't know. Not for sure. And I couldn't say anything, not without proof."

"Something has possessed William Davenport," Jerry said. "Or he's allied himself with something very dubious. I've known him and his style, his energy, for too many years to think that was just him, no matter what he may have learned. And if you knew it and didn't do anything about it—"

"I couldn't," Henry said again. He shoved his chair back from the desk, crossed to the windows to pull back the curtains. The windows faced east, and the sun was strong enough to make both men wince, but Henry stared out at the pool house anyway. "I only suspected because Bill asked me to stand in for someone last week—he'd been doing something with a smaller group, teaching new students, and one of the men was ill, and they couldn't put it off...."

That made sense, Jerry thought. Davenport had never had any respect for Henry's talent—which was real enough, even if it wasn't disciplined, and even if Henry was lazy and didn't always show at his best. If Davenport didn't believe Henry was any good, then he would have assumed that Henry couldn't actually feel what was going on. "But you sensed—something," he prompted, and Henry shrugged.

"I thought something was off. Bill wasn't himself—it wasn't like him to bother with the novices, especially when he'd already said they weren't a very promising group. I thought at first maybe Mac—Don McKenzie, I think he's after your time—had leaned on him to make him do it." His hand was tight on the edge of the curtain, crumpling the expensive linen with its stenciled patterns. "Then.... There was just something wrong, something very dark, and it took everything I could muster to pretend I hadn't noticed."

"So why the hell didn't you say something to your Magister—whoever, McKenzie?" Jerry glared at him, remembering the sudden inaudible rush of power, standing there by the pool knowing he'd never been as strong as Davenport alone and that he certainly wasn't as strong as Davenport plus whatever power he carried. And then Alma, thank God, interposing her will and shield, buying him time.... He shook the thought away—it wasn't even twenty-four hours after, he had a right to be a little shaky still—and narrowed his eyes at Henry. "Or have you been playing politics again?"

Henry didn't look away from the pool. "Not me. I learned my lesson last time."

"Like hell."

"Don't start." For a second, Henry sounded unutterably weary, and that pulled Jerry up short. "It wasn't me," Henry said again. "But, yes, there was an—issue, some accusations and complications about six months ago, and I didn't want to say anything. Especially since I'm morally certain that no one else at the ritual noticed a damn thing. What was I going to do, go to Mac and say, hey, Bill Davenport's playing with nasty toys, only nobody else noticed but me? You really think that's going to go over well? Knowing what the big boys think of me? Oh, Kershaw's willing, and he's got money, but—not much talent." He controlled himself with an effort. "I did wonder if that's why he didn't want to do anything with the tablet. It's a thing of light, definitely."

"That's why you invited us to the ritual," Jerry said. "Reliable, unbiased witnesses."

Henry let the curtain fall, cutting off the sunlight again. "Yep."

"Thanks a lot."

"I had no idea he'd do anything like that," Henry said. "It doesn't make sense."

It didn't, Jerry thought, unless the thing, whatever it was, had recognized the Aedificatorii Templi, recognized the presence of a member of a lodge committed to the Great Work. Davenport had been part of it once himself, had repudiated it, and he'd never liked Jerry. The two things together might have been enough, for a creature like that.

"What are you going to do about it?" he asked, after a moment.

Henry seated himself again, steepled his fingers in front of his chin. "I'll talk to Mac. There's no other choice."

Jerry sighed. "If you want, I can write you a statement. Say what I experienced. Or McKenzie can contact me himself. I'm willing to back you up on this, Henry."

"Thank you." Henry's eyes flickered closed, just for an instant, visible relief.

"There is one thing you could do for me," Jerry said.

Henry gave him a suspicious look, and Jerry met it guilelessly.

"I'd like to spend some more time with the tablet, and I've got some references back at the hotel that would be very helpful. Let me borrow it for the day, if you would. I can at least give you a decent translation."

Henry hesitated, but finally sighed. "I want it back. It's important."

"You have my word," Jerry said. "I'll bring it back tomorrow."

"All right," Henry said. He went to the glass-fronted cabinet, brought out the well-wrapped bundle and handed it across the desk. "Just—be careful."

"Believe me," Jerry said, and slipped the packet into his pocket. "I will."

This man fought him. Managing him was no easy task, but then one worth having was not. He had knowledge and power both, not enough, but more than the first man, the hapless Vittorio Gadda. That one's mind had been small, filled with nothing but concerns for the family he left behind, with the fear he would lose his job. This one – he had thoughts worth knowing.

And yet he fought harder. There were times, almost, that he broke free. He could not, of course, and if he did it would regain control. But he was strong, a priest and scholar, nothing to be trifled with.

He did not want to get on the train. He struggled on the platform, enough that no doubt it looked odd, a man hesitating to board when he had a ticket, letting the others pass him. "Are you coming, sir?" a man asked. Uniform, cap. This man's mind provided the information. The conductor.

"Yes," it said, and they stepped aboard. It was easier once the train started, once they were in the compartment. There was no way to get off, and so this man stopped fighting. It wished it could believe he was defeated, not just marshaling his strength. He was no fool, this one. It felt a heady kind of power in that. There was power in the struggle. And each bit of power made it stronger.

It had hoped there would be real power in California, but there was not. These rites were tasty but no more than that. Money, yes. Some money, and a little energy. But not what it hungered for. Kings and emperors had not been enough for it. Certainly there was no one here worthy of its attention. This man would do until it found a better.

And then it would ascend again to the heights of power it craved.

Lewis stared at the square of lead sitting in the middle of the table in Jerry's room, silk and burlap unfolded around it. It didn't look like much, just a slab of metal incised with letters and symbols that he didn't recognize. Mitch held out a pack of cigarettes;

Lewis took one, lit it without thinking, and drew in a long breath of smoke.

"All right," Jerry said. He opened his notebook, unfolded a sheet of paper. "Here's the transcription of the Latin, with my translation. Most of it is pretty standard, very similar to the invocations you see on the more elaborate curse tablets—Henry wasn't wrong about that, at least. It's only here at the end that we get the crucial part." He pointed. "Diana in all your aspects, heal the wounds and strengthen the bonds that here imprison this spirit of the underworld, through the power here embodied in these tablets."

"Tablets?" Alma asked. She laid a cautious finger against the metal, pulled it back as though she'd been shocked. "Oh. That's—"

"Potent?" Jerry said. "Yes. And, fortunately, of the light. But, yes, tablets, plural."

Mitch eyed the lead warily. "What you're saying is that this was intended to imprison an infernal spirit? So it is a binding."

"That would be my best guess," Jerry answered.

The metal gleamed dully in the overhead light, the air conditioning unit throbbing beneath the curtained window. It was only roughly square, with what looked like silver nail heads in each of the four corners; the lines of Roman letters and spiky Etruscan symbols covered the entire surface. The once-sharp edges were blurred, worn and polished bright, and there were other bright spots among the letters, as though something had rubbed against it. Without thinking, Lewis reached for it, and caught his breath as his fingers touched the metal. It was—not hot, not exactly, and not quite a shock, either, but there was something live there, like the leap of a pulse beneath his fingertips. Like the power he'd felt at the ritual, the deep strength that had blocked whatever it was that Davenport had done—

"Use the silk if you have to touch it," Jerry said impatiently, and looked back at his notes.

"Silk is an insulator," Alma said. She touched his arm gently. "And this—it has a lot of power."

Lewis nodded slowly. "It's... hot? I don't know." He used the silk scarf to turn it over, not sure what he was looking for—he could still feel the power buzzing in it, but not as strong, not as startling now that he knew it was there—and saw an odd geometric design carved into the tablet, along with another block of letters. They were Roman, but there weren't any spaces between the words, and he looked at Jerry. "What does this say?"

Jerry pushed his glasses up again. "Ah, that. The symbols are attributes of Diana, various aspects, and the inscription asks her to punish anyone who disturbs the tablets. Again, plural. This must have been part of a larger working."

"That can't be good," Mitch said. "Look, Jerry, what are we trying to do here? Or are you just curious?"

Jerry glared at him. "It seems highly probable that this tablet is one of a set meant to hold—something, an infernal spirit, a demon—imprisoned in Lake Nemi. The tablet was placed in the first year of Claudius's reign, which would make the demon something associated with Caligula."

"Which even I know is bad news," Mitch said. "But what are we doing with it?"

Jerry ignored him. "Suetonius says that Caligula interfered with the succession of the priesthood of Diana's shrine, thus desecrating the shrine, and he also profaned Diana's holy lake by building the ships that are currently being excavated. No one was supposed to sail on the lake, you see. So I would assume that this thing that the tablets bound was somehow part of the general profanation of the temple fane. And I think we can also assume that it is what we all sensed in Davenport."

"Can we?" Alma asked. "You've said for years you didn't like Davenport's methods, and that he was going to stir up something nasty one of these days."

"Granted," Jerry said. "But Henry told me that Davenport started off excited about this tablet, and then dropped it completely. I think that's significant."

"I'll buy that," Alma said, and Mitch nodded.

"Ok. So what are we doing with it? It's Henry's lodge and Henry's problem. They're in a lot better place to deal with Davenport."

"Henry's consulting his Magister," Jerry said, "and I said I'd back him up if he needed evidence."

Lewis looked up sharply. That didn't sound very satisfactory at all, and from Alma's expression, she agreed.

"Will they?" she asked.

"I also thought I'd call Bullfinch," Jerry said. He glanced at Lewis. "Geoffrey Bullfinch. He's—an expert in these matters, I suppose you'd say. If Henry's lodge won't act, or can't, Bullfinch definitely will."

Alma grimaced—thinking of the expense of the long distance call, Lewis thought—but nodded. "Go ahead. It's a good idea."

Jerry shoved himself to his feet, limped to the telephone. "Long distance, please." He gave the number, listened, and hung up with a quick thank you. "She'll ring back when she gets through," he said, and met Alma's gaze squarely. "Look, I'd prefer to take action myself, but—you're right, it's not our lodge. Now that they know, they'll have to do something, and they're a large and powerful group. They will deal with him. And if they don't, Bullfinch will."

Mitch stubbed out the last of his cigarette. "Which brings me back to my question, Jer. What exactly are we doing here?"

Jerry looked at the tablet. "I want to know what this thing is," he said. "I want to know what they're up against. Just in case."

"In case what?" Mitch asked.

Jerry reached for his cigarette case, and busied himself lighting one.

Alma said, "In case Henry's people can't handle it. In case something else goes wrong. I agree with Jerry on this one."

"Ok," Mitch said again. "So what's our next step?"

"I have an idea there," Alma said. "Lewis?"

Lewis gave her a wary look.

"What we talked about before," she said. "If you're willing."

"My— the dreams?" It felt weird to be talking about it, especially in front of the others, and he braced himself for disbelief, for mockery.

"Yes."

It was his choice, Lewis realized. She wouldn't say anything more unless he agreed. Mitch might talk about her bullying people, but that wasn't her style, not in anything this important. And he wanted to help. He still wasn't sure about this whole lodge thing, about magic and this network of lodges—it still sounded like something out of the pulps, or out of Uncle Arturo's tales of Masonic conspiracy—but he was sure of what he'd felt at Henry Kershaw's house. That rush of power, the unprovoked attack, the sheer malevolence behind it.... "Ok," he said. "I'm game."

Alma's smile warmed him to the core. "Lewis is a clairvoyant," she said. "He dreams true. Maybe he can see something for us."

Mitch nodded. "Good thought."

"That's very useful," Jerry said. "A mirror, maybe, or black ink in a silver dish—"

"Something simple," Alma said, firmly.

"Simple would be good," Lewis said.

"Simple is about all we can manage on short notice," Mitch said.

At Jerry's instruction, Lewis seated himself at the low table, and Alma slid the tablet in its wrappings so that it lay between his upturned palms. He imagined he could feel the power radiating from it, warm like sunlight on the edges of his hands. He turned his hands so that his palms faced in, and felt the heat gathering, tingling in his palms.

"Relax," Jerry said softly. "Close your eyes, let your mind drift. Just relax."

Obediently, Lewis closed his eyes, took a deep breath, trying to find his way back into the images of his dreams. He could remember most of them, the dog, the women, the lake, Davenport with his hand outstretched, but they were all clearly memories, nothing new. His foot itched. His eyes snapped open, and he rubbed the arch of his foot, grimacing. The warmth in his palms was fading. "Sorry."

"It's Ok," Alma said. "Try again."

Lewis took another deep breath, closed his eyes again, but there was nothing but the red dark behind his eyelids. "I'm not—this isn't working."

"It's Ok," Alma said. "Let's take a break."

Lewis pushed himself up from the table, went to stand by the window, brushing aside the curtain so that he could stare out onto the heat of Hollywood Boulevard. Below him, a limousine negotiated the late afternoon traffic, the chauffeur in the open driver's compartment rigidly ignoring every other car on the road. It wasn't working; whatever talent he might have, it wasn't looking very useful at all.

"Diana Nemorensis," Alma said. Lewis didn't turn, still watching the limousine creep forward. "Jerry, what about this?"

"Gil's denarius?"

Lewis glanced over his shoulder, saw Alma holding out the blue box, saw the flash of gold as Jerry extracted the coin. Suddenly he was back in the wood, under the trees. A circle of lake as perfect as the moon lay below him; torches flared on the shore, and a congregation in white robes lifted their hands to the sky. The image was gone as quickly as it had appeared, and he blinked, shook his head hard.

"Lewis?" Alma's voice seemed weirdly distant, and he shook his head again.

"Whoa."

"He saw something," Jerry said. "Didn't you?"

"I—yes," Lewis said. He let the curtain fall, turned to face the others. "Why now?"

"Because of this," Jerry said. He held up the coin. "This is Diana of Aricia."

"So there's a connection to the tablet," Mitch said, and Jerry nodded.

"Indirect, but yes, a connection."

"Maybe that's why—" Alma began, and blushed. "I keep it in my dresser drawer."

And the dresser was next to the bed. Lewis felt his own cheeks heat. "But why me?"

There was a little silence. "No offense," Jerry said at last, "but you were there."

"Alma's about as clairvoyant as a rock," Mitch said, with a grin.

"The binding was done in Diana's name," Jerry said. "It's a logical connection. And if a demon has been loosed—" He shrugged. "That's what we swore our oaths for. Anyone who's sworn to the Great Work probably feels something. We just happened to have a closer connection."

Lewis glanced at Alma, half expecting her to grin and shrug, but she was nodding, her expression perfectly serious. "So you want me to try again?"

"If you're willing," Alma said.

Lewis settled himself in front of the tablet again, and Jerry set the coin at its foot. The gold caught the light, blurring the figures.

"Relax," Jerry said again. "Close your eyes, relax, and let your mind drift."

It's not working. Lewis bit back the words, made himself sit still a little longer. What he really wanted was to be flying back to Colorado, all of this behind him—no more rituals, no more weird stories, dreams and visions, just the cold air at altitude and the deep green of the pines below. And suddenly he was in the grove again, staring at the lake below. The torches were gone, but the lake itself was ablaze with light, as though buildings floated on the water. Music played in the distance, drums and pipes and the rattle of a tambourine; there were voices, and a shriek caught between pleasure and pain. At his knee, the white dog snarled in answer, her hackles raised.

His eyes flew open, the image vanishing, and Alma met his gaze across the table.

"Try again," she said, before anyone else could say anything, and he closed his eyes obediently.

He was on a patio, stone tiles cool beneath his feet, the air sweet with resin, sparks streaming up from pitch-pine torches to rival the stars. The sound of voices was much louder, and even though he couldn't understand the words, he couldn't miss the note of hysteria, laughter hard and high like an estaminet right behind the lines. There was a smell of wine, too, and incense, and under it the tang of vomit, and out of the corner of his eye he saw a man in white sag helplessly over a railing.

In the center of the patterned floor, on a circle spoked like a wheel, a girl was dancing, naked except for ribbons at her wrists and ankles. He felt himself blush, looked away to see a handsome young man resting on a couch. There was a wreath in his golden hair, and a wine cup in his hand: the emperor of the world, Caligula. He lifted his head and Lewis saw clearly into his eyes. There was nothing human there, only a darkness so deep and hungry that nothing, no act of man, could be more than a momentary satisfaction.

Lewis wrenched himself out of the vision with a gasp, caught himself on the edge of the table.

"Easy," Mitch said.

Alma eyed him carefully. "Are you all right?"

Lewis nodded. He could still smell the resin smoke, reached for a cigarette to take the taste out of his mouth.

"What did you see?" Jerry asked.

Lewis lit the cigarette, took a long breath of the smoke. "I saw it. The thing that attacked you." The look in its eyes haunted him—he'd thought he'd seen everything in France, but that bottomless malice was more frightening than anything he'd ever imagined. Treat it like photo recon, he told himself, just pictures, just like the bodies tangled in the wire after a night assault could become nothing more than dots, a pattern on a photographic plate. "You were right, Jerry, it was Caligula, and it's—" He stopped, not able to find a word large enough for what he'd seen.

"Tell me exactly what you saw," Jerry said again.

Lewis took another long pull on his cigarette, marshalling the words the way he'd ordered his reports in the war. The woods, and the dog, and the ships, and then Caligula and the thing within him. He shook his head, still groping for the words, and Alma patted his shoulder.

"That's not good," Mitch said, half under his breath.

"No," Alma said. "It has to be stopped."

Jerry handed her the coin and began folding the tablet back into its wrappings, taking more care than was strictly necessary. "Why the hell doesn't that operator call back?"

"You know how long it takes to get a trunk line," Mitch said. "When you can get one."

"I'll call Henry, warn him what he's dealing with," Jerry said. "It'll light a fire under him."

He moved to the telephone, lifted the receiver. Lewis looked at the others. "Isn't there something more we should do?"

"Like what?" Mitch's tone was gentle, easing the sting. "He hasn't done anything, Lewis. Not that we can go to the police about. And his own lodge is going to have a better idea of how to find him, how to stop him. He's on their turf."

"And they're a solid group," Alma said. "I may not agree with the way they do things, but they're of the light. They will stop him."

The force of the vision was fading, the details disappearing like a dream, and he was glad to let it go. "And Davenport's not Caligula," Lewis said. "It's not like he can order up orgies and murder. This isn't Rome."

"Exactly," Alma said.

"I got Henry," Jerry said. "He's going to call his Magister, and some others. They're on it."

"Good," Mitch said.

"I told him we'd help if they needed it," Jerry went on. "And I asked him to let us know what happens."

"Thank you," Alma said. "Do you think they'll call? If they need us?"

"They'll call," Mitch said.

The telephone rang then, and Jerry grabbed for it, pivoting awkwardly on his artificial leg so that he stumbled against the bed. "Ballard." He listened for a long moment, his frown deepening. "Can't you keep trying? He might—oh, I see. All right, thank you."

He hung up the phone very carefully, and turned to face the others. "Bullfinch isn't answering. The operator says he's unavailable."

"What does that mean?" Lewis blurted.

Jerry shrugged. "Out of town, gone into retreat, I have no idea. The operator just said the San Valencez exchange says they can't reach him and don't know when they will be able to."

"On a job, maybe," Mitch said, and Jerry shrugged again.

"God knows."

"Which leaves this to Henry," Alma said. "And his lodge."

"They'll handle it," Mitch said. "You said it yourself, they're solid. But it's in their hands now." He paused. "Look, let's call it a day. We've earned a break, to get this out of our heads. I had a conversation with one of the bellhops yesterday, and he gave me a card for a nice little dinner and dance spot not too far from here. We're in Hollywood, we might as well act like it."

Lewis nodded. That was exactly what they needed, something normal, or as normal as a Hollywood nightclub would be.

"Our last party went off so well," Jerry said, but he didn't look disapproving.

Alma gave a reluctant smile. "All right. Give me time to change, and we'll do that."

It was solidly dark by the time they'd all bathed and changed. Lewis shaved hastily, put on his one good suit, and couldn't suppress a soft whistle as Alma emerged from the bathroom. He'd seen the blue dress before, but it looked good on her, flattering her height and her eyes. She'd found a ribbon flower somewhere, and pinned it to her hat, and the curls that peeped out by her ears shone like gold.

"I don't suppose Mitch and Jerry would be willing to wait a little bit," he said.

"Not Jerry," Alma answered, but she let him kiss her anyway, and pulled away before he could smudge her lipstick too badly. There was enough of a promise there that he held her wrap without complaint, and they rode the elevator down to the lobby under the attendant's incurious eye.

Mitch had gotten directions from the bell captain, and led them down Hollywood Boulevard as though he belonged there. He was careful to keep at a pace Jerry could manage comfortably, though, and Lewis hung back a little himself, enjoying the feeling of Alma's hand on his arm. There were palm trees everywhere, tall and exotic, and he craned his head as they passed, wondering if there were coconuts in them. Surely that would be too dangerous, but he couldn't see for sure.

Ahead of them, Mitch paused, pointing to something across the street. "Or we could just take in a movie."

On the far side of the boulevard, a line of palm trees in stone planters led back toward a square-pillared concrete-colored building. There were painted columns on the left, and paintings like in an Egyptian tomb lined the long walls. The sign above the entrance read, in enormous fake-historical letters, Grauman's Egyptian. Alma reached across and whacked him with her purse. From the way he hunched his shoulder, she hadn't pulled her punch, and Lewis couldn't really blame her.

"I think we've had enough Egyptian theater on this trip," Jerry said.

The dinner club was like something out of a movie, with a huge doorman in a brass-buttoned uniform who examined the card Mitch handed him with great care before touching his peaked cap and allowing an underling to open the door. There was a hat check girl in a short-skirted uniform that showed the tops of her rolled stockings, and an orchestra in white dinner jackets playing respectable jazz. A discreet tip got them a pleasant table toward the side of the dance floor, and Lewis was glad to see Alma relax a little. A waiter in a red jacket took Jerry's drink order, and returned with glasses and a coffee pot, from which he proceeded to pour a round of gin sours. Lewis tasted his cautiously, decided that the gin had come from a clean bathtub, at least, and Jerry lifted his glass.

"A semi-successful trip, anyway."

"Which is about all you can hope for with Henry," Alma said, and they touched glasses.

The food was good, too, and they ordered a second round of drinks, and then a third. Lewis thought about asking Alma to dance, but after the conversation he'd overheard, he didn't think it would be a good idea to rub it in. Jerry was in a surprisingly good mood, though some of that might be the gin, and Lewis didn't really want to spoil that. So of course Mitch asked her to dance instead, and he watched with mild envy while Jerry told him a long and apparently pointless story about a dig he'd worked on once in Egypt.

Then as Mitch and Alma passed them for the third time, her eyes met his, and she lifted a hand, beckoning. He wasn't about to turn that down, but he waited until Jerry hit a stopping place before he rose to cut in, and he and Alma turned gravely at the edge of the dance floor, neither one of them a very good dancer, but both enjoying the chance to hold each other in public. The music stopped, the band leader announcing a break, and Alma brought him back to the table, fanning herself as she sat down.

"I suppose we should start back."

Jerry fished his watch out of his pocket. He'd had a fourth

drink while they were dancing, something dark and dangerous looking, but he still seemed good-humored enough. "It is getting late. And I promised Henry I'd give him back the tablet tomorrow morning."

Lewis sighed softly—he'd managed to forget about magic and curse tablets and mysterious obligations—but Mitch nodded, and signaled for the check. Lewis winced at the prices, but put in his share without complaint. It was worth it to have danced with Alma in a Hollywood nightclub. They paused at the door, collecting hats and Alma's wrap, and the doorman looked them over.

"Call you a cab, boss?"

Mitch made the mistake of looking at Jerry, who shook his head.

"We're fine, thanks," he said, and strode briskly out the door, his cane tapping on the pavement. Lewis looked at Alma, who rolled her eyes, but followed.

The street was much quieter than he'd expected, the traffic noise from Hollywood Boulevard distant and muted. It seemed darker, too, as though the streetlights were further apart.

And that was foolish, he told himself, and smiled as Alma took his arm. She tucked her other arm through Jerry's, her heels loud on the pavement, and Mitch glanced over his shoulder, grinning. Then there was a movement ahead of them, shadows detaching themselves from a doorway, and Jerry released Alma's arm, freeing himself to use his cane.

"Hey, now," Mitch said. There were three of them, three big guys in work clothes, one with a sports coat that showed almost forest green in the streetlight, the others in shirtsleeves. "We don't want any problems."

Lewis stepped in front of Alma. The guy in the coat moved like a knife fighter, moved like trouble.

"You got 'em anyway," one of the others said, to Mitch, and the third man stepped wide to flank them. A razor glinted in his left hand.

"You don't want to do this," Mitch said. "You're making a mistake—"

The guy in the coat made a sudden rush, heading for Jerry. Lewis hesitated, trying to keep an eye on the guy with the razor, keep himself between him and Alma. Jerry turned slightly, pivoting on his good leg, and reached under the back of his jacket. He came up with a pistol, small, maybe a .22, polished steel, and fired once. The man in the green coat staggered back, blood blossoming on his pale shirt, and Jerry turned again, bracing himself with his cane.

"Get down, Mitch—"

Mitch ducked, but the other two were already running, feet loud in the quiet street, and Jerry pointed his pistol at the sky instead.

"Oh, my God," Alma said. She caught Lewis's hand in hers, her grip punishingly tight.

Mitch knelt by the man in the green coat, checking his pulse, and looked up with a shake of his head. "He's gone."

"Yes," Jerry said, but Lewis could see him shaking.

"All right," Mitch said, and pushed himself to his feet. "Three against one, but, Ok—"

"You and Lewis take Alma back to the hotel," Jerry said. He tapped his wooden leg with the cane. "Who's going to arrest a wounded veteran who's been set upon by thugs?"

"Especially if he's protecting his girlfriend," Alma said. She unlaced her fingers from Lewis's and nodded to him. "Jerry's right. The two of you go on. We'll take care of this."

Lewis looked at Mitch, saw the same reluctance in his eyes, but they both knew she was right. There'd be a lot more questions asked if they were all there, and they would be questions he didn't know how to answer. There wasn't time to hesitate, someone would have heard the shot—maybe that was even a siren he was hearing now—and Mitch nodded slowly. "All right. We'll come after you if we don't hear."

"Go," Alma said, and they turned away.

Chapter Eight

The sirens were definitely getting closer. Jerry took a deep breath, and wrapped his arm around Alma's waist, pulling her against his side. She leaned in stiffly, still shocked, and the first beat cop came charging around the corner, revolver drawn. Jerry lifted his cane, showed his right hand empty as well.

"Thank God! Officer—" His voice cracked: embarrassing, but probably useful. He cleared his throat. "This guy—we were attacked—"

"Hold it right there, buddy," the cop said, but he lowered his weapon. Behind him, a car turned into the street, siren grinding to a halt. Its revolving light cast flashes of blue down the length of the street, flickering off the bricks and narrow sidewalk. More cops appeared, and a second car, disgorging a pair of men in cheap civilian suits.

"Thank God," Jerry said again. "I didn't know what to do."

"Ok, pal." That was one of the civilians, tall and lean and graying. Jerry could see his eyes moving, taking in the body and the cane and the wooden leg, drawing a picture already. "What's your name?"

"Jeremiah Ballard. This is Alma Gilchrist."

She nodded, wide-eyed, had the sense to say nothing.

One of the uniformed men had a notebook out, was scribbling in it, while another one knelt beside the body, feeling for a pulse.

"This one's a goner, Lieutenant," he said, and began searching the pockets.

"Ok, Mr. Ballard—"

"Doctor," Jerry said, gave a little shrug and a wincing smile. Better to fix it now and look pompous than have to correct him later. "It's Doctor, actually."

"Dr. Ballard," the lieutenant said, with a lifted eyebrow. "So what happened here?"

"We were out for the evening," Jerry said, "Al—Mrs. Gilchrist and I. We thought we'd walk back to the hotel, get a little air, and— this guy jumped out of the doorway. He had a knife—" Yes, the uniformed man had found it, was chalking the pavement to mark where it had fallen before another man took it away. Jerry tapped his wooden leg with the tip of his cane. "I'm not much good in a fight, not since the War. But I couldn't let him hurt Alma."

"Did he say anything?" the lieutenant asked. Behind him, the cop was scribbling in his notebook, while the second civilian had gone to stare down at the body, his face expressionless.

"He wanted money," Jerry said. He looked at Alma, saw her nod. "I saw the knife, and he was coming at us."

"Get his gun," the lieutenant said, and the uniformed man put away his notebook. Jerry let him pat him down, felt him pull the little automatic from the holster at the small of his back.

"That's it, lieutenant," the cop said, and handed it over. The lieutenant looked at it for a minute, handed it back to the cop.

"You got a permit for that, Dr. Ballard?"

"Yes."

"How about an address?"

"I'm from out of town," Jerry said. "Colorado Springs. I'm staying at the Roosevelt Hotel."

"You ever seen this guy before?"

Jerry shook his head.

"He have any reason to think you two would have money?" the lieutenant asked.

'I have no idea," Jerry said.

"Hey, Mike." That was the other civilian, still staring at the body. "Guess who we got here? Sammy Lukeman."

"No kidding," the lieutenant said. "Ok, Dr. Ballard, you and Mrs. Gilchrist here are going to have to come down to the station with me. I've still got a few questions you can answer."

Jerry heard Alma take a breath, and he nodded as calmly as he could. "Of course."

The police station smelled of stale smoke and disinfectant, and the coffee they were offered tasted as though the pot had never been cleaned. Jerry sipped at it anyway, wishing for more sugar, but Alma tasted hers once and put it aside. He glanced sideways at her, wondering if he should offer his hand, but her expression was closed, and he looked away again.

They'd been through the questions again on the ride to the station, and once more separately, before the lieutenant—Morton—had brought them back to the interview room and left them there. "I'm sorry, Al," he said quietly, and she gave him a half smile. There were shadows under her eyes like bruises.

"Not quite the night we had in mind," she said.

"Maybe we should have just gone to the movies," Jerry began, and the door opened. Morton waved his stenographer to a chair, and sat down opposite them again.

"Well, so far your stories check out, except for one little thing." He looked at Alma. "I can't find you registered at the Roosevelt."

"Oh, my God," Alma said, and Jerry caught his breath. He'd forgotten, they'd both forgotten, that she'd registered as Lewis's wife. He opened his mouth, trying to think of something that wouldn't make her look like a whore.

"She's—" he began, groping for something, anything, and Morton pinned him with a look.

"I'd like to hear this from Mrs. Gilchrist, please."

The color rose in Alma's face, but her voice was mostly steady. "I'm registered as Mrs. Lewis Segura."

Morton lifted an eyebrow, though it couldn't have been a huge surprise. The stenographer smirked over his notebook. "So is it Gilchrist or Segura?"

"It's Gilchrist," Alma said.

"I don't see that this is really relevant," Jerry said. He tried to make his tone pleading rather than aggressive. "I'd really like not to cause anyone any more trouble."

Morton ignored him. "So you're not married to this Segura, either?"

"No," Alma said. Her cheeks were flaming. "I'm not."

"You get around, honey."

"Hey," Jerry said, and Morton looked at him.

"As for you, Dr. Ballard. Mr. Kershaw vouches for you like you said he would—and for Mrs. Gilchrist, lucky for her—and he's sending his lawyer to take care of the paperwork. You'll have to have a hearing on this."

We're from out of town, we need to get home—Jerry closed his mouth on the words, knowing they were pointless. Maybe Henry's lawyer could sort things out, figure out a way to get them out of it, but in the meantime, nothing good could come of protesting. "Ok," he said, and did his best to sound meek and unthreatening.

The lawyer arrived within the hour, brisk and competent. He checked the various papers, had them sign some and vetoed others—without complaint from Morton, Jerry noted—and finally led them out into the waning night. There were cabs waiting, and the lawyer signaled for one.

"Er, you do have money—"

"Yes," Jerry said, and opened the door for Alma. "The guy didn't get anything."

"Good," the lawyer said. "Very good. Er—"

"Tell Henry we'll call him in the morning," Jerry said firmly, and levered himself in next to Alma. He gave the cabbie the address, aware that the man was eyeing them with undisguised curiosity, and gave Alma a wary glance. She sat unmoving, eyes straight ahead, profile as stark as if it had been carved from stone. "I'm sorry," he said, after a moment. "I—I screwed up, Al. I didn't think."

She looked at him then. "I don't know whether to laugh or cry. Oh, my God, Jerry, I can't ever come back here again. And what will they think at the hotel?"

"It's Hollywood," Jerry said, with more confidence than he really felt. He patted her shoulder. "It will be all right."

"Easy for you to say," she said, but the stiffness had eased from her face.

Alma curled up on the bed around what was left of the shreds of her dignity. If Jerry hadn't saved them all from possible death, or at least serious injury, she'd have to kill him herself.

She stretched one hand out on the soft, cool white sheets, closing her eyes as her fingers opened. She could hear what Gil would say, his voice soft and rueful. *You get what you pay for, and you can't have your cake and eat it too.* The price of an unconventional life was not being respectable. She'd never been willing to do the things she'd need to do to be respectable. She'd never been able to imagine fitting in to a life so circumscribed, so narrow. A world without flying or magic. A world without Gil and everything they'd built together. It couldn't be worth it.

She hadn't liked Gil the day she'd met him. He'd seemed arrogant, dismissive, if not outright offended that the new ambulance driver assigned to the corps was a woman. "Well, what are we coming to," he'd said in a slow Midwestern drawl, like her mere presence was going to bring on the apocalypse. "We've got a girl driving the bus."

Reacting would have proved his point. Too emotional, too irresponsible to be given the awesome responsibility of saving men's lives. And so she had been cool. No, cold. Professional. She'd spoken to Lt. Colonel Gilchrist as little as possible and only in the line of duty. Until the day he'd been sprayed with shrapnel from an explosive shell.

Ambulance drivers didn't just drive the bus. Usually they were the first medical attention a wounded man received, and sometimes the only treatment. Especially if the wounds weren't life threatening, and the man was stubborn. She'd spent two hours with a lamp set up, picking splinters of metal out of his back with tweezers. Most of them were tiny, little razor sharp needles that had been smoking hot when they'd cut through jacket and shirt and undershirt to lodge in his skin. Tiny, yes. And none of them dangerous in themselves. But infection killed more men than wounds, and they'd come through a filthy jacket on their way in. Every single one of them could be dangerous if they suppurated.

It must have hurt, her pulling each one out with tweezers, nipping at lacerated flesh with metal pincers, then dabbing it with raw alcohol, but he sat still like she told him to, occasionally swearing a blue streak and then asking her pardon.

"I've heard it all before, Colonel," she said. And of course she had. By that time she'd been there four months and there wasn't a lot she hadn't seen or heard.

After that he treated her differently, with a cautious kind of respect, even if he no longer looked her up and down like a doll. She supposed that she'd earned his regard in some sense. In muddy, shapeless clothes it was hard to tell she was even female unless she spoke. She blended in, just Al. Pretty soon everyone had stopped apologizing for swearing in front of her. She'd stopped being female in any meaningful social sense, which suited her fine. Days and nights blurred together in a haze of exhaustion. There was only the corps.

Until the day Mitch was hit. He brought his plane in, wing dragging, and she could tell from the edge of the flight line that it was both plane and man to blame, and was running out on to the field with her kit before the props stopped rotating, Gil one step behind her. She jumped up on the wing and leaned over Mitch, his hands on the controls and his eyes pressed shut, his lap full of blood.

"Ok," Mitch said calmly. "I'm going to die now."

"Don't be ridiculous," Al snapped. "Gil, help me get him out of here. Get his shoulders." She could already see. If it had been an artery he would have passed out long ago. It wasn't going to kill him. Just cost him his life.

Gil rode with him in the ambulance, hunched in the back holding his hand, while she'd jolted over roads rutted by artillery caissons, rutted through mud and fill all the way down to the Roman stones beneath. Afterwards, when he was delivered to proper surgeons, she'd stood a moment by the ambulance, thinking about Mitch's jokes and his thick Southern accent, his cool head and his offhand gallantry, the way he made the absurdly difficult seem effortless in the air. She'd begun to think of him as a friend, and even though he lived she wondered what the day had killed in him.

Gil came up behind her, leaned on the ambulance and lit a cigarette. They wouldn't let you smoke in the hospital, not with the oxygen tanks around. He inhaled and blew out a long stream. "Crap," he said quietly.

Al didn't trust her voice to say anything.

In a moment he put his hand on her back. He didn't say

it was ok, because it wasn't. He didn't say that he knew she'd done all she could, because she had. He just stood there, his hand on the back of her shoulder, and after a moment she leaned against it.

The hotel room door opened and Alma heard Lewis' quiet step. He was probably looking to see if she was asleep.

"I'm not," Alma said, opening her eyes.

Lewis sat down on the edge of the bed, looking characteristically sheepish. "Are you ok?"

"Fine," Alma said.

Lewis must have already talked to Jerry or Mitch. He looked around the room uncomfortably. "Alma, you know this isn't what it looks like."

Her gaze was perfectly steady. "It's exactly what it looks like, Lewis. We are sharing a bed, and we're not married." She could hear the ghost of Gil in her voice, *call a spade a spade, Al. We're spades.*

Lewis swallowed hard. "If..." he began.

"Shhhh." Alma sat up, putting her fingers to his lips. His skin was warm beneath her hand, a stubble of beard on his chin. "Don't." His eyes were hazel, and there was a tremor of hurt there. She put her hand to the side of his face. "It has to be about us. Do you see? It's not about anyone else or what they think."

After a moment he nodded. "I do see." Lewis shifted around, coming to sit so that she leaned back against him, his arm around her shoulders. "I've never met anyone like you," he said.

"I don't think there is anyone like me," Alma said, and she couldn't keep her voice from shaking a little. "I'm a strange bird."

"Well," said Lewis, after a moment, "I expect we all are."

Dawn was showing gray outside the curtains by the time Jerry got back to the room. He was moving a lot slower than usual, his face drawn with what looked more like pain than exhaustion, and stood now in the middle of the room, swaying slightly, before he finally managed to get up the energy to strip off his suit coat. Mitch watched long enough to be sure he wasn't actually going to fall over, then got up to fetch the bottle he'd left in the dresser drawer. He collected the tooth glasses, poured a stiff shot for each of them, and pressed one into Jerry's free hand. The other man blinked, startled, then drained it at a gulp. He held it out, and Mitch refilled, it, trying to read Jerry's expression. There was nothing there, though, just flat blue eyes staring at nothing, the lenses of his glasses catching the light. Mitch had learned long ago that what was said didn't matter just as long as there was a human voice, and he added another splash of bourbon to the glass.

"C'mon, Jerry, drink up."

Jerry blinked again, thoughts coming back from wherever he had been. He took another swallow, then stretched to set the glass on the bedside table. "It's Alma I feel worst for."

Mitch hesitated, not knowing how to respond.

"I forgot," Jerry said. "I didn't think about how we registered, I just thought it would be easier this way."

"We none of us thought," Mitch said. "And it was Al's idea, remember."

"Gil would have thought," Jerry said.

That was unanswerable, though if Gil had been alive, Alma might not have cared as much. Mitch said, "He was a better liar than any of us."

The ghost of a smile flickered across Jerry's face. "Can you imagine what he'd have done if he'd been here?"

Carried it off with panache and a line of bullshit second to none, Mitch thought, but it felt too raw still to say. "I'm almost scared to think."

"Yes—" Jerry stopped abruptly, wincing. "God. Help me get my leg off, will you?"

He dropped heavily onto the edge of the bed. Mitch gave him a wary look, beginning to be really worried now. He couldn't remember the last time Jerry had actually asked for help. He got Jerry's pants off, feeling the scars pull in his own low belly as he took the other man's weight, started on his shirt before Jerry shook himself and started to cooperate. The belt and straps that held the wooden leg in place looked like an instrument of torture, and from Jerry's expression that wasn't far from the truth at this point. Jerry started to heave himself into a better position, but Mitch put a careful hand on his good knee.

"Drink," he said. "Let me do this."

For a second, he thought Jerry would refuse, but then he reached for his glass again and took a long swallow. Mitch turned his attention to the buckles, undoing the wide straps. He'd known they had to be tight to do any good, but he couldn't help grimacing at the grooves they'd left in Jerry's skin. He tugged the leg free, and winced again at the rubbed raw skin. Jerry flexed the knee, the absurd stump wagging. There wasn't much more than five or six inches left, barely enough to fit into the carved socket.

"There's some cream in my Dopp kit," Jerry said.

"Right." Mitch found the tube after a quick search, brought it back to the bed. Jerry took it, began to smooth the ointment onto the stump, face tightening.

"So," Mitch said. "When did you start carrying a gun?"

"Packing heat," Jerry said, with a snort of something like laughter. He closed the tube, reached for his drink again. It seemed to be hitting him harder than usual, but that wasn't necessarily a bad thing. "Since this." He lifted the stump. "I didn't think it was wise to rely on fisticuffs."

And if he could say 'fisticuffs,' Mitch thought, he wasn't that drunk. Or maybe he was, nothing ever seemed to stop Jerry from talking. "Probably not."

"The police kept it," Jerry said. He leaned back against the headboard, eyes half closed behind his glasses.

"I'd expect them to," Mitch said. He took a swallow of his own drink, letting the bourbon burn its way down his gut, fire to match the dull pain that had started where the scars had pulled. It happened now and again, as he'd been told it would, adhesions pulling loose, old scars newly inflamed by an injudicious movement. It would only be a problem if he bled—there were still shrapnel fragments in there somewhere—or if the pain got worse, and became something he didn't know. But this was the same as always, and he sat still, waiting for it to ease away.

"Gil made me get a .22," Jerry said. "Said he knew I liked big guns, but he thought discretion was better."

Mitch smiled in spite of himself. Yeah, that was Gil, all right, a double entendre said with a straight face, and just enough connection to demonstrable truth that no one could point a finger. "That's Gil."

"Yeah." Jerry's voice broke then, and Mitch looked away from the naked grief on his face.

"Go to sleep, Jer," he said, gently, and got up, wincing, to put out the overhead light. Jerry slid down onto the pillows, setting his glasses aside, and Mitch switched off the bedside lamp for him. He should go to bed himself, he knew, but he could feel the pain settling in for a while, not agonizing, but enough to keep him awake, keep him from finding a comfortable position until whatever he'd strained loosened up again. He settled himself in the armchair instead, bending one leg and then the other until he found a workable position.

Outside the curtains, the light was getting stronger, the sky a paler gray, the room filled with familiar shadows. Jerry was asleep or passed out or anyway silent and unmoving, the stump tucked under the sheet, and Mitch felt the familiar bleak sorrow wash through him. It wasn't fair, and never would be fair, and no one could expect it to be fair. At least he could still fly. He shifted his weight again, finding a new position, trying to focus on the memory of flight, the feel of the air around him, lift, control, freedom.... He closed his eyes, conjuring up the Terrier's controls under his hands and feet, the instrument panel readings optimal, but even as he lost himself in the daydream, he felt the tug of the old fear. Someday even flying might not be enough.

Chapter Nine

They ordered a late breakfast at the diner down the street from the hotel, lingering at their table while the bored waitress erased the blackboard and wrote out the lunch specials and the cook and the dishwasher called back and forth in Spanish, lifting their voices to be heard over the clatter of pans and the scrape of the spatula on the griddle. Jerry sipped his third cup of coffee, wishing his headache would go away. His stump still hurt, too, in spite of extra moleskin: it was looking like a day to be endured. Of course, they were all looking a little rough, Alma with dark circles under her eyes, Mitch with ghostly stubble on his cheeks. Even Lewis looked only half awake, and he hadn't bothered with a tie. Alma was wearing slacks, and her plain blouse was buttoned almost to the chin. And that Jerry felt bad about.

"I'm sorry," he said again, and Alma looked up sharply from the remains of her pancakes.

"So am I. I don't really like being taken for a—a floozy."

Jerry pushed his glasses back up onto his nose. "It wasn't entirely my idea. In fact, if you'd gone when I told you to—"

"We'd've been down at the police station bailing you out at three in the morning," Alma snapped. "If they'd even let you go."

"At least you wouldn't be worrying about what some cop thought about you," Jerry said.

"Some cop," Alma said. "The entire precinct, more like. Not to mention the clerk at the hotel. They all think I'm— well, at best, they think I'm some cheap little round-heels with no more sense than morals. Or they think I'm a hooker."

"How do you think I feel?" Jerry glared at her. It felt good to snap, good to let out some of the pent-up misery. "I can either look like a four-eyed cripple who doesn't know enough to know he's being had—"

"Thank you very much," Alma said.

"Or I can look like the kind of guy who'd screw his best friend's wife." Jerry stopped abruptly, aware of shaky ground, aware, too, that Lewis was scowling at him and the waitress was listening with interest. He felt the blood rising in his face, and abruptly Alma began to laugh.

"Oh, Jerry," she said. "What a mess."

"You see, kids?" Mitch said. "All better now."

"Go chase yourself," Alma said, but she was smiling.

Jerry grabbed the check, counted out a buck and change. Lewis gave the cook a glowering stare as they made their way out, and Jerry wondered what the man had said. Alma hadn't noticed, though, and Lewis offered her his arm. On the sidewalk, Mitch paused to light a cigarette, and Jerry stopped gratefully, trying to settle his leg better. At least his headache seemed to be gone.

"What's the damage?" Mitch said quietly. "I didn't get a chance to ask last night."

"I need to call Henry's lawyer," Jerry said. "It was clearly self-defense, and the cops knew the guy—somebody said he'd just got out of jail on an assault charge. Muscle for hire, and perfectly willing to try a little freelance mayhem on his off night."

"Not the brightest," Mitch said.

"No. But there will almost certainly have to be a hearing, and I just want to try to arrange it so Al doesn't have to testify."

"You think that's likely?" Mitch sounded dubious, and Jerry shrugged.

"I'm going to try."

Back in the cool of the lobby, Jerry stopped at the front desk, more to rest his leg than because he expected there would actually be any messages. To his surprise, the clerk turned away from the pigeonholes with a slip of paper in his hand.

"Yes, Dr. Ballard, there was a phone call for you. The gentleman said it was urgent."

Jerry looked at the note—Henry Kershaw, please call as soon as you get this—and then looked where the clerk was pointing, to the row of telephone booths tucked into a side hall.

"Thanks," he said, and stumped off toward them. The others caught up to him quickly, and Mitch gave him a look.

"What's up?"

"Henry wanted me to call him." Jerry wedged himself into one of the narrow booths. His leg didn't bend right, stuck out awkwardly, and he tried to pretend that he was propping the door open on purpose. It was probably about the hearing, he thought, and braced himself as he lifted the receiver.

"Number, please."

He glanced at the paper, read off the number there.

"One moment."

"Did he say what he wanted?" Alma asked. Her voice was a little high, and Jerry guessed she was thinking about the hearing, too. He shook his head, wishing he could be more reassuring.

"Just to call."

Voices spoke in his ear, the operator and Miss Patterson. He gave his name, but Miss Patterson didn't noticeably thaw. Then Henry's voice crackled in his ear.

"Jerry! We've got a problem."

"About last night?" Jerry felt something cold settle in the pit of his stomach. If he couldn't keep Alma out of this….

"What? No, no, that's not important—"

"It kind of is to me," Jerry said. This was the Henry who'd always driven him nuts.

"I told you, George will take care of all that," Henry said. "Don't sweat it."

"I'm thinking about Al," Jerry said.

"Listen," Henry said. "Bill Davenport's done a bunk."

"What?" Jerry blinked at the telephone as though the cabinet had suddenly sprouted wings.

"You heard me."

"Yes, but—" Jerry stopped, reordering his thoughts. "Are you sure?"

"I've got a man on retainer," Henry said. "A private investigator. After you called last night, I thought I'd have him check up on Bill. He's skipped town, and cleaned out his bank account, and I bet I know one person he paid out of it."

Jerry paused again, digesting the other man's words. "You

think Davenport had something to do with this."

"It's not a bad neighborhood where you were," Henry said. "And George said the guy you shot was hired muscle. And Davenport picked you to attack at the Ploiaphesia. The thought crossed my mind."

"Son of a—" Jerry stopped himself. Ok, it was possible, possible that Davenport and/or whatever he was working with had decided they were enough of a threat to warrant an attack. But he couldn't see what he'd done to frighten them.... The tablet, of course. Davenport knew he was one of two or three people in the country who could both translate it and recognize it for what it was. But that didn't get them much further. "What happened?"

"My guy went to Davenport's office at the college, and he hasn't been there since he got back. They're not real happy with him, either, by the way. He was supposed to give an opinion on some bronzes they had, and he never showed."

"Henry." Jerry closed his eyes, prayed for patience.

"So, anyway," Henry said. "He checked the apartment Bill kept over in Glendale and called me from there. He said it looked like Bill left town in a hurry."

"Hell." If Davenport was gone, and had taken his dubious ally with him.... No, he still couldn't make it make sense. "Ok, what now?"

"I want to talk to you about that," Henry said. "Can you come to the house? Right away?"

Jerry frowned at the cabinet's polished veneer. "Why?"

"I want to put the tablet somewhere safe," Henry said. "And I think we need to figure out what to do about Davenport."

Both points were inarguable, and Jerry sighed. "All right. We'll take a cab, be there as soon as we can."

He hung up the phone, turned to face the others. "Davenport's skipped town."

"That's interesting," Mitch said. "I wonder—well, I wonder where and why?"

"I wonder how," Alma said. Her face was intent.

"Henry said his apartment is in Glendale," Jerry said. "I wonder...."

Mitch nodded, comprehension dawning. "Maybe Lewis and I should check it out?"

"Check what out?" Lewis asked.

"Grand Central's in Glendale, actually," Alma said.

"Oh." Lewis nodded. "Yeah, Ok, we could probably find out if he caught a plane." His voice trailed off as though he wasn't sure why they'd bother.

"If he's run," Mitch said, "he's not just Henry's responsibility anymore."

Jerry nodded. "Henry wants the tablet back, and I think I'd be happier if he had it. And he wants to talk with us. Al, why don't you and I deal with Henry, and let Mitch and Lewis check out the flights?"

"Yes," Alma said, and looked at Lewis. "Let's do that."

They took a cab from the hotel up and over the Hollywood hills, wound down past the trees of Griffith Park toward Glendale. There were a dozen questions Lewis wanted to ask, most of them some variation on 'what the heck do you think we can do about this Davenport guy anyway,' but he knew better than to say anything like that with the cabbie listening in. He still wasn't quite sure he believed in possession, in demons—well, except that the Church said they were real, and Father Mira had certainly believed in them. Lewis could still remember the scandal from when he was six, his best friend Nelo dragged stumbling into the church with his mother calling down the Virgin's wrath on the woman with the evil eye who had cursed her son. He'd followed to see what was wrong, and she'd turned on him, proclaiming that it was his fault, because his father was a Bolshevik and a heretic and his grandmother was a witch and he was a child of evil. *But Grandmother goes to Mass every day,* he'd protested, and Nelo's aunt had hissed at him, *because she needs to.*

Father Mira had straightened things out, though. He'd blessed Nelo, given him prayers to say to ward off the weakness in his legs, and told Mrs. Gabarra to take him back to the settlement house, too, and give him more milk like the ladies there said. *It's not the evil eye that's at issue here,* he'd said, *it's the evil tongue. That's how the demons catch you, they tempt you to say things you'd never mean if you only drew breath before you spoke. The next time you would say such a thing, recite an Ave first. Our Lady will protect you from evil.* A part of him, the part of him that would always be six years old, standing in the beeswax-and-incense-smelling nave while the grown-ups shouted, and wished the priest were still alive to ask about all of this. Except that then he'd have had to explain about Alma, and that Father Mira would never have tolerated. Especially since Lewis couldn't honestly say he repented of anything about it.

The cab pulled into the circle at the end of the terminal, and they both climbed out, Mitch leaning back to pay and add a tip that made the cabbie touch his cap before he pulled away.

He straightened, looking up at the tower, and Lewis said, "Ok, now what?"

Mitch gave him a crooked smile. "Isn't this where we go beat somebody up?"

"I think it helps to know who to hit," Lewis said, and Mitch laughed.

"I'm kind of off hitting people anyway, after last night." He tipped his head to one side. "Let's talk to Nomie first, he pretty much knows everything."

"Nomie?"

"Nomie Jones," Mitch answered. "He manages the hangars here. He was Gil's mechanic, he'll take care of us."

"Ok." Lewis trailed after him through the terminal, listening with one ear to the drone of engines overhead. They found Nomie in the hangar's main machine shop, supervising a boy with a face red from sunburn and acne as he broke down the motor of a ratty-looking Jenny. Jones himself was a skinny dried-up little man with the weathered face of a jockey. He gave the red-faced boy a last dubious look, but stepped willingly enough into the relative cool of the hangar itself. A steady breeze came in the open doors, cool on the skin: out of the southeast, Lewis knew without thinking, and perfect for flying. There had been three or four bright shapes against the clear blue as they crossed the tarmac, and at the far end of the hangar, a girl in jodhpurs was standing with her hand on the wing of a bright yellow two-seater, nodding her head earnestly as the pilot gave last-minute instructions. Jones saw where he was looking and gave a cackle of laughter.

"Listen, Nomie," Mitch said, before the older man could say anything. "I need a favor."

"What's in it for me?" Jones asked, but Lewis thought there was a certain wariness beneath the teasing tone.

"My undying gratitude," Mitch answered, and Jones grinned, but the wariness didn't leave his eyes.

"Then I'm your man."

"I need to find out if a particular person caught a flight east, probably yesterday," Mitch said. "But maybe today. You know anybody who'd be able to tell me that?"

"Maybe," Jones said. "You want to tell me what this is about?"

"We had some trouble night before last," Mitch said, carefully, "and that led to some more problems last night. Major Ballard ended up shooting a man."

"No shit," Jones said. He sounded impressed, Lewis thought, but not particularly surprised. "I know a guy in the DA's office might be able to help with that."

"Thanks," Mitch said. "I'll take you up on that. But right now we're trying to find out about the guy who set us up."

Jones paused. "Janie might know."

"Can we ask her?" Mitch asked.

"I'll introduce you," Jones said dubiously. "She's a nice girl, Cap."

"And I'm a nice guy," Mitch said. "And so's Lewis."

Janie turned out to be a nicely-rounded brunette in a pretty flowered frock and high-heeled pumps tied with rose-colored ribbons that matched her nail varnish. The flower in her hat was the same delicate color. She couldn't have been more than eighteen, and Jones handled her like a kitten that hadn't quite found its feet. She worked in the tower, she said, in answer to Mitch's careful questions. Oh, not in the *tower*, just in the office, but all the tickets came through there. Mitch gave her his best smile, and she allowed as how she could probably check that for him, see if Mr. Davenport had taken a flight.

"Give me five minutes," she said, with a smile that would have put most movie stars to shame, "and as soon as Miss Barnes is out of the way, I'll check the flight logs."

"And I'll buy you your milkshake," Mitch said. "Since you're missing your break for me."

"Chocolate, please," she said, with a giggle, and skittered away. Mitch watched her go, his expression almost wistful.

"She's a nice girl," Jones said again, and Mitch gave him a look, his expression suddenly weary.

"I'm not likely to forget it, Nomie, am I? Let's get the kid her milkshake."

Lewis trailed after them through the lower level of the terminal, feeling distinctly useless. Mitch was a lot better at making nice with pretty secretaries—they liked him better anyway, all soft southern accent and courtly manners, the easy charm of a born gentleman. Lewis didn't have the looks to pull it off, too swarthy, too foreign, with none of the suave grace of a Valentino to mitigate it.

Outside, the engine noises changed, and he stopped under one of the open arches to watch a big trimotor line up on the runway. The pilot was good, brought her down with only a single bounce, and taxied sedately up to the terminal. The door popped open, stairs unfolding, and the passengers began to clamber down, while a couple of guys in company coveralls began hauling suitcases out of the baggage compartment in the tail.

"Western from Salt Lake," a voice said at his elbow, and he turned to see a tall man in a green work shirt, his tie tucked into the buttons. He was obviously a pilot, and Lewis nodded.

"Nice landing."

"Frank's good," the other man said, with only a hint of envy. "Who are you with?"

"Gilchrist Aviation," Lewis said. "Out of Colorado Springs. Yourself?"

"Milton Air. I'm on the San Francisco run."

Ok, Lewis thought. Status established. "Fokkers?"

"Fords. We've got one Kershaw Terrier, but those babies are expensive."

Lewis nodded. "Yeah. But solid. Easy on the passengers."

The other man gave him a second look. "You guys fly one? I'm Steve Garvey, by the way."

"Lewis Segura." They shook hands, and Lewis went on, "My boss says they're cheaper to maintain in the long run."

"Wish I could convince Landis of that," Garvey said.

"Say," Lewis said. He could feel himself tensing, made himself relax and smile. "I don't suppose you were flying yesterday."

"Yeah." Garvey gave him a curious look.

"Did you take an older guy, wavy hair going a little gray? Sharp dresser?" That was a guess, since he'd only seen him in the white robes of the ritual, but Lewis was willing to bet Davenport dressed every bit as well as Jerry. "Traveling alone."

"Nope, not me." Garvey shook his head for emphasis. "How come?"

"He talked to us about passage back east," Lewis said. The lie came easier than he'd expected. "We gave him a fare, but he hasn't gotten back in touch. I'd like to know if we should wait around or not. Otherwise we're going back empty"

Garvey shook his head again. "I haven't carried anybody like that. But one of the other guys might have."

The story seemed to work, and Mitch and Jones were still sitting at one of the little tables, Janie between them trying to look grown up. Lewis wandered back through the hangars, stopping in every bay, but none of the other pilots remembered carrying anybody matching the description. One of the mechanics, a gangling redhead, allowed as how he might have seen a guy like that at the telegraph office, but that was all. Lewis thanked him anyway, and started back toward the terminal. The telegraph office was still open, and he hesitated by the door, but couldn't come up with a good excuse for asking. Western Union guarded its patrons' business.

Mitch and Jones were still at their table, though Janie had disappeared, presumably heading back to work, and Lewis's steps slowed. He hated going back with nothing, and he glanced again at the Western Union office. In the magazines, guys were always digging telegrams and half-finished messages out of the trash, but he couldn't see himself getting away with that. Maybe it was time to try this seeing thing again. It had worked before. He rested his shoulder against one of the arches, let his eyes cross just a little, trying to picture what had happened the day before, what the redhead had seen. He felt his breath slow, the engine noise receding, caught a glimpse of—yes, Davenport at the counter, passing two slips to the clerk. And then the image was gone, and he swayed, dizzy, before he caught his balance. He pressed his hand hard against the concrete of the arch. If he was going to try this, it was probably time he asked Alma to teach him properly....

"I know what you are doing," a woman's voice said, in Spanish.

He looked up, startled, and an older woman in a maid's uniform locked eyes with him.

"You should know better." She had one hand in the pocket of her apron, and he knew she grasped her rosary.

"I'm sorry," he said, in the Spanish of his childhood, and her eyebrows rose.

"Then you most certainly should know better—"

"I'm sorry," he said again. "But it's important, señora, I promise. I'm trying to prevent harm. A grave evil."

He wasn't entirely sure where those words had come from, but they seemed right. The woman regarded him a moment longer, then nodded, slipping her hand out of her pocket. "What do you seek?"

"A—man," Lewis said, with just enough hesitation that he thought she understood. "Older than I by some years, gray at the temples. A well-dressed man, I think, and traveling alone. I need very much to find him."

She was silent for a moment. "There was such a one yesterday. I clean the offices here, you understand, and I was at the telegraph when he came in. A dark one, that, so I made myself very small. But he was here, and he sent two telegrams—which I think you saw? But I do not think he took an airplane."

"Thank you," Lewis said. Impulsively, he caught her hand, squeezed it gently. "Thank you very much."

She colored, and for an instant Lewis saw the girl she had been, young and slim and bright-eyed. "Be very careful, my son," she said, and turned away.

Lewis made his way back to join the others, knowing from their expressions that their luck hadn't been much better. At Mitch's nod, he pulled out a chair and joined them.

"Any luck?"

"Just with Janie," Jones said, with a grin that didn't reach his eyes, and Mitch sighed.

"He didn't buy a ticket under his own name. He might have been using someone else's, or he might have hitched a ride off the books, of course."

"I don't think so," Lewis said. "I asked around the hangar. Nobody there had carried anybody like that. He was here, though, and sent a couple of telegrams."

"How the hell did you find that out?" Jones demanded.

"I found somebody who saw him," Lewis said. "So I don't have any idea who it was to, or anything like that."

"That's not much," Mitch said, and sighed. "Jerry said he lived in Glendale, this is probably the closest Western Union office."

"Yeah." Lewis rested his elbows on the table, glad to be off his feet. "Ok, now what?"

"Back to the hotel," Mitch said. "And hope Al and Jerry turned up something better."

Chapter Ten

Alma and Jerry didn't talk much on the way to Henry's house. There wasn't really a conversation she wanted to have in front of the cabbie. Everything she could think of would end with "Don't you think Gil would have said that it is our problem?"

Of course Gil would have. He would have considered it work put before them, a mess that had landed on their doorstep, and hence their problem. If you sign up to save the world, it isn't always exactly convenient. You do the work that is set before you. That's the company plan.

She'd been lazy since Gil died, lazy and demoralized. That wouldn't do in the long run. They had to get back up on the horse and try again. If that's what Jerry was doing, she ought to back him up, not provide an impediment. After all, she expected as much from him.

It was with that in mind that she got out of the car in Henry's drive, the houseboy coming down to hold the door for her and then for Jerry in turn. Miss Patterson was nowhere in evidence, and Henry came to meet them just inside the door himself.

"About last night," Jerry began.

Henry cut him off, leading them at a quick pace toward his office. "It's all settled. I've sent a man to Union Station to check on outbound trains, but of course it's too much to expect that Davenport would still be hanging around the station. He's had hours, and it's a busy terminal. Hell, he may have even left yesterday."

Jerry's jaw clenched, and not entirely from stumping down the hall at Henry's pace, so Alma forestalled him. "Yes, we'd thought of that. We've sent Mitch and Lewis to Grand Central."

"Oh, good." Henry looked pleasantly surprised as he rounded

his desk, and Alma shut the office door behind them as Jerry sank into the chair. "They'll be able to get more out of aviators than my man will."

"Yes, that was what I thought," Alma said patiently. Henry never would have doubted that Gil had two brain cells to rub together, but she was, after all, only a girl. Even if that was calling mutton lamb, as she was thirty-eight.

"The real question isn't where Davenport is," Jerry said. "But what he plans to do."

"What it plans to do," Alma said.

Henry sat down on the other side of his desk, running one hand through his hair distractedly, and Alma thought that Henry really did look distressed. He might prefer the glamour to the actual work, but he did have a sense of responsibility. "And how are we supposed to guess what an infernal entity thousands of years old wants?"

"Not simply blood," Alma said logically. "If it just wanted to kill, the thing to do would be to lie low in Davenport's body and commit murders under the radar."

"Do we know it hasn't done that?" Jerry asked. "This is LA. Surely there are unsolved murders?" He looked from one of them to the other.

Henry swallowed. "We don't know that," he said finally. "What we do know is that we have to catch that thing and stop it before Davenport can do anything else."

"It's not Davenport," Jerry said, shaking his head as though bothered by a pesky fly. "It doesn't matter about him, don't you see? And that's why the police can't stop this. They can arrest Davenport, but the entity can jump to a new body. They'll take Bill Davenport away in handcuffs, and tomorrow one of the policemen will be its host. Only we won't know who. This thing can keep jumping from one host to another, so it doesn't matter who they arrest. It's going to keep doing this until we banish it or bind it."

Henry put his elbows on the desk. "How do we do that?"

"I don't know yet." Jerry's eyes were frank. "But I do know we'd better not lose track of him."

"If he left by plane," Henry began.

"He could have gotten a long way since yesterday," Alma said. "But fortunately we still have the tablet."

"A material link," Jerry said, as Henry frowned. "The entity was once bound by the tablet, so the tablet can serve as a material link for an operation intended to find it."

Henry nodded slowly. "Ok. What do you need me to do?"

"A candle would be nice," Alma said. "And an atlas." She glanced around the bookcases in his office. "I expect you have an atlas?"

"Of course," Henry said, getting up and rummaging around on one of the shelves. "What else? Do you want to use the temple?"

Jerry looked at Alma, then shook his head. "Not if it hasn't been cleaned since Davenport used it. We're fine in here. I assume you've got regular house wards?"

"Of course," Henry said, setting a taper in a bronze Mexican candlestick down on the desk beside the Motorist's Atlas of the United States.

Alma let out a deep breath and sat down in the chair as Jerry got up, trying to compose herself. He put one hand on her shoulder briefly, and she smiled up at him. "Just like old times," she said.

Jerry nodded, reaching in his pocket and pulling out a steel handled penknife. He flicked it open one handed, the sharp blade catching the light of the candle flame as Henry pulled the curtains at the window. "Which way is…."

"That way," Alma said, nodding toward the door.

Jerry smiled. Jerry's lack of a sense of direction was a long standing joke. He turned around, his back to her, facing east, and she heard him take a deep, centering breath. Henry sunk back into his desk chair, and Alma closed her eyes. This part was Jerry's, and she had best use the time to relax.

Another breath, and Jerry began, the Hebrew syllables falling resonantly from his lips. "Ateh malkuth ve-gevurah ve-gedulah le-olahm." She did not need to see the movement of the blade tracing patterns of fire across his body. She could feel it like a familiar whisper, like the rustle of silk. "Amen." She could feel the knife lift again, marking the pentagram in the air, feel it like the glow of the candle before her.

The sound of his footsteps was muffled by the thick carpet, but she felt him pass her, journeying clockwise around her to face the bookcase to the south. Again the movement of the knife, blade channeling will.

Another set of steps, now to the windows that let over the swimming pool, his back to Henry as he inscribed the symbol to the west. It felt like a breath of rain, as though a cool wet wind had stirred the curtains, and Alma bent her head. The first time she'd seen this she'd been frightened. Gil had reached over and squeezed her hand. Now it was comforting.

Again, and Jerry was facing north now, another inscription before he moved back to where he'd begun, sealing the circle he had traced around. "Before me, Raphael," Jerry said, his back almost against hers. "Behind me, Gabriel. On my right hand Michael, and on my left Uriel. About me shines the pentagram, and within me the six rayed star."

Alma opened her eyes. Though nothing had physically changed, the room seemed lighter, cooler. Jerry bent his head for a moment like a man in prayer, then turned about, closing the penknife. "I think we're ready."

"Ok," Henry said.

Wordlessly, Alma flipped open the Motorist's Atlas, turning to the road map of southern California, while Jerry unwrapped the tablet and laid it on the desk beside her. It gleamed dully in the candlelight. She took a deep breath and reached up to unfasten the chain around her neck, pulling the necklace off and laying it in front of her. She'd gotten used to wearing her wedding ring on a chain around her neck when she flew, because she hated having anything on her hands, and now it seemed like a compromise. She wore it next to her heart, not on her finger as a reproach to Lewis. Nor could she bear to leave it off entirely. There might be a time when she did. Almost surely someday there would be a time when she did, but not now.

Henry's eyebrows rose, but he said nothing.

Alma refastened the chain, resting her right elbow on the desk and looping the chain around her ring finger, raising her arm at ninety degrees to the surface, so that the wedding band hung free beneath her palm an inch or two above the atlas. It turned slightly as it swung, the script inside the band catching the light. "Ok," Alma said, looking up at Jerry.

He nodded and moved the tablet closer, until the fingers of her left hand rested lightly on the edge of it. "She's going to find the connection," Jerry said quietly to Henry. "A creature like that leaves a big footprint, and we have a material connection with the tablet."

Metal. Alma closed her eyes again, her fingertips just touching the edge of the tablet. Incised metal. Lewis had tried to see, had tried to open a window into the past using his untapped clairvoyant potential. Alma had none, but she knew how to use what she had. Metal from the breast of the earth, lead forged long ago. Metal in her other hand, the gold ring swinging in the loop of its chain, turning and catching the light of the candle flame. Red fire. Forger's fire. Tablet and ring were both born of flame, both born from the breast of the earth.

Show me, she whispered silently. Not Jerry's focused will, not the power of words, but more primal than that. Like calls to like. Flame calls to flame, metal to metal, and the tablet to the creature it bound so long.

And the last piece. Earth rendered into symbol, not in the banishing pentagrams of Jerry's ritual phrases, but in the prosaic and easily understood symbols of the road map. Here are the Sierra Nevadas, here Banning Pass. Here is the highway that runs across the desert to Las Vegas, here, just as she had seen it from the air days ago, a ribbon on the map making plain the memory in her mind, the snake of black asphalt through red land. The map was a skillful symbolic representation, everything to scale, and like the best correspondences there was nothing occult or obscure about it. Anyone could understand it. And hence it had more power, not the power of secrecy but of omnipresent belief.

Show me. She felt the pendulum begin to move, the ring swinging in wide circles. It tugged. It pulled. This way. She heard Henry stir, and perhaps he would have said something, but Jerry forestalled him.

"Give her time," Jerry said.

There was a rustle, and for a moment the pendulum hesitated. Paper moved. Jerry was turning the page in the Atlas. She must have tracked off one border or another.

Show me. Not nearly so far north as Las Vegas. The desert unspooled in her mind, rail lines running straight as a ruler across the land, like looking down from 5,000 feet, cruising along. Williams Junction. Flagstaff. Gallup.

Another stirring. She was running off the map again, Jerry turning the pages, flying east as though she were winged herself, flying into afternoon. The shape of the plane raced ahead of her on the ground, her beloved Jenny. Albuquerque was an oasis of green, round circles of irrigation bright against the desert, growing oranges and lemons in the May heat.

The tracks turned northward and now so did she, her shadow out over her right wing. Northward toward Colorado. Just south of Trinidad she saw the train, a streamlined silver streak against the earth, the Santa Fe's Chief laboring up the grade at fifty miles an hour. The plane paced it, circling.

Somewhere far away the ring was circling too, turning in a tight knot over the page of the atlas.

"There's nothing there," Henry said. "Why the hell would Davenport go there?"

"He's on his way to Chicago," Alma said, her voice sounding thready, as though the wind had taken it from her throat. "He's on the Chief."

"The express train to Chicago," Jerry supplied. "Well, that's great."

Alma opened her eyes, letting the ring down where it stood. It lay on the paper, the circle of gold just touching Trinidad, Colorado.

"He must have left last night," Henry said.

"Early last night," Alma supplied. "The Chief leaves Los Angeles at six pm."

Jerry nodded. "Hire some thugs to kill us, hop on the Chief, have a nice dinner while the deed is done with miles between you and the ones you want out of the way."

"Can you catch him?" Henry asked.

"With an airplane?" Jerry looked over the top of his glasses.

"No, with a bicycle," Henry snapped. "Of course I mean with your Terrier."

"My Terrier," Alma said. She was owner and pilot both, while the amount Jerry didn't know about aviation would fill volumes.

"Don't you have planes, Henry?" Jerry asked mildly.

"I have lots of planes," Henry replied. "But I also have mail routes and passenger routes, and I can't cancel scheduled flights to send my pilots out chasing the Chief all the way to Chicago."

"Because that would cost a lot of money," Alma said sharply. "That's a hell of a lot of fuel, Henry."

Henry got up and went to the southward wall, lifting a rather ugly painting to reveal a wall safe beneath. Alma waited while he turned the knobs, then opened the door and drew out an envelope. He counted, frowning, and then handed the contents to her. "Think that will do it?"

Twenty-five twenty dollar bills.

"That will take us to Chicago," Alma conceded. She met his eyes firmly. "Are you chartering us to catch your man for you?"

Henry put his hands in his pants pockets, his coat bulging out over them. "Gil wouldn't have charged me for expenses."

"Gil isn't here," Alma said. "And you look like a millionaire. While I am not."

Henry sighed. "Ok. You win. Catch Davenport for me and I'll cover all your expenses."

"You'll cover our expenses whether or not we catch him," Alma said briskly. "We use the fuel either way."

"Fine." Henry offered his hand reluctantly. "You drive a hard bargain."

"You could always use your own plane," Alma said sweetly. "But I expect you'd lose a lot more than five hundred dollars plus whatever else."

"I'm not writing you a platinum ticket," Henry grumbled, but he shook her hand firmly. "I'll be behind you in a day or two on one of my planes as a passenger. I needed to get back to New York anyhow for the launch of the *Independence*."

"Your new zeppelin?" Jerry asked, looking up from apparent fascination with the road atlas while Alma bargained.

"Yep," Henry said with satisfaction. "Maiden flight. New York to Paris. I'm taking her up next week."

"Sounds like fun," Jerry said, pushing his glasses up his nose. "How soon can you leave?"

Alma looked at her watch. "In the morning."

"Oh for the love of…."

"Henry, it's nearly two o'clock. By the time we got to Grand Central and got fueled it would be four. And it's a big field. We'd have to wait for a takeoff time between the scheduled traffic. If we're lucky we'd be in the air by five, and we're flying east. Unless it's absolutely critical I'd rather not make a night leg, and it's not critical." Alma slipped the chain back around her neck, the ring disappearing down the front of her shirt. "We can get to Chicago ahead of him, especially since we know where he's going and can take a more direct route. We can fly straight from Gallup to Denver and cut hours off. And there are a couple of other short cuts further east." She looked at Jerry. "We'll leave first thing in the morning. I'll go to Grand Central now and file a flight plan. We can keep abreast of his progress as we go and we'll send you a telegram if anything changes."

"For which we'll need this," Jerry said, tapping the tablet and taking a silk handkerchief out of his pocket.

Henry shook his head. "It's a good thing I trust you people," he said.

"It certainly is," Alma said. "I'd like to see you explain this to your pilots." She got to her feet. "It's always a pleasure, Henry."

"For some value of pleasure," Henry said.

It had taken most of the afternoon and evening to get the Terrier re-rigged for the flight to Chicago, and it had only been Henry's intervention that had gotten them the supplemental tank from Kershaw Aviation's shop down the road. Mitch and Lewis had bolted it in place, rigged and tested and retested the fuel lines and the switch-over valve, and then they'd ditched the extra seats and strung a baggage net across the back of the passenger compartment. Not that they'd be carrying that much—they didn't have that much, just what they'd brought to Hollywood, but Jerry flatly refused to leave his books behind. And he was probably right that they'd need them, Mitch thought. Assuming that they managed to catch up with Davenport—with the thing that was riding him, anyway, and also assuming that they could figure out what to do about it.

Mitch looked around the passenger compartment again, checking that the remaining seats were bolted down, and that the narrow cot they'd gotten from the Kershaw shop fit tightly into the chocks. The Terriers were designed to take luxury fittings, like the cot with its thin, hard mattress—daybed, the shop manager had called it, or 'chaise'—but he'd never installed one before. But this was going to be a long flight, sixteen hours at the absolute best, assuming they got fueled up fast each and every time, and never had to wait for a runway. And there would be hard work to do at the end of it.

Mitch flexed his fingers, working knuckles he'd bruised the day before when one of the wrenches slipped, and swung down the steps to begin his walk-around. They had to stop Davenport, or the thing that was wearing him, but he wished they had a better plan for how. The sun was only barely up, throwing long shadows across the tarmac, sending his own shadow back toward the hangar. Everything was in order, the big rotary engines gleaming with oil, the control surfaces perfect, and he looked back toward the terminal, shading his eyes. Yep, there they were, Alma in the lead, Jerry beside her, his jerky movements unmistakable as he fought to keep up, and Lewis was behind them, lugging Jerry's bag as well as his own. Lewis was willing, Mitch allowed. He was a good pilot, and he was willing to help without being asked, and he was willing to work with Jerry's moods, so if he was what Alma wanted, Mitch thought, more power to him. But if he screwed up, hurt her in any way—Mitch nodded once. He wouldn't let that happen.

"With the tablet at least we can find it," Jerry said, as they came into earshot, "but after that—banish or bind it, those are our only options, and I don't see how to do it yet."

Alma was looking a little frayed around the edges, Mitch thought, and Lewis was starting to look positively mulish. "Good morning," he said, with all the good humor he could muster, and Alma gave him a grateful glance. "Did you get the legal stuff straightened out?"

"Yes," Alma said firmly, before Jerry could expound on the topic. "We'll have to come back for a hearing, but Henry's lawyer got them to agree that we could carry on with normal business until then."

"That's a relief," Mitch said. He grabbed Jerry's suitcase, swung it up into the plane. It landed with a thud, and Alma shook her head.

"How are we for weight, anyway?"

"Fine," Mitch said. "Lewis and I went over the figures three times, and we've got ample margin. Even with the supplemental tank full."

Lewis tossed his own bag up the stairs, followed it more gently with Alma's, and heaved himself aboard.

"We're cutting it close," Jerry said. He shook his head. "He – it – must be about twenty hours from Chicago by now."

"We'll make it in eighteen," Mitch said. "Maybe less."

Jerry looked as though he wanted to say something more, but Alma interrupted him. "We're next after Western's Early Bird. Better get settled." She held out a clipboard. "We're going a little northerly, there's weather to the south."

Mitch nodded, glancing down the list. Salt Lake, North Platte, Iowa City, and then Chicago: the first leg was the longest, but it should be easy flying, daylight all the way. They wouldn't have to worry until they got to Iowa City, and then it would be even odds whether they could get in and out before full dark. Iowa City had lights, more or less, for the mail planes, but he'd been through there before. Which meant he wanted the last leg, and the first.... He'd been going to ask Lewis to take the first leg with him, but it looked like Alma could use a break. "Why don't the two of you take it easy to Salt Lake? Jerry can keep me company up front."

For a second, he thought Jerry was going to protest, but then he shrugged and tucked his cane under his arm to make the climb into the cabin. Alma said simply, "Are you sure?"

"Yeah." And he was, he thought, as he climbed into the cabin behind her. He was flying: it didn't so much matter where, or with who, or into what, as long as he was in the air.

Jerry had worked himself into the copilot's chair, wooden leg braced carefully against the edge of the rudder pedals on his side. Mitch double-checked that everything was switched to his side, the copilot's controls completely disabled, and began running down his checklist. Outside, another set of motors sprang to life: the Early Bird, on its way north to San Francisco.

"Sorry," Jerry said, without looking at him. "I'm—this has me worried, Mitch, that's all."

You and me both, Mitch thought. "We'll figure something out," he said, and flipped the starter switches. The big engines coughed to life, sputtered, settled to their familiar rhythm. Mitch waited, adjusting the mixture, testing flaps and rudder, while the Early Bird lined itself up into the wind and lifted neatly into the air.

"Flag," Jerry said, lifting his voice to be heard over the noise of the motor.

That was the one thing you could trust Jerry to notice, but Mitch glanced out the side window anyway, saw the flagman waving from the end of the runway. He gave the Terrier power, let it bounce along the taxiway that ran parallel to the runway, feeling the extra weight of fuel in the tail. The flagman signaled a final time, waving him onto the runway, and he kicked the rudder gently, pointing the Terrier's nose down the midline. He gave her more throttle, easy at first, then harder, the Terrier waddling down the runway like an elderly goose. She'd be fine once some of the fuel burned off, but it took longer than usual to get the tail up, longer still to get her off the ground. She climbed slowly, scratching for altitude, and Mitch kept the power up for longer than usual, leveling off at 6000 feet. That was going to make things interesting over the Rockies, he thought, and did a quick calculation to see how much fuel they would have burned by the time they had to claw their way over the mountains. They'd be down to close to a normal full load, by his rough reckoning: that was manageable. And Alma and Lewis were both good, they could handle it.

The sky was clear above him, vivid blue, the sun glinting off the tip of the right wing. There were a few low clouds, thin enough to see through, and Jerry had his nose pressed to the side window, looking out and down. You couldn't blame him, Mitch thought. There was nothing like it, nothing in this world.

And that was trite, but he'd never been the one to find the definitions, the one who put things into words. That was Jerry's job, and from the almost wistful smile, Jerry was having just as much trouble articulating it. And that was Ok. The joy was enough. It had made the War bearable, survivable: there had always been the moments, between the mud and the killing and the misery, when his wings caught the air and he soared for an instant outside himself. It was still there, as reliable as breathing, the beat of the motors and the easy ride of the Terrier. It would always be there, he told himself, and once again believed the lie.

Lewis and Alma each had a window. They'd never be able to fly otherwise, but looking out opposite windows sharing a thermos of coffee, not being in the cockpit was bearable. Alma wasn't sure whether Mitch meant for her to take the second or third legs, but it didn't matter. She and Lewis would both take the cockpit, and Jerry could sit on the chaise where he could get his leg up.

Alma craned her neck, looking ahead. Mitch was about to thread the Banning Pass, and Mount San Gorgonio raised its barren head above the tree line, more than 11,000 feet. Maybe someday it would be possible to fly over the peak – that day might not be far away – but for now they had to thread the pass just as cars and trains did.

Lewis came over to look out her window, kneeling on the floor to get a better view. It was breathtakingly beautiful, and so was the expression on his face as he looked out, rapt and delighted. Alma suppressed the urge to ruffle his carefully combed hair.

Lewis glanced at her sideways, as though he had caught her looking at him, had guessed what she was thinking. "Will you teach me?" he said.

Alma caught her breath. "I'm not sure I can," she said.

"Is it forbidden?"

"No." She shook her head. "But I can't teach you things I don't know. Your mix of talents is very different from mine. I can show you some basic things, but oracular work.... It's entirely different from anything I can do. For that matter it's different from anything Mitch and Jerry can do. We can all show you a few things, but you'd need a different master to go very far, someone whose talents are more like yours." Alma put her hand on his arm. "Lewis, the oracular talents are very complex and can be unnerving. Are you sure you want to do this?"

"I have to if I'm going to be any use," Lewis said.

Alma searched his eyes. "You don't have to do this for me," she said.

He nodded slowly. "I know. But do you think I can just go home and forget about it while you and Mitch and Jerry are doing this? That's the choice, isn't it? I can bow out or I can figure out what to do."

"Yes," she said. Alma looked down at her hand, and laced her fingers with Lewis'. "This is part of my life, Lewis. Part of who I am. You don't have to do it. But I'm not going to stop."

"I know that," Lewis said. He looked like he was fumbling for words. "I wouldn't want you to. I like you different."

"I like you too," Alma said, and put her arm around him, drawing him close to look out the window side by side as clouds as thin as veils drifted from the mountain peak.

Chapter Eleven

They took off from Woodward Field a little after noon, Alma at the controls as the Terrier rose into the gentle air. They'd been lucky with the weather so far, she knew, but to her relief it looked as though that luck was going to last a little while longer. The clouds and rain were staying well south of them, and while there was supposed to be a front coming into the California coast, they'd be ahead of it all the way to Chicago. The Terrier was sluggish with the extra fuel, climbing slowly, the controls heavy under her hands, but the engines were all running steadily. She glanced at the instrument panel, confirming RPMs and airspeed and the rate of climb. Everything was in order; it was just the extra weight that she'd have to get used to.

"That extra tank makes a big difference," Lewis shouted, and she nodded. She was getting used to the way that he sometimes seemed to read her mind when they were in the air, one pilot matching another.

"Yeah. It'll be better when we burn some of it off."

"What's the height of the pass?"

"8700 feet," Alma answered. "I want to take us up to 10,000 if the weather stays good."

Lewis gave her a sidelong glance. "Will she make it with this load on?"

"She should," Alma said. She smiled back at him. "I know she'll make 9500, and that's plenty."

"Ok." Lewis hoped he didn't sound as dubious as he felt. He liked a bit more air between himself and the ground.

Jerry had settled himself on the chaise, propping up his bad leg among a scatter of books, while Mitch sank into one of the rear facing chairs. He unwrapped the first of the sandwiches they had bought in Salt Lake City, and took a bite. Turkey. That was fine.

It had been a long six hours in the cockpit, and he was glad to let Alma take the controls for a while. They'd left the door open, and he could hear their voices off and on, but the words were drowned by the roar of the engines. They were still climbing, he could feel that, throttle well open, straining for the altitude they'd need to cross the Rockies. He looked back at Jerry, still frowning over his books, and finished chewing the bits of sandwich.

"So," he said. "What are we going to do when we find this guy?"

"That's what I'm trying to figure out," Jerry said distractedly, paging through one of the books on his lap.

"Can we talk about this for a minute?" Mitch's voice was sharper than he'd intended, and Jerry looked up.

"Sure," he said, adjusting his glasses. Jerry tended to forget they were supposed to be a team, not the Jerry show, sometimes. They needed to work this out together.

"Ok," Mitch said slowly, "The way I see it we've got three problems. One, we've got to find this guy. We're reasonably sure we can do that. We ought to get into Chicago five or six hours ahead of the Chief, so we can get onto him at the station. Two, we've got to bind or banish this thing and get it out of Davenport. I've got no idea how we're going to do that. And three, we have to make sure it doesn't jump into one of us while we're trying to do number two."

Jerry nodded. "I'm in agreement on all of those, though I think we actually need to address the third one first. If it can jump into one of us, we're in serious trouble. I think the only reason it didn't try to do that back at Henry's house is that it was surprised and scared. If we'd grabbed it there we could have dealt with it. A consecrated Temple, plenty of trained people for the operation, and frankly Henry's basement to tie Davenport up in while we worked it out. But it surprised us too, and we didn't get the jump on it when we could have."

"I don't usually tackle somebody and tie them up because they flex a little psychic muscle," Mitch said.

"Well, no." Jerry grinned. "Of course we don't. That's because we're the good guys."

Mitch tipped his hypothetical white hat. "And now we can't nab Davenport. I suppose Lewis and I could ambush him, mug him, knock him out and haul him back to the plane, but…."

"And then do what with him?" Jerry grimaced. "First of all, I have no idea how to bind that creature yet. Secondly, what do we do with him on the plane? We don't have nearly the energy we'd need to keep it in a protective circle, even if we used Lewis, and he has no idea what he's doing."

"And that brings us back to the thing jumping," Mitch said grimly. "If we can't keep it from jumping into one of us, we can't risk contact."

"That's what I'm working on now," Jerry said. "We need an amulet, a sigil. Something that we can wear or carry that will protect the bearer. Otherwise, you're right. This is too hot to handle." He waved a book in Mitch's direction. "There are a lot of things we could do if we had proper equipment and time. And the right materials. But…."

"We can use Henry's machine shop at the airport," Mitch said. "There's probably equipment we could use as a burin, and there's sure as hell plenty of sheet metal. Lewis has a pretty good hand in the shop. I've seen him do some nice fancy cuts."

"Engraving on metal would be better than on paper with ink," Jerry said.

"Less likely to get wet or torn."

Jerry nodded. "On silver would be ideal."

"We're going to get into Chicago between eleven and midnight," Mitch said. "You think Henry has silver lying around his machine shop at two in the morning?"

"Ok, no. Ideally we would need to consecrate the burin at the hour with the correct planetary correspondence to the sigil we desire to grave."

"We've got five hours," Mitch said. "And those are the hours we have before the Chief gets in. So one of them better be the right hour."

"And then of course we should create the correct sigil. The problem is that the most obvious power to call upon to bind it is Diana, which suggests we should use one of the sigils of the moon. But most of them have the opposite effect of what's intended. They're for opening or revealing, for activating oracular talents or making plain what is hidden. I suppose, of course, we could use a non-specific protective device, but…."

"Like…." Mitch probed.

"A sigil of Sagittarius would be appropriate, since Diana has a clear correspondence with archery, but I would prefer to get a specific invocation in. Give me a moment, here." Jerry pulled his pocket notebook out and started scribbling with the stub of a pencil.

"Ok." Mitch leaned back and ate his sandwich.

Lewis glanced at the altimeter again, listening to the engines straining. 8680 and still climbing, though the air was rougher here, lifting and dropping the Terrier at irregular intervals. A lot rougher, he amended, as the bottom seemed to drop out of his seat. The mountains loomed ahead, bare rock too steep even for snow, the peaks higher than the plane itself. Alma was frowning, her hands white-knuckled on the wheel.

"We could go north to South Pass," Lewis said.

He thought she would have looked at him, but the Terrier bucked again, and there was a thump and a curse from the cabin. "We're all right," she said.

"It's less than 8000 feet," he said. "South Pass."

"It's an hour longer," Alma said. "We'd have to put down in Cheyenne then, too."

And Cheyenne was a lot busier than North Platte, a regular stop for passenger planes as well as the mail carriers. They wouldn't just lose time in the air, they'd lose it on the ground as well. The Terrier dropped another ten feet and rose again almost as quickly. This was the way to go, if they could just get the altitude. He glanced at the numbers he'd scribbled on the edge of the flight plan: they would be burning about twenty gallons of fuel per hour, maybe a little more given that Alma was running rich, and the supplemental tank held forty-three gallons. It was getting close to time to switch over to the main tanks—in the next half hour, maybe sooner. And that meant they'd be crossing the mountains with a full normal fuel load: tight, but doable.

"We'll need to switch tanks soon," he said.

"Ok." Alma's hands were steady on the controls, the muscles of her forearms bunching and relaxing as she eased the plane up another hundred feet. "We should probably do it sooner. I've had to keep the mix richer than usual to get us going."

Even as she spoke, the port engine misfired. Lewis swore under his breath, his heart racing, but then the engine caught again. "How about now?" he asked.

"Now sounds good," Alma agreed.

Lewis leaned forward, remembering the procedure Mitch had drilled into him. Open the right valve, open the left valve, count twenty seconds—the port engine missed again, but he kept counting. The Terrier was designed to fly on any two of its three engines, that was no problem. The main thing was to keep the fuel flow steady, and make the transition without getting air in the lines. Twenty seconds, and he reached between the seats to close the valve on the supplemental tank. He held his breath, waiting for the engines to falter, looked sideways to see Alma's knuckles white on the control wheel. The starboard engine missed, caught; the Terrier steadied again under Alma's touch. And then the needle twitched on the main fuel gauge, a sure sign that the gas was flowing, and Lewis allowed himself a sigh of relief. Alma grinned, shook her head.

"It's always something."

The altimeter was hovering at 9200 feet, mountains rising on either side higher than the plane. Below them, Lewis could make out the thread of a road tracing the narrow pass, but there was no other sign of human presence.

"I'm going to hold her here," Alma said. "We're at the peak, no point trying for more."

Lewis nodded, and let himself relax into his seat.

"There." Jerry thrust his notebook under Mitch's nose. "What do you think?" There were pages covered in scribbles, bits of mathematical formulas and Hebrew letters, a square of numbers like a strange acrostic puzzle, all the things that made up Jerry's work. Balanced against the swaying of the plane, he stabbed the pencil at an elaborate square design made up of symmetrical swoops and curves alternated with triangles and an elaborate hexagram. "That."

Mitch's brow furrowed. "I think that's going to be impossible to engrave."

"It's the best possible sigil," Jerry said. "I've transliterated Diana Nemorensis via numerology, then used the Hebrew letters corresponding with each number to create a grid, then calculated the best way to have a single line pass through each number in correct order to make a symmetrical design…."

"We're talking about a machine shop, not a jeweler," Mitch said. He twisted around. "Hey Lewis! Can you come back here a minute?"

"Go on. I've got it," he heard Alma say, and Lewis climbed out of the copilot's chair and came back.

"Can you engrave this?" Mitch asked as Lewis came between the chairs.

Lewis took the notebook and turned it so the light from the window hit it better, running his other hand through his hair. It had escaped from its pomade and didn't lie flat like Valentino's. He looked doubtful, but replied, "I suppose? I'd give it a try. Something about fourteen inches square…."

Jerry snorted. "Fourteen inches. If we all want to wear amulets as big as dinner plates around our necks."

"Well, it does say to put on the armor of light," Mitch said, cracking up at the visual implied. "I suppose we could use rotor covers or something. Sort of like a breast plate."

"What?" Lewis blinked. "Isn't that the Advent service?"

"Mitch is being stupid on purpose," Jerry said. "We need it engraved on an amulet you could wear or carry in your pocket."

Lewis looked at it and regretfully shook his head. "I don't think I can do that," he said. "I've never done work that fine. To try it I'd need a jeweler's burin. There's no way I can do that on something maybe three by three on shop equipment."

"I told you," Mitch said. He reached over and rapped Jerry on the forehead. "Simplify, Jerry."

"Lout," Jerry said. "If you don't care if it works or not I can just put any damn thing on there." He picked up his books again.

"Back to the drawing board."

"We'll be coming into North Platte in about an hour, " Lewis said.

"Ok," Mitch nodded. "I'll take the next leg shotgun if it suits you." He glanced over at Jerry, his nose back in the book. Maybe Alma could get something more useful out of him.

Lewis ducked back into the cockpit and settled into the copilot's chair. They were leaving the mountains at last, and the ground beneath them showed trees as well as broken rock. The air was easier now, a tail wind carrying them, and a glance at the controls showed that Alma was running a leaner mix of fuel.

Alma glanced over at him. "I couldn't hear most of that. Are they onto something?"

"I don't think so," Lewis said, frowning. "Mostly bickering."

"They do that."

"They wanted to know if I could engrave some sort of symbol for us to wear." Lewis shook his head.

"A protective sigil." Alma seemed unflustered, her hands light on the controls. "Like the one on the plane."

Lewis put his head to the side. Thin clouds were starting to build below them, nothing serious, a thin veil obscuring the ground. "What?"

Alma gestured toward the back of the plane with her head. "The roundel on the tail. It's a protective sigil. Gil and Jerry worked it out and painted it on all the Gilchrist planes. It's on our business cards and stationery too. And on the sign on the hangar."

"Oh." He thought for a moment. He supposed there was no harm in painting a protective sign on a plane. That wasn't witchcraft. More like wearing a St. Christopher medal. "What's the Bible verse?"

"They have pierced my hands and feet. I can count all my bones," Alma said promptly.

Lewis blinked. "That's depressing." He looked at her sideways. "Why the hell would you paint that on an airplane for protection?"

"Don't ask me," Alma said. "That was Gil and Jerry."

They came down the eastern slope of the Rockies into the mail field at North Platte in the declining light of the early evening. Lewis climbed out to stretch his legs while Mitch supervised the refueling, and walked along the length of the runway past the old gas beacons, metal pots half as tall as a man squatting on wheeled trolleys, ready to be lugged into place. He'd landed with worse light back in the war—he'd landed more than once by the light of a dropped flare, heart in his throat and an Act of Contrition on his lips. He'd been lucky each of those times, lucky and good; North Platte to Iowa City—another lighted field, a night stop for the mail planes—was nothing in comparison. It would only be an hour past sunset by the time they got to Iowa City. And Mitch would take the last leg into Chicago's Municipal Field. He walked back toward the Terrier, stretching carefully. He'd only taken the controls a couple of times, but it was easy to tense up as though he'd been flying, particularly in the mountains.

Alma and Jerry were nowhere in sight when he got back to the plane—in the end of the hangar that served as a control center, probably—but Mitch was sitting on the cabin steps, smoking. The fuel truck had pulled away, and Lewis frowned.

"We're not using the supplemental tank?"

Mitch shook his head. "No need. I hate the way she handles with it full, anyway."

Lewis paused. "We could probably make Chicago in one hop with it full. Cut out the ground time at the very least."

"You've got guts," Mitch said. His smile softened the words. "I thought about it, but we'd be cutting it awfully close. I just don't see the need to take that much of a risk. Especially since Jerry hasn't figured out what to do yet."

"These—sigils," Lewis said. He pronounced the word carefully, tasting it on his tongue, trying to decide exactly what he wanted to know. "Will they really keep this—is it a demon?—from possessing any of us?"

"That's the plan," Mitch said. "Technically, I don't know if this thing is a demon, exactly, but it's certainly not a creature of Light."

Lewis blinked, not sure if that actually answered his question, or just raised more, and Mitch pushed himself to his feet.

"I wish I knew what it wants—but maybe Jerry will have figured that out, too." He ground out his cigarette and started for the hangar.

Lewis ran his hand through his hair, wondering again just what he'd gotten himself into. Demons, possession, magic.... Alma. He supposed that was what it came down to: this was Alma's world, and he wanted to be part of it. He reached into his pocket, found the half-empty packet of cigarettes and lit one, inhaling the familiar tobacco. He had choices, he couldn't kid himself there. He could walk away—Ok, maybe he couldn't actually do that, or at least he didn't want to, didn't want to leave Alma, but he could say to her, Ok, this is too strange for me. I don't want to be part of this magic, this lodge business. She'd made it clear that it had to be his choice, and Mitch had pretty much said the same thing: he had to choose, not just follow because Alma wanted it. She would keep him on as a pilot, as her lover, it would just mean he wouldn't be part of things like this.... And that wasn't good enough. Whatever happened, he wanted to be with her. To be at her side.

"I wish I knew what I was doing," he said, and rested his hand against the Terrier's aluminum skin.

Mitch and Alma came back from the hangar together, Alma with a paper bag in her hand that turned out to contain more sandwiches. It was cooler under the shade of the wing than in the cabin, and Lewis wolfed down half of one while they waited for Jerry.

"I got the control tower to radio ahead to Iowa City, let them know we'd be coming in after dark," Mitch said, "and they said they'd have the field lit for us. They wouldn't radio Chicago, though, said we'd have to do it from Iowa City."

"I suppose I understand it," Alma said. "Most people aren't going to want to make a night flight. But—"

"We'll be into Iowa City around ten," Mitch said. "The tower will still be open at Chicago, and they'll wait for us. Not to worry."

"I'm not worrying," Alma said.

Mitch lifted an eyebrow at her, and, reluctantly, she smiled. "Ok, maybe I am, a little."

"We'll be fine," Mitch said. "Lewis will take us to Iowa City, and I'll get us to Chicago."

Lewis nodded his agreement. He would have liked to add something, but there really wasn't anything more to say.

"Right," Mitch said. "Now—where's Jerry?"

Alma looked over her shoulder, and Lewis said, "There."

Jerry was limping toward them as fast as he could, his artificial leg dragging awkwardly in the clipped grass. "I got hold of Henry's hangar manager at Chicago," he called. "I told them we were doing a test flight, that we'd need to use their shop when we got in. They'll leave the key for us at the tower."

"Nice work," Mitch said.

Lewis nodded agreement. That would make things easier, all right. He'd been imagining something out of Black Mask magazine, picking locks—or, since he had no idea how you actually went about picking a lock, climbing in through a window or something—and not having to worry about the night watchmen or the police was definitely a relief. "Are we ready, then?"

"I'd say so," Mitch answered, and looked at Alma.

She nodded. "As ready as we're going to be."

Lewis settled himself into the cockpit, Mitch in the copilot's seat to his right. They ran down the checklist—Lewis was pretty sure he had it memorized by now—and the flagman waved them out onto the grassy runway. There was a nice gentle breeze, just enough to lift the windsock on its pole outside the hangar. Lewis pointed the Terrier into the wind and opened the throttles.

He had to admit that the Terrier was much easier to fly without the weight of the supplemental tank. She climbed easily past 6500 feet, low enough to see the landmarks in what was left of the daylight, and Lewis leveled out, adjusting the fuel mixture as they reached a cruising altitude. There were clouds on the horizon, blending into the deepening dusk, and he glanced at Mitch.

"Did we get a weather report?"

"Alma did," the other man answered, and twisted in his seat. "Al? Weather report?"

"Sorry." Alma scrambled forward, handed the typewritten sheet to Mitch. "High clouds, maybe a little more wind, but otherwise it's still fine. Tomorrow and the day after—that may be another matter."

"Thanks," Lewis said.

"With any luck at all," Mitch said, "we won't be flying then."

Lewis looked for wood to touch, but there wasn't any, and contented himself with tapping his own head.

The clouds were definitely closing in with the night, gray hummocks and rills filling in the sky around them, sheets of pale haze that thickened as he watched. The air would be smoother above them, Lewis knew, but he didn't want to be landing through the cloud deck in the dark when he didn't have to. He pushed the wheel forward just a little, letting the Terrier descend decorously, a hundred feet, three hundred, a thousand, and leveled off again when he thought they were well below the clouds. The sun was low enough behind them now that it was below the clouds, too, striking last flecks of reddish light from the landscape below. Mitch checked his notes, gave him the compass reading, and they flew on into the deepening night.

The air was a little choppy, just enough to require attention and strength to keep the Terrier mostly level. Lewis thought the weather report was probably right, there would be weather coming in behind them, sending out feelers ahead of the storms. Below them, the countryside was mostly dark, a cluster of town lights occasionally passing beneath the wing. That, at least, was nothing like France, where the night flights had been broken only by the flash of artillery, and he was grateful for it.

"Keep an eye out for the beacon," Mitch said. "We should be seeing it pretty soon."

Lewis nodded, his eyes flicking from the compass to the invisible horizon and back again. For a few long moments, there was nothing but darkness and the drone of the engines, the instrument panel glowing softly, the dimmed lights of the passenger cabin barely passing the cockpit door. And then, so faint at first that he thought he'd imagined it, he caught the first flash of the beacon, the edge of the beam sweeping out into the night. They'd barely been off by three degrees: he smiled, and steadied the Terrier on the new heading.

Iowa City was waiting for them. The lights came on as he made his first approach, circling over the beacon to get his bearings, and it was easy enough to let the Terrier down onto the well-manicured runway. He taxied to a stop beside the hangar, and they climbed out again so that they could top up the main fuel tanks as quickly as possible. Lewis lit cigarettes for himself and Alma, and stood for a moment letting the night breeze play over him. It had been a hell of a long day, and it looked like it was going to get even longer. Maybe he could catch a catnap on the way to Chicago….

"Nice landing," Alma said, and exhaled a plume of smoke. "I still don't much like night flying."

Lewis shrugged one shoulder. "At least we have lights." And nobody's shooting at us, he added silently. The way things were going, saying it aloud felt like tempting fate.

It didn't take long to finish fueling and to radio Chicago to tell them they were coming. Alma settled down in the seat in the back as Mitch prepared for takeoff. She didn't even need to have a look at him. The Terrier was his baby, and he had the smoothest hand with it of all of them. Jerry didn't look up either.

"So, Jerry," she said. "How is it?"

Jerry folded the book down. "It isn't," he said quietly. Certainly his voice wasn't audible in the cockpit over the engines. "I'm not sure this can be done, Al. Not with what we have and the time available. I'm not sure I can design something that's actually bombproof that's small enough and that we can make with the materials we can get and that we can do in a couple of hours. And if it doesn't work…." He shook his head.

Alma frowned, leaning forward. She knew she couldn't be heard in the cockpit either. "Look, resisting possession is about will, right? That's what it comes down to in the end. It's about knowing you have sovereignty over your own body, and having the will to make it so."

Jerry let out a long breath. "Of course it is," he said quietly. "But do you think most of us believe that?"

"Jerry…."

"We don't believe that we have that kind of control. We don't believe we have the right or the strength or the ability to say no to a demon. And so it controls us." Jerry ran one hand through his hair. "We call upon external aid. We ask Diana or St. Christopher or whomever to help us. We say, I am weak, my dear, carry me. I am lost. Find me." His blue eyes met hers. "Everyone needs it sooner or later, Al."

"I know," she said. "I have."

He reached over and took her hand, folded it in his. "I know you have. And I'm glad I could be here."

She squeezed his fingers. "I am too, Jerry."

He looked away. "You know, after the war, you and Gil...."

"You don't need to say it," Alma said.

"If you and Lewis work out, I couldn't be happier for you."

Alma searched his face, and then nodded slowly. "Thank you, Jerry."

He drew himself up with effort. "So. About these sigils...."

"It has to be strong enough for us to believe in. That's the important thing. Not being consecrated at the right hour of the night in the right phase of the moon. All of that is secondary to belief."

Jerry sighed. "I think a sigil of Sagittarius on one side and the crescent moon on the other is the best we can do given the constraints. That's probably simple enough for Lewis to engrave on a small piece of metal." He shook his head. "I'm giving up on the quill taken from the left wing of a male gosling and the virgin parchment...."

"Or any other kind of virgin," Alma said.

Jerry gave her a quicksilver smile. "Or any other kind of virgin. Consecrate the burin with perfume of the art.... I don't suppose you have any perfume?"

"Not with me." The plane had leveled off, and Alma turned and called to the cockpit. "I don't suppose either of you have some cologne?"

Mitch didn't look around but shouted back. "I've got a bottle of Musgo Real after shave in my kit. If you want that."

"What's in it?" Jerry called.

"I don't know."

Alma rolled her eyes. "I'll find out," she said, undoing Mitch's case. She found the bottle and unscrewed the cap, taking a deep sniff and handing it to Jerry. "Vetiver," she said. "Sandalwood."

Jerry sniffed and nodded sharply. "That will do. Musgo Real it is!"

From the cockpit, Lewis could be heard querying Mitch, "We're going to do a magical thing with Musgo Real?"

"Better than Burma Shave," Mitch said.

They followed the Chicago beacon into the Municipal Airport, the rotating beams of light like a landlocked lighthouse. Mitch brought the Terrier down between the lines of boundary lights, his eyes roving from the instruments to the barely-visible field and back to the instruments. His gut shrieked that they were turning, right wing pitching up, but he ignored the sensation, focusing on the turn indicator. It showed straight and level: his body was lying again, no surprise there. He stole a glance at Lewis anyway just to check, saw him relaxed and easy in the copilot's seat, and then he was below fifty feet, the ground rising to meet his wheels. He let the Terrier stall, and dropped neatly onto the runway.

It was just a little before midnight, but they were not the last expected flight. One of the passenger lines was scheduled to land just before one, so there were still lights on in the terminal, and a handful of porters waiting by the main entrance. Mitch taxied the plane to the only available hangar, and began shutting everything down while Alma and Lewis went in search of coffee, and to fetch the key to the Kershaw machine shop from the tower. He had just finished setting the chocks when Jerry came down the steps. He looked tired and a little drawn, and Mitch guessed the leg was beginning to hurt again. He knew better than to ask, though, and said only, "Do we have a plan?"

"Of course," Jerry said, so brightly that Mitch gave him a wary look.

"I'm serious."

"I do have a plan," Jerry said. "I just didn't say it was a good one."

Chapter Twelve

"Oh Adonai most powerful, who hast established all things in thy wisdom, who didst choose Abraham to be thy faithful servant and didst promise that in his seed shall all the nations of the earth be blessed…." Jerry intoned solemnly, his hands raised before him.

Lewis found his mind wandering, much as it had in long ago days as a choir boy and an acolyte. This "operation" seemed about as long as a full Mass, and not entirely dissimilar. There were endless invocations and readings, including the entirety of Psalms 8, 11, 27, 29, and 32 before Alma put a stop to it with apparently several more Psalms to go. "I think God has the gist of it," she said. "And it's nearly two, Jerry. We have to have time to make the actual sigils."

He'd already cut the sheet metal into 3 inch by 3 inch squares and made a small hole in each for a chain or string to go through. Well, after Jerry had endlessly blessed Henry Kershaw's shop equipment. Any fear and trepidation Lewis had felt at the darkened shop and talk of demons had vanished in the face of Jerry reciting Psalms 51 and 72 over the miter saw and anointing it with Musgo Real after shave. Instead, this all began to feel just a little silly.

Which was probably not the proper frame of mind, given that he still had to engrave the four pieces of metal. If Jerry ever got done summing up the entire Old Testament.

"…Thou who has appeared unto thy servant Moses in the form of a burning bush, and hast made him to walk upon dry feet through the Red Sea, who gavest the Law to him upon Mount Sinai, Thou who hast granted unto David kingship and unto his house thereafter…."

Mitch shifted from foot to foot, a solemn expression on his face, his eyes downcast as though in church. He looked like an overgrown choirboy too, and Lewis had a sudden vision of a row of well-scrubbed children lined up in a pew in order of height from Mitch at the end about fourteen all the way down to a little boy still in skirts holding on to his sister's hand. There was the sharp, clean smell of the pine boughs adorning the plain glass windows, the spicy scent of cinnamon. There were cakes on the altar where there ought to be bread, or cookies maybe, wrapped in different baskets and cloths, some of them still warm. Their scent mingled with the smell of beeswax from the candles. A woman's voice rose in sweet song, accompanied by an old fashioned harpsichord. "Silent night, holy night…."

Lewis blinked. Jerry was still running on, having got up to King Solomon. That was not Lewis' memory, not his own thoughts. Christmas Eve, yes, but not the Mass, not the familiar words, not the priest at the altar. This was entirely different, and yet the same in spirit. A different Christmas Eve, a different home.

He glanced over at Mitch, who still stood with his head bowed. Was this Mitch's memory? Had he somehow shared it for a moment, thinking too of church as a child, half lulled to sleep by Jerry's voice?

Alma cleared her throat, catching Jerry's eye. Her meaning was clear. Wrap it up. They were running out of time.

"Yes, um," Jerry inserted suddenly, his lengthy recap breaking off. "Moving right along." He lifted up the four small squares of metal. "May these pentacles be consecrated by Thy power that we may obtain virtue and strength against all Spirits, through Thee, Most Holy Adonai, whose kingdom endureth without end." Laying them on his handkerchief, he handed them to Lewis. "You can start engraving now."

"Thanks." Lewis took them carefully, for all that they were pieces of metal he'd cut himself less than an hour before. He laid them out and then chose one, picking up the burin carefully. Sweat stood out on his brow.

Mitch touched his arm lightly. "They don't have to be perfect," he said. "It's the intent that's important."

Obscurely that made him feel better. There would be time

another day to ask Mitch about what he'd seen, whether it was real or just his imagining, but he held on to that feeling of peace. There was something stable about Mitch, solid and bright beneath whatever darkness overlay it. His hands were cutting, tracing the symbols dark on bright, but he was only half aware of them. Yes, there was a darkness there, something the color of old blood beneath affable charm. There was a shadow, and against it the flame burned all the brighter. A decision reached, an acceptance sought again and again. He couldn't name it, didn't need to, but it stood at the core of Mitch, just as Mitch stood at his shoulder.

"Very nice," Mitch said, as Lewis lifted the first amulet and turned it over, ready to begin the back.

"This one's for you," Lewis said. "It has you in it."

Alma's eyebrows twitched.

Hers was the second one. He made the first cuts with care, the long semicircle of the huntsman's bow the twist of her smile. She was strong, stronger than anyone, practical and competent. And under it was joy. For all the sadness that came to her eyes when she spoke of Gil, she had no regrets. Alma never would. Courage came from joy, and for her life would always be sweet no matter what it held. It drew him to her in laughter and tears alike to share in that evergreen strength.

"This one is for Alma," he said, his fingers tracing the crescent moon. The new moon pale over forests of dark cypress trees, fragrant wooded glens cathedrals beneath the stars….

Jerry's was hardest, as he'd expected. Mercurial, brilliant, shifting as the seas. It didn't want to take. His hands slipped on the burin, the lines wavering, and he pressed it back, like holding on to the controls bucking in an unexpected thermal. There was strength there too, strength in yielding, the inexpressible, immovable permanence of the sea. Water yields. It gives, it pours, it shapes itself to whatever contains it. And yet it is nothing but itself, flowing with unimaginable might, unfathomable depth. Jerry yielded. But he did not surrender.

"This one's for you," he said, placing it in Jerry's palm still warm from his hand. There was a quick flash of amazement there as he felt it, and Lewis thought yes. That is how it should be, each suited to the one it belonged to, hallowed by the craftsman's love. He could not speak names of power, recite rituals to consecrate. But these were made of his love and concern, and that had power of its own.

The last one. The one for himself. He had been mistaken that Jerry's was hardest. The hardest was his own. A wave of fear washed over him. He could not make something that would protect himself. He didn't know how.

The shape of the moon mocked him, the hunter's bow eluded him. Darkness moved with a thousand whispers. They would never get back. They would never make it. If everything depended on him, they would die. He stood in memory beside the downed plane, tugging at Robbie's jacket, searching for a pulse. If it were up to him, it was over. Night crawled around him.

A dog howled, high and longing. Then another, and another.

That was as it was in the first dark, when man knew no fire. There was the pale moon rising to cast her light, heralded by the long song of the wolf. They were not foes but friends, packmates brought among men to work at their sides, and their presence made the night safe.

Lady of Hounds, Lady of the Crescent Moon, bright protectress.... The metal shone bright, burnished with her light.

It had been a dog that had saved them, some farm dog who led the old Frenchman to the downed plane, creeping out at night across lands that were once his before they were claimed by war. An ordinary black and white dog, leading a man through the woods. "Please help us, please..." He didn't speak French and the man spoke no English, but their uniforms spoke for them, Robbie's blood spoke for them.

The hunter's bow, dark on bright, hunter's truth. I kill that I may live. Lady of the Hunt, Lady of Wild Places....

The amulet glittered in his hand as though it were made of glass, cool and smooth beneath his touch.

"That's beautiful," Alma said softly as he lifted it, turning it around in the light of the incandescent bulb. "I had no idea you could do that."

"Neither did I," Lewis said shakily.

Alma unfastened the chain around her neck and slid one

end through the hole in her amulet, letting it slide down to rest against her wedding ring.

"You did good work," said Mitch. He nodded solemnly. "Let's anoint each one of these, and then take the working wards down."

"So that I can check into a hotel later with my three identically reeking gentlemen friends," Alma said, giving Lewis' hand a squeeze. "I always like all my boys to smell alike!"

"We won't be checking in anywhere soon," Jerry said, casting a glance at his watch. "The Chief gets here in about an hour."

They took a cab to Dearborn Station under slowly paling clouds, the sky red as a furnace in the east. Red sky at morning, Mitch thought, stifling a yawn. They'd done well to get in ahead of the weather. The clock in the massive tower showed a quarter to five. Jerry paid off the cabbie, and they pushed through the doors into the main hall. It was busier than Mitch had expected, the station already springing to life. Shoeshine boys were already waiting for patrons, and the first bundles of the day's papers were opened beside the newsstands, vendors whose sour faces said they'd seen everything deftly pinning a sample to the stand before folding the rest away. The milk train was just in, and a steady stream of passengers, mostly laborers in dungarees with lunch pails in hand, made their way toward the streetcar stops across West Polk. A trio of younger men with too-sharp suits and weary eyes had stopped at the lunchroom counter, were ordering eggs and coffee from the Harvey girl in her old-fashioned uniform, while a couple in evening dress walked slowly past them, the girl giggling as she leaned on her boyfriend's arm. The left-luggage office was open, and they stopped to check their bags, Alma tucking the claim tickets into her purse. She had changed into a plain shirtwaist, a little crumpled from travel, and the same blue cloche she had worn before.

"The Chief's on time," she said, as they drifted back into the enormous main hall.

Mitch slipped his hand into his pants pocket, feeling for the amulet. The rough lines were reassuring, armor against the worst that could happen. He felt heavy, stupid from lack of sleep, and shook himself hard. "Ok," he said. "So now what?"

"We find out where he's going," Jerry said impatiently. "We follow him."

"Yes, but how?" Lewis asked. He rubbed his chin, dark with stubble. "I mean, isn't there something, I don't know, magical that would work better?"

"That's more likely to attract its attention," Jerry said.

"More than us flailing around?" Lewis said.

"You may have a point," Alma said, with a quick grin. "But we've only got ten minutes to come up with a better plan if we're going to."

"It's very simple," Mitch said, and hoped it was true. "Me and Lewis will wait by the gates and follow him. Al, you and Jerry stay in the concourse—the benches over there, maybe, they're discreet. You're the ones Davenport knows best, he could care less about me, and he's never met Lewis at all."

Alma nodded.

"We'll follow him," Mitch went on. "You back us up, catch him up if he gets past us. Otherwise, you'll stay here, and we'll either come back for you or have you paged."

Jerry nodded reluctantly. "We'll have to collect the luggage anyway if he's going to a hotel."

"Which I, for one, hope he is," Alma said. "What I wouldn't give for a nap right now!"

"What about a cup of coffee instead?" Lewis said, but she shook her head with regret.

"No time. The Chief will be here any minute."

"Right," Mitch said, with more confidence than he actually felt. "Come on, Lewis."

They made their way through the main concourse and through the swinging doors to the head of the platform. Porters were already swarming the platform, and a conductor stood by the open gate of Track 9, checking his watch. The air was much warmer all of a sudden, and stank of coal smoke, diesel and hot metal. Already there were other people waiting—a young man carrying flowers, an older couple arm in arm, a handful of drivers and servants in uniform—and Mitch picked a spot in the lee of the newsstand, trying to make himself inconspicuous. Lewis bought a paper, and folded it back to pretend to study the racing pages.

A bell clanged in the distance, the sound quickly drowned in the heavy chuffing of the engine and the long screech of brakes. The Chief pulled slowly into the platform, stopping with a last rush of steam and a clatter as the conductors began to open the doors. Mitch straightened and saw Lewis tuck the paper under his arm. The first passengers bustled past the gate, hurrying toward the main concourse. Mitch saw the boy with the flowers embrace a tall girl in a plain hat, and the older couple stoop to welcome a tired-looking woman with a pair of toddlers in tow. There were businessmen, lots of them, porters trailing them eagerly; couples, the men in good suits, the women in smart hats and well-cut traveling sets; another family with a squalling baby; a pair of college boys arguing with a porter over a trunk—

"There," Lewis said. He nodded toward the gate. "There he is."

Mitch looked where he'd indicated. Sure enough, it was Davenport, looking a little haggard in his good gray suit. He had dispensed with a porter, and was carrying his own suitcase, striding briskly along as though he had someplace to go. Mitch pulled himself away from the wall, and let himself blend into the crowd a few yards behind him, Lewis at his heels.

In the main concourse, Davenport stopped and looked around as though he was getting his bearings. Mitch brought his hands to his face as though he were lighting a cigarette, peeping between his fingers and the brim of his hat. It must be hell, that thing wearing Davenport like an old overcoat, trapped screaming inside his own head while the creature used him, body, mind, and soul.... Davenport was strong, he always had been, but clearly he'd been no match for this thing. Mitch just hoped the amulets would be protection enough, once they figured out how to confront it.

Davenport was moving again, heading for the main doors. The crowd was thinner there, attenuated by the sheer size of the concourse, and Mitch hung back, not wanting to be seen. Out of the corner of his eye, he could see Alma angling toward them, carefully casual, and he risked waving her back. She saw and slowed her steps. Davenport was at the door, heading for the waiting taxis, and Mitch hesitated. He was too far away to follow if Davenport took a cab, but he didn't dare get closer. There weren't enough people there to cover him. Then Lewis brushed past him, reaching into his pocket for his cigarettes, came out the doors ahead of Davenport and stopped to light a match. Beside him, Davenport spoke to the cabbie; the man touched his cap and tossed Davenport's suitcase into the trunk, then held the door for him. Mitch pushed through the doors as the cab pulled away, and saw Lewis standing beside a second taxi.

"He said the Great Northern Hotel," Lewis said.

"Right," Mitch answered, and slid into the seat behind him.

"Great Northern?" the cabbie asked, and Mitch reached into his pocket, dangled a five dollar bill over the cabbie's shoulder.

"Your buddy who just left," he said, and the cabbie gave him one quick and comprehending glance. "We want to go where he goes."

"Cops or private?" The cabbie grabbed the bill, and put the taxi into gear.

"He owes us money," Lewis said.

"He said he was going to the Great Northern," Mitch said, "but we'd like to be sure."

"You got it, boss," the cabbie said. "He ain't got far."

Mitch leaned back in his seat as the cab slid into the line of traffic four or five cars behind Davenport's cab. They made their way quickly down Dearborn Street, traffic still light enough that it was easy to keep the other cab in sight. In the end, though, it didn't really matter. Davenport's cab pulled up decorously in front of the Great Northern Hotel, and Davenport climbed out, collected his bag, and headed into the lobby. Their own cabbie looked over his shoulder with a grin and a shrug, and at Mitch's nod pulled into the curb just shy of the dark gray canopy.

"That's got to be the easiest five bucks he ever made," Lewis said, as the cab pulled away.

"Yeah." It was, Mitch thought, starting to be an expensive trip all around. Through the glass doors, he could see Davenport at the massive desk, obviously booking a room, and he reached for his cigarettes, buying time to see if Davenport was going to go to his room or just check his bags and head somewhere else. But, no, the clerk had summoned a bellboy, and they were trailing off into the depths of the lobby. "Ok," he said aloud. "I guess it's time we got a room."

Lewis winced at that, and Mitch clapped him on the shoulder. "Wait here, make sure Davenport doesn't come back down."

The Great Northern's lobby was enormous and old-fashioned, with a huge skylight two stories high and an enormous carved marble clock on the mezzanine above front desk. They'd made an attempt to make it look more modern by laying rugs over the ornate marble tile, and by painting the ironwork green and gold, but it still looked like exactly what it was, a grande dame settling reluctantly into middle age. Gil would have had a story to match the place, Mitch thought, some excuse that went with the marble scrolls around the clock and the picture gallery on the second floor—White Russian countesses and stolen crown jewels, something straight out of Oppenheim. He'd be lucky if he could get the clerk to give him a room at all.

He still hadn't worked out what to say when he reached the counter. The clerk was a young man, maybe twenty, so fair Mitch doubted he shaved more than twice a week. There was a copy of Black Mask face-down on the ledge beneath the bank of pigeonholes, and Mitch suppressed the instinct to smile.

"The guy who just checked in," he said. He reached into his pocket, brought out his wallet to flash his pilot's license, and took it away again before the clerk could get a good look at it. "Bill Davenport. I'm looking to get two rooms as close to his as possible. Across the hall would be best."

The clerk blinked. "Sir, I'm not sure—"

"There won't be any trouble for the hotel," Mitch said. "I can promise you that."

"Sir—" The clerk stopped again, tried for sophistication. "Sir, if it's divorce—"

Mitch shook his head, gave an easy smile. "No, nothing like that. And nothing to get the cops involved. It's a matter of— well, there's a letter written by a lady, an actress, and the studio wants it settled. Very quietly, if you understand me. It's just a matter of making sure he keeps his part of the deal." He slid another five dollar bill across the countertop.

The clerk looked quickly down, then nodded. "Oh. That's—I

suppose that's all right. But there's to be no trouble."

"None in the world," Mitch said.

The rooms weren't as nice as the rooms at the Roosevelt, Alma thought, but they would certainly do. Somehow Mitch had arranged it so that she nominally had the room directly across from Davenport, and the three men had the room next door, but the connecting door was unlocked, and Lewis lugged his suitcase in with hers. She held out the bag of doughnuts she'd bought at the station, and Mitch accepted one, his eyes closing in pleasure as he bit into it.

"Thank God," he said. "I was starving."

"I didn't know if we'd want to risk the restaurant," Alma said. "Or room service."

"This is good for now," Lewis said, with a quick smile.

There was a noise from the hall, a door opening, and she turned quickly to look through the peephole. It was Davenport's door, all right, and Davenport himself, setting his shoes out to be shined. It seemed extraordinary that he should think of that, or that the demon should. She watched him close the door again, and turned back to the others. "I think he's settling in for a while. He just put his shoes out."

"I could stand a nap myself," Mitch said. He did look beat, his eyes red and tired, and Alma nodded.

"Why don't you and Lewis get some sleep? Jerry and I can keep an eye on things here."

For a second, she thought Lewis might protest, but Mitch nodded. "Sleep, then a shower. I may never wear Musgo Real again."

Lewis looked back at her. "You sure you don't want me to take the first watch?"

"I slept on the plane," Alma said. It was more or less true, even if it had been more of a doze than solid sleep. "Go ahead."

She waited until the door closed behind them, then reached for another doughnut. They were good, fresh and sweet, and she let herself savor it. Maybe later they would order lunch—it was Henry's dime, and that reminded her, she should probably wire him for more cash if they were going to be in Chicago for a while.

"What do you think he's after, Jerry?" she asked.

"I wish I knew." Jerry had stretched out on one of the twin beds, his coat draped over the back of a chair, his hat and tie set neatly on top of it. He hadn't taken off his leg, just rested it on the mattress, the wooden knob that served for a foot nearly denuded of rubber. Another thing she needed to fix, Alma thought, and pulled the stool of the dressing table closer to the door. It wasn't very comfortable, but that ought to help keep her awake.

"Something like this," Jerry said softly. His glasses lay beside him on the pale coverlet, and his eyes were closed. "It wants power, Al. Power and death and sorrow and destruction. Corruption. Those are the things it needs, that it feeds upon. I've been thinking...." There was a long silence, long enough that Alma wondered if he'd nodded off, but then he opened his eyes again. "The ancient sources generally agree that Caligula's reign started out quite reasonably—he was genuinely popular, did things like stop the treason prosecutions Tiberius had begun at the end of his reign, when he was getting old and paranoid. And then he fell ill with a fever. His life was despaired of, but he recovered. And his first act then was to order the deaths of two of his dearest friends who had offered their lives to the gods in exchange for his. The rest—everyone knows. Murder, depravity, madness—"

"He made his horse a senator," Alma said. "That's one thing I remember."

"And a priest," Jerry said. "Though that was fairly benign. He declared himself a god in AD 40, and proceeded to behave as though he did in fact have god-like powers of life and death. Supposedly there was a day at the games when he ran out of criminals before he ran out of wild beasts, so he picked a random section of the crowd, and sacrificed them instead."

"And we have to stop it." A shiver ran up Alma's spine. Caligula reborn.

"Somehow," Jerry said. He swung himself upright. "Look, I'm not going to be any use here. Chasing Davenport around the city is not going to be my strong suit. There's material at the Oriental Institute that can help us—maybe—find a way to bind this thing." He was knotting his tie as he spoke, sleeking his hair into shape again.

"Don't you want a nap first?" Alma asked.

Jerry picked up his hat and cane, gave her a sideways smile. "The rest of you did all the work getting us here. It's about time I did something useful."

He slipped out the door without waiting for her answer, and Alma shook her head. "Oh, Jerry," she said, softly, and settled again to listen for Davenport's door.

Chapter Thirteen

Alma had just checked her watch for the fifth time—ten o'clock—when she heard water running in the bathroom next door. A few minutes later, the connecting door swung open, and Mitch poked his head in, hair still damp from the bath.

"I don't suppose there are any doughnuts left," he said. "Where's Jerry?"

"He went to the Oriental Institute," Alma answered. "He said the library there has things that might help him figure out what we do next."

Mitch found the paper bag, and retrieved the last doughnut. "That would be good. Look, I'm going to order us some sandwiches and coffee, but why don't you take a nap till they get here?"

Alma started to protest, but a yawn overtook her. Mitch grinned, and she smiled ruefully. "You're right. Wake me the minute he moves."

"He'll have to get his shoes back first," Mitch said. "Go to sleep, Al."

She refrained from pointing out that Davenport might have packed more than one pair of shoes, and retreated into the adjoining bedroom. It was a mirror image of the other, the beds on the opposite wall, but otherwise identical. The men had drawn the shades, but the cloudy light filtered in around the edge of the window. Lewis was asleep in the far bed, stripped to shorts and undershirt, clothes folded on the nearest chair. The other bed was barely mussed, just the pillow tugged free of the blankets: typical, she thought, that Mitch would sleep so neatly, almost as though he was never there.

She pulled off her dress and hung it up in the narrow closet, and after a moment's hesitation unhooked her stockings. If they had to move fast, she'd have to go bare-legged, but it was worth it to be able to sleep in comfort. She fluffed up the pillow on the unoccupied bed, and Lewis said softly, "Al?"

"I thought you were asleep," she said.

"Not really." He gave her a sleepy smile. "There's room to share, if you want."

"Yes," she said, and he folded back the sheet, leaving her half the narrow bed. She slid comfortably down against him, fitting herself to his arms, and laughed softly at the lingering scent of Musgo Real on his hands.

"What?"

"You smell like Mitch," she said, and settled deeper into his arms.

She woke to the sound of voices and clinking china in the other room. Lewis was gone, and she reached for her watch, frowning. It was after one o'clock, and she untangled herself from the sheets, feeling the muscles tighten at the base of her neck and in her arms. It had been a long flight, but all things considered, she felt surprisingly good. She dressed quickly, ran a comb through her hair, and pushed open the connecting door.

"Oh, good," Mitch said. "I was just about to wake you."

"What's up?" As promised, Mitch had ordered food, and there was a coffee service and a big plate of sandwiches on a wheeled table. Alma reached for a sandwich, and took a quick bite.

"Davenport got lunch delivered about five minutes ago," Lewis said. He was sitting on the stool by the door, a cup of coffee in his hand. He grinned. "No shoes, though."

"Give him time," Mitch said.

Alma poured herself coffee as well, managed to finish it and most of a second sandwich before they heard a knock at Davenport's door. Lewis was on his feet in an instant, peering through the peephole.

"It's the bellhop," he said. "With the shoes."

"Right." Mitch set his cup aside. "Sounds like he's moving."

Alma nodded, reaching for her purse.

"So what's the plan?" Lewis asked.

"You go down to the lobby," Mitch said. "Since Davenport doesn't know you. We'll stay here, just in case he does something else, and we'll follow when he leaves."

"And meet me in the lobby?" Lewis said.

"You follow him," Mitch said. "That's the main thing. We'll catch you up."

"Ok." Lewis picked up his coat and hat. He'd shaved at some point, and looked almost entirely respectable.

"Do you have cash?" Alma asked, and he nodded.

"I'm good for now."

The door closed softly behind him, and Alma looked at Mitch. "You're good at this."

"I have unplumbed depths," Mitch answered, with a wry smile. "Al, I'm making it up as I go."

Across the hall, Davenport's door opened. Mitch pressed his eye to the peephole. "Ok," he said, his voice suddenly tense. "This is it. Hat and coat—and he's headed for the elevators. I can't.... Wait, he's caught one. Come on."

One thing, Alma thought, there were plenty of elevators. They caught one almost at once, reached the lobby in time to see Lewis whisking out the main door. Mitch lengthened his stride to catch up, and as she hurried at his side, Alma caught a glimpse of Lewis making his way south on Dearborn. Davenport had to be ahead of him, but she couldn't see him, and didn't spot him until they caught up with Lewis at the next intersection.

"Well?" Mitch asked, and Lewis looked over his shoulder.

"He went up there."

He nodded to the iron stairs that led to the elevated railway station across the street. Mitch looked at the stream of cars, the white-gloved policeman with his whistle directing traffic, and muttered something under his breath. But then the policeman gave another shrill blast, stopping the cars, and they joined the other pedestrians hurrying up the steps.

Luckily, the platform was crowded. Alma allowed herself one quick glance to be sure Davenport was there—yes, there he was, at the far end of the platform, looking distinguished and a little impatient—and melted back behind Lewis. The train arrived with a screech of brakes, and she hung back with the others until they were sure Davenport had gotten aboard, and then stepped into the next car. Lewis forged his way down the corridor until he was almost at the connecting door, where he could see into Davenport's car, and Alma dropped reluctantly into one of the wooden seats. The train lurched into motion.

She had only the vaguest idea of Chicago's geography. Jerry knew the city well, of course, he'd been a student here, but he wasn't with them. She hoped one of the others had thought to buy a guidebook, or something. They were heading south, though, she could tell that much, under skies that were steadily darkening. She hadn't thought to bring an umbrella or a raincoat, either, and hoped they wouldn't get caught in a downpour. Lewis was still standing by the connecting door, relaxed and easy; after the first few stops, she decided there would be plenty of time to get off when Davenport did, and she let herself relax a little.

The train made its way slowly along the elevated tracks, brakes scraping on every corner. The buildings were close on either side, backs of tenements and apartments and shops, so that she wondered how anyone stood the noise. You'd get used to it after a while, she supposed, but still. Five stops, seven, ten.... The train kept heading steadily south, the crowd thinning with every stop, until Lewis had to take a seat, or become too conspicuous. Alma craned to see the station signs. Forty-Seventh Street, Fifty-First, Fifty-Fifth. The train slowed again, and she saw Lewis rise to his feet. The train pulled into the Fifty-Eighth Street Station, and she followed Mitch onto the platform. There weren't so many people here, but Davenport seemed oblivious, and headed for the stairs as though he was in a hurry to get where he was going before the rain came.

At least it was easier to keep him in sight along these streets. He was heading east now, past houses and open lots and the occasional neighborhood shop. Trees rose ahead, a public park, and Lewis looked over his shoulder.

"Why would he—is he meeting someone, do you think?"

"No idea," Mitch answered, but his voice was faintly worried.

Alma took a careful breath as they plunged into the tree-shaded walks. Whatever Davenport wanted here, at least she could feel the ground beneath her feet, the familiar solidity of earth untrammeled by the city. It was a comfort, if it came to a confrontation, to know it was there for her. They skirted a lagoon without stopping, and came out on the park's eastern edge. The buildings were more crowded now, square, handsome buildings in brick and granite, and she realized they had reached the University.

"Mitch," she began, and he answered, "Yeah. I see it."

A new building rose ahead of them, its sign proclaiming it the Oriental Institute Museum. Davenport looked neither right nor left, heading up the steps into the shadowed doorway.

"Isn't that where Jerry was going?" Lewis said, and Mitch nodded.

"We'd better find him," Alma said.

The museum downstairs was not open yet, plastered walls still waiting for paint, signs proclaiming that soon it would be a luxurious and modern home for the University of Chicago Oriental Institute's famed collection of Middle Eastern antiquities. The building was new and very large, boasting the best amenities scholars could want, and if the museum was not yet open the library and reading rooms on the second floor lacked nothing. Certainly the collection of classical works belonging to the University of Chicago was impressive. It was even better than it had been when Jerry finished his doctorate here in 1916.

He'd been twenty-seven then, a promising young scholar in the field. Whatever disadvantages anyone had dared to mention had been long since overcome. He'd worked on a dig in Palestine and another in Turkey, studied with Dorpfeldt and written a paper that earned the approbation of Arthur Evans. Perhaps some of his theories were a little outré, especially in terms of giving so much credence to early syncretic elements as evidence of cultural influence, but Evans had become a colossus by going out on a limb. Risk is how societies, and men, advance.

The war had changed all that, of course. Mathematics had proved useful for artillery, but it was being fluent in Italian that had sent him to Venice, to defend the city against the Austrians. And then there had been Gil.

He'd tried to return here, in the fall of 1919. He'd been more than welcome, a special assistant to a professor who had believed in him. A wound is an honorable thing, of course, especially one taken in the saving of precious civilization from the barbarian hordes. But there had been blood clots in the damaged foot, the last one cutting off circulation so that it swelled up alarmingly, the skin stretched tight like the surface of a balloon. Given the choice of his foot or his life the decision was logical. He read Seneca in the hospital, hoping it would serve.

A few weeks and he'd be back at work. Surely. But Stoicism did not conquer facts. A cold Chicago winter stretched ahead, living in rooms in a boarding house on an upper floor that he could not get to in his wheelchair, still too weak to transfer from wheelchair to bed without help. He'd sent a casual letter from the hospital. Doing fine, pesky foot. And he'd known or at least hoped what would happen.

Gil looked better. Well, a corpse would look better than Gil when he'd seen him last, in the hospital in Venice just before he'd been shipped home. They hadn't thought Gil would live. They hadn't known the war would end. Jerry had said goodbye, Gil wavering in and out of consciousness, knowing it would be final.

And now he sauntered in, his hair more gray than brown now, and the lines in his face deeply graven, but with a bounce in his step. "Come on, Jerry. We're here to spring you."

"Spring me?" He'd still been taking morphine by injection then. His head wasn't clear.

"We're taking you back to Colorado. Now don't worry about a thing. You'll go in top comfort by air, just like you were the President!" Gil came over and put his hand to Jerry's brow. "And you know Alma is as good as a nurse. She's seen it all in the ambulance service. Better than a boarding house, and you know it."

He did know it. He knew perfectly well he couldn't live alone, but he'd hardly dared to hope….

Alma's smile was warm. "How are you doing, Jerry?"

"I'm fine," Jerry said, looking from Gil to Alma, her conservative black hat looking incongruous on her. He'd never seen her dressed like that, never seen her dressed like a lady. "I'm just fine now."

He'd gone to sleep on the plane, an injection of morphine to ease the discomfort of travel, the pain of being jostled over and over. He'd gone to sleep to the white noise of the engines. Alma sat beside him, her profile sharp against the window as she read a book. She looked up, caught his drowsy gaze. "We'll be home soon," she said as he drifted off.

Nine years ago, now. He'd probably never go in the field again, not with his leg, and if he couldn't go in the field he was more or less useless to any faculty. Still, there was utility in synthesis, and he was welcome at the Oriental Institute even if thirteen years meant that most everyone he had known at the University of Chicago were gone. He still had some contacts, still had the respect of some fellow scholars, even if they did feel terribly sorry for poor Dr. Ballard, whose career had seemed so promising.

He kept abreast of the work, of course, and still took every journal. He even wrote some, mainly reviews of other scholars' work that he liked to think were sparkling with dry wit. He'd been able to keep up with that even during Gil's final illness. He'd like to think it was a contribution.

At least, Jerry thought, looking up from the table in the main reading room, he'd kept abreast enough to have an idea of where to look for the information he needed. There had been some very promising work on Ephesian Diana since Hogarth's excavations before the war, new votive material that was being worked on by a veritable army of graduate student translators. It was quite possible that the correct form of an Artemisian binding could be inferred. Hopefully it would not involve anything impossible, like sacrificing a bull.

Not that he had a moral objection to the sacrifice of bulls. Jerry ate beef. No different from slaughtering a steer for consumption, but not something they could manage easily in one of Henry's aircraft hangars. Now, on a farm....

Jerry looked up as the door to the reading room opened. He blinked. For a moment he thought he was imagining things. He'd been concentrating so hard on the subject of Davenport and the *animus infernus* that he imagined him there.

But no. There was Bill Davenport standing in the doorway next to the docent, staring at him with what could only be described as a look of horror.

Jerry looked back. Anything he'd meant to say died on his lips, suddenly very, very aware of the amulet in his pocket. He stared at Davenport—no, at whatever it was that wore Davenport—and it stared back.

And then, suddenly, it let out a horrible, bloodcurdling scream. Or maybe it was Davenport who screamed, the terrible plea of a man in anguish, and turned around and dashed for the door, nearly knocking the elderly docent down in the process.

Jerry got to his feet faster than he would have thought possible. He hurried around the table, his only thought that he couldn't let it get away, couldn't let it jump into some perfectly innocent graduate student who happened to be walking in, into the secretary at her typewriter in the front office or the plasterer just inside the museum doors on his ladder. He had to stop it somehow.

There were the stairs, and he had just reached the head of the stairs to the main lobby when he heard another scream below. Grabbing the rail, Jerry manhandled himself down the first few steps, enough to see. Just as Davenport had come down the stairs Mitch, Alma and Lewis had been walking in the front doors. Lewis was still holding the door open, Alma just ahead of him, Mitch a step in the rear.

The secretary looked up from her desk. The plasterer turned around. An old man in a three piece suit stood arrested by the secretary's desk, a letter in his hand.

Jerry felt it gather, like a leopard tensing to spring. Trapped. Cornered. There was no way out. This was a trap prepared by the hunters, by Her hounds. For one moment Jerry saw it all in tableau, and then it leaped. There was no other way to put it. It was like the invisible shimmer of air, a sudden wave of heat, as it sprang at Alma.

Her eyes met its. For a moment Jerry thought they would darken, change, that he would see her become nothing. And then it recoiled like a cat that has sprung at a bird and unexpectedly met a window pane.

Davenport screamed again, his head flung back as it rebounded, and then he ran at the doors with all his strength, shoving them out of Lewis' hand. The door caught Mitch full in the chest, knocking him back against the wall, his head cracking on the ornamental marble, and Davenport ran past him like a quarterback with a clear field sprinting for the touchdown.

With Lewis at his heels. Lewis didn't hesitate, just turned in pursuit.

Mitch staggered up, shaking his head and lowered it like a bull. It took a lot of punishment to get to Mitch, Jerry thought, as Mitch took off after Lewis, his coat open and his tie flying.

Jerry hurried down the steps, altogether too aware of the docent behind him, recognizing the elderly man by the desk as one of his former professors, Dr. Keating, someone who surely knew both him and Davenport by sight.

"What in the world?" the docent exclaimed. "I have no idea!"

"That was William Davenport," Dr. Keating said with astonishment. He looked at Jerry sharply, taking in his foot and his harried manner both. "And Ballard?"

If he was ever going to be able to set foot in here again, Jerry thought, he'd best make a good story of this. "Dr. Keating," he said. "It's good to see you, sir. That was Davenport, all right. But I have no idea what the difficulty was." He gestured to the docent. "I've been working here all morning, until this gentleman showed in Davenport who took one look at me, screamed and left. I had no idea I was so alarming!" Jerry grinned. "Bill's always been a bit odd, but the last few years…."

"Those two men…." Keating began.

Alma blinked winningly. "They held the door for me. I couldn't say."

Jerry came over and took her arm. "Dr. Keating, may I introduce a very particular friend of mine? This is Mrs. Gilchrist. She was doing some shopping while we are here in Chicago and came to meet me for lunch. Alma, darling, are you all right?"

"Of course," Alma said brightly. "Just a little startled. I had no idea archaeology could be so exciting."

"You'd be surprised," Keating said dryly. "It's a pleasure, Mrs. Gilchrist. And Ballard, it's good to see you around again. We've missed you here."

"Thank you, sir," Jerry said.

Keating shook Alma's hand. "He was one of our brightest lights. I hope we can lure him back one day."

Jerry found himself inexplicably warmed by the sentiment. "I hope so," he said. "I truly do, Dr. Keating."

It was some minutes before he and Alma could extricate themselves from the conversation, and by then there was no point in abandoning his notes spread all over the table in the reading room upstairs. Alma's quick glance outdoors on the pretext of seeing if that was indeed thunder she thought she heard showed no sign of Mitch, Lewis or Davenport.

"They could be blocks away by now," Alma said quietly as Jerry zipped his papers inside their worn leather case.

Jerry shook his head. "I should have considered that Davenport might come here too. We were students here at the same time."

"If I'd had any idea where we were going…." Alma began.

"How would you have called anyway? You would have lost him if you'd stopped to use a phone." Jerry straightened up, looking around the reading room with something like regret. There was so much more he could research, so much he wanted to do, if only to satisfy his own curiosity.

"I just hope Mitch and Lewis are ok," Alma said.

"I do too." Jerry pushed in his chair and headed for the stairs, everything neat behind him, smelling of leather and oriental rugs. "At least we know the amulets work."

Alma nodded. "That was scary. But yes, they do. At least we know that now." She took his arm, squeezing his hand as she did. "Good work, Jerry."

Her hounds coursed it. Their pursuit was relentless. It had no idea how they had picked up the scent. So much distance left between, so much ground crossed so quickly…. Superhumanly quickly, in this strange world. Continents and seas could be traversed in days rather than months. Surely it was only through Her that they had followed!

Her hand was on them. It could see that. They wore Her power like a shield. It should not have tried to jump into Her priestess. That had nearly been fatal. It had nearly been caught between, unable to take a new host and unable to return to the old. It had hurt.

Moreover, it was exhausted. It must rest. It must recover its strength.

But the hounds were relentless. They did not rest. They followed it still, and if it paused they would be upon it.

The only solution was distance. It must put miles between them so it could rest. It must lose them long enough to gain respite, no matter the danger that entailed.

And then it must kill them. There is, in the end, only one way to get a hound off the scent.

Chapter Fourteen

Lewis skidded to a stop at the curb, earning a warning shout and a raised fist from the driver of a delivery van. Davenport scrambled on, dodging traffic in a chorus of horns, and in the far lane a carthorse backed and plunged in its traces, garbage scattering from the overfilled wagon. Someone yelled something, and half a block away the cop directing traffic turned to see what was going on. Lewis swore, shifting from foot to foot as he waited for a break in the traffic. He wasn't sure how far he'd come, only that they were going west, towards the Stockyards, more or less, at least from what he remembered of a week spent in the city seven years ago. He hoped Davenport didn't know it any better, but he had a sinking feeling he might. He craned his neck to see Davenport, moving briskly away, and Mitch slid to a stop beside him, breathing hard.

"Davenport—?"

"There." Lewis saw a break in the traffic, darted forward, heard Mitch curse as he followed. They were just in time to see Davenport turn a corner, and Lewis broke into a trot, Mitch at his heels. He reached the corner, slowed as he realized they were indeed on the edge of the Stockyards, and then saw Davenport taking the steps to the L station two at a time.

"He's taking the train," he said, and Mitch caught his arm.

"Slowly," he said. "We don't want to spook him any worse."

Lewis paused. That made some sense, although he wasn't sure how much worse it could get. Well, no, there was a lot worse. There was scared enough to attack, scared enough to try for a new body, a new host. He had seen it, in the Institute, and was only grateful that it had gone for one of them rather than a stranger, and was even more grateful that the amulets had worked. He was very aware of his own, clattering against the change in his pocket; he could still see the instant of fear as Alma braced herself, the relief as the thing rebounded and returned to Davenport's body. "Are there other entrances, do you think?"

"Just there," Mitch said, pointing up the street. "He can't get out that way without us seeing him."

"He's going to take the train," Lewis said, and Mitch glanced at him.

"Do you see that, or what?"

"It just makes sense," Lewis said. "He'll stand out like a sore thumb in the Stockyards in that suit." *And so will we, if we have to chase him there.* "I bet he's trying to get back to the Loop. We can't chase him there without it looking pretty funny."

"It looked pretty funny back at the Institute," Mitch said. He nodded. "Ok, let's see if we can follow without him noticing."

They paid their nickels and edged onto the platform, trying to keep out of sight. At least there were maybe a dozen people there ahead of them, and they hung back in the shade of the overhang. Lewis caught a glimpse of Davenport's hat, the gray hair untidy beneath it, and ducked back out of sight. "What do we do once we catch him?" he asked.

Mitch touched the back of his head, wincing, and resettled his hat so it wasn't pressing on the bruise where he'd hit the wall. "I was hoping you wouldn't ask that. That's more Jerry's department."

Lewis gave him a look. "Seems to me we might be better off with a plan."

"Yeah, you might be right." Mitch glanced down the platform again. "I don't want to lose him, that's the main thing. We don't have to take him now—in fact, I think we'd better not, not when we don't know what to do with him, and when there's too much risk that he might—jump—somewhere else." He paused. "If we could get him off somewhere by himself, I suppose we could hit him over the head and tie him up until the others got here…."

His voice trailed off doubtfully, and Lewis shook his head. "I'm not thrilled with that idea."

"Me, neither," Mitch said. "I just—we'll follow him, see where he goes to earth. Then we get Jerry and Al to help."

The sound of an approaching train drowned any protest Lewis might have made. He really didn't like the idea of mugging anybody, even Davenport, even knowing what Davenport was, and he especially didn't like it in a strange city where the police were notoriously capricious in their corruption. He had a feeling Mitch was applying the first principle officers learned in the War: making a decision mattered more than what the decision actually was and whether it was right or wrong.

The train slowed and drew up to the platform with a squeal of brakes. Lewis saw Davenport get into the middle car, and he and Mitch climbed into the car behind him, shouldering their way up closer to the front of the car so they could see when he left. The train lurched into motion, moving north along the elevated tracks.

It was a long ride back toward the center of the city, and too noisy in the car to say anything, especially the things Lewis really wanted to ask. Except for one thing, he thought, and leaned closer to Mitch.

"Alma. She's all right?"

Mitch nodded. "The, um, things you made, they work. She'll have been scared—hell, I was scared—but she'll be fine otherwise."

Lewis nodded back. He'd been terrified himself, seeing that unnatural shimmer in the air, movement and purpose where his eyes told him there was nothing at all. And to see it leap for Alma—He shuddered in spite of the muggy air. The amulets worked, that was the main thing. They were safe as long as they carried them. He just wished that felt a little less like stalemate.

Davenport stayed on the train all the way north to the intersection with the Loop, and climbed off among a flurry of businessmen and clerks and stenographers. At least it made it easy to stay back in the crowd, Lewis thought, and concentrated on keeping Davenport in sight.

For a few minutes he thought the man was heading back to the hotel, but then Davenport turned south again, blending with the crowds heading for the La Salle Street station a few block away. Mitch muttered a curse, lengthening his stride to keep up, but even so, Davenport disappeared through the doors while they were still across the street. They had to wait for the traffic to clear again, stopped in the concourse to look around frantically. There was no sign of Davenport. Lewis took a breath, trying to steady himself. If Davenport wasn't visible, maybe he could be Seen the other way. He let his eyes cross, trying to find the calm, the space he'd somehow found at the airport in Los Angeles, but nothing came. There was just the noise of the train station, footsteps and voices and the shriek of metal on metal from the platforms. Mitch looked up at the schedule board.

"It's only locals now, the big east-bound trains don't leave for an hour—"

"He'd need luggage," Lewis said, with more confidence than he felt. Maybe he didn't, probably a demon wouldn't need it, and if it was running, all it needed was to find someone else to jump to—

"There," Mitch said, with sudden relief. "There he is."

Lewis lifted his head, saw the gray suit and hat moving toward the door. "He must think he shook us."

"Yeah." Mitch moved easily through the crowd, staying far enough back to keep Davenport in sight without risking being seen. It was after five o'clock, and the offices were closing; it was easier to lose themselves in the crowds. Davenport didn't seem to be as worried now. He kept walking north, not racing the traffic or hurrying to make a light, just keeping a steady pace. Maybe we've got him, Lewis thought. They might be heading back to the hotel, or at least that was vaguely in the direction they were going. He checked a street sign as they passed. No, they were north of the Great Northern now, and turning west again. A white marble building loomed ahead: another train station, Union Station, and Davenport was striding briskly through its doors.

"What the hell?" Lewis said. Mitch gave a shrug, his eyes fixed on Davenport as he approached the ticket window.

They were too far away to hear, but Mitch was studying the signs above the ticket windows. "That's for the locals," he said. "That doesn't make sense—"

Unless it wasn't Davenport, Lewis thought. All of a sudden, the hat, the suit looked different, darker; the set of his shoulders was different, the cadence of his stride. He reached into his pocket, found the mechanical pencil he always carried, and caught up with the gray-suited man.

"Excuse me, sir," he said, and the man turned, prepared to be annoyed. Not Davenport, not even much like him, only roughly of a height and heavier, older. Not Davenport at all. "I think you dropped this?"

The stranger looked at the pencil, shook his head. "Not mine, son."

"Sorry," Lewis said, and the stranger headed on toward the gate.

"What the hell do you think you're doing?" Mitch demanded.

"It's not him," Lewis said. "It's not Davenport."

"What?"

"It's not him," Lewis said again. He shook his head. "I don't know where we lost him, but we did."

"Goddammit," Mitch said. He didn't bother to lower his voice very much, and a pair of secretaries gave him a wary look. He slipped his hat off, ran his fingers through his hair, wincing again as he touched the back of his skull. "How—Lewis, can you See him?"

"I tried before," Lewis said. "And I didn't get anywhere. But I'll try again."

Mitch looked at him. "When?"

"At the other station. La Salle."

"And you didn't see him?"

"I couldn't focus on him," Lewis said. "Couldn't find him. I'll try—"

"No." Mitch looked suddenly very tired. "You won't find him because he isn't here. And hasn't been for a while. We've been chasing an illusion."

"What?"

"It, Davenport, whatever—it made us see what we were looking for," Mitch said. "See him, follow someone that looked like him—probably the first person who looked at all like him, any guy in a gray suit. And our own desire to see him did the rest. Stupid, stupid."

"The minute we questioned whether it was him, it wasn't," Lewis said, slowly. "That's what… broke the spell?"

"It's me who's the idiot," Mitch said. "I should have guessed he'd try something."

There was a grumble of thunder from outside, and Lewis glanced up to see the skylights darkening. The clouds that had been lurking all day chose that moment to open up, and he shook his head. "That's all we need. Ok, what do we do now?"

Mitch took a deep breath, shook himself hard. "Wait for this to ease off, for a start. There's no point getting ourselves drowned."

"I'm for that," Lewis said.

"Then...." Mitch touched his head again. "Back to the hotel, join up with Jerry and Al—maybe Jerry got something useful, since we sure as hell didn't. Davenport probably won't come back for his bags, but we've got the tablet. We can still track him with that."

Lewis nodded. He was suddenly aware that he hadn't eaten since noon, and he jerked his head toward the lunch counter. "Ok. In the meantime, what say I buy us dinner?"

Mitch paused, and managed a reluctant smile. "You know, that's the best idea I've heard all day."

Alma waited by the elevator while Jerry inquired for messages at the front desk of the Great Northern Hotel. She knew from his expression that there were none before he returned to her. "Nothing?" she asked anyway.

Jerry shook his head. "Unless Mitch and Lewis came back ahead of us and are already upstairs. They haven't left a note at the desk and they haven't called."

Alma let him usher her into the elevator. "I wish we knew where they were."

"So do I," Jerry said worriedly. "They could be anywhere. I don't think there's any use in hunting all over town for them." He waited until they were out of the elevator and in the room before he finished his thought. "We've got the tablet. We could dowse for them on a Chicago street map if they're still after Davenport, but chances are it's a moving target. They'd be long gone before we could get a cab and get there."

"Let's save that option," Alma said. She too was worried, but she wasn't sure that running off half cocked and charging all over town was a good plan. And of course they weren't in the room. Even the most cursory inspection revealed that no one had been in the rooms since they'd left, not even the maid. Who probably ought to have been by now, since it was mid-afternoon. Alma poured herself a cup of the now long cold coffee and went to stand by the window looking down at the street. Back to the west the light was obscured by massive thunderclouds building, a classic Midwestern storm still miles away, the clouds purple beneath, burnished with fire above.

"I'm sure they're fine," Jerry said.

"I'm not," Alma said.

"Mitch has a good head on his shoulders and Lewis isn't fragile." Jerry came and stood beside her, his hands in his pockets. When he stood up straight he topped her by four inches. "You don't have to carry us all, all of the time."

"I don't?" Alma gave him a sideways smile, sipping the cold coffee.

"No." Jerry pushed his gold framed glasses further up on his nose. "God knows we've all leaned on you too much. It's probably not been good for us. Good for me." Jerry frowned down at the street. "I couldn't stay here alone ten years ago. That's absolutely true. And when you and Gil needed me, I have no regrets about being there. None. But being back in Chicago has made me start thinking, Al."

"About getting back in the field?" She took another sip of the coffee. "You should, Jerry. You can teach. You can translate. Ok, maybe not a dig in Mesopotamia, but there are a lot of things you can do, a lot of things that the world needs you to do. That's building the Temple too."

"I know." Jerry shrugged. "But it's not that easy. I've been out of it for a long time. There aren't faculties lined up waiting to hire me."

"Still, you could put out some feelers."

"I could."

Alma leaned back on him, bumping him with her shoulder affectionately. "I'm not trying to get rid of you, Jerry."

"I know that too." He bumped her back. "But you have Lewis now."

"I do. Whatever this is." Alma grimaced. "I don't know, Jerry."

"He's not Gil."

"Of course not." Alma shook her head. "There was only one Gil."

"Thank God," Jerry said. "I'm not sure the world would have survived two."

Alma grinned, as he'd meant her to. "We should call the hangar," she said. "That's the other place Mitch and Lewis might have left a message."

Jerry waited while Alma put through the call, eventually getting Henry's shop manager on the phone, who said he'd seen nothing of Mitch and Lewis at all, though he thought the Terrier was swell. He didn't mention that his shop inexplicably reeked of Musgo Real, which Alma thought was a mercy.

"Oh, and there's a telegram for you here, Mrs. Gilchrist. Mr. Kershaw sent it from St. Louis last night." Which explained why Alma wasn't getting the usual nonsense from the shop manager once he discovered that Al Gilchrist was a woman. She was a friend of Mr. Kershaw, the big boss on the west coast, who could have a pet aviatrix if he wanted one.

Alma debated for a moment the wisdom of going down to Municipal Field and getting it or not, but Mitch and Lewis were still missing with no idea when they'd turn up. Besides, Henry was unlikely to have put anything bizarre in a telegram that would be seen by dozens of people, especially when he knew he'd have to send it to the shop since he had no idea where they would be staying. "Would you mind opening it and reading it to me?" Alma asked, feeling Jerry perk up beside her.

"In St. Louis flying southern route stop," the shop manager read. "Will be in NY tomorrow pm late stop. My man found Davenport cable stop. Bought ticket on *Ile de France* leaving Friday stop. That's all there is, ma'am."

"Thank you," Alma said, jotting it down on a piece of hotel stationery beside the telephone. "I appreciate it. Would you mind giving me a ring at the Great Northern Hotel if there's another cable or message?"

"Sure thing," the shop manager said. "Hope Mr. Kershaw's test flight is going ok."

"It's going fine," Alma said. Jerry was craning over her shoulder trying to read the note. "Thanks for everything."

She hung up and passed the message to Jerry, whose eyebrows rose. "Henry's in St. Louis?"

"He had to get back to New York for his airship launch, remember?" Alma said. "He's flying the southern route, LA to St. Louis rather than through Chicago. It looks like he laid over in St. Louis last night." She shook her head at the note. "But that's not the important thing. The important thing is that now we know where Davenport is going. He got tickets on the *Ile de France* out of New York for tomorrow." Alma let go of the note and swore. "Goddamnit. They've probably missed him. The *Commodore Vanderbilt* left Chicago for New York forty minutes ago, at three o'clock. It will get into New York tomorrow morning in plenty of time for him to make an afternoon sailing."

"Unless Lewis and Mitch tailed him to the station," Jerry said. "In which case they're probably on the *Commodore*."

"If they could get a seat at the last minute," Alma said. "It's a premium express train."

Jerry blinked. "Al, how in the hell do you always know the train schedules everywhere in the country?"

"It's our competition," Alma said. "The main reason people fly is to get somewhere faster than the train. So I need to know when the trains leave and how fast they can get you there. Otherwise how do you think I would ever sell a ticket? We can leave when you like and get you there sooner. It's the only advantage we've got. The train is safer and a lot more comfortable."

"I mean, how do you keep all those schedules in your head?"

"How do you keep Latin and Greek?"

Jerry shrugged. "Point taken. So what do we do about Lewis and Mitch?"

"If they're on the *Commodore* there's not a thing we can do about them," Alma said. "Except for us to pack up and fly to New York. It's a long flight for one pilot, but I can do it if I need to." An awfully long flight, she thought to herself. And one not well begun late in the day with no sleep the night before. A night flight by herself.... Alma walked over to the window again. The flag on the pole across the street stood out, flowing beautifully dead east.

The clouds were building, the slanting light already gone.

That was the other problem with air travel. The *Commodore Vanderbilt* would keep going through the night for anything short of massive blizzards. This thunderstorm would close Municipal Airport within the hour. And there was no way she'd take off in the Terrier with a full fuel load right into the teeth of a storm this size even if the airport didn't close. She wouldn't do it in her Jenny at home, much less with a plane she knew less well that frankly handled like a load of bricks when they had the auxiliary tank full.

"I think we're going to have to go tomorrow," Alma said. She held a hand up to forestall Jerry. "Look out the window. There's no way. But if they're on the *Commodore* with Davenport, you and I can take off in the morning and try to catch up to them."

"We won't get there before the *Ile de France* sails," Jerry said. "Even I can do that math."

"But Lewis and Mitch will," Alma said. "I'm glad Mitch has plenty of cash with him."

"I am too," Jerry said.

Chapter Fifteen

The rain had slowed by the time they finished eating, but it was still steady enough to soak through the shoulders of Lewis's jacket and drip disconsolately from the brim of his hat. The vague feeling of content that had come with the hash and fried eggs was long gone. His socks squelched in his shoes, and while he might have been this physically miserable since the War, it hadn't been more than once. Mitch looked just as damp and maybe even less happy, and the elevator operator gave them a sympathetic glance.

"Still raining? It's supposed to keep it up all night."

Mitch looked about ready to explode. Lewis mumbled something polite and placating, and then they'd reached their floor. Mitch knocked, not bothering with the key, and Alma opened the door and fell back as though they'd startled her.

"What are you doing here? I thought you were on the *Commodore Vanderbilt*."

"What?" Mitch stared, damp hat in his hands.

Lewis shrugged off his coat, feeling a damp patch still between his shoulder blades. Since the war, he hated having to stay in wet clothes, and wanted nothing more than to get changed. "Why would we do that?"

"You lost him," Jerry said.

Mitch sailed his hat onto the dresser with unnecessary force. "Yes, we lost him. We chased all over the damn city after an illusion."

"He's going to New York," Alma said. She brandished a sheet of the hotel's notepaper. "Henry sent a telegram. Davenport's got tickets on the Ile de France."

"Why?" Lewis asked. He kicked off his shoes and socks, but

the cuffs of his pants were clammy around his ankles.

"I don't know," Jerry began, and Alma interrupted.

"It's more important that we stop him first. What happened?"

"We followed him back to downtown," Mitch said baldly. "He tried to shake us in traffic, then he took the L. Then he went to the train stations, La Salle Street first, then Union Station. That's where Lewis realized something wasn't right. Somehow—and I don't know when, or how—he managed to send us off after an illusion."

"Dammit, Mitch, how could you?" Alma exclaimed.

"Because I'm stupid," Mitch snapped. "How was I to know he was going to New York?"

"It's my fault," Lewis said. The wet clothes were sticking to his skin, chill and nasty, and he shivered. "I was leading—he must have fooled me somehow, and if I hadn't suggested we eat—"

"You what?" Alma glared at him, and Lewis met her eyes squarely.

"We waited at Union Station for the rain to let up, and we had something to eat while we waited. I'm sorry, Al."

"It wouldn't have made any difference," Jerry said. "The *Commodore Vanderbilt* left at three."

"You should have been on it," Alma said unreasonably.

"And how the hell were we supposed to know that?" Mitch demanded.

"Because you've brains, no matter how hard you try to hide it, and talent to spare." Alma ran her hands through her hair. "Both of you. Damn it, he's sailing tomorrow."

"All right." Mitch glared at her. "We'll fly out—"

He was interrupted by another crash of thunder, and Alma shook her head. "Not tonight, we won't. Not in this weather."

Mitch went to the window. "It'll clear. We'll be fine."

"No, it won't," Alma said. "That's the storm front that's been behind us since California—"

"I can handle it," Mitch said.

Lewis looked from him to Alma's furious face. "Well, I can't. Not with the supplemental tank full, and maybe not even with it empty. They're going to close the airport anyway."

Jerry gave him a look that was almost grateful. "Lewis is

right," he said. "We won't get out tonight."

"Then what the hell—" Alma bit off the rest of what she'd been going to say, shook her head hard. "We can't afford to lose him. Not with what it can do."

"He has to stay Davenport a while longer," Jerry said. "If he wants to sail on the Ile de France, he has to stay Davenport."

"That's true," Mitch said.

"If we take off first thing tomorrow, with a full fuel load," Lewis began, and Alma nodded.

"Ok, it's eight hundred miles, give or take, to New York."

Mitch reached for a scrap of paper, found a pencil and scribbled for a few minutes. "We can't do it in one hop. We'll have to stop to refuel."

"Are you sure?" Alma came to look over his shoulder.

"I'm sure," Mitch said.

"But—"

"We'd be landing on fumes," Mitch said. "Trust me on this one, Al."

She nodded reluctantly. "So if we leave first thing—we might be able to go at first light, if we use Henry's name, and plan to leave before any of the commercial flights want to go. If we could leave by five, we could make it by one. We might just be in time to make the sailing."

"Or to stop him from sailing," Jerry said. "One or the other."

"We might make it by then," Mitch said, but he sounded doubtful.

"Assume the worst," Jerry said. "We miss the Ile de France. What are our options?"

"Catch another boat?" Lewis said, when no one else spoke.

"We'll be behind him all the way," Alma said, "and we'll have to dowse for him when we get there. But, yes. That's a possibility."

"Make sure he really did take the Ile de France," Mitch said, with a wincing smile.

"Point," Jerry said.

"We wire Henry," Alma said. "We tell him that Davenport gave us the slip and to look out for him. If he can do anything—well, I doubt he can, but on the off chance, at least he'll know."

"Henry's in New York?" Mitch asked.

"For the airship launch," Jerry said.

"Oh, right." Mitch touched the back of his head again.

"Maybe he can come up with an excuse to stop him," Lewis began, then shook his head. "No, sorry, that would only make it—jump—again."

Alma nodded. "And that's the one thing we really don't want. Let it think it's shaken us, and we'll catch up with it in France."

Lewis looked from one to the other. Mitch's temper had cooled, and there was a new ease, a comfort, between Alma and Jerry, as though they'd come to some understanding. "But what does it want?" he asked, and there was a little silence.

"I don't really know," Jerry said, after a moment. "I do know that, almost by definition, it can't be good."

"But—" Lewis paused. "Ok, I know this sounds bad, but hear me out. How bad can it be? This is one guy, an archeologist—a college professor. What can he do? You're talking about sailing to France and letting everything back home go hang so that we can chase him. Isn't there—I don't know, some other group who could take over, or something? Like Henry's lodge, or that Bullfinch guy you called in California?"

"I don't know anybody else," Alma said. "Not any more. It all fell apart after the War, Lewis, we just—there didn't seem to be much point, after everything we'd been through. Saving the world—most people didn't think it was possible. Gil was one of the few who thought we could keep trying."

Jerry touched her shoulder, a casual, intimate gesture that made Lewis blink. "What it wants," he said. "If I'm right, what it wants is what Caligula had, absolute power over an empire that exists to serve and sate it alone. No, it can't get that from Davenport, though it can, if it tries, feed its bloodlust. Think about Jack the Ripper. This thing could use one body to kill, and then move on, and the truly responsible creature would never be caught. It would probably enjoy making someone like Davenport do that, too—there's extra pleasure to be gained from forcing an unwilling host to commit atrocities, and Bill, whatever I may think of his scholarship, he's not that kind of man.

"And that's the least it can do. It's new to this world, it hasn't found its feet yet, but it's already deduced there's not much for it here. Who could it possess in America that would give it the kind of power Caligula had? The President? Not really. He doesn't have enough money, and there are too many checks on his power. A millionaire, a Morgan or a Vanderbilt—Henry, even—they have the money, the social standing, but not the political clout. But in Europe, or in a colony…." Jerry shook his head. "There are people who have that kind of power right now, and this creature will figure out how to reach them. We can't let that happen."

Lewis nodded slowly. He could see the pictures Jerry conjured up, and knew there were places where that kind of power still existed. It didn't matter that they'd won the War, some things never changed. People never changed.

"It's what we do," Alma said. "It's what I do. I made a promise."

"To Gil?" Lewis asked.

Alma nodded. "To Gil, and to God, and to the lodge, to the Builders of the Temple. But to myself most of all."

They took a taxi to Municipal Field in the thinning light, the sun not yet up, but the eastern sky glowing behind the last of the previous day's clouds. It had taken four telephone calls and a good deal of pleading, but Henry's manager had gone to bat for them, and the controller had grudgingly agreed to let them take off before sunrise, provided they didn't require field lights, and would pay the overtime for the fuel boy. Alma had winced and agreed, and the manager—currying favor with Henry, Mitch guessed—offered to supervise getting the plane gassed and ready. They pulled up at the hangar, and the manager sent a mechanic to help load the baggage, while Mitch made his walk-around and Alma collected the latest weather reports. She came back shrugging, handed him the sheaf of flimsies, and Lewis came to look over his shoulder.

"Not bad," he said, and Mitch shrugged.

"Could be worse." They were both whistling in the dark, and knew it: the storms that had gone through Chicago the night before were still ahead of them, not building, but not diminishing any, either. It would be a rough ride all the way, even if they didn't overtake the front. At least they'd gotten what passed for a decent night's sleep on this trip. Mitch stretched a final time, and touched the sore place on the back of his head. It was a lot better this morning, and only hurt when he actually pressed on it, but he'd seen stars when he'd hit the wall, all right. He'd been a little worried there for a moment.

Alma and the manager were talking about something—probably the flight plan, Mitch thought, but before he could join them, Alma had turned back toward the plane.

"We're fueled up and they're ready," she said. "And I think the controller wants us out of here as soon as possible."

Mitch nodded. "We're just—there he is."

Jerry was limping toward them, a paper bag in his hand. "Breakfast," he said, and hauled himself into the cabin.

"Thanks," Mitch said, and followed him aboard. He settled himself in the cockpit, and looked up in mild surprise as Lewis took the co-pilot's seat.

"Alma and Jerry are talking about what to do once we catch the thing," Lewis said, and Mitch nodded.

They ran through the last checklist, flipped the ignition and adjusted the choke until the big radials were humming nicely. The flagman was waiting for them, waved them onto the field ahead of a big Ford with Powers Air Transport stenciled on its tail. Lewis grinned.

"Nice to have pull."

"Henry's name counts for something," Mitch said.

The Terrier was sluggish with the supplemental tank, and took most of the length of the field before it rose reluctantly into the air. Mitch kept the throttles open for a long while, letting the power build, and finally leveled out just above the patchy cloud cover. He could see a heavier wall of clouds ahead, and hoped the winds would keep pushing it ahead of them. They'd be cutting it close, impossibly close, but if everything went right, they might just be able to catch the liner. He ran the numbers again in his head, calculating. Maybe, maybe if he pushed it, if everything went just right, they could make it without stopping.... If they could take the shortest route, if they decided not to worry where they crossed the Alleghenies, didn't bother staying in range of emergency fields, if they didn't hit headwinds: it was so close, just on the edge of impossible. He glanced out the window, seeing

Lake Michigan beneath the wing, blue flashing in and out of the spotty clouds. He didn't have to commit to anything until they were over Ohio, and that was a couple hours' flying. He'd see how it went, and decide then.

An hour and a half in the air, and he was pretty sure they weren't going to make it without a stop. And if they stopped, they weren't going to make the liner. The clouds had closed in, and he'd dropped down to 3000 feet to get under them, the Terrier bouncing and leaping in the unsteady air. He was pretty sure they were burning fuel faster than he'd planned, but they were running on the supplemental tank, and there was no gauge to check. He looked out the window again, looking for the grain silos outside of Fostoria. In the right-hand seat, Lewis looked up from the clipboard.

"What about Canton? I've got a listing for McKinley Field."

Mitch considered. Land at Canton, top up the wing tanks without filling the supplement tank, that would save time—no, if they were going to do that, better to press on further, burn a bit more fuel. "What's beyond that? Is there something at Altoona? Allentown?"

Lewis reached for the Rand-McNally with its listings of roads and airfields. The Terrier rocked again, and Mitch tightened his grip on the controls. The weather was getting worse as they closed on the front, the clouds dropping lower ahead of them, heavy with rain.

"Towanda Legion Airport," Lewis announced, and grabbed for the clipboard as the Terrier dropped. "Full fuel service, grass field. North and west of Scranton."

"Ok," Mitch said, and adjusted his grip on the controls.

Half an hour more, and the rain began. Mitch lifted the Terrier, looking for clear air above the clouds, but they gained a thousand feet, and they were still in broken cloud, thunderheads towering to the east. Mitch swore under his breath, then louder as he fought the controls. There was a series of thumps from the cabin, one of Jerry's books gotten loose, and a moment later Alma fought her way to the cockpit door.

"How's it looking?"

"See for yourself," Mitch answered.

"Damn it to hell." She clung to the doorframe as the Terrier lurched and fell off to the left. "It's no good, is it?"

"Cleveland," Mitch said, grimly. "I'm putting us down at Cleveland." He couldn't risk taking his eyes off the controls, but he knew she heard the regret in his voice. "I'm sorry, Al."

The air was a little easier to the north, but it took most of his strength to muscle the Terrier down onto the grass. It was raining hard still as he taxied onto the verge, and he sat for a moment in silence after he'd shut down the engines. Lewis scrambled out of the other seat, back into the cabin to let down the steps, and a moment later Mitch saw him and Alma running across the grass toward the administration building, Lewis's jacket held over their heads in lieu of an umbrella. It didn't make any difference, Mitch thought. They weren't going to make it in time—they'd have to catch another ship, figure out some other way to get to Paris, and then start the whole lousy process all over again. And in the meantime, Davenport, or the thing that rode him, it would have all the time in the world to do whatever it pleased. Jerry had talked about Jack the Ripper, the dry pedantic voice not quite able to quell the horror. Mitch had seen something like it once, behind the lines, a girl—not a nice girl, maybe, sharp and demanding, and expensive, too, but she hadn't deserved to die like that, gutted like a fish in her little second-floor apartment, the sheets and mattress so soaked in blood that they'd thought for a moment they were red satin. And the girl, so carved up he hadn't registered her as human at first, and then had thought it had been a bomb, artillery, even though it couldn't have been, the rest of the room untouched, except for the blood. They'd caught the guy—he'd been eager to confess, to explain why he had to do it—and they'd tried and hanged him, but it wasn't something Mitch could ever get out of his mind.

If he hadn't lost Davenport in Chicago—if he'd had the sense to think that it would use its powers, would try to distract them, they wouldn't be in this mess. They could be on the train, almost to New York already, with plenty of time to get tickets and get on board without him seeing them. But, no, he'd fucked it up again, and people were going to pay for it. Just like they always did.

"Mitch?" Jerry spoke from the cockpit door, balancing himself carefully. "Take a break, why don't you?"

Mitch sighed, untangling himself from the controls, and Jerry stepped back to give him room. "What now?"

"We regroup," Jerry said. "We refuel, we fly on to New York, we buy tickets on the next ship out. And who knows, maybe the *Ile de France* will have been delayed."

Mitch glared at him, unable to believe what he was hearing, and Jerry gave a shrug.

"What else can we do?"

Mitch shook his head, but he knew the other was right. "Yeah. I suppose you never know."

They were on the ground for almost two hours before they could get clearance to take off again, stuck behind the commercial flights that had been delayed by the same storms. At least the front had moved on, and weakened as it went; the air was rough, but the ceiling was higher, and they rode easily over the Alleghenies, and came down at last into Flushing Airport a little before three. There was tie-down space behind the middle hangar, and Lewis and Mitch secured the Terrier while Alma disappeared into the administration building. She came back shaking her head, squinting in the returning sunlight.

"It's gone. Sailed on time."

"Damn it," Mitch said, and dug his toe into the grass.

"I'm going to call Henry." Alma's voice wasn't quite steady, and Lewis put out a hand, then let it drop as though he'd thought better of it. "I'll let him know what happened, and then—then we'll figure out what to do."

Chapter Sixteen

Alma disappeared into the hangar, Lewis at her heels, and Mitch reached for his cigarettes, and lit one as though it would help. Jerry took one, too, squinting against the smoke. He looked for a moment as though he was going to say something, but there was nothing to say, and instead he lowered himself awkwardly onto the plane's steps.

"You Ok?" Mitch asked, and Jerry nodded.

There was still nothing to say. Mitch leaned back against the fuselage, the metal warming as the sun came out, finished his cigarette and ground it out on the wet grass. And then Alma was back, hurrying now, Lewis at her heels with an amazed grin on his face.

"I talked to Henry," Alma called. "We're going on the *Independence*."

"What?" Mitch pulled himself upright, and Jerry looked up sharply.

"He's got space for us?"

"Apparently. He was in a hurry, there must be a million things to do," Alma said. "But he said if we were at the Fort Tilden air station by seven, he'd have two cabins for us."

"We'll get there ahead of Davenport," Jerry said. He smiled slowly. "We'll maybe even have time to prepare something, some place to hold him, a good way to deal with this thing."

Lewis said, "It's on the other side of Queens, they said, Fort Tilden, about an hour by taxi. We've got plenty of time."

"Damn," Mitch said. He shook his head. "It's nice to catch a break for a change."

Lewis nodded.

"Do we know if there's a weight limit?" Jerry asked. He was

thinking of the books, Mitch guessed, and Alma shrugged.

"Henry didn't say."

"It's a luxury liner," Mitch said. "They must expect people to bring luggage."

"I can prioritize," Jerry said, struggling to his feet.

Alma ran both hands through her hair. If she was trying to tidy it, Mitch thought, she wasn't succeeding. "All right," she said. "Be at the hangar by seven. For the first flight of a luxury transatlantic airship. Oh, my God." She shook her head. "I haven't a thing to wear."

Jerry snickered. Lewis gave her a startled look, as though he'd never expected to hear such a comment cross her lips. And he probably hadn't, Mitch thought. That wasn't Alma's style at all.

"I'm serious," Alma said. She looked at her watch. "My God. There's just no time."

"You've got that blue dress," Lewis said, carefully. "It's very nice."

"It's not nice enough," Alma said. "You're lucky, you can wear your suit the whole time—"

"I've got an idea," Mitch said, before they could start another quarrel. "There was this girl I used to know...." Easy Edie, they'd called her back home, before she'd run, first to Charlestown and then to Baltimore and finally New York City, her mother trying valiantly to put a good face on it, saying she was an actress.... It was easy not to think of how he'd found her, a perfect bottle-blonde Ziegfield girl, cynical and cheerful and frankly mercenary. "She was a, um, a dancer, in the Follies. She came from my home town, and when we were demobbed, I came home through New York and I looked her up. I spent a couple of weeks squiring her and her girlfriends around town, and I remember there was a shop here in Queens—there's a good chance you might find something there."

"Really?" Alma gave him a wary glance. "I don't have a whole lot of cash left."

"That won't be a problem," he said. "Edie was always—careful."

They rode the streetcar down to the bridge, and got off among old-fashioned buildings with signs in Yiddish as well as English.

The neighborhood had the same closed, faintly exotic feeling as the streets where Lewis had grown up, where everybody had a secret language and you turned a dumb immigrant mask to the outside world. It was odd to be a stranger, to be on the outside, and he knew they were being watched as they made their way along the sidewalks. They were looking for the Misses Greenberg's, Mitch said, and he found it quickly enough. It was a street-level storefront, with an arrangement of what looked like expensive hats in the window, and a severe and lanky woman presiding over the showroom. She gave them a comprehensively disapproving glare, and Mitch put on his best smile.

"Good afternoon, Mrs. Feurzeig. I know you won't remember me, but I'm a friend of Edie Goodwin—Edie Goode, she is now."

She blinked at him from behind glasses as gold as Jerry's, but the name and the soft accent earned a grudging nod.

"Edie always said that if a person needed nice clothes on short notice, this was the place to come," Mitch went on. "My friend Mrs. Gilchrist, here, she needs an evening frock, something suitable for ocean travel. For tonight."

"Tonight?" Mrs. Feurzeig looked dismayed.

"We're leaving on the *Independence*—the new airship—tonight at seven," Alma said. "I didn't bring anything appropriate."

Mrs. Feurzeig gave them a reproachful look—she was clearly used to improvident men—and stepped back behind the counter. "Miss Greenberg!"

Miss Greenberg was as round as Mrs. Feurzeig was skinny, a sweet-faced, graying woman in an old-fashioned high-necked blouse. Mrs. Feurzeig explained the situation, and they both turned to study Alma.

"Stand up straight, dear," Miss Greenberg said, not unkindly, and Mrs. Feurzeig tipped her head to one side.

"She's very tall."

"I like her that way," Lewis said, in spite of himself, and surprised an elfin grin from Mrs. Feurzeig.

"Yes, but hems still aren't that short, Mr.—Gilchrist, is it?"

"Segura," Lewis said, and hoped he wouldn't blush.

Neither woman seemed taken aback, but then, if they made

clothes for Ziegfield Girls, they'd probably seen everything. Lewis relaxed, and saw Alma's frown ease.

"Right," Mitch said. "We need some things, too. Jerry, why don't you and I take care of that?"

"Yes," Jerry said, shaking himself out of what looked like fascinated contemplation. "Let's do that."

The bell above the door jangled as they left, and Lewis turned his attention back to the women.

"Shoes," Mrs. Feurzeig said, and Miss Greenberg shook her head.

"I doubt we have anything that would fit. Pity."

"What do you have with you?" Mrs. Feurzeig asked, and Alma blinked.

"Black pumps."

Mrs. Feurzeig gave a martyred sigh, but Miss Greenberg said cheerfully, "Better than brown, anyway."

"The eau de nile?" Mrs. Feurzeig began, and Miss Greenberg shook her head.

"No green, not with her skin."

"But not blue—"

"Not baby blue," Miss Greenberg corrected. "But midnight—"

"Ink," Mrs. Feurzeig said. She gave her partner a look of triumph. "The slip with the silver starburst."

"Yes." Miss Greenberg nodded decisively, and Mrs. Feurzeig disappeared into the back of the shop.

"Starburst?" Alma said, looking over her shoulder. "God, I hope Mitch was right. I really don't have that much cash left."

"I have some, too," Lewis said, and hoped it would be enough. He'd never been in this position before, Alma's acknowledged lover, and it felt strange. Strange, but good, and he dared to pat her shoulder.

Mrs. Feurzeig returned with an armful of royal blue fabric which she shook like a conjuror's handkerchief so that it became a narrow slip with a darker band around the hips. In the center of the band was a beaded and sequined shape like an exploding firework, and more beads scattered across the skirt.

"Oh," Alma said. Lewis glanced at her, startled, and surprised a look almost of longing on her face.

"Ah," Miss Greenberg said, tipping her head from side to side. "All right, dear, let's try it on."

The two women herded Alma into the back, and Lewis settled into the armchair that was obviously reserved for husbands and protectors. He remembered other men talking about the tedium of waiting while their wives tried on dresses, or laughed at the folly of women's fashions, but he thought he wouldn't mind. Not when Alma had that look on her face, like she was getting an unexpected treat. And in that dress, her slim legs naked except for stockings …. He set his hat carefully in his lap, and tried to think of something else. Mitch was busy buying socks and underwear. He just hoped they'd think to buy him a spare undershirt, too.

Alma appeared more quickly than he would have expected, and Lewis gave a soft whistle. There weren't a lot of reasons to dress up in Colorado Springs, and he and Alma had never bothered to make occasions. He'd seen her in nice dresses at Easter and at Thanksgiving, a well-cut tweed suit for business, but never anything like this. The royal blue—exactly the color of Schaeffer Ink—flattered her tanned skin and golden hair, and the narrow cut made the most of her height and curves. The starburst caught the light, heavy silver sparkling at the center of her hips. On some women, probably most of the ones who shopped here, it would have been blatant advertisement; on Alma, it was … challenge? And one he'd be glad to meet. Victoria would never have worn such a thing, but on Alma it looked entirely right. The neck scooped low, revealing a hint of lace.

"Wow," he said, and Alma grinned, twirled, the skirt flaring.

"It's beautiful, isn't it? But—"

"Beads," Miss Greenberg said, and Mrs. Feurzeig produced a tray. Alma reached for a strand of silver, but the other women shook their heads as one.

"Not with your skin, dear," Miss Greenberg said.

Mrs. Feurzeig poked unhappily through the tray. "You really ought to take more care, you know. You can't get away with neglecting yourself forever."

"I'm a flyer," Alma protested.

"You're much too tall," Mrs. Feurzeig said, but Miss Greenberg laughed.

"An aviatrix, dear, not a circus flyer. Aren't you?"

"Yes, exactly," Alma said.

Mrs. Feurzeig unearthed a string of ivory pearls that were interspersed with rhinestone-studded spheres. "Maybe these?"

Miss Greenberg nodded thoughtfully, and Alma turned again in front of the mirror.

"You look beautiful," Lewis said. He wondered if she had dressed up for Gil. Alma turned full circle, the skirt swirling, and he saw a shadow cross her face, and guessed she was thinking of Gil, too.

Mrs. Feurzeig saw the same shift of expression. "Now, understand, it's not silk, but you treat it like silk, it'll go on looking like it. The appliqué is all hand-done, but there's no need for alterations. Forty dollars, and we'll throw in the beads."

"Forty dollars," Alma began, and Lewis stood up.

"We'll take it," he said. Alma looked at him, and he gave her his best smile. "You could always bill Henry for it."

"As what?" She was trying to sound indignant, and failed.

"Travel expenses?"

She snorted. "I don't think he'd buy it."

"Ok, take it out of my pay." Lewis grinned, and Alma leaned close.

"I'll take it out of something," she said softly, and disappeared into the back to change into slacks and blouse again.

Mrs. Feurzeig was smirking, and Lewis felt his face heat. She said nothing, however, just wrapped dress and necklace in tissue and brown papers. Alma reappeared, her ordinary self again, and took a deep breath as she opened her purse.

"It's worth it," Lewis said, and she smiled again.

"I hope so."

They made it back to Flushing Airport in time to re-pack the suitcases, cramming in their new purchases, while Alma changed back into her old blue day dress. It was starting to look a little tired, Lewis thought, and was glad she'd had the chance to pick up something nice. Jerry sorted his books, picking a few he could leave behind—or, he said brightly, transfer to their suitcases. They wouldn't be over the weight limit. Lewis gritted his teeth and took a couple of volumes, and the others did the same.

There was a surprising amount of traffic on the roads that led to the Rockaways, and on the last bridge it came to a near standstill. Searchlights swept the air in the distance, pale fingers of light against the purpling sky, and more lights hazed the air above the tree line. And then at last they turned into the Naval Air Station, and Mitch leaned out to give their names to the young sailor on duty at the gate. He consulted a harried-looking civilian, who consulted a clipboard, and waved them through. The Navy airship hangar loomed ahead, enormous and somehow flimsy, its walls crisscrossed with braces. More lights picked out "Fort Tilden" painted along the side, and a pale semi-circle of silver-gray poked out from behind it like a tarnished moon. It was almost unimaginably huge, Lewis thought. He'd hunted balloons, of course, a change of pace from aerial recon and then from escort duty, but those had been much smaller, pale and flabby, nothing like this streamlined monster.

They made their way toward a second makeshift barrier, where MPs and civilian cops held back a crowd of sightseers. There were reporters, too, photographers jostling for the best shots, and men with notebooks collecting man-on-the-street impressions. A couple of newsreel cameras had been set up, huge boxy things on tripods that looked too small for their weight, and a man with his cap on backwards was peering through the viewfinder of one as he turned its crank.

"Mrs. Gilchrist?"

Lewis turned with her to see a homely young man in a well-cut suit hurrying toward them. "I'm Joe Palmer," he said. "Mr. Kershaw's assistant for the flight. He wanted me to meet you, be sure you got aboard all right."

"That's very kind of him," Alma said, offering her hand, and one of the reporters called, "Hey, Joe! Who's the dame?"

Palmer gave Alma an apologetic glance. "Would you mind giving them a brief interview, Mrs. Gilchrist? It's better if we can keep them happy."

Keep them fed, Lewis thought, not liking the idea. But it was Alma's call. She lifted her eyebrows, and he could almost see the thoughts chasing themselves across her face. In the long run, there was nothing bad about getting Gilchrist Aviation into the papers in conjunction with Henry Kershaw. "All right," she said. "But, truly, brief—"

Palmer was already turning away, a practiced smile on his face. "This is Mrs. Alma Gilchrist, of Gilchrist Aviation, a colleague and a guest of Mr. Kershaw's. Mrs. Gilchrist, this is Stu Mather, of the *Daily Mirror*."

Alma's eyelids flickered as she registered the tabloid's name—even people from Colorado knew the *Mirror*'s reputation for racy reporting—but she smiled gamely.

"Friend of Mr. Kershaw's?" Mather said, and she gave him a blank look.

"My late husband and I did a good deal of work for Mr. Kershaw." She included Lewis and the others with a wave of her hand. "These gentlemen are some of our test pilots."

"No offense, Mrs. Gilchrist," Mather said, "but Kershaw's got a woman running tests for him?"

"I have some of the finest pilots in the West working for me," Alma said, and there was iron in her voice. "Lewis Segura, here, won the DSC in France. Mitchell Sorley is a decorated ace, with seven confirmed kills. We're a small company, but Mr. Kershaw recognizes quality."

"So what exactly are you doing for Kershaw?" Mather asked.

"I'm sorry," Alma said. "I really can't go into detail. I'm sure you understand."

"And the last gentleman?" another reporter called, notebook ready.

Alma paused, gave a sudden, wholly mischievous smile. "I'm sorry," she said again. "I really can't discuss Professor Ballard's presence."

That was one in Kershaw's eye, Lewis thought, and hid a grin. Flashbulbs popped, and Alma turned to Palmer, poised as a movie star. He took her arm, shaking his head at the reporters.

"That's all, boys, let the lady get on board."

Once inside the barriers, stewards in white jackets hurried to take their luggage. Palmer had cabin tags for them, and once the bags had been weighed—Jerry's was three pounds under the limit, Lewis noted—the stewards whisked them away. Here under the airship's shadow, Lewis had to crane his neck to see it clearly, the silver-gray skin curving gracefully up into the sky. It was topped up and ready, he guessed; the mooring lines were taut, sailors from the station keeping a watchful eye on them, and there was another cluster of men at the top of the mooring mast, where the *Independence*'s round nose just met the tower. A hatch was open in the hull there, a crewman leaning out, arms folded on the edge of the opening: but of course the gas was held in internal cells, Lewis thought, not in the rigid hull.

He looked back along the ship's enormous length, and picked out the engine nacelles jutting from the hull. They were silent still, the huge propellers unmoving. Each blade was as tall as a man, and elegantly curved. The gondola seemed very small to hold cabins and lounge and dining room, never mind the cockpit—bridge, he supposed it would be, on something like this, like on a ship. But then he saw the double row of windows let into the lower curve of the hull, and realized that at least some of that space had been moved into the frame. That meant that the gas cells would be above that; he wondered how many there were, how much gas it took to lift a ship like this.

If you came in on it over the top—you'd have to take it in a dive, the gunners would be in the engine nacelles and in the gondola, maybe in the nose, but there'd be a window of vulnerability directly at the top of the frame where none of the guns would reach. Get up in the sun, dive as hard and steep as you can—and load with incendiaries, that was key—you'd only get one good shot, but it would probably be enough, one phosphorus bullet into the hydrogen cells should send it up like a Roman candle. The trick would be getting away afterward: side slipping was safer, but gave the gunners a chance; pull up too fast, and you'd tear your wings off. But the ship would burn. He could almost see it, tail pitching up, flames running eagerly up the tipping frame, fragments of canopy and burning bodies falling like tears of fire—

"You look like you're figuring out how to light her up," Mitch said, in his ear, and Lewis shook his head.

"I'm glad I never came up against one of these." He could picture the machine gunners tucked in under the engine nacelles, hanging out the end of the gondola, and shook himself hard.

"Me too," Mitch said.

A cluster of radio microphones had been set up by the rolling stairs that led up into the rear of the gondola, and Jerry paused for a moment, eyeing them. "I suppose it would be too much to expect Henry not to give a speech."

"Yes," Alma said. "It would."

"This way," Palmer said. He consulted another crewman waiting at the base of the steps. "You're the last to board, except for Mr. Kershaw."

"Then we'd best get moving," Alma said. "Thanks for your help."

"Oh, you'll be seeing more of me," Palmer said cheerfully. "I'm coming along for the ride, and Mr. Kershaw said I was to be sure you didn't lack for anything."

"That's very nice," Alma said, and started up the stairs.

Lewis followed, checked as they both realized that the *Independence* was moving. It wasn't much, not more than a ship at the dock, but it was enough to shift the airship's fold-down stairway back and forth along the platform. A crewman leaned out, ready to help, but Alma judged her moment, and stepped across without a wobble. Lewis followed, and heard Jerry swear. He glanced back, and saw the crewman hauling him aboard.

They found themselves in a glass-walled space at the very tail of the gondola, only a polished brass railing running at waist height and a few equally polished struts impeding the view. At the moment, the view was mostly of dirt and sailors, ready to manhandle the airship away from the tower, but at altitude, Lewis thought, it would be spectacular.

"Observation car, sir," the crewman said, helpfully. "The stairs to the promenade are forward."

"Thanks," Lewis said, and followed the others.

The stairs were real stairs, not a glorified ladder, and Jerry pulled himself up without hesitation. Lewis allowed himself a sigh of relief, and looked around. The windows he'd seen from the outside ran along the wall here, offering a slanting view of the ground and a few sailors clutching ropes, while toward the center of the hull was a low wall upholstered in dark gold brocade.

Behind it was a low platform set out with tables and chairs—all made of aluminum, Lewis saw—and already a dozen people had gathered there. An officer with a clipboard hurried toward them.

"Mrs. Gilchrist and party?"

"Yes," Alma said.

"Welcome aboard." He was a young man, but there were streaks of gray in his hair: another veteran, Lewis guessed. "I have your cabin numbers here, but we'll be taking off directly, and you may want to watch? Hors d'oeuvres will be served, and there will be a champagne toast once we reach the three-mile limit."

"Good for Henry," Mitch said, and the officer grinned.

"We have a full cellar on board as well, sir."

"That," Jerry said, "is the best news I've heard today."

"Second-best," Mitch said, with a meaningful glance around the promenade, and Jerry sighed.

"All right, second-best. But it's very close indeed."

"Let's find a table," Alma said.

They took the last open table beside the low wall, and tugged the chairs around so that they could all see out the windows. It was odd, Lewis thought, to be able to shift furniture—strange that it wasn't fastened down, strange that it wouldn't affect the trim. But the *Independence* was simply too large for that to matter.

Jerry rested his cane against the wall, and stretched his leg cautiously. "I read somewhere that every passenger on board here could run to the same side of the lounge to see some passing sight, and the pilots wouldn't even notice."

"I wouldn't have thought it," Lewis said, looking around. "But now—" He stopped, looked quickly away from the tall redhead in the white lawn slip-dress. Not only was the fabric sheer enough that he suspected she was wearing next to nothing under it, but he thought he recognized her. "Isn't that Celena Moore? The singer?"

Mitch glanced over his shoulder, eyebrows rising appreciatively. "Not to mention Miss Mary Holliday, the Sparkling Starlet."

"You've been reading Winchell," Jerry said, and ostentatiously refused to look.

"I read a while ago that Henry'd been seen with Mary Holliday,"

Alma began, and broke off as a waiter appeared with a tray of hors d'oeuvres. Instead of serving them, he set it on the table with a bow, and Lewis realized each of the tables had been served a similar dish.

"There's coffee and soft drinks," the waiter murmured deferentially, "and if the gentlemen would like something stronger—"

"Yes, and so would the lady," Alma said, with a smile.

"Very good, ma'am." The waiter backed away.

"Ah," Jerry said, leaning forward. "Henry's making his speech."

Lewis craned his neck to look, and saw Henry and another man, obviously a reporter, talking cheerfully behind the microphones. Flashbulbs popped all around them, and then Henry lifted his hand in something between a wave and regal acknowledgement, and disappeared from view.

"We should be taking off soon," Lewis said.

Even as he spoke, he felt the floor tremble faintly: the engines had come on, though he could hardly believe the giant machines made so little difference. Across the table, Alma met his eyes, and he stood up, holding out his hand.

"Come on. Let's watch from the promenade."

She nodded, and they hurried down the short flight of steps. At the very bottom of the row of windows, they could just see the heads of a few sailors, doing something out of sight—backing them off the mooring tower, Lewis guessed. The *Independence* was definitely moving now, moving backwards like a car in reverse, the ground slipping slowly past.

"Excuse me, ma'am," the waiter said, arriving with a tray. "Sir."

Lewis took the drinks, cocktails in china cups, and as he handed one to Alma he realized that the airship was moving forward now. "Look," he said, and the ground began to drop away from them, slowly at first, and then more quickly, picking up speed as the airship rose.

"We're in the air," Alma said, and shook her head. "We've taken off."

Lewis looked down at his drink, the liquid steady in the cup, the deck solid underfoot. It didn't seem real, didn't seem possible, and as he looked up again he saw the same disbelief in Alma's eyes. There was beach beneath them now, the bright flicker of surf, and then dark water, *Independence* rushing east into night. Further up the promenade, an older couple turned away from the windows with a sigh and a smile, and in the golden light of the lounge the Sparkling Starlet gave an effervescent laugh.

"This isn't flying," Lewis said. "Well, I mean—you know what I mean. It doesn't seem real."

Alma nodded. "It docs feel like a flying carpet, doesn't it? Like magic. But it is real, and it's getting us to France three days ahead of Davenport."

Lewis grinned, and lifted his cup to hers. "To magic."

"To magic," Alma echoed, and for a second there was a shadow on her face. "We'll need it."

Chapter Seventeen

The dining room of the airship was a mixture of Spanish Colonial and science fiction, sort of Mission meets Mars. It was absolutely hideous.

"Nice job, Henry," Mitch muttered, looking around.

"Oh my God," Jerry said.

Lewis blinked.

The combination of cowhide and aluminum was baffling. "The tickets were four hundred dollars apiece. It's lovely," Alma said in a low voice, pointedly waiting for Mitch to pull out her chair for her. "Henry's comped us, and we appreciate it so very much."

"Right." Lewis pulled out her chair instead. His one suit needed pressing and looked distinctly out of place in the elegant dining room. But no one was looking at him. Alma had the distinct impression she was drawing eyes in a way she usually didn't. It was the dress, she thought, ink blue and dancing with fireworks. Even Mitch was looking at her admiringly, and that was unusual.

Jerry settled into his own chair and unfolded his napkin. "It's hideous and you know it. I don't understand how good style can elude…."

"Jerry," Mitch said. "Can it."

To Alma's surprise, Jerry did. He looked up almost cheerfully. "Ok then. How about some wine?" He glanced at Lewis. "International waters. They can break out the bottles."

"Sounds good to me," Mitch said.

The wine was good and the food what one would expect on a train, which was all the more remarkable for being prepared in the air. Though they weren't seated in one of the prime locations beside the slanting windows, they could see the stars outside.

The sense of motion was much smoother than in an airplane, but it still felt very strange to Alma – not being in the air, but being in the air while sitting at a table eating a late dinner with so much space around her. It was a little surreal, but by the end of dinner she thought she might be getting used to it.

"We may as well relax," Mitch said, pouring himself another glass of wine. "Davenport's on the Ile de France, and there's nothing we can do until we get into Paris. So we might as well enjoy the flight."

"There's a lot we can do," Jerry said. "We have to figure out what we're going to do once we catch him. That's the big thing. Isn't it, Al?"

"Humm? Yes," Alma answered half attentively. She was still glancing around the room. The nicest tables by the observation windows were the big spenders, and the reporters were the ones by the kitchen doors. She didn't see Henry anywhere, which seemed odd, but perhaps he was staying in the cockpit for this first part of the flight of his new airship. She would be.

"Do we have to do that now?" Mitch asked. "Jerry, we're all dog tired. We'd do better off getting a good night's sleep and tackling it in the morning. We've got all day tomorrow and all tomorrow night to figure it out. Let's get some rest tonight."

"We could go over...." Jerry began.

"No," Alma said firmly. "We can't. Lewis and I are going to bed. Good night." She stood up and took Lewis' arm as he scrambled politely to his feet.

Their cabin was tiny, more like the cabin in a Pullman car rather than the cabin of an ocean liner, with upper and lower bunks and a small built in dressing table that you could sit at if you perched on the lower berth. Lewis took off his jacket and hung it neatly while Alma surveyed the room.

"We could close the upper bunk up," she said. "And just share the lower. If you don't mind being close." There was something about the way the stars moved outside the tiny window, warm with friendship and a good bottle of wine. She sat down to unfasten her stockings. "I don't travel like this," Alma said, rolling the left stocking down carefully so as not to snag the silk. "I'm not used to luxury. Would it be terrible for us to enjoy it a little? There's something romantic about this. About sleeping in the air with neither of us having to worry."

Lewis nodded, unfastening his tie and taking off his shirt. He hung it neatly with his coat in the tiny wardrobe, probably to wear again before washing, given the limited choices they had with them. He frowned. "Don't you think you were a little hard on Jerry back there?"

"Jerry wants to sit up half the night chewing over every classical reference he can think of," Alma said. "Which we can do in the morning." She rolled the right stocking off and shook it out, then stood up to unhook her garter belt.

Lewis was still frowning. "I mean making it so obvious that you were going to bed with me," he said. "I mean, given his feelings.... It just seems like rubbing his nose in it."

"I share a bed with you all the time," Alma said confusedly. "Jerry knows that perfectly well."

"I know he knows," Lewis said, standing there in undershirt and trousers, his brows knit. "And he's a good sport. He's a nice guy, Alma. But you can't expect him not to be hurt considering."

Alma blinked. "Considering what?"

"Considering how he feels about you." Lewis swallowed. "I know you don't feel the same, and I'm not saying you should. I'm glad you don't. But it's still got to be hard on him."

Alma blinked again. Lewis ran one hand through his hair, mussing the pomade, and suddenly what he was saying made sense, in a completely confused way. "Oh Lewis," she said, standing up and putting her arms around him. "You're so kind. But there isn't anything to worry about. Really. Jerry and I are friends. I promise you he's not in love with me."

Lewis met her eyes, but the worry didn't leave his. "I don't know how you can say that," he said. "The way he is about you.... Al, there's something there. You can't deny that."

Alma took a deep breath. She'd hoped it wouldn't come to this, though she supposed that was a forlorn hope. It would eventually. Gently, she put her hand against his stubbled cheek. "Lewis, Jerry has never been in love with me. Jerry was Gil's lover."

Lewis looked utterly thunderstruck. "What?"

"Jerry and Gil were lovers for a long time. Jerry's very protective of me. He doesn't want me to get hurt. But he's not in love with me and never has been."

"But you.... But Gil...." Lewis seemed to be searching for words.

"It wasn't a sham marriage if that's what you're thinking," she said. His cheek was warm beneath her hand. "I loved Gil passionately and he loved me. But he also loved Jerry."

"And you approved of this?"

Alma met his eyes. "Jerry and Gil were together long before I met Gil. Jerry approved of me."

Lewis shook his head like a fighter who'd taken one too many punch. "I can't believe that you...."

"Jerry thought I was good for Gil. And I was." Alma swallowed. She would not let herself choke up, not like someone too weak to talk about it. "Jerry had a career that was going to take him all over the world, working at one dig and another, getting home a few months out of the year. And Gil and I.... We wanted to build something together. I'd spent my whole life running from one post to another. I wanted to go home. And Gil wanted a home. We wanted children. That never happened, but...." Alma swallowed again. "But it might have. And then there was Jerry's leg and Gil got sick and...." Her voice cracked, so she stopped.

Lewis was looking at her, a curiously blank expression on his face. "Why would you do something like that?"

"Why would I choose freedom and flying and going home to Colorado and to share my life with two wonderful, fascinating men? Why wouldn't I?" She willed him to understand, searched for words. "I wish I could show it to you the way it was to me. I wish I could make you see. I know it's strange, but you know I'm an odd duck. I've never wanted an ordinary life."

Lewis swallowed, his eyes searching her face like he was looking for the right words too. "But Gil.... Everybody says that he was a great pilot. That he was so good. And Jerry. He's brave and...."

"And you like him and can't imagine that he could be a brave man and a good officer and queer?" Alma's voice was a little harsher than she meant it to be.

"Jerry's not effeminate. I mean, even with the books and the Latin...."

"Nor was Gil," Alma said tartly. "I promise you he was perfectly capable. I certainly never had any cause for complaint."

Lewis swallowed again. "And you were ok with this? With Gil and Jerry?"

Alma took a deep breath, finding a smile. "I was very happy. Truly I was. When Jerry lost his leg, Gil and I took care of him, and when Gil was sick, it was me and Jerry. It was harder on him than me, I think. I could mourn and everyone respected that. Jerry had to act like he was just a good friend. And I have the planes and the company and Jerry doesn't have any of the things he wanted, not even Gil. It's not anyone's fault of course – his leg, the war. But it's been hard on him. And hard on him to see me with you when he's alone."

Lewis took a step back, as though he would step out of her arms, but the edge of the berth was at his back. "It's a lot to think about, Al."

"I know." She looked away, blinking at the irony. "When Gil told me about Jerry long before we were married he expected me to drop him like a stone. But I told him I had to think about it. That I didn't have enough data to make a decision." Gil had been taken aback by that, steeled for the blow, not expecting quirky curiosity, a bevy of questions about exactly what he and Jerry did. A key turned. Something suddenly made sense. "I don't suppose I understood it then. What he was trying to tell me about different kinds of love. You and Gil are so very different, such different men, and yet...." She was skating perilously close to words she had not said. "I would never want you to be just like Gil. You're you, and he was himself. There are so many different shades of love, Lewis. If he were alive, I don't know how I would choose." If Gil were alive and she'd met Lewis.... Alma shook her head. Gil would have to suck it up. She'd told him in the beginning that she believed in Free Love. And he'd not have a leg to stand on, not with Jerry for eleven years. He'd abide by her choice. More than anything else, they'd always been fair to one another.

But it was Lewis who mattered now, Lewis who stood looking

at her like he'd never seen her before. "I don't understand," he said.

"I know." Gil had given her time to think, time to ask all the questions. It had never occurred to her then how that must hurt.

"Alma, you're...." Lewis broke off, inarticulate in the face of it. "You mean a lot to me. This is just.... I like Jerry." He said the last almost helplessly, as though it flew in the face of all.

"Jerry is like a brother to me," Alma said. "Whatever you think or whatever you decide, don't take it out on him. It was my decision to marry Gil knowing exactly what the score was. Nobody has done anything to me."

Lewis nodded slowly, his eyes troubled. "Ok, Al."

She lifted her hand to his cheek again. Gil had done just that. Ok, Al, he'd said. Take all the time you need. Think about it all you want to. I'll be here.

"I'll be here," Alma said. "Take all the time you need."

Alma turned over in the narrow bunk, looking for a warmth that wasn't there before she remembered. The *Independence*'s engines droned steadily, a gentle vibration through everything, and she lay for a moment listening to it, staring at the bunk above her. There probably would never have been a good time to have that conversation, but last night, when she had been floating on wine and luxury and good-fellowship—it seemed especially cruel.

She rolled over, not quietly, but there was no sound from the upper bunk. And, to be fair, she'd promised to give him all the time he needed, just as Gil had done for her. He deserved that, deserved the time to think things through. She slipped from under the covers, dressed quickly, slacks and her one pretty blouse, and closed the cabin door softly behind her.

Breakfast was already being served in the lounge, though her watch proclaimed that it wasn't quite six in the morning. A smiling steward offered her a window table, but she shook her head, and said she needed to stretch her legs. What she needed was privacy, a little space to herself to think things through, but that wasn't going to happen here. She walked the length of the promenade, then up the central corridor, past the most expensive cabins to the locked door that led to the control cabin, and back again. The crew was up already, stewards at work in the passenger area, flight crew in their padded coveralls taking a shortcut at the change of the watch. She was in the way, at loose ends, and she found herself back in the lounge, taking the offered table. The steward brought her a pot of coffee, fine china badged with Republic's crest and *Independence*'s crossed flags, waited while she chose poached eggs on toast, and slipped silently away again.

Outside the slanting window, she could see the sea, the sun glittering from the dark surface. They were high enough that she couldn't really make out individual waves, just the occasional flash of white that was a higher swell, and the airship's ride was so smooth that she couldn't tell if those breaking crests were driven by wind or just by random chance. She'd never flown over open ocean herself, of course, so she had no comparison to work with.

She sipped her coffee and wished Lewis were there. Maybe if she hadn't told him, if she'd made something up to explain why she knew Jerry wasn't in love with her—Jerry wouldn't have contradicted her, and he probably would even have understood. But she couldn't do that to him, any more than she could do it to herself. She had loved Gil, passionately and completely; he had loved her, and Jerry, too.

She closed her eyes for an instant, remembering a dinner, the three of them for once on leave at the same time, hers beginning and Jerry's ending. They had lingered over coffee and grappa that tasted like well-aged kerosene, and though she'd known she should excuse herself, let Jerry have his last night, she couldn't quite bring herself to do it. She and Gil had only just come to an understanding; she wanted every minute she could steal. Jerry gave her a grin, rueful and unrepentant—no, he wasn't leaving, either—and Gil threw back his head and laughed.

"You know, there is another option."

Alma blinked, and then blushed, and when she could look up again, Jerry's face was just as pink. He managed another smile anyway, and shrugged one shoulder. "I'm game if you are, Al."

"Right, then," Gil said, and beckoned to the waiter.

They found their way back to Gil's lodging, a narrow room above a shop, almost filled by an ancient four-poster bed. Alma blushed again, and Jerry looked at Gil, his expression not quite a challenge.

"Ok, now what?"

"I think you two should kiss," Gil answered, and Jerry looked at her.

"Ok, Al?"

If she said no, it would never be mentioned again; she could walk away and neither of them would blame her. But she would always regret what might have been. She took a step closer, turned her face up to his. "Yes," she said.

They traded kisses for a while, her and Gil, her and Jerry again, and then Gil and Jerry, exciting in ways she'd never imagined. And then they'd found their way into the featherbed that nearly smothered them until Jerry kicked it onto the floor. She ended up on her knees between them, Jerry's big hands cupping her breasts, pulling her hard against his chest, while Gil worked her with his fingers, bringing her to a shaking climax. Afterward, she lay watching while Gil took Jerry, too fascinated and aroused to think of jealousy, finally fell asleep on Gil's shoulder while Jerry sprawled on his other side, and woke before dawn to find Jerry already dressed, peaked cap in hand. He'd kissed Gil, who barely stirred, then came hesitantly around the end of the bed to kiss her as well.

It had never happened often, maybe twice or three times more, but it had been a delicious secret, a hint of spice among the three of them. She did not, would not, regret a moment. If it cost her Lewis—surely it would not. He had accepted her as she was, pilot, the company owner, and now the lodge. Surely, surely, he could come to accept this, too.

The steward appeared with her breakfast, offered another pot of coffee, and she smiled and nodded, her mind still worrying at the problem. There was no need to tell him more than she already had, not now, not ever—she curbed her thoughts with an effort. She had promised to give him time, and she would give him time, treat him carefully, as normally as she could. There was more than enough to keep them busy until they got to Paris.

It was with a sense of immense satisfaction and subtle well-being that Jerry settled himself in the airship's lounge. True, he couldn't enjoy his coffee and his cigarette at the same time, due to all smoking aboard the *Independence* being relegated to the interior smoking lounge, so he'd had his cigarette first and was now settling in for coffee. There were very few people in the lounge, though the sun was high, streaking in through the right side windows.

Jerry glanced at his watch. Only seven am in New York. He hadn't reset it yet. But they were somewhere mid Atlantic, and the sun had climbed much higher here. Ten o'clock? The airship's crew would know, crossing six time zones from New York to Paris. Forty hours on the crossing – it was incredible, actually. Months and months on tiny, crowded disease ridden sailing ships reduced to this, cruising along in the clouds across thousands of miles.

A fragment of poetry came back to him, something a friend had given him once, before war and all of that, disjointed bits that almost made a verse. It had caught him at the time, a student of archaeology; because the poet addressed the future archaeologist who might someday parse his words. *I care not if you bridge the seas, or ride secure in the cruel sky…but have you wine and music still, and statues and bright-eyed love?*

Not a thousand years to conquer the sky. Twenty years, perhaps, since the words were penned.

"Music," Jerry said, "And bright-eyed love." He flipped open the late edition of yesterday's *New York Times* left folded neatly on the side tables for the lounge's patrons. Reviews of the gallery openings of inexplicable painters. A rather good review of a show he'd never heard of. Jerry had little patience for theater. Gil had always laughed and said that if it happened less than a thousand years ago Jerry wasn't interested. Two thousand, Jerry had replied. Plautus had nothing on Euripides.

Gallery showings…. Was there nothing except paintings by experimental moderns? Jerry flipped the page.

Noted Archaeologist Found Dead. Dr. William C. Davenport, an internationally recognized authority on Roman antiquities and member of the faculty of the University of California at Los Angeles, was found dead this morning in his hotel room.

Jerry blinked, then read the article twice over with a mounting sense of panic.

Dr. Davenport's body was found just short of noon by the chambermaid, who notified authorities. The cause of death was undetermined at press time, but appeared to be natural causes. Dr. Davenport was en route to his dig in Italy, where he is engaged in the excavation of the Nemi ships at Aricia, a find described by Dr. Davenport himself as "quite extraordinary." Dr. Davenport had arrived the previous evening by air, and was scheduled to sail for Europe today. "His death is a tragedy for the profession," said Dr. E. M. Compton of Columbia University. "He was one of the brightest lights in the field of Classical Archaeology."

Jerry got to his feet, the paper clenched in his hand. He hurried down the narrow interior corridor of the airship to his own room.

Mitch was combing his hair in front of the tiny dresser mirror, the comb carefully dampened.

"Davenport's dead," Jerry said.

Mitch looked around, frowning. "What do you mean, Davenport's dead?"

"I mean he's dead," Jerry said, waving the late edition of the *Times* at him. "He was found dead yesterday before the *Ile de France* sailed."

"Dead?" Mitch said again.

"Dead! It's not like you to be this stupid! Dead!" Jerry expostulated. "Davenport is dead. Yesterday morning. While we were trying to figure out how to catch the Ile de France, he was already laid out by the coroner."

"Crap," Mitch said succinctly. "The damn thing's jumped."

Jerry nodded. "And we have absolutely no idea where or to whom."

Mitch ran his hand through his hair, ruining his careful combing job. "In New York twenty four hours ago. He could have jumped to anybody. To the maid. To somebody else staying in the hotel. To...." He shook his head. "Anybody. It could have jumped to anybody going anywhere in the world."

"Meanwhile, we're on an airship bound for Paris," Jerry said. "And even if Henry will blow another thousand dollars letting us bum a ride back on the return trip, it will have five or six days' lead on us in New York. It could literally be anywhere in the world."

"Alma's going to pitch a hissy," Mitch said.

"Alma's going to have to live with it," Jerry said. "And she's going to have to live with the fact that we're not any good without Gil. We're not even really a lodge anymore." Jerry pulled up, swallowing. No, he would go on. It was time to say the thing he'd been thinking, that they'd all been thinking whether they admitted it or not. "Maybe it's time to pull the plug on the Aedificatorii Templi."

Mitch looked away, as though there were some answer in the unmade upper bunk or the wardrobe door. "We have oaths, Jerry. We can't walk away from those."

"We don't have to have a lodge to live by our oaths," Jerry said gently. "Mitch, you know we haven't worked effectively as a lodge since Gil died."

"We were pretty good in Henry's hangar the other night," Mitch said. "The amulets worked. They probably saved Alma's life."

"We were, and they did. And Lewis is a nice guy. But he's a completely untrained oracular talent, and none of us have the faintest idea how to train him." Jerry shook his head. "Be realistic, Mitch. We're not a lodge. We're a bunch of drifters who maybe one day were going to amount to something."

Mitch's mouth tightened. Eleven years ago he'd been a hero, a handsome twenty five year old with a good education, a nice guy with girls dripping off him, a real live flying ace better than you see in the movies, cleft chin and clipped jaw and big blue eyes. He'd even been picked to do some goodwill trips before he came back to the states after the Armistice, the very picture of a good American boy. Now what was he? A guy who lived in an apartment over his friend's garage and flew planes.

Not that Jerry could talk. Mitch at least had a regular job.

"I'm sorry," he said.

Mitch shrugged. "Jerry, we've got to keep going. It's what we do. It's all we've got." He paused as though he were searching for words. "We're a team. And we have oaths. In the end it doesn't matter whether we won or not. It just matters that we were true to ourselves and each other."

Jerry dropped his eyes. "I know," he said.

"You're pissed because it got away. I'm pissed because it got away." Mitch ran his hand through his hair again. "We screwed up. I lost it in Chicago, and that's my fault, not Lewis'. Lewis didn't know what it could do. He's the new guy, and I was in charge. Mea maxima culpa. So we need to sit down and figure out what to do next."

"I'm also pissed because it killed Bill Davenport," Jerry said. He hadn't meant to, but he did anyhow. "He was a pain in the ass and I didn't like him, but I knew him for twenty years, Mitch. And nobody should die like that."

"Aw, crap," Mitch said, as though he'd just realized something. "I'm sorry, Jerry."

"It's not as though he was a friend," Jerry said. "We were in school together. That's all. He was insufferable even then, stuck on himself and endlessly self promoting. It's not like I cared about him or something."

"Of course not," Mitch said. "But it's hard to lose one of your guys. Always is, even if the guy is an ass." He clapped Jerry on the shoulder. "Come on, Jerry. Let's tell Alma and Lewis. And then we'll figure out how to track down this thing. It's going to pay for it. And we're the ones who will bring it in."

"How the hell are we going to do that?"

"We've still got the tablet. We can dowse for it again. It can run but it can't hide, Jer." Mitch's hand was on his back, steering him out of the compartment. "We can follow it wherever it goes, like bloodhounds on a scent."

"That's true," Jerry said. And that made the nauseated feeling a little less.

Chapter Eighteen

Henry was making himself scarce again. Jerry leaned against the promenade railing, staring at the ocean a thousand feet below. He supposed it made sense: this was the *Independence*'s maiden voyage, though by the time Henry let paying passengers on board, especially celebrities and reporters, Jerry was sure all the kinks had been well worked out. Henry never bet except on a sure thing. And maybe that was it, Henry making sure his bets stayed good, but beyond a glimpse at the champagne toast on launch, and occasional quick sightings in the public areas, they'd seen more of the airship's chief pilot than they had of its owner. Not that Jerry hadn't enjoyed his brief conversations with the pilot—Georg Federman, his name was; Henry had lured him away from the Zeppelin Company with the promise of better pay and quicker promotion—but they did need to talk to Henry, and preferably before they landed in Paris. He'd sent a note forward to the control car after lunch, but there'd been no response.

Maybe at dinner, he thought. Surely Henry would have to put in an appearance then. The Sparkling Starlet was looking a little neglected, and one of the reporters had managed to insinuate himself into her circle. Henry would want to control that interaction as much as possible. He moved away from the rail, trying to decide what to do until then. Maybe he'd grab a cigarette, then fetch some books from his cabin, and take them into the lounge where he could spread out a little. The airship's movement was smooth enough that nothing was going to roll away—smoother than a plane, smoother than a train or even a liner, so smooth that he barely needed his cane. Alma had said she could get used to traveling like this, and so could he.

"Dr. Ballard?"

Jerry turned to see Joe Palmer coming down the promenade from the bow of the ship. "Yes?"

"I'm glad I found you. Mr. Kershaw got your note, and said if you were free, he could see you in the observation car."

Clever Henry, Jerry thought. The observation car, with its glass walls, had proved unnerving for most of the passengers. Everyone had dutifully visited, and just as quickly left, most of them pleading the chill of the unheated space. Jerry hadn't liked it much himself, but it was the most private public space on board. "Thanks," he said aloud. "I'll head straight down."

The stairs into the observation car were some of the steepest, and it took concentration to negotiate them without looking like a cripple. The car was empty, except for Henry, and Jerry spoke before he'd reached the last step.

"Davenport's dead—"

Something tingled on his skin as his foot touched the floor, like a door closing, and Henry straightened, turning to face him

"Yes. I saw the *Times*."

Not Henry, Jerry thought, the air cold on his skin. It wore Henry's body, Henry's face, but he could feel the darkness behind its eyes. The amulet was still in his pocket, hooked onto his watch chain; he didn't dare reach for it, it would protect him just as well there, and he took a step backward, groping for the stair rail. His hand struck something cold and solid; he knew if he turned, he wouldn't see anything, but there was no escape that way. That had been the tingling, the trap snapping shut, sealing them off from the rest of the airship.

"You were right," the creature said. Its smile was a deliberate parody. "We do need to talk."

"If you say so," Jerry said. It took a step toward him, and he stepped away, keeping as much distance as he could between them. His options were terribly limited: the thing couldn't jump to him, and probably wouldn't want to, Henry was a better host, but he still hadn't figured out how to exorcise it, how to bind it, and Henry was stronger than he was in any case… It was backing him toward the wall of windows, he realized, and put out his free hand to guide himself along the rail. He mustered his will, focusing it like a knife, said, "What's your *name*?"

The creature gave Henry's good-humored laugh. "Oh, please. Do you think I'm really that stupid? And you, of all people, can't force me."

It stalked closer, and Jerry backed away again, letting his hand slide along the railing. It took a sharp turn, and in the same moment his shoulder hit the corner of the car. Trapped, stupid, a stupid, terrible mistake.... He shifted his grip on his cane, and the thing smiled.

"You're lucky that I might have a use for you," it said. "If you are suitably cooperative."

"Unlikely," Jerry said, dry-mouthed. "Look, this is not a good plan for you—"

"Oh, I disagree," it said. "You haven't even heard my offer."

"Not interested."

The creature smiled. The expression wasn't Henry's at all, but something much older, a depth of experience lurking in its eyes. "You're clever," it said. "Clever enough to make those charms you carry. I could use such skill, and I'm willing to offer you something in return."

"You don't have anything I want," Jerry said.

"Gil," it said.

The name was like a punch to the gut. Jerry let out his breath not quite soundlessly, shook his head hard. "You can't do it. You can't raise the dead."

"You don't know what I can and can't do," the thing said softly. "I have more powers than you have ever imagined—more than you have ever read about in all your books. And I can do better than raise the dead. Serve me, serve me well, and you can choose a body, young and healthy, never touched by war—Kershaw's young pilot, perhaps? You seemed to get on well with him. And I will call Gil's soul to it, and he will be yours again."

"No," Jerry said, but he couldn't help imagining it, Gil alive again, alive and healthy, able to breathe without coughing, no more bloody handkerchiefs and useless cures.... And with Gil alive to lead them, they could fight this thing—Alma would kill him, he knew, if Gil didn't do it first, and the thought steadied him enough to shake his head again. "No."

"Pity," the thing said, without particular regret, and pinned him with a look. Jerry heard the window slide open behind him, and felt the first blast of frigid air. He couldn't move, couldn't speak, could only with enormous effort tighten his hold on the railing. The thing in Henry's body moved closer, laid a hand on his shoulder, fingers closing tight enough to leave a bruise.

"We are flying at eleven hundred feet," it said softly, "or at least that was the altitude when I left the control car. It's a very long way down, and you'll be conscious for most of it. You'll be falling, seeing the lights recede from you, your life receding, and all the way down you'll know. Perhaps you'll even be conscious when you hit the water, when every bone shatters, your organs rupture, one tremendous flash of agony as you die. And I will savor every shrieking breath, every second of your fall."

Jerry shuddered, tried again to move, and the creature smiled. "Such a tragic accident! Such a shame, a pointless end to a disappointing life." It tapped Jerry's wooden leg with its foot. "And so easily arranged. So easy for a cripple to stumble, such a foolish mistake to have a window open—"

Oh, God. Jerry couldn't form a better prayer, and reached instead for craft, found a word and directed it not at Henry, not at the thing that wore him, but at the barrier that sealed the observation car. The creature kicked his leg again, sending it sliding; he lurched and fell forward, head and shoulders in the slipstream, tie whipping back like a flag.

And then there was a shout from the stairs and the thing was hauling him back in, a terrible mockery in its eyes.

"My God, Dr. Ballard—" That was Palmer, hurrying toward them, and Henry slid the window shut.

"Yes, that was a little too close. Jerry, are you all right?"

"Yes." Jerry's lips were numb, as though he'd been hanging in the freezing air for hours. "Yes, I'm fine." He pulled himself upright, straightening his tie and jacket, and Henry shook his head.

"Make a note, Joe, we need to fix those windows so they don't go all the way back. Damn, that was—close."

"But it didn't happen," Jerry said, and dredged a smile from somewhere. "Don't worry, Henry, I won't make that mistake again."

"Be sure you don't," Henry said, and slapped him hard on

the bruised shoulder. "Does that take care of what you wanted?"

"Oh, yes," Jerry said. He felt sick, swallowed hard. "Yes, that takes care of that."

"Good," Henry said. The creature smiled again behind his eyes, and he turned away, heading for the catwalk that led to the control car.

Jerry took a deep breath, his heart slowing, and Palmer gave him a worried look. "My God, how did that happen?"

"My foot slipped, I think," Jerry said.

"Are you sure you're all right?" Palmer looked as though he wanted to offer his hand, but Jerry waved it away.

"I'm fine," he said again, and willed it to be true.

Lewis knotted his tie—not the same tie he'd been wearing the night before, but the same suit, the same shirt—and stooped to check his hair in the mirror. It was mostly tamed, and his cheeks were smooth: as presentable as he was going to get, and he shrugged on his jacket. Alma had dressed already, gone with Mitch to grab a cigarette and to see if they could find Henry, and he wasn't entirely sorry. He still didn't know what to think of what she'd told him. He didn't really want to think about it, if he was honest, didn't want to keep wondering about Gil. Gil and Alma, Gil and Jerry, Gil and Alma wanting kids.... It was probably Gil's fault they didn't, he thought, and then was ashamed of himself, embarrassed at even thinking such a thing. But it wasn't right, putting Alma in such a position—except that Alma said she was, had been, happy, and he couldn't disbelieve her. He had always known she'd been happy with Gil, even if now he couldn't figure out why. Take all the time you need, she had said. He wished he didn't need any time at all.

He made his way down to the lower deck, where the washrooms were, aware that everyone else was heading for the dining room and he would need to hurry. He pushed open the door, checked as he saw Jerry leaning over the further washbasin. There was a sour smell of vomit.

"Jerry?"

He saw a shudder run through the other man's shoulders, head still lowered. "Yeah."

"What happened?" No point asking if something was wrong, that much was obvious.

Jerry didn't answer at once, turned on the taps hard to rinse the sink, and when it was clean, splashed water on his face. "It's in Henry."

"What?"

"It's in Henry," Jerry said again. He reached for a towel, dried his hands and face. He looked suddenly old, face gray and strained. "He tried to pitch me out the window of the observation car."

"Damn," Lewis said. That was—he couldn't imagine anything worse, anyone worse for it to take over.

"Yeah," Jerry said again, with the ghost of his usual smile. He pulled off his glasses, and rubbed the bridge of his nose. "We are screwed."

Lewis took a breath, shoved away those words. They couldn't afford that now, not if they were going to do—something, anything. "Are you hurt?"

"No." Jerry put his glasses back on, straightened slowly. "Scared. It's—a long way down."

Lewis nodded, feeling an unwilling sympathy. You could never completely get over that fear, the knowledge that if the wings failed, the engine died, you lost control in any of a hundred ways, you'd fall out of the sky, with no chance of recovery. And it wasn't even something that hit you once, and went away. Every glitch in the engine, every flutter in the controls, every time someone got the drop on you: the abyss was always there, always waiting. All you could do was learn to live with it, and kill the other guy first.

"Sorry," Jerry said. "I'm Ok."

"What do we do now?" Lewis asked.

"Tell Al and Mitch," Jerry answered. "And hope one of us comes up with something."

Jerry's color was better by the time they reached the dining room, and he was moving with a semblance of his usual care. Alma and Mitch were already at their table, Alma glorious in her royal blue dress, and for a crazy instant Lewis wished they didn't have to tell her. But her expression was already sharpening, and

Mitch looked up from the menu, frowning.

"What's wrong?"

Jerry pulled out his chair, seated himself awkwardly before he answered. "It's got Henry."

"What?" Alma grimaced, lowered her voice. "Jerry, are you sure?"

"I'm sure." Jerry concentrated on unfolding his napkin, his eyes on his plate, bright with the Kershaw emblem. "He—it—tried to kill me."

Lewis took his seat next to Alma and tried to focus on the menu. Soup, trout, tenderloin of beef on toast.... His stomach roiled.

"How—" Alma began, but the steward interrupted her, offering a tray of cocktails. Jerry drained his, and motioned for the steward to bring him another.

"Easy, Jer," Mitch said.

Jerry glared at him. "Mitch, the man tried to push me out the window of the observation car. I think I'm entitled to a second drink."

Alma let her breath out with a whoosh. "Well," she said.

"Yeah." Mitch grimaced.

We're screwed, Lewis thought. He unfolded his napkin, set it carefully on his lap. Really and truly fucked. No way out, no way off until they got to Paris.... A familiar cold settled on him, his hands steady on the silverware. He could kill Henry, of course. It wouldn't be easy, he didn't know what the thing, the demon, could do to stop them, but on balance, he guessed he could kill Henry, Henry's body. There were lots of nooks and crannies on the ship, dark places to lie in wait; it could be done. The problem was, that wouldn't get them very far. If they were caught, or even suspected, they'd be in serious trouble. No one was going to believe some crazy story about demons and possession. And, more importantly, the thing might jump again. Kill Henry, and it would need another host; it might not be able to take any of the four of them, but there were forty more bodies aboard the airship, too many choices. Too big a risk to take the easy way out.

Alma's eyes widened, and Lewis looked sideways to see Henry making his way through the dining room. He was playing the gracious host, stopping at every table with a word and a grin, accepting the compliments as his due. He looked unchanged, at least on the surface, still the same tall, distinguished businessman. But on a closer look, darkness trailed him, fumed from him like strands of smoke. He was making his way toward their table, as inexorable as a snake, and Alma pressed her foot against Lewis's beneath the table. She managed a cool smile as Henry loomed over them, resting one hand on Jerry's shoulder. Lewis looked up, meeting the creature's eyes, and felt the hairs rise on the back of his neck. How could anyone not see the darkness there, a gap opened into something dark and dank and terrible, smelling of dead ground and old bones....

"Alma," Henry said, the creature said. "I'm sorry I haven't had much of a chance to see you this trip."

"Oh, that's quite all right," Alma said. We know you have other commitments."

"It's a pleasure to have you on board," it said. It was entirely sincere, Lewis realized; it was enjoying every moment of this game, secure in the knowledge that it would win. It tightened its grip, and Lewis saw Jerry wince. "Did Jerry tell you about our earlier conversation?"

"He certainly did," Mitch said.

"I don't know if I made it clear," the creature continued, "but the offer I made him was really for all of you."

"Offer?" Alma said, with just the right note of curiosity.

"Hasn't he told you?"

There were two spots of color high on Jerry's cheeks. "I hadn't really had the chance."

"Oh, well, then." Henry smiled. "I'll let Jerry tell you, and you can talk it over. In the meantime, I hope you're enjoying yourselves."

"Immensely," Alma said, and dredged a smile from somewhere. "It's an amazing ship, Henry. You should be proud of it."

She was speaking past the demon, Lewis realized, to the man trapped in his own body, and the demon couldn't quite hide its frown. It mastered itself in an instant, managed a parody of Henry's easy grin.

"Thank you. She's a beauty—the best in the world, even if it's me who says so." It paused. "And, please, don't wait too long to decide. I can't hold my offer open forever."

"Of course not," Alma said, stiff-lipped, and Henry turned away. Lewis watched him go, pausing at one table and then another, exchanging an intimate smile with Mary Holliday.

"If you were a dog, you'd be growling," Alma said. "Stop it. Look—friendly. As though we were having a good time."

She was right, of course, and Lewis made himself relax, smile. Alma pressed her foot against his again, and looked at the others. "Ok—"

The waiter interrupted her, bringing the soup course, and he was followed by the wine steward, offering a Montrachet. Mitch accepted it with a smile, and the steward filled their glasses, leaving the bottle in ice as though they were in an earthbound restaurant. Lewis sipped at his soup. It was rich and creamy, but he barely noticed the taste.

Alma swallowed a spoonful. "What was the offer, Jerry?"

Lewis looked at his plate. He didn't really want to hear, didn't want to see Jerry have to explain himself, abase himself—and that was exactly what the thing wanted, he realized. It was keeping track of Jerry's humiliation, just as it was sowing malice and discord throughout the dining room. Celena Moore was blushing, her expression surprisingly insecure; two of the reporters were glaring at each other as though they were contemplating a fistfight. Palmer looked like a scolded puppy as he trailed after Henry.

"Jerry," Mitch said.

Jerry put his spoon down carefully, not meeting anyone's eyes. "It's not possible, you know. What he offered." He looked at Alma then. "He said he could give us Gil."

Mitch sat up a little straighter, blinking as though someone had hit him.

Alma said, "Oh."

"It's not possible," Jerry said again, and Mitch shook his head. "Then why offer?"

"Because it likes misery," Jerry answered.

Alma said, "It cannot raise the dead. We know that, and it knows we know that. What was it proposing?"

"That we choose another host," Jerry said. His voice was tight, remote. "And it would bind Gil's soul to that new body. After we had done it good service, of course."

"Of course," Mitch said. "Could this thing really do that?"

"Probably," Jerry said.

Lewis looked at Alma. She was sitting very still, as composed as a statue, nothing at all alive except her wide eyes.

"This is—this has to be tempting," he began, groping for words, and her calm shattered into movement, reaching across the tablecloth to close her fingers tightly over his.

"Of course it's tempting," she said. "It was meant to be, that's what it does. But we can't, and that's an end to it."

Lewis returned the crushing grip. He didn't dare look at Jerry, didn't want to see what he was feeling....

"Gil would murder us," Mitch said, and Jerry laughed.

"We'd deserve it, too."

"Yeah." Mitch reached for the wine, topped up glasses that had barely been touched. "Ok, what do we do now?"

Alma squeezed Lewis's hand a final time and leaned back to smile at the waiter approaching with the fish course. "We finish our lovely dinner," she said. "And then we'll talk."

Chapter Nineteen

After dinner they assembled in Mitch and Jerry's cabin. Alma perched on one end of the lower berth while Jerry sat on the other. Mitch leaned against the wall beside the dressing table and Lewis stood with his back to the door. Alma crossed her legs, looking from one to the other, but everyone was silent. Lewis thought this was one of those moments when nobody knew what to say, not even Mitch, who usually had the right words. It was Gil's ghost, Gil's ghost and the creature's offer, and Lewis took a breath. It was the last thing he wanted, Gil back, but the man had been their leader, and they needed him desperately right now. Hell, Lewis needed him, and they'd never met. *Just loved the same woman*, a mocking voice whispered in the back of his mind. *If you can call it love.* He shoved the thought away, and straightened a little.

"I know I don't know anything about this," he said, slowly, "But if the thing out there can do it—can we, I don't know, call up Gil's spirit, ask for his help? At least he knew what he was doing, and I sure the hell don't."

Jerry gave a bark of laughter, but Alma looked at him with a startled smile.

"We sure as hell can't call his spirit into some stranger," Mitch said, scowling.

"I didn't mean that," Lewis said. "Not what that thing was offering. I know that's bad. But—I don't know what you can do. What's possible here."

"It wouldn't do any good," Jerry said, and tilted his head back against the wall of the berth.

"We can't raise the dead," Alma said, still smiling, her voice gentle. "And while we might be able to reach Gil's spirit if we could find a competent medium, I don't know what good it would do us even if there was one on the ship. No, we're the lodge. This is for the living to handle."

Lewis couldn't help feeling a sort of unworthy relief—Gil was a hard act to follow—and Mitch shook his head.

"Ok. We know what we're not doing. Anybody got any ideas about what we should do?"

"I think we need to go to Italy," Jerry said.

It was to everyone's credit that nobody swore.

"Why would we go to Italy?" Alma asked, frowning.

"We're chasing the demon," Mitch said. "Which isn't in Italy."

Jerry drew himself up, something of his old confidence returning. "That's the problem. We're chasing it. And it can jump into literally anybody, as we've just seen. So we make it chase us."

There was a moment of silence. Lewis wondered if he were the only one to whom that seemed a bad idea. "Why would it do that?"

"Because it's going to need time to find the right person to take over," Jerry said. "I mean, I can think of three or four candidates off the top of my head, men who have the kind of power it's looking for—Stalin, for a start, or maybe Ataturk—"

"Mussolini?" Alma said.

Jerry nodded. "Il Duce. He's certainly ambitious enough, and he's got control of the Parliament. King Zog of Albania. Moving further afield, Chiang Kai-Shek. But to get to them, it needs time to prepare, time to insinuate itself into their circles. And we can make that very difficult. So it needs to get rid of us, and we need to meet it on ground of our choosing."

"Which still begs the question of exactly how we're going to get it to follow us," Alma said. "I'm not arguing with the premise, Jerry, but I'm not making the connection."

"We know how to bind it for another two thousand years, and we will unless it stops us." Jerry paused, looking around the cabin.

Mitch looked startled. "We do?"

"It thinks we do," Jerry said. "Otherwise it wouldn't have tried to kill me. Otherwise why lure us on to the *Independence* at all? It could simply have left us in New York." He shook his head.

"No, it thinks that we're onto it, and that we have the power to bind it. We're a threat to it. Otherwise—it's like Alma said, why not just run? It's not as though we can prove to any authority what's going on, and its ability to jump from one host to another negates any ability to tie it to its crimes."

Alma let out a long breath. "But do we, Jerry? If we yell 'can't catch me!' and get a demon to chase us, what then? As you saw this afternoon, these amulets aren't protection against physical harm. They're not going to do a lick of good if it decides to just shoot us. Or shove you out a window again."

"That's true," Mitch said. He looked at Jerry keenly. "Do you actually know how to bind this thing?"

"I know where to bind it," Jerry said, "And that's the beginning. We need to go to Lake Nemi, to the Shrine of Diana at Aricia where it was bound before. We need to undo what let it out."

Lewis frowned. "I know I don't know a lot about this stuff, but what if the thing that freed it was unburying the Roman ships? We can't rebury them. That's a big project, right? With the Italian government and hundreds of people involved."

"It's not the ships per se," Jerry said. "It's something that was buried in connection with the ships. I'm guessing the tablets themselves – the one we have is part of a set. I would guess that the tablets were put aboard the ships and the ships were deliberately sunk."

Mitch asked the question Lewis had been thinking. "Why would they do that? Weren't these big, fancy ships?"

"Go back to the beginning, Jerry," Alma directed. "Tell them the whole story the way you told me."

Jerry pushed his gold-rimmed glasses back up on his nose, his face animated with his enthusiasm for the subject, and Lewis glanced sideways at him. He was handsome, maybe, in a weathered way, the lines of chronic pain bracketing his mouth, or maybe that was just being forty-two. He wasn't pretty and didn't look like he had been, at least not in the way Lewis would have expected. But there was something attractive in his face when he talked about something he cared about. Lewis could see that.

"Ok, to start with, it was sacrilege to build the ships at all. Diana's Mirror is a very small lake, and for hundreds of years before the period of Caligula it had been forbidden to boat on the lake. It was ok to fish from the bank, but no boats were allowed. The lake belonged to Diana. For Caligula to build two gigantic pleasure barges on the lake was a desecration." Jerry shrugged. "Of course, Caligula did a lot of that. If you told him that something was forbidden he'd do it just to prove he could. And he'd already desecrated the Shrine for what might have been political reasons, or might just have been because he wanted to."

Mitch frowned. "What was that?"

"The priest of Diana, the Rex Nemorensis, was selected in a very peculiar way. I know you've read Fraser's account, so…."

"I don't remember it," Mitch said. "How about you recap?"

He did remember, Lewis thought. This was for his benefit. It was like Mitch to make sure nobody was left behind and nobody was embarrassed about it.

"The priest had to be a fugitive slave, a wanted man. He had to challenge the current King of the Grove to a trial by combat. The two of them would go into the woods, and whichever came back alive was the winner and would serve as Diana's priest for the rest of his life." Jerry glanced around at their faces. "So you see it had to be a desperate man to try it. If he lost he would be killed. And if he won, he'd have an honorable place for a few years, until another challenger killed him. Or he might hold it for quite a while, at the cost of death after death in the wild wood."

"The hunter's bargain," Lewis said, and wasn't aware he'd spoken until he realized they were all looking at him. "Life for death."

"Exactly," Jerry said. "The Rex Nemorensis embodies that lethal math."

Lewis didn't think any of them were strangers to that. It was what war came down to in the end – kill or die. He could see how it must go, the desperate man going into the woods in misty morning, a knife in his hand, knowing that the king of the grove is waiting. He knows the woods better, and he's waiting along some game trail, at some place where the path divides in the forest. Perhaps they will stalk one another by day and meet at last by night, while the crescent moon sheds her cool light in benediction over death….

"Anyway," Jerry said, "Caligula either had some political problem with the Rex Nemorensis who was serving when he came to the throne, or maybe he just didn't like the guy. But in any case he bought a famous gladiator and brought him to Nemi. There the gladiator 'ran away' and challenged the King of the Grove. It was a set up, and of course he won. It was sacrilege for anyone to interfere in the choosing of Diana's priest that way, a serious desecration of her shrine. Nobody had ever done it before and as far as we know nobody ever did it again. It was shortly after that when Caligula had the Nemi ships built on the lake. There's been a lot of speculation that they were the site of some of his most horrific murders, including possibly the murder of his sister Drusilla, though other accounts say she died of a fever."

"Nice guy," Lewis said. His skin crawled.

"Yeah." Jerry pushed his glasses back up on his nose. "Anyhow, after Caligula's murder, his uncle Claudius came to the throne. It appears that Claudius tried to set a lot of things right. The tablet we have definitely dates from the first year of Claudius' reign based on the consuls serving, and it suggests that Claudius tried to appease the goddess by sinking the pleasure ships in the lake, giving to her all their treasure and getting rid of the offending things at the same time. I'm guessing that the plaques were aboard them and that they bound the *animus infernus* that had possessed his nephew."

Lewis shivered again. He could see it too clearly, the scene conjured by Jerry's words. Another misty morning, the lake like black glass, the middle aged man standing on the shore, a fold of his toga over the back of his head in a way that Lewis had never seen. He was making a long speech, some of his words slurring together, others enunciated too carefully, but there was power in it. Power and sorrow. He had loved his nephew before the demon claimed him.

Just like it had now taken Henry.

"It's pretty clear that Claudius invoked Diana to bind the creature, and that she did so. We need to figure out what Claudius did and see if we can do the same thing," Jerry said.

"She wants us to," Lewis said. "That's what I've been dreaming," He blinked, trying to piece it together. "All the dreams about the lake and about things hunting in the dark, even about Davenport the first time, before I met him. There's a white hunting dog, a white hound."

Jerry nodded seriously. "That's one of Diana's aspects, yes."

His eyes unfocused, Alma's fingers blurring together. He had been on the verge of something, carried in the flashes of vision, and now it came suddenly clear. "She leads the pack, and they hunt by her will. They wear her mark, and they hunt in her name. Diana's Hounds."

Mitch looked startled, but Alma didn't. "The amulets," she said. "We wear her mark. We're her hounds."

Lewis nodded slowly. "She'll help us. She wants to. I don't know why she doesn't just...do something." He swallowed. He was talking about her like she was real, a pagan goddess, who surely ought to be on the same side as a demon if anything. But it didn't feel that way in his gut. It felt like she was asking them for help. That was why she showed him things, why these visions came so clear. "I think she needs us," he said.

"Of course she does," Alma said gently. "How else does any spirit work in the world?"

"Ok," Mitch said. "Let's think about going to Italy. But first we have to get off the airship in Paris." He glanced at Jerry. "Without getting killed along the way. The airship is supposed to arrive in Paris at eight am tomorrow morning. We've got ten hours to stay out of that thing's way. So the first thing is that nobody wanders off alone. We stay in pairs. Jerry, that means you're with me."

Jerry nodded tightly.

Mitch unfolded from where he leaned against the wall. "The other thing that making it chase us will do is make it less likely for it to hurt Henry. It's not enough to get rid of the thing. We need to get rid of it without harming Henry."

"That's not going to be easy," Jerry said warningly.

Mitch looked at him sharply. "Think about it. We don't leave our own behind. Henry was our lodgemate once. It's not his fault he's possessed by this thing. We get it out of him without harming him."

"It probably is his fault," Alma said. "And ours too. We wired Henry that Davenport had lost us in Chicago and that he was on his way to New York. How much do you want to bet that old Henry couldn't resist going to confront Davenport by himself? And he didn't have an amulet."

Jerry hit his forehead with his palm. "Of course he did! That's just like Henry! He trotted over to the hotel as soon as he got our telegram, ready to handle Davenport alone."

"And it jumped into him," Mitch said grimly.

"I should have known. I've known Henry long enough." Alma let out a deep breath. "Ok, let's give this a try, Jerry. Once we get to Paris we'll head for Italy by train and see if he'll chase us. But you'd better have figured out what we're going to do when we get there."

"Believe me, I mean to," Jerry said fervently.

Jerry said he was going to sit up and work on it while Mitch curled up on the upper bunk in their room, so Alma and Lewis went back to their own cabin. Even spooned together, sleep eluded Lewis for a long time, and when at last he did sleep it was briefly and restlessly. Alma seemed an enormous weight on his arm, pressing him down into the mattress, and it wasn't long before he rolled over, staring at the ceiling above.

"Can't sleep?" she asked. Her voice was clear, not muddled by sleep.

"No," Lewis said. He ran his hand over the day's beard on his chin. "I keep waiting for the other shoe to drop." He wasn't surprised she was lying awake. He would be too, if he were her. "Listen," he said awkwardly, "About Gil…."

"He would never want me to do something like that," she said. "Never." He felt the splash of one tear hitting his arm, but her voice was angry. "It only made the offer because it's in Henry, and it knows it would hurt me. That's how it works, Lewis. It feeds on misery and fear and pain. It's feeding off me right now, and I don't know how to stop it." He heard her choke back a sob, tightened his arms around her, not knowing what to say.

"What we had was beautiful and wonderful. And it's over." Her voice sharpened. "Things happen. No one gets forever. We were so lucky, Lewis! For a few years we had everything."

Lewis bent his face against her hair. He couldn't do anything about the demon, or even about its offer. All he could do was be a shoulder for her, and he'd do that if she'd let him. He wouldn't let it take her. No matter what.

Alma raised her face and kissed him hard, breathlessly, as though she could devour him, and Lewis leaned into it, his arms tight around her. This was the way to break it, he thought. It fed on misery. There was no sustenance for it in love.

When she looked up her eyes were bright. "I'm ok," she said, and there was no tremor in her voice. "I'm fine."

"Sure," Lewis said. "Sure thing."

"I just couldn't sleep," she said.

"Me either." Lewis twisted enough to glance at his watch. 3:30 am. He wondered where they were. Possibly over England, or nearly so. He wondered if this might not be the most fantastic time to be in the observation car, crossing sleeping Britain by night, the lights of towns and cities winking up into the sky, clustered like threads of light on a spider's web.

Alma huffed. "Can't sleep just because we're trapped on an airship with a demon?"

"Yeah." Lewis grinned. "Oddly enough, it makes me nervous."

She gave him a sudden sharp look. "You're serious."

Lewis paused. "Yeah," he said, after a moment. "There's something—not right somewhere."

"Can you see where?" She gave the word the little twist that said she meant more than ordinary sight, and he closed his eyes obediently, trying to find the stillness that let him reach outside himself. His mind stayed stubbornly blank, and he shook his head.

"Nothing. Sorry."

She shoved her hair back from her face, smoothing it into some semblance of order. "If you've got a bad feeling there's probably something wrong. Let's get up and go see."

"Truly?" He'd never seen this before, this kind of rock-bottom faith in him. She would get up in the middle of the night and go wander around just because he said he had a feeling something wasn't right. And this.... This was like a cold place in the pit of his stomach, the absolute unshakable certainty that something was badly wrong.

"You're a clairvoyant," Alma said. "If you have a feeling, that's good enough for me. And the number of things that could be wrong beggars the imagination."

"Ok," he said, and leaned over to hunt for his pants. "Let's get dressed then."

The door that separated the passenger areas from the crew compartments and the cargo holds was unlocked. That wasn't exactly surprising, Alma thought, you wouldn't want to block access in an emergency. What was a little surprising was the dark green leather that covered both sides of the door, quilted like the upholstery of a sofa. Soundproofing, maybe, though the airship was astonishingly quiet in operation. She let it close softly behind her and looked around. The crew corridor was more brightly lit, the lamps utilitarian, and through gaps in the ceiling she could see the duralumin girders of the frame rising up into the dark.

"Ok," she said, and looked at Lewis. "Where to?"

"Up." His face looked different in the harsh light, harder and younger at the same time, oddly unfamiliar. She hadn't seen him like this before, except maybe once in the blurred aftermath of a dream.

"Ok," she said again. Stairs or ladders? There must be one or the other, and they needed to get out of the main corridor, out of sight—

Ahead of them, a cabin door swung open, and a man in a striped flannel bathrobe stepped out. Lewis started forward, but she flattened her hand against his chest.

"Mr. Palmer," she said, softly.

He turned, blinking, sleep fading to a frown. "Mrs. Gilchrist? What are you doing here?"

If you're going to tell a lie, Al, make it a whopper. She could almost hear Gil's voice, could see him standing by the mantel with its electric fire, Jerry with his new wooden leg propped up on a footstool, shaking his head at both of them. Their second Christmas in Colorado, that had been, when things were starting to go well again.

"Good, I'm glad I didn't have to wake you," she said. "Has Mr. Kershaw told you why we're on board?"

"No." Palmer looked from her to Lewis and back again.

"Henry received some crackpot letters," Alma said. "Threats against the *Independence*. He didn't think it was anything serious at first, but later—he had reason to wonder. So he asked us to come along. And now—Mr. Segura has had some indications that there might be trouble up in the hull. Maybe with the gas cells."

For a mercy, Palmer didn't ask what those indications were, just blinked at them for a moment. "No wonder he's been worried," he said. "Do you want Captain Brooks? Or one of the pilots?"

"I think actually we want you," Alma said, and smiled. "We just want to take a quiet look around—it may only be an attempt to create bad publicity."

As she'd hoped, those were magic words. "Of course, Mrs. Gilchrist," Palmer said. He glanced back at his cabin door, and she said, "There's no need to change."

"And no time, if there is a problem," Lewis said. He was falling into the spirit of the story, Alma thought. "I just hope I'm wrong and we only lose some sleep."

"All right," Palmer said, and tightened the belt of his robe. He was wearing sturdy-looking slippers, Alma saw with some relief. "Where do you want to go?"

"Up," Lewis said again. "There's—there's a catwalk along the bottom of the gas cells, right? I'd like to take a quiet look there."

"If there's a problem with the gas, it would show up in the control car," Palmer said, but he didn't sound entirely sure of himself.

"It should," Lewis agreed. "But I'd just like to take a look."

"Ok," Palmer said. "Which catwalk?"

Lewis hesitated. Alma said, "There are two?"

"Yes," Palmer answered. "We have both hydrogen and helium cells—we need the hydrogen for the extra lift, and it's a good deal cheaper to valve it to balance the fuel consumption than to waste the helium. Mr. Kershaw's idea was to place the hydrogen cells inside the helium cells, so that the helium protects the hydrogen from any sparks. It reduces the danger of fire dramatically—but my point is, there are two catwalks that give access to the cells, one at the bottom of the helium cells, and the other running, well, through them, to reach the hydrogen cells."

Lewis's lips thinned. "Let's start with the hydrogen."

Palmer sighed. "I was afraid you'd say that."

The stairs that led out of the main corridor were narrow and steep, like the ladders on the ship that had brought her and Gil home from Italy. His ghost, his memory, was very present—couldn't help but be, she thought, but at least this was a clean thing, not the creeping misery at dinner.

At the second landing, even the perforated ceilings ceased, and the fabric of the gas cells loomed above them. Battery-powered headlamps hung on a board at the bottom of the next ladder, and Palmer took one and flicked it on, motioning for them to do the same.

"Safety lights," he said. "There's no electricity further up, for obvious reasons."

Alma switched on her light and followed Palmer up the next set of stairs. They emerged onto the lower of the two catwalks, a duralumin grid that stretched to either side into the darkness. The gas cells hovered above them, held in place by a padded metal net, and in the far distance her light just picked out the lacy girders of the frame. Lewis turned his head slowly from side to side, letting the light sweep across the gas cells and the narrow catwalk. It was only a couple of feet wide, with a thick rope stretched between the girders for a handhold, and it arrowed on into the darkness beyond the reach of their lights.

"The main catwalk," Palmer said. His voice seemed hushed, smothered by the weight of fabric above them. "It runs the full length of the ship."

Lewis looked around again, and met her eyes with an apologetic shrug. "Up further," he said. "The hydrogen cells?"

"This way."

They walked another fifty feet toward the airship's bow before they came to a second ladder. It was a real ladder this time, stretching up into darkness, surrounded by hoops that if they wouldn't break a man's fall would at least keep him from damaging the gas bags. Alma tilted her head back, and spotted the second platform maybe thirty feet into the air. It seemed to lead into the gas cell itself, and in spite of herself she caught her breath. Lewis gave her a look, his face set under the headlamp, and she nodded.

"Will you be all right, Mr. Palmer?" She waved toward his slippers, and he shrugged.

"I'll manage. You've got me a little worried now, Mrs. Gilchrist."

"You don't know how much I hope it's all a false alarm," she said, and started up the ladder after Lewis. Her arms were feeling it by the time she reached the catwalk, and she stopped to catch her breath, turning her head slowly to get her bearings. They were in a gap between two of the cells, right at one of the main rings of the frame. She could see it, overhead and to either side, the duralumin pierced with holes to reduce the weight. On either side, the gas cells swelled, drab gray fabric with an odd sheen from the chemicals that made it impermeable. The catwalk did lead into them, she saw, or rather, the cell was divided on either side of the walk, draped over it like washing on a line. The opening looked like the mouth of a cave. Lewis started toward it, feet silent and careful, but she caught his arm.

"Do you—did you see anyone?" she asked, and hoped he'd understand what she was really asking.

He paused, his eyes focusing on her, and seemed to come back to himself. "I don't think—there won't be anybody there," he said. "Or there shouldn't be."

"Be careful," she said.

"The manual controls are at the mid-point," Palmer said nervously, and Lewis nodded.

"I think we're fine. But let's just take a quick look."

Alma nodded, reassured, but couldn't help ducking her head as they passed under the gas bag's shadow. Inside, the air was still and felt weirdly heavy; her light played across the dull fabric, taut and plain, and the unpainted duralumin of the walkway. She looked down once, and her light fell through the grating to the main catwalk thirty feet below.

"There," Palmer said, and pointed past her shoulder. She looked where he was pointing, and her light fell on a red-painted panel set between two of the posts that held the catwalk's rail. Lewis studied it, frowning.

"Hey, Palmer? Am I reading this right?"

"What?"

Alma pressed herself against the nearest stanchion as Palmer pushed passed her, and peered over his shoulder. The dials didn't make a lot of sense to her, but it seemed as though they ought to be closer to the midline, not dropping down toward eight o'clock.

"That can't be right," Palmer said. He tapped the nearest dial, with no result. "It looks like we're valving hydrogen, but it's much too early—"

"What should it be reading?" Lewis asked.

"Between two thousand and twenty-two hundred," Palmer said. "I don't understand. These have to be wrong, or Captain Brooks would be doing something about it."

"Al," Lewis said. "You and Palmer check the next cell aft, see if it's the same. I'll go forward."

"Right," Alma said. "Come on, Mr. Palmer."

He made no protest, shuffled along after her in his bathrobe and slippers. They came out of the first gas cell into another gap, the frame ring looming in on them, and Alma ducked into the next cell without hesitation. The control panel was in the middle there, too, and the needles were creeping down toward eight o'clock.

"My God," Palmer said, and shook his head.

"We'll check one more," Alma said, grimly, and kept moving aft. In the next cell, the panel was bigger—it was a bigger cell, Palmer said, farther away from the passenger section—but the needles were below eleven hundred, and falling.

"We need to get down to the control car," Palmer said. "We have to tell them."

"Back the way we came," Alma said.

Lewis appeared at the entrance to the forward cell just as she reached the ladder. "Either all the hydrogen cells spontaneously sprung a leak, or somebody's opened the valves."

"We have to tell the captain," Palmer said again. "My God, Mrs. Gilchrist, if we keep valving hydrogen at this rate—"

"Emergency controls," Lewis said. "Can we close the valves from here?"

"Not on this level," Palmer said. "All the panels say the main valves are closed, it must be the automatic valves that are open—they're supposed to open if the pressure gets too high, it's to keep the cells from being damaged. But it's not possible that all of them jammed open—"

"Can we get to them from here?" Lewis asked, and Palmer shook his head.

"You'd have to go back down, climb up the riggers' walks in the frame."

"Damn," Lewis said.

"Mr. Palmer," Alma said. "Go tell Captain Brooks what's going on, see if he can't get someone to the automatic valves as quickly as possible. We'll make sure none of the main valves are open." She paused, not sure she wanted to know the answer. "How long do we have?"

Palmer shook his head. "I don't know. It depends on when the valves opened. I just—I hope we can make the coast."

"Go," Alma said, and the young man shook himself, slid down the ladder toward the main catwalk.

"I'm not sure I think much of Kershaw's—its—plan," Lewis said, after a moment.

"It doesn't need Henry to live," Alma said. "Doesn't need any of us to survive. It can jump to a rescuer, anyone who comes to see what happened. And our deaths will nourish it." She shivered. "All right. Let's check the main valves just in case."

"And hope Kershaw doesn't have any more surprises up his sleeve," Lewis muttered.

Chapter Twenty

The sound of the engines didn't change. Perhaps it was some subtle shift in the sense of motion, some tiny change in angle of declension. Mitch couldn't have said what it was. But it was enough. He was a pilot, and it woke him.

Mitch sat up, bumping his head on the ceiling. He was in the upper bunk aboard the *Independence*. Jerry slept in the bunk below, still fully dressed and wearing glasses, a book opened across his chest.

"Something's wrong," Mitch said.

Jerry stirred, eyes opening at the sound in Mitch's voice.

Mitch glanced at his watch. Eight minutes after four. They shouldn't be descending, not yet. The airship's course was supposed to skirt the coast of southern Britain, passing over Lands' End and then more or less following the coast as far as Portsmouth, when it would turn a little south, making for Le Havre and the coast of France, straight as an arrow from there to the airfield outside Paris. At ten after four they ought to be over the Channel, or perhaps making landfall in Cornwall.

"Wait here," he said, and got to his feet, hurriedly putting his shirt back on over his undershirt and tucking it into his pants. He slid his feet into his shoes without socks. "I'm going to get Lewis."

"Ok," Jerry said bemusedly. He looked still half asleep.

Mitch went into the corridor, pulling the door shut behind him. All was quiet. Of course the passengers were asleep at four in the morning. He knocked softly on Lewis and Alma's door. There was no answer, so he knocked louder. "Lewis? Alma?"

No answer again, so he tried the door. It took a moment's glance to see that they weren't there. No sign of a struggle, just gone.

"Damn," Mitch said softly. He hurried down the corridor toward the dining room, feeling the wrongness in the base of his belly. A one, maybe two degree angle. That was nothing. But it was wrong.

The dining room was deserted. The tables had been laid for breakfast but it was too early for even the stewards to be awake. Mitch padded over to the port side windows, a broad sweep down the side of the gondola that in daylight afforded a magnificent view of sea and sky. Now it was overcast and even the stars didn't show.

But there were stars beneath. To the left and rear a chain of lights hung on the horizon, a curve of glittering gems against the darkness. Mitch had flown these skies himself, ten years ago, and it only took him a moment to get his bearings. The lights behind were Brixham and Berry Head, the generous curve the shape of Tor Bay. The airship had crossed the neck more or less over Plymouth and now took off across the dark waters toward France. A hundred miles to Le Havre on this diagonal course, though it must be less than sixty to Cherbourg.

Which was not good news. If they were prematurely descending it would not be a tragedy to do it over England. Bournemouth had a good airfield if they could turn north. Portsmouth would be nearly ideal, though he didn't think they'd get so far at this rate of descent. But this.... A sharp right rudder would turn them south to Cherbourg. Otherwise there was a hundred miles of gray, rolling waves before they crossed the coast again.

Mitch almost ran back down the corridor, caught Jerry at the door coming out, his cane in his hand. "We're descending," Mitch said. "Way too early. We're over the Channel and I'd guess we're a hundred miles out from Le Havre."

"Um," Jerry said. "That's not good."

"You're right. That's not good. Crashing in the English Channel is not good, Jerry," Mitch snapped. He could feel the adrenaline coursing through his veins, the same elongation of moments he'd always felt in combat, like there was all the time in the world for everything. "We've got to get to the cockpit."

"The pilots...."

"Would be turning hard to port if they were able to," Mitch

said grimly. "We could make Bournemouth easily on that course. Come on, Jerry. And watch my back."

It could be a technical problem, a jammed rudder or the like. But somehow that seemed awfully coincidental.

The door was locked, of course. And of course nobody answered his knock, not even when he pounded on it. The small glass porthole showed nothing, just a dovetail of wall that revealed nothing.

"Open up!" Mitch shouted. "Emergency!"

There was no response.

"Oh shit," Jerry said quietly, under his breath. At an extreme angle the wall did show something, a spatter pattern of scarlet against the white.

Mitch put his ear to the door, listening. He thought he heard a faint moan. "Anybody there? Are you hurt?"

The faint moan again.

"Here." Jerry thrust his cane at Mitch. "Break the glass and use the loop to reach in and catch the latch from the inside."

"Thanks," Mitch said, grabbing it. There was a reason he was glad Jerry was a damned genius. He stepped back and swung, but it took several blows to break the glass. Then he put the cane through loop down, feeling around for the latch.

"Help..." a weak voice murmured. "Gott in himmel....." He trailed off with a gasp.

The pilot Federman, Mitch thought. He was German, hired away from the Zeppelin Company. "Is that you, Federman?" Mitch called. "Hang on. We're coming."

The loop of the cane caught the latch and Mitch levered it up, the door swinging open.

"Oh damn," Jerry said softly.

Captain Brooks was dead on the floor beside the control chair, shot in the head. It was his blood that had made the spray of scarlet across the wall. Federman lay almost behind the door, half against the wall. He'd been shot in the chest, and one glance was enough to tell Mitch he probably wasn't going to make it.

That knowledge was in his eyes too as Jerry went down laboriously beside him. He looked at Mitch, and he knew.

"Who did this?" Jerry said, checking his pulse with one hand, the other keeping his balance on the gore streaked floor.

"Mr. Kershaw...." Federman said, his mouth twisting with pain. "He is a madman. He came in and said he had to talk with us.... He shot Captain Brooks...."

"And you tried to take the gun," Jerry said, his eyes tracking the bloody footprints across the floor, the position where Federman lay. "You struggled and he shot you point blank."

"He is mad...." Federman whispered. "Mad. He reset the controls. I do not know...." His eyes twisted up to Jerry. "There are forty passengers, forty innocent people...." His breath caught on a sob of pain.

Mitch slid into the pilot's seat, dashing blood from the controls with his left hand. No time. And all the time in the world. There were no lights ahead, only dark sea.

"Listen," Jerry said evenly. "Mitch, Captain Sorley there, is a top pilot, an ace. You tell us what you can and we'll get you down. Mitch can fly anything that was ever built. Right, Mitch?"

"Yeah," Mitch said, his eyes roving over the controls. Elevator controls. Rudder. And these gauges – pressure dropping? There was something wrong outside of the cockpit, something badly wrong. "Jerry, close that door and latch it. Use your cane to jam the latch. We don't want it getting back in here." He couldn't bring himself to say Henry's name. That thing wasn't Henry, who would never in a million years do this, who would never in a million years kill these innocent people and wreck his own airship. To be trapped in your own body, unable to stop it while it destroyed your life's work, while it shot down men in cold blood....

The rudder didn't answer. Not that he'd expected it to. That would be too easy. A turn to port for Bournemouth. A turn to starboard for Cherbourg.

"Ok, Federman," he said calmly. "Tell me what these pressure gauges mean."

Lewis ducked back into the tunnel that led to the controls for the nearest hydrogen cell. At least the design was meant to be simple, something any idiot could read and follow. The handwheel for the main valve was underneath, a lock-bar holding it in place. He crouched to get better light on it, tested the bar and then the wheel itself: it was, as far as he could see, closed tight. He moved on toward the airship's tail into the next cell—the main valve was secure there, too—and then the next. It looked as though Palmer's guess was right, and it was the automatic valves that had been sabotaged. And that made sense: they were designed to open easily, to keep the pressure differentials from damaging the cells. It was the logical place for a saboteur to go to work. Especially one with access to all the memories of the man who'd designed and built the ship, and no need to worry about self-preservation....

Alma met him on the ladder platform, shaking her head. "All the main valves seem to be closed."

"Here, too," Lewis said.

"Does it feel to you like we're nose-down?" Alma began, and a single sharp report sounded from below.

"Gunshot," Lewis said. It made no sense, you'd have to be insane to fire a pistol inside the hull, with only a few layers of fabric between you and an explosive gas, a gas that needed only a single spark, a bullet ricocheting from a girder, to burst into flames. But the thing in Henry wasn't human and didn't think like that.

"This way," Alma said, and slid down the long ladder. Lewis followed, his skin crawling. The thing was loose, he could feel it watching, somewhere, and he came off the ladder in a crouch, spinning to take in the full circle. The beam of his headlight flashed over gas cells and empty girders. Alma started down the stairs, into the lighted corridor beneath them, and Lewis heard her swear. Fifty feet ahead, Palmer lay sprawled across the width of the corridor, blood seeping from beneath him. A telephone handset dangled from its cord above him. Alma stooped to touch his neck, then straightened and reached for the handset.

"Is this the control room?"

Apparently not: she made a face, and spoke more loudly. "No, Palmer's been shot. There's a problem with the automatic release valves in the hydrogen cells, it looks as though they're jammed open. You need to get to them right away—what do you mean, you can't?"

She put her hand over the mouthpiece, looked back at Lewis.

"He's locked them in their cabins. The off-duty riggers." She took her hand away. "I don't know where the duty men are, but they're not responding. We'll come and let you out—"

"No," Lewis said, and flattened them both against the corridor wall. He put his finger to his lips, and pointed up through the gap in the ceiling. A light was moving along the lower catwalk, coming toward them.

"Scratch that," Alma said, softly. "You'll have to break yourselves out. We are going after the saboteur before he does any more damage." She hung up the handset and looked up at the moving light.

Lewis tugged them into the center of the corridor, switched off his light and Alma did the same. They could hear the footsteps now, steady, confident, coming closer with every stride.

"Mr. Kershaw?" The voice came from aft, and the footsteps stopped.

"Yes? What is it?"

"Sir, there's a problem, I can't find the Chief—"

The pistol spoke again, and there was a cry and a thud. Alma flinched, and Lewis bit back a curse. There was a moment of silence, and then the footsteps started again, moving away.

"We have to stop him," Alma whispered.

"Wait," Lewis said. They couldn't afford to hurry, not when Kershaw, the creature, was armed and they weren't. The same icy armor that had protected him in combat was descending on him, slowing his heartbeat, quickening his thoughts. Weapon first, he thought, and then—the best we can do is harry him, keep him from doing anything else to the ship, and hope the captain can fix whatever's wrong. He looked up and down the corridor, seeing nothing but the smooth fabric-covered panels. Nothing here that would do them any good. The footsteps were fading, almost out of earshot, and he turned back to the stairs, started slowly up. Palmer had been in pajamas, but the man Kershaw had shot was duty crew and might have something useful on him.

The catwalk was dark, lit only by light seeping though the gaps from the corridor below, but Lewis didn't dare light his headlamp. He eased forward and saw the body first as a break in the light. He knelt beside it, feeling for a pulse—none, and when he rolled it toward him, he realized the man had been shot in the face. From the marks on his coveralls, he was one of the riggers. He heard Alma swear again, and she dropped to her knees beside him.

"Dead," he said, softly, though she could see it as well as he could. He was already going through the man's pockets, unbuttoning the overalls, came up with a rigger's knife and a smaller knife with a folding blade. He handed that to Alma, kept the rigger's knife for himself, and in the leg pocket found a narrow aluminum wrench. He gave that to Alma as well, and pushed himself to his feet.

"There," Alma said softly, copying him. She pointed into the darkness.

"What?"

"I saw—there," she said again.

This time, Lewis saw it, too, the glow of the creature's headlamp, moving away from them, toward the stern. There would be control wires there, access to the engines, a thousand ugly possibilities, and he hefted the rigger's knife. "Let's go."

Mitch studied the controls, trying not to look ahead into the darkness of the Channel. One wheel for the rudder, currently jammed and unresponsive. One wheel for the elevators. It had a little more play, but he hadn't tried to do more than get the nose up a little, concentrating instead on getting them turned toward Cherbourg.

"Otto," Federman said faintly.

Mitch didn't look back, didn't want to see the life ebbing from him. A nice kid, they'd spoken in the smoking room, the pilot delighted with his new job, the new ship.

"What was that?" Jerry asked, gently.

"Autopilot," Federman said. "Otto—a joke...."

"Yes," Jerry said. "How do we disengage it?"

"The column at the end of the chart table," Federman said. "The lever, red handle. Pull that, then the foot brake."

"Ok," Jerry said, dubiously.

"You'll have to do it, Jer," Mitch said. "If that frees up the rudder—"

"Yeah, I get it," Jerry said. He staggered to his feet, limped toward the chart table that stood behind the pilots' position. The autopilot was obvious once it was pointed out, a duralumin cylinder that rose maybe a foot above the tabletop. The controls were on the far side, from Mitch's perspective, and Jerry stood for a moment, studying them.

"The red-handled lever," he said. Federman must have confirmed it because he went on, "Ok, there it is. And then the pedal."

Mitch put one hand on the rudder, kept his other hand on the elevator wheel. "Go ahead."

He heard a crunch of gears, presumably Jerry hauling back on the lever, and then a heavy metallic thunk.

"Ok," Jerry said again, sounding nervous, and Mitch felt the elevator move. The rudder stayed frozen, though, even when he pulled harder. He took a chance, hauled on it with both hands, but it still wouldn't budge. He felt the nose pitch down, and grabbed for the elevator wheel again. There was a bubble gauge on the panel in front of him, and an artificial horizon, and he concentrated on bringing them both level, the airship sluggish under his hands. That might just be the size and the lack of normal lift, but he didn't like it.

"I have elevator control," he said, "but no rudder." He craned his neck to see the gas board, but it was too far away to read the dials clearly. "Jerry, how's the pressure looking?"

There was a silence, and when Jerry spoke, his voice was a little higher than normal. "Um. Ok. Looks like we're still losing hydrogen, but the helium cells seem to be Ok."

"Good," Federman said, "We can fly on that…." His voice trailed off alarmingly, and Mitch heard Jerry stumble across to him.

"Easy now," Jerry said. "Gently."

"A good thing we went with Mr. Kershaw's design," Federman said, more strongly. "One man if he must can fly it…."

"A very good thing," Jerry said, soothingly. There was a rustle of fabric, and Federman gave a grunt of pain.

Mitch looked at the altimeter. Six hundred feet, and steady—or maybe not. The needle was creeping down, slow but inexorable, and he turned the elevator wheel to lift the nose a few more degrees. Not too far, the frame wouldn't stand an abrupt angle, but enough to point the big ship upward. 590 feet.

"Hey, Federman," he said. "If I'm still losing altitude, what do I do?"

There was no answer, and Mitch risked a glance over his shoulder. Federman lay with his eyes closed, Jerry fumbling with the bloody fabric over his chest.

"Federman," Mitch said again. They were holding altitude a little better, but the nose was starting to swing north. A wind out of the south, he guessed, and pulled as hard as he could on the rudder. It gave, just a little, and *Independence* swung back to its original heading.

Jerry said something, voice soft and gentle—repeating the question in German, Mitch realized. There was a pause, and then Federman answered, gasping, and Jerry shushed him.

"Ja, so, Junge. Bist du still."

Mitch looked back again, saw Jerry smoothing the hair away from Federman's forehead. The pilot was breathing in short, painful gasps, and Jerry's face was set and tired.

"What did he say?" Mitch asked. "Come on, Jerry."

"Ballast," Jerry answered. "Drop ballast to gain height. And—dynamic lift? Something to do with the engines?"

"Yes," Mitch said. That he understood, increasing the engines' power and lifting the nose, spending speed to get lift. But in an airship—there was no natural lift, they'd still need gas—"Jerry, you'll have to drop ballast for me. I think it's that panel to the left."

"Ok," Jerry said, and hauled himself to his feet again. "Yes, Ok, this is it. It's water ballast. There are four, no, six tanks, it looks like they're along the keel? I assume I want to drop water evenly from all of them?"

"If you can manage it," Mitch said. "I can compensate a little."

"From the middle first," Jerry said, "and then the ends…."

"Now would be good, Jerry."

"Ok."

Out of the corner of his eye, Mitch saw Jerry pull a brass lever. There was a distant rumble, more felt than heard, and Jerry hastily pushed it back up to the closed position. He did it again, and then a third time. This time the *Independence* pitched up, and Mitch shoved the elevator wheel over to bring the nose down again. A pencil rolled off the chart table—the first time in the entire trip that there had been the slightest unsteadiness.

"More?" Jerry asked.

Mitch looked at the altimeter. 560 feet. "Yeah."

Jerry pulled three more levers in quick succession. The *Independence* staggered, but Mitch had been expecting it this time, and she leveled out almost at once. They were gaining altitude again: 575, 590, 605, leveling out at 620 feet. Mitch allowed himself a sigh of relief. *Independence* would fly on helium alone, Federman had said. If they could keep this altitude, they could probably make Le Havre....

"Shit," Jerry said. "We're losing pressure in cell 14."

Lewis had taken off his headlamp, wrapped it in his handkerchief to muffle the light. He kept it pointed at the catwalk, his hand cupped to hide as much of the glow as possible. Alma had turned her light off entirely and had her hand on his belt as they felt their way toward the stern of the ship. Maybe it was his imagination, but he thought the dark had faded a little, that they were creeping toward dawn. Or maybe his eyes had just gotten used to the dark. The airship shivered under them, a strange, uneven movement, and Alma's hand tightened for an instant.

They had left the passenger compartments behind long ago, and the crew's quarters as well, and had reached the part of the ship where the heavy cargo was carried, holds like boxes bolted into the curve of the frame below them. Most of them were empty, Lewis saw, or only lightly loaded: passengers might make the trip for status, but hard-headed businessmen weren't going to risk their money on a maiden voyage.

He paused, scanning the catwalk ahead, searching for the flicker of light that had marked the creature's progress. For a long moment there was nothing, and then it came again, further away, and—higher? Yes, higher, he thought, and in the same instant realized that they were approaching the tail. The gas cells were smaller here, where the frame tapered toward the huge fins that held the elevators and rudder. The light vanished, hidden behind the curve of the gas cell, and Lewis risked uncovering his own light.

"He's going up into the tail," he said, and Alma switched on her headlamp.

She made a small noise of surprise, and Lewis looked down to see a car—a Peerless coupe, fabric roof folded and secured with half a dozen straps—strapped in the cargo bay below them.

"Oh, Henry," Alma said, and her breath caught on the last word. "Wait—what's that?"

Lewis looked where she was pointing, and his own breath came short. Below the catwalk, below and beyond the box that held the car, a body lay on the fabric of the hull. It was struggling, he thought, adrenaline jolting through him, and then he realized that the body wasn't moving, at least not of its own volition. What he had taken at first glance for blood or oil was a tear in the hull, slowly spreading wider as the weight of the body stretched the overburdened fabric. It was like any airplane fabric, you could walk on it if it was whole, but get a rip, a tear—a bullet hole or two—and the taut fabric split at the slightest stress.

"Oh, my God," Alma said, and caught his arm. "Lewis—"

"There's nothing we can do," he said. The tear was spreading, disappearing beneath the body's legs. They dropped, first one, then the other, and then the body tilted forward, vanished into the night.

"Oh, God," Alma said again.

Lewis crossed himself. "He was dead already," he said, and hoped it was true.

Relieved of the body's weight, the tearing stopped, but now the edges of the fabric were flapping in the wind of the airship's passage. Smaller tears were starting to appear, the edges of the fabric shredding: it would go soon enough, Lewis knew, ripping away until it reached a stable point. Probably at the girders, he guessed, and was glad the hull didn't need to be intact to fly. As long as they could keep Henry from releasing any more of the lifting gas, the *Independence* would stay in the air.

"Damn," Alma said, and he looked back to see her studying the valve panel at the base of the gas cell. "He's jammed it open."

"Hell." Lewis looked from her to the catwalk curving up into the dark of the tail. Henry, the creature, had to be stopped before he did anything worse, but if they could fix the valve—

"Go," Alma said, and tugged the wrench out of her belt. "I'm going to see if I can close this. And then I'll go forward and tell the captain what's going on."

It wasn't a great idea, but it was the best one they had. "Ok," Lewis said, and started along the catwalk. It rose under his feet, curving up as the airship's body tapered, and he paused to cover his light again. In the renewed darkness, he thought he saw movement up toward the tail, movement and then the quick flash of a light. It had to be Henry, anyone else would be showing a headlamp, and Lewis started forward, whispering an Act of Contrition. Knife against gun was not good odds, but he ought at least to be able to keep the bastard too busy to do any more harm.

"I can't close the valves from here," Jerry said. He didn't look at the dead man on the floor, couldn't spare him the sorrow. "We're still losing pressure in cells 14 and 15."

"Ok," Mitch said. "And the hydrogen?"

"Gone, mostly," Jerry answered. "I've got zero readings in all the hydrogen cells." *Independence* would fly on helium alone, Federman had said, but not if they kept losing gas at this rate.

"I don't suppose the radio works?"

Jerry looked over his shoulder. "The tubes are smashed."

"Goddammit!" Mitch controlled himself instantly, his hands never moving on the elevator controls.

"Do we drop more ballast?" Jerry asked. It was the only thing he'd figured out how to do that might be of the slightest utility.

Mitch hesitated. "Not yet," he said at last. "Does the telephone work?"

Jerry blinked—what, call up Paris and ask the operator to send a fleet of rescuers? And an exorcist, perhaps? Then he saw what looked like a field telephone set up beside the dials that displayed engine output. Or something like a field telephone, he thought, as he limped over to it. The ones he remembered from the War threw off too many sparks. "Maybe."

"Can you reach the engineers? Anyone?"

"I'll try," Jerry said. There was a handwritten list taped to the cabinet that housed the batteries: short-short-long was the port-side rear nacelle. He turned the crank, the old skills coming back, but there was no answer. He tried again, without result, then rang long-short-long for the forward starboard nacelle. This time the line clicked, and a voice said, "Captain?"

Jerry hesitated. "Captain Brooks has been shot."

"Oh, good job, Jerry," Mitch said. "Reassure them right away."

"What? Who is this?" the voice in the telephone demanded.

"A friend of Mr. Kershaw's," Jerry said. "Someone's trying to sabotage the ship."

"Yeah, I know that. How do I know it's not you?"

You don't. Jerry bit back the words as probably counterproductive, looked over his shoulder at Mich. "What do you need me to tell this guy?"

"Tell him we're losing gas," Mitch answered. "I need more power from the engines, everything he can give me to keep from losing any more altitude than we have to."

The telephone was squawking at him again, and Jerry said, "Be quiet. We're in a serious situation here. We are losing gas—have lost hydrogen and are losing helium. We're losing altitude, and we need more power."

There was a little silence, and the voice said, "I told you we were descending." There was a pause. "Ok, I'm upping the rpms, but I can't give you any more without unbalancing the ship."

"Can you contact the other engine nacelles?" Jerry asked.

"Are you kidding? Look, you're in the control room, you call them." There was another pause. "What the hell's going on?"

"There's a guy with a gun loose on the ship," Jerry said. "Jam your door closed and stay out of trouble."

"Jesus," the man said.

"Stand by," Jerry said. "I'm going to try to get the other engines to answer." He hung up without waiting for a response, turned the crank again. Short-long-short was the forward nacelle on the port side, and to his surprise, he got an answer. He gave the same orders, watched the rpms creep up again on the dials, and tried the aft nacelles again, with no result.

"That's feeling a little better," Mitch said.

"You're getting, um, 1480, 1490 rpms on both the forward engines," Jerry said. "The guy I talked to said he couldn't give you more or the ship would go out of balance."

"It'll do for now," Mitch said. "Where are we with the helium?"

Jerry stumbled back across the control car, bracing himself on the chart table. "Um. Pressure's still falling in cells 15 and 16. The leak's stopped on 14. It's holding at sixty percent of full."

Mitch adjusted the elevator wheel. "Well, that's something." He didn't sound convinced, and Jerry didn't believe it either.

Lewis eased forward along the catwalk as it rose into the tail girders, the muffled headlamp tucked in his pocket, knife in his hand. Outside, dawn was coming, the fabric lightening enough for him to make out the shapes of the girders, the patterns of guywires and crosspieces and the access ladders. He could see the creature, too, a shadow moving against the bigger shadows, a flash of light against the girders. It was heading for something, he thought, it had a destination in mind—the control wires, for a bet, the cables that moved the rudder and elevators. They'd be most accessible here, at the point where they exited the hull.

And that needed to be stopped. He placed his back securely against a girder, looked up to study the pattern of ladders and catwalk and frame. Going up the ladders was the last thing he wanted to do, just asking the thing to shoot him, but there didn't look to be a good alternative. Up to the central catwalk, then, and across. With luck, the creature would be looking for him on the lower level, and wouldn't expect him coming from his own level.

He swung himself onto the first ladder, moving as quickly and as quietly as he could manage, his skin crawling. The thing was out there somewhere; if it saw him, he was a sitting duck, trapped in the ladder's cage. The words of the Ave rolled in his mind, matching the rhythm of his climb: Ave Maria, gratia plena…. And Diana, too, if she was listening: he could use all the help he could get, all the hunter's stealth he could muster.

At the top of the ladder, he rolled out onto the catwalk, crouched for a moment to catch his breath and his bearings. The light was definitely stronger now, the hull paler gray, the frame and the ladders dark against it. He could see what had to be the controls for the rudder and elevators, a tangle of dark shapes against the fabric of the hull. Henry was there, the creature using him, using his knowledge of the ship to destroy it, a moving shadow busy in the dark.

Light spilled then, a section of the hull rolling up and away, letting in the dawn. Lewis could see Henry's body silhouetted against it, realized he was going not for the internal controls but for the cables and gears that lay outside the hull: harder to fix, in the little time they had left.

He shoved himself to his feet, not daring to think, hurried down the catwalk, heading not for the ladder, but for the girders themselves. They came together here in a final frame ring no wider than the height of a man. If he could pull himself along them—he stretched, found a handhold and hauled himself up. Yes, there were handholds, the holes that lightened the metal spaced comfortably, and he dragged himself up onto the beam, let himself slide along its length until he reached the final ring. Henry was still stooped over something outside the hull, leaning out into the air, and Lewis reached for the rigger's knife. But, no, he couldn't be sure of his aim, not with a knife he didn't know, and instead he fumbled in his pocket and drew out a handful of change. He slung it at Henry with all his strength, heard the grunt of surprise and the tinkling of the coins falling through the girders, ducked behind the girder as Henry turned, gun ready.

"Kershaw!" Lewis shouted. His voice was distorted by the hanging fabric, but Henry leveled the gun anyway and Lewis ducked as low as he could behind the nearest girder. Henry fired, once, twice, and then the hammer clicked on an empty cylinder. Lewis launched himself across the frame and scrambled onto the catwalk, but the creature was already charging, gun clubbed in his hand. Lewis blocked the first blow with his forearm, tried to bring up the knife, and the creature struck again, grazing his forehead as he dodged back and away. Lewis fell back, and the thing pushed past him before he could strike, footsteps suddenly loud on the catwalk. It was running down the middle of the ship, toward the bow, the gas cells, and Lewis swore and started after him.

"Kershaw!" he shouted again. "You can run, but we'll find

you. We know where to bind you—"

It was darker under the gas cells, and he stopped to pull out his headlamp, switched it on again. He risked taking off the handkerchief, shone the light ahead of him, but there was no sign of the creature. He took a deep breath, and plunged further into the dark.

Chapter Twenty-one

Mitch hauled on the rudder again, worked it back and forth in the hope that somehow that might free up whatever was jamming the controls. It wasn't anything in the control car, he was pretty sure of that, guessed it was somewhere in the tail, maybe in the rudder gears themselves, but that didn't matter unless he could actually fix it. They were still losing altitude: 450 feet now, and he could see the waves distinctly in the rising light, along with the first shadow of the coast. But that wasn't the problem, or wasn't the worst problem. The wind had been rising with the dawn, steady out of the southeast, and the airship wanted to turn with it, turn north and west and away from the land. He risked letting go of the elevator again, used both hands on the rudder, and thought it gave a little before the nose dropped too far and he had to grab the elevator wheel again.

"Jerry!"

"Yes."

Mitch looked over his shoulder. "I need your help here."

"Ok." Jerry stumbled toward him, bracing himself on the chart table and the back of the captain's chair. He looked like hell, Mitch thought, gray-faced and unshaven and determined, and guessed he himself didn't look any better.

"Take the elevator wheel," Mitch said. "Hold it just like this."

"Ok," Jerry said again, and braced his hip against the pilot's chair. He took the wheel gingerly, blinked as he assessed the resistance, and then nodded. "Ok, I—I think I've got it."

"Keep the bubble in the center," Mitch said. "See there? Just like a level."

Jerry nodded, and Mitch slid out of the chair, took the rudder in both hands. He planted his feet, turned the wheel as hard as he could left and right and left again. It barely moved, maybe an inch or two of play, but he thought as he tried it again that it was moving just a little more. Yes, he was sure of it, it was moving further—if there was something in the gears, maybe this was chewing it up, giving him a little more control. There was a warning twinge in his groin, the old scars pulling, but he ignored it, tried a few short hard turns to the right. Pain blossomed, but he thought the wheel gave just a little more.

"Mitch," Jerry said.

"Keep the bubble in the center," Mitch gasped, and threw all his strength against the rudder. Yes, this time he was sure it moved, and he turned it back and forth again. There was maybe a twenty-degree arc of movement, and he turned it hard again.

"Mitch, I'm losing it," Jerry said.

"Hold on just a little longer—"

"I can't." Jerry's voice was rising again. "Damn! I'm sorry—"

There was a slithering sound, Jerry's leg slipping on the metal floor, and Mitch caught the elevator wheel. "It's Ok," he said. "I'm not going to get much more rudder."

Jerry pulled himself away, swearing at himself, and Mitch slid back into the pilot's chair. His belly was on fire: he'd torn something, all right, and he was willing to bet he'd be pissing blood for a day or two. If he lived that long. He put that thought aside and checked the instruments again. 410 feet, and nose down. He adjusted the elevator wheel, brought the *Independence* slowly back to a nose-up attitude, looked at the heading. With the rudder pushed as far right as he could get it, they were just maintaining the direct course for land. If they could gain some altitude. At this rate of descent, they'd never make it.

"Jerry," he said again, and hoped his voice sounded more or less normal. "I need you to drop some more ballast."

"Ok," Jerry said. He dragged himself to the panel and began flipping levers. There was the shudder of the water leaving the tanks, and Mitch touched the elevator again to compensate. *Independence* steadied, but she didn't rise.

"More."

"Ok."

Mitch stared at the altimeter, willing the needle upward. It moved, but only slowly: 420 feet. 425. "More."

"That'll empty the tanks," Jerry said.

"Do it."

"Ok." Jerry flipped the levers, left them in the open position. "That's it," he said. "That's all there is."

"Ok," Mitch said. 430 feet, and—steady? No, falling, but more slowly. Maybe it would be enough. He felt as though someone had dipped him in acid from the waist down, the old injuries screaming. "Jerry. Give me your tie."

"What?" Jerry was already loosening the knot, though, pulled it free of his collar. "Here."

Mitch looked at it and decided he wasn't going to be able to manage. "Actually, you do it. I want you to pull the rudder wheel as far to the right as it will go and tie it in place."

"All right," Jerry said, fingers busy. "Are you all right?"

In spite of himself, Mitch snickered. "I'm crashing an airship, Jerry. How are you?"

There was a moment of silence, and then Jerry snorted. "Idiot. Now what?"

"Hope we're light enough to make the coast."

Alma ducked out from under the last of the helium cells—number 9, she thought it was, a little aft of center. She had heard the noise of the ballast releasing, not just once, but several times, and guessed the pilots were trying to compensate for the leaking gas. She'd managed to get a couple of the valves partially closed, but on most of the cells the damage was too great, and she was beginning to think it was a waste of time. She hadn't seen Lewis since she'd left him in the tail, and that was a cold knot of terror that she refused to consider, refused to allow into her thoughts. Instead, she continued forward and gave a gasp of relief as she saw a telephone station. The buttons were clearly labeled, and she pressed the one that said "control car." The bell jangled in her ear, but there was no answer.

There had to be a pilot, she thought. She'd heard the ballast drop, someone had done that—someone was flying this thing—

"Yes?"

"Jerry?" She heard her voice scale up with shock.

"Al? Where are you?"

"Lower catwalk, between cells eight and nine," she said. "What are you—"

"The thing killed the captain and the pilots," Jerry said. "Mitch is flying us."

Oh, thank God. They were alive, all more or less accounted for—except for Lewis. She said, "Where—how bad is it?"

There was a mumble of voices, Jerry presumably consulting Mitch. "Not good. We're at 210 feet and Mitch can't stop the descent. We're still about a mile off the coast." Jerry paused. "There's a nice sand beach, if we could only get there."

"Can you drop ballast?" she asked.

"We've already dropped it all," Jerry said, with some asperity.

"What about the passengers?"

"I have no idea," Jerry said. "I managed to get hold of a steward, told him to deal with it."

And that was the right choice, Alma admitted. Worry about getting the ship down in one piece, that was the main thing.

"Have you seen Henry?" Jerry asked.

"Lewis went after him," Alma said. "He—the creature—shot a bunch of the crew." She shook her head. "He's the least of our worries, right?"

"Right." There was another pause before Jerry spoke again. "Mitch says we'll be in the water in twenty minutes if we can't gain some height."

The ballast was gone. What else could they drop? Cargo? "The car," she said aloud. "Jerry, tell Mitch I can drop one more thing, probably 700, 800 pounds."

She replaced the handset without waiting for his answer, hurried back down the catwalk toward the cargo sections.

It had been getting lighter for a while now, must be almost dawn. She could even read the numbers on her watch—4:45—and colors were seeping back into the world, the red of the instrument panels, the green of her slacks, the oxblood browns of the steamer trunks on the cargo pads below. Overhead, the gas cells looked weirdly shrunken, the lower parts of the cells hanging loose in their netting.

She heard footsteps then, coming toward her, and flattened

herself against the rope railing and lifted the wrench. Hopefully the gas bags would help conceal her—but, no, she knew those steps, and she risked calling.

"Lewis?"

"Al?"

The footsteps stopped, and she stepped out onto the catwalk, the wrench still ready just in case. It was Lewis, though, Lewis alone, and she sagged with relief.

"I lost him," he said. There was a bruise on his forehead, and a streak of blood over his eye, but otherwise he looked unharmed.

"Never mind." She caught his hand, and pulled him after her along the catwalk. "We've got to get that car overboard."

He didn't hesitate, swung himself down into the box that held the car. Beyond it, Alma could see the opening where the fabric of the hull had been torn away, a huge square that stretched from one girder to the next. She could see the ocean through it, waves entirely too close. Jerry had said 200 feet, but she doubted they were that high.

"The floor swings down to make a ramp," Lewis shouted. He reached into the car's open body, released the handbrake. "Once I get her loose—"

They could drop the ramp and the car would fall free. "I'll help," Alma said, and ducked under the rail to let herself down onto the platform. Here for the first time she could feel movement in the ship, the faintest wobble and shimmy of the ramp. She'd felt worse in her own planes, she told herself, and stooped to unfasten the ties.

"Cut them," Lewis called, and she nodded, reached for the knife he had given her, and began sawing at the leather straps. It seemed to take forever, hacking and pulling, but finally the first one parted, and she began working grimly at the next one. She could see the sea out of the corner of her eyes, rising closer, could even smell the salt air. Another strap gone, a guard chain released. She started for the rear wheel, saw Lewis already slicing through the first strap.

"The ramp release?" she called, and he pointed.

"There, I think."

Yes, that was it, heavy greased rope caught in a brake, pulleys running overheard. Lewis cut the final strap, scrambled back to join her. She could see where the hinges lay, a foot or so from the end of the platform: it should be enough to stand on, but the ramp had been designed to lower gently, its end traveling only a few feet to the ground. Let it go like this, with nothing to stop it, and the whole thing could tear loose—

"I'll boost you to the catwalk," Lewis said.

She shook her head. "Hold my waist."

He frowned for a second, then nodded, wrapped one arm tight around her waist and hooked his other arm and a leg into the holes in the nearest girder. Alma hauled back on the brake lever. For a second, she thought it wasn't going to move, but then the drum turned, the weight of the platform and the car pulling the free end down toward the gap in the hull. The drum spun, rope whining, and the ramp fell away, the car rolling and then sliding, tumbling backward off the end of the ramp. It hit a girder with a resounding crash, and vanished through the hole in the hull. She heard it hit the water, a heavy splash. More fabric split where it had hit the girder, tears running through the skin like cracks in ice. But they weren't falling any more, she thought. They might even be rising—

"Come on, Al," Lewis said. "We've got to get forward."

"What?" She was moving anyway, dragging herself past the dangling ramp, Lewis's arm still steadying her, his body close behind her as they pulled themselves up the ladder to the catwalk.

"We've got to get forward," he said again. "We don't want to be here when we hit."

She blinked again, and then understood. There was nothing here between the frame and the catwalk, just the duralumin girders that would crumple like paper when they hit the ground. They needed to be forward, where the crew and passenger compartments strengthened the lower part of the hull.

"Yes," she said, and let him drag her forward. A horn went off somewhere toward the bow, an urgent, two-toned warning, and they began to run.

"Flares?" Mitch asked.

"Done," Jerry said.

The alarm was howling: no need to ask about that. Whatever could be done for the passengers was being done. Alma had bought them a few hundred yards, maybe just enough. "Tell the mechanics to get out of the engines," Mitch said, and a moment later heard Jerry relaying the order over the telephone. "Leave me full power, and get the hell out. Then you sit down."

The sun was up before them, their shadow racing over the water. Ahead rose the beach south of the Le Havre airfield, a strip of sand maybe a hundred feet wide, and a rugged sandy hill rising up from it. Not what he would have chosen to crash into, but better than the water. The tail would be in the channel, but the passenger sections would be on land. Light flashed above the airfield, flares answering their own, clearing the field for an emergency landing. He pulled on the elevator wheel again, struggling for more lift. Just a little more, just enough to clear the hill, just enough to reach the runway....

There was nothing left. *Independence* had given him everything she had, she wasn't going anywhere but down. She was fighting it still, he was fighting it, but there wasn't enough gas left to carry the heavy frame any longer.

There were people on the brow of the hill, waving and shouting, but they'd have to look after themselves. There were rocks in the water, he saw them now as they dropped lower, a big cluster that would rip the control car right off the frame. He tugged the rudder left, praying that the wind he'd been fighting would help them now, felt the ship start to swing. They passed it, twenty-five feet up and a yard to the right. Sand ahead, a hundred feet of sand. Mitch released the rudder, hauling the elevators up a final time, and dropping the tail. He heard a splash, felt the airship stagger, and then the nose fell hard, slamming against the hillside. The windows shattered, and he flung up his arms to cover his head and face. He heard, felt the frame snapping behind him, but the control car stayed intact. He lifted his head slowly, saw Jerry staring at him from the captain's chair.

"Are you all right?"

Mitch considered the question. He was bruised, there were

some cuts on his arms—and maybe on his scalp, there was a spot that stung like fire—and the old wound in his gut clawed at him, but they were alive. "Yeah. Come on, we've got to find Al and Lewis."

The alarm was wailing as they ran forward along the catwalk. Past the cargo bays, past the fuel tanks—please, God, well past the fuel tanks, Alma thought, and kept running, their feet loud on the metal grate. The ship was wallowing under them, heavy, heaving movements, the nose pointing up so that they were running uphill. It wouldn't be long now, she could tell from the sounds, from the way the catwalk pitched up. Lewis grabbed her by the waist, pulled her down to the grating and pinned her under him, covering her body with his own. The nose jerked up—he'd known it was coming, she realized, seen the moment, and she squeezed her eyes tight against his shoulder. There was a sound like a thousand guitar strings snapping, and the catwalk slapped her back, knocking the wind from her. More crashes followed, and then the groan of bending metal. Under them the catwalk bent and buckled, but Lewis held them firm, his head pressed against her neck. The alarm cut out, and there was just a last screech of metal. And then, blessedly, silence. The air smelled of salt and spilled diesel oil. Alma caught her breath, coughing, and Lewis eased his weight a little, careful still to keep hold of the grating. They were lying at an angle, she realized, and as she struggled to sit up, she saw that the catwalk had been torn from its brackets only ten feet behind where they lay. It had twisted, too, and she grabbed the nearest stanchion for balance.

"Lewis?" Her voice was a croak; she swallowed hard, and tried again. "Are you all right?"

"Yeah...." He pushed himself up and off her, going to his knees. The cut on his head was bleeding again, a new bright thread trickling down into his eyebrow. "You?"

"Yeah." She sat up, muscles protesting, feeling the bruises on her back and sides. Beneath them, the frame was solid, only a little crushed, but toward the stern the frame was shattered, caved in around the tattered remains of the gas bags. The frame had broken completely in two toward the tail, which, she realized, was attached to the forward part of the ship only by the fabric covering.

Lewis had pulled himself to his feet, and was surveying the wreckage. "This way," he said, and pointed.

Alma took his hand, and let him help her up. The tilted catwalk felt stable enough underfoot, but she wanted out of the broken shell. One of the frame rings had cracked, pulling the girders apart, and it would be possible to climb down its slope to the ground. Or, rather, to the torn fabric of the hull, the waves already starting to seep through, and Lewis held up the rigger's knife.

"We'll cut our way out."

Climbing down the girder was easier than it had looked. Alma balanced on the girder's last point, the water lapping at her toes, while Lewis slashed a hole in the heavy fabric. It parted reluctantly, and Lewis climbed out onto the sand and turned to steady her. She braced herself on his forearms and he swung her out and down, so that she landed on the dry sand above the lapping of the waves. She giggled then, unable to stop herself.

"What?"

"I've just been in an airship crash, and I didn't even get my feet wet...."

Lewis smiled, but wrapped his arm around her waist, offering support.

"I'm not hysterical," Alma said.

"I know. But we should keep moving. In case Henry—" He didn't finish the thought, but Alma nodded, and they struggled further up the beach, stopped at the base of the hill to look back. People were streaming down the rugged slope, civilians and men in uniform, and Alma guessed they must have come down near the field at Le Havre. *Independence* lay broken in the low surf, the nose a good third of the way up the hill, bent up at a strange angle. The tail was shredded, sinking in the deeper water offshore, but most of the passenger section was on land, and already people were climbing out of the windows, helped by crew and by the rescuers from Le Havre. The control car had hit the sand just at the base of the hill. All the windows were broken out, but the car itself seemed intact, which should mean that Mitch and Jerry were all right....

"My God," Lewis said, and she clutched his hand. It was hard to believe, looking at the wreck, that anyone could have survived. But there were a dozen people on the sand beside the observation car, people she recognized, had spoken to; there was Celena Moore, being helped down by a pair of French army officers, and the Sparkling Starlet, to her credit, was holding someone else's child. The older couple from the launch were standing arm in arm, staring up at the wreckage.

And then she saw them, Mitch steadying Jerry on the yielding ground. They saw her, too, and Mitch lifted his free hand and waved. Alma felt tears sting her eyes as she hurried toward them and grabbed them both in a tight embrace.

"Easy, Al," Mitch said. "We're Ok."

"Are you?" Alma let them go and leaned back to look at them. There was blood in Mitch's hair, and they both looked wrung out. "You look terrible."

"We're all right," Jerry said. He looked back at the wreck. "The—thing?"

"Got away from me," Lewis said. "I'm sorry."

"No," Alma said. "You did what mattered, kept him from doing anything more to the ship."

"We wouldn't have gotten this far without you," Mitch said.

"Anyway, what we said before still holds," Jerry said. "We can't kill it—well, we could maybe kill Henry, but it would still jump."

"And that means Italy?" Mitch asked, with a groan. "Oh, my Christ, the tablet."

"Right here," Jerry said, and tapped his jacket pocket. "I thought it was better not to let it out of my clutches."

"Genius," Mitch said, and Jerry rolled his eyes.

Alma took a breath, looked them all up and down. Bedraggled, yes, but a few minutes' work in the train station's restrooms would make them presentable. "Italy," she said. "Do any of you have any money?"

Mitch fumbled in his pocket, checked his wallet. "I've got the rest of what you gave me, Al. A little over a hundred, American."

"And I've got about fifty dollars," Jerry said, "but no passport." He gave Mitch a wry smile. "Not so much of a genius after all."

“I don’t have my passport either,” Alma said. “We’ll have to manage.”

Lewis tucked his wallet back into his pocket. “Ten bucks. And a fifty-franc note I kept for luck.”

“If we can get to Paris,” Jerry said, and frowned. “We do go through Paris, right? I know someone who can take care of our papers for us. And we can also pawn things there. We’ll need more than a hundred and sixty dollars to make this work.”

Alma nodded. “All right,” she said. “Let’s go.”

Chapter Twenty-two

Fortunately trains left Le Havre for Paris nearly every hour during the day. They made the first train of the morning with ten minutes to spare, Mitch buying tickets in rusty French, but with a charming smile that encouraged the girl at the ticket counter to see nothing else. They looked terrible, like bedraggled drifters, but there was nothing to be done about it. They could clean up in the washroom in the station a certain amount, but there was nothing to be done about the tear in Lewis' pants, or the blood on Mitch's shirt. Water would not entirely remedy that.

There were no empty compartments, and so the four of them had to split up, Mitch politely begging the pardon of an old woman, a young woman and a little girl of three for intruding on their family outing. By Rouen they had ascertained that he had flown in the Great War, and he had ascertained that they were returning to Paris with grandmere so that she might stay some time and assist in the upcoming months until the accouchement. It was all quite friendly. Mitch hoped the other three had found compartments as agreeable. Lewis had looked pretty worn out.

Mitch hurt. The adrenaline surge of action had worn off. He'd torn something loose and he knew it, shifting around uncomfortably in his seat. He excused himself to the ladies and went to the washroom. Not a surprise to see blood in his urine. Mitch grimaced and washed his hands carefully. It would pass. Hopefully it didn't mean anything important.

When he came in the young woman looked up keenly. "You are troubled, M. Sorley?"

"Quite well," Mitch said, taking his seat again very gingerly. "A twinge, Madame."

She had kind brown eyes beneath a pink cloche, and she

reached under the seat to her bag, pulling out a bottle of Calvados. "It is for my husband, but he would not mind having a drink with you. He lost his right arm in the Marne, and I am certain you should drink together were you here."

"I couldn't possibly," Mitch began, surprised at how well the pleasantries came back to him. If he just didn't move much....

"We know pain," her mother said brusquely, taking the bottle and pouring a drink into a water glass. "Drink."

"Thank you, Madame," Mitch said, and downed it in one gulp.

After that the world was a kinder place. Indeed, by the time they pulled into Paris at Gare du Nord two and a half hours later, Mitch was feeling a vast sense of peace. Which probably had a lot to do with Calvados and no sleep and adrenaline let down, but he'd take it where he could.

Mitch bid a warm goodbye to his compartment mates, and stood on the platform trying to get his bearings. He didn't think he'd been in this station before. He vaguely recollected that Paris had half a dozen, and this wasn't one he'd visited. People were getting off the train, the conductor politely assisting by opening compartment doors. This was the last stop for the train.

A man hurried by, pulling his hat brim down, an abstracted look on his face, and Mitch felt his heart skip. It could be wearing him. It had to be wearing someone. On the unlikely chance that Henry had survived the crash, surely he would be at the center of a firestorm of questions and investigations. Most likely Henry was dead. Either way, it would have jumped. And it could be anyone.

But there was no recognition in the man's face. His eyes slid past Mitch entirely and he vanished into the crowd.

"It could be anyone," Alma said at his elbow and Mitch jumped a half mile. She gave him a wan smile.

"How was your trip?" Mitch asked. Jerry was coming down the platform toward them, moving about as stiffly as Mitch thought he looked.

"Well enough. And you?"

"Fine," Mitch said.

Jerry joined them, his face nearly gray. "Do you suppose there's any chance of breakfast? Or lunch? It's noon and I haven't eaten."

"None of us have," Mitch said. "Let's find an exchange so I can change a ten and we'll get something to eat."

Alma glanced down the platform. Porters had rushed out to carry bags and now the disappointed ones were approaching people who obviously didn't need them asking to carry bags. She gave one of them a fish eye and he backed off. "I think we probably got out of Le Havre ahead of it," she said.

Jerry nodded, his voice low. "I didn't see anyone else at the station when we left who looked like they'd come straight from the crash site. Even the rescuers would be sandy or wet if nothing else."

"Probably a rescuer, not a passenger," Alma said thoughtfully.

Jerry nodded. "More resources. Most of the passengers won't have ready money or passports, and certainly aren't going to be able to leave for a while."

Lewis had joined them, coming and standing behind Alma, not quite touching. The cut on his head had stopped bleeding and he'd washed, but with a day's growth of beard and the fresh cut he looked like a deadly ruffian, a man to be given a wide berth. "How many of the passengers do you think survived?"

Alma saw Mitch's mouth tighten and gave him a quick glance. "More than would have without Mitch," she said. "There are a couple of dozen people alive in Le Havre this morning who would be dead now otherwise."

Mitch felt his chest unclench and he nodded stiffly.

"That's a win," Alma said gently, "And not a little one for them and everyone who loves them."

"Yeah," Mitch said. He'd take it that way. There was no point in dwelling on Federman or Brooks or any of the others. No point in dwelling on Henry. He'd think instead of the others, the white jacketed waiter, his dark skinned face seamed with blood from a cut on his head, carrying an unconscious woman out of the observation car, the pretty starlet with someone's crying child in her arms. Waiter and starlet both had people at home, people who would not have telegrams and tears, and at last a memorial service beside an empty coffin for someone lost at sea. He'd call it a win.

Jerry put his hand on his shoulder. "Let's go find some lunch," he said.

The Café des Pyramides had not gone up in the world since the War. When Jerry was a student it had hardly been particularly salubrious, and now they blended in far too well with the midday clientele. That would have been more encouraging, Jerry thought, if he hadn't overheard the waiters muttering to each other as he made his way back from the cabinets. They had decided, however, that if Lewis was a wanted man, it was better to keep serving him peacefully, and try to get the reward later, so Jerry thought they were safe for now. No need to mention that to the others, though.

He settled himself back at the table—far enough in the shadowed back of the café that their presence wouldn't discourage the other patrons, and added a tot of brandy to his coffee. Mitch was drinking his neat, and looked like he could use it.

"Ok," Lewis said, in a lowered voice that wasn't going to convince anyone of his good intentions. "Now what?"

"Money," Jerry said, succinctly. And then clean clothes, a valise to make them respectable, and a plan. He wasn't sure what he could do about the rest, but he was pretty sure he could get them cash. Lewis blinked, then unbuckled the strap of his wristwatch and slid it across the table.

"Ah," Mitch said, and did the same. He fumbled in his pockets, and came up with a silver penknife as well, slipped a gold signet ring from his finger.

"If I had any sense, I'd wear earrings," Alma said. She handed over her watch, and reached for the chain that held her wedding ring and the amulet.

"Not the ring," Lewis said, and Mitch nodded agreement.

"The chain, then," Alma said. "It's gold."

Jerry hesitated, but they would need every franc he could raise. And, God willing, they would redeem it all in the end. Four watches, his watch fob and chain, Alma's chain and the penknife.... It would have to do. He swept everything into his pocket, and pushed his chair back.

Lewis looked at him. "You know a reliable pawn shop? I like that watch."

"This is Paris," Jerry said. "We're going to need a little help."

"I'll come with you," Alma said. She glanced at Lewis, who gave her the smallest of nods.

"We'll be back in a couple of hours," Jerry said. "Stay here, and try not to get into any trouble."

Mitch gave him a tired grin. "Not much chance of that," he said.

The studio was only a Metro stop away, and a few blocks further down a narrow side street. Jerry hadn't remembered the cobbles as being this uneven, but then, he hadn't been back in Paris since he'd lost his leg. He hadn't really thought about the three flights of stairs up to Paul's garret, either, but he tipped his hat to acknowledge Mme. Flammand's snarl of greeting, and started up the first flight. Alma followed, with a wary glance over her shoulder.

"I hope her bark is worse than her bite."

"It never used to be."

Jerry was sweating by the time they reached the top floor, and his stump was starting to burn again. He rapped on the studio door with more force than he'd intended, and it was flung open in his face, a squat bear of a man scowling out at him.

"I told you—" He stopped abruptly, the glare turning to a grin. "Jerry? I thought you were in America for good."

"So did I," Jerry said, and they embraced.

Nothing had changed, Jerry thought, except for the one thing that mattered. Paul Vallerand now wore a patch over his right eye, and tinted glasses over that. He touched his cheek below his own eye. "You never thought to mention this."

Vallerand shrugged. "What was there to say? The war was hell for everyone."

"Your work?"

"I lose depth perception, I gain a new sense of composition," Vallerand said, and the boundless enthusiasm was there, unchanged. "Wait till you see. Look, together you and I make one entire pirate."

Jerry laughed in spite of himself. "Paul, you're mad."

"And this surprises you? But who is the lady?"

Jerry made the introductions quickly, and Vallerand waved his hand toward the back of the studio. A lanky redhead was sitting on the edge of a worktable, smoking, and an exquisitely posed model stood on the dais, a length of fabric held to her chest, the rest falling away to leave her back completely nude.

"You remember Robin Beriault," Vallerand said, and the redhead lifted his cigarette in greeting. "Ok, kid, that's it for today."

The model relaxed, wound the fabric deftly around herself—himself, Jerry realized—and slipped behind a screen. "It's good to see you again, Robin," he said.

"But what brings you to Paris?" Vallerand asked. "And—forgive me for asking—in this kind of shape. You look dreadful."

"I need your help," Jerry said frankly, and Vallerand waved him to a chair. He cleared another for Alma, and pulled over a carved chunk of wood that might have been intended for a footstool. The model emerged from behind the screen, a thin, ash-blond youth with an odd elegant face that went badly with his workman's clothes.

"Tomorrow?" he asked, and Vallerand nodded.

"Same time."

"Ok," the boy said, and let himself out.

"So," Vallerand said, as the door closed behind him. "Are you in trouble?"

"Not yet," Jerry said. "But I need money and papers for myself and Alma, and I was hoping you could help. We—were in a crash, and lost everything."

"Money," Vallerand began, shaking his head, and Jerry shook his head.

"Sorry, that was badly phrased. I need your help pawning some things."

"Oh, that I can do," Vallerand said. "Auntie's always happy to help. But papers—"

"What sort of papers?" Beriault asked, sliding off the table, and Vallerand threw up his hands.

"This is not the war, Robin. They arrest you for things like this."

Beriault shrugged one shoulder. "If they find out."

"We need to be able to travel," Jerry said. "To Italy. Alma speaks Italian, but no French. And you know me. Can you do anything for us?"

Beriault cocked his head to one side. "Yes. Yes, I can make up some identity cards—no, passports—that will work, I think. You'll have to be British, though. That's what I have."

"You promised you weren't doing that anymore," Vallerand said.

"I'm not." Beriault's face softened. "I swear, Paul. These are just the leftovers. Otherwise I'd have a lot more options."

Vallerand paused for a moment, then shook his head. "Ok. This once. But, Jerry, if you're caught—"

"We didn't get the papers here," Jerry said. "That's understood."

"Ok." Vallerand took a deep breath. "Ok, then. What have you got for Auntie?"

Jerry reached into his pocket, pulled out the bundle of watches and jewelry. Vallerand spread it out on the worktable and extracted Alma's chain. "I can't take that," he said. "Men can't pledge ladies' jewels. You know that."

"I didn't. It never came up," Jerry said, but he handed the chain back to Alma.

"Right," Vallerand said. "I'll be back in an hour or so. And in the meantime, Robin can do your passports."

"Thank you," Jerry said, and clasped Vallerand's hand.

"Thank me when you see what I can get you," the artist answered. "Auntie's not been as generous as she used to be."

Beriault was already rummaging in a pile of boxes stacked between the long windows. "Ah, here we are," he said, and pulled out what looked like a handful of passport folders. "It'll take me a bit to fill them out and do the stamps. Make yourselves comfortable—have a smoke, have a drink. We're out of coffee, but there's wine on the shelf. And you can pour me a glass while you're at it."

Jerry did as he was told, poured glasses for each of them, and he and Alma returned to their chairs. He stretched his leg, the stump aching, lifted his glass to Alma. "Salut."

"To you, too," she said. "You know some interesting people, Jerry."

"I knew Paul when I was in school," Jerry said. "He and Robin had a studio together then. Except Robin was the one with the money, because he was really good at drawing his own."

"I never did," Beriault said, without looking up. "Straight forgery only."

He'd spoken in French, and Jerry translated for Alma's benefit. "If you say so, Robin. But, anyway, I hoped they'd be able to help us."

Alma nodded. "I still say you know some interesting types." She paused. "Why did Mr. Vallerand keep talking about his aunt? I mean, even I know that much French, the plume de ma tante, and all that."

"Auntie is the Crédit Municipal," Jerry said. "The city pawnshop. It's a government monopoly here, Al, and if you want to borrow more than a few francs, you have to show your identity card and proof of residence. Which I don't have. So Paul will do it for me."

"Only in France," Alma said, and took another swallow of her wine. "Is that a Baedeker?"

Beriault waved a hand, and she collected the guidebook, buried herself in the timetables.

The passports were ready and drying in the sun by the time Vallerand returned. He handed over the money—Jerry whistled appreciatively at the amount—and with it a bag with bread and sausage and a bottle of wine. "For the train," he said, and Alma took a deep breath.

"Thank you," she said. "You've been—you're being so kind."

"A pleasure, Madame." Vallerand flourished a bow. "And one more thing." He disappeared behind a second, larger screen that hid his bed, returned with a pair of cheap cardboard suitcases. "Props," he said. "Take them. And perhaps Madame could wear this?"

He held up a plain gray frock, respectable and Parisian, and Alma took it gratefully.

"I could just kiss you, Monsieur."

Vallerand cocked his head, and Jerry translated. Vallerand laughed. "Please do!"

That didn't need translation. Alma grinned, and gave him a hug, then vanished behind the screen to change. Vallerand found her pumps as well, and a pair of cotton stockings for later; there was a second-hand store in the next block, a little out of their way, perhaps, but anything else they needed they could probably purchase there.

"Thank you," Jerry said, and embraced both men.

"Be careful," Vallerand said. "And tell me the story when it's over!"

"I'll do that," Jerry said, and let them out into the hall. It was awkward, trying to carry a suitcase and maneuver himself down the stairs, and Alma rolled her eyes and took it from him. He started to protest, and made himself stop. He couldn't afford for his pride to delay them.

The second-hand store was where Vallerand had said, and they bought spare shirts and underwear, then made their way back to the cafe. Lewis and Mitch were still there, the table covered now with the remains of a second meal, and Lewis was glowering at the waiter. Mitch gave them a look of relief, and pulled back his chair.

"Are we ready? These guys were getting a little antsy."

"We're ready," Alma said. "We've got a train to catch."

The train left Gare de Lyon at 6:40, winding its way slowly through suburbs, over iron trestle bridges and brick right of ways, until factories and apartment buildings gave way to trees and houses, branches hanging thick over the track in a canopy of spring leaves. The west slanting sun made a hypnotic play of light across them, flashing over the windows. Lewis put his head against the glass and slept.

He woke to darkness, his mouth feeling as if it had been stuffed with cotton. If he had dreamed he remembered nothing.

"Good morning, sleepy head," Mitch said. He was sitting on the seat across, only the small side light illuminating the newspaper he was reading. "Or should I say good night? Jerry and Alma wanted to talk without waking you up, so they're in the other compartment. Or were hours ago. It's coming up on midnight."

"Oh," Lewis said, still trying to get his bearings.

"We could fold the bunks out if you'd like to lie down and get comfortable," Mitch said.

"Ok." Lewis got up stiffly and moved things around. The two

seats folded into one lower bed while a top bunk pulled down from the wall, also exposing a second window high up.

Mitch moved like an old man, Lewis thought. "If you don't mind taking the upper..." he said.

"No, that's fine." Lewis' eye fell on the front page of the folded paper. He didn't read French, but the picture said it all. "Is that...."

"Deadly Airship Crash Kills Fourteen?" Mitch nodded. "That's *Independence*. On the front page of the late edition."

It certainly looked impressive in the picture, the broken body of the airship across the beach, tail section in the water, while French Marines scrambled over it.

"The *Independence*, a new American airship en route from New York to Paris, crashed early this morning at Le Havre," Mitch read aloud, translating as he went. "Fourteen people are confirmed dead, including both of the pilots and three of the engineers. Miraculously, only two of the passengers were killed, Mr. Palmer of Los Angeles, and Mrs. Grogan of New York, who was struck on the head. The other dead include numerous crew members. Four passengers remain missing. 'It is a miracle,' said M. Jourdain, President of the Air Safety Commission of France. 'Given the nature of the catastrophic failure, it is little short of a miracle that all aboard were not killed.' While initial search and rescue operations were conducted by the Marines of the Cruiser of War Marengo, currently berthed at Le Havre, responsibility has now been taken over by Sûreté."

Lewis blinked. "Isn't that police?"

"The equivalent of the Bureau of Investigation," Mitch said. "Which means they found a bunch of bodies with bullet holes and have a lot of questions about them. Notice they mention Palmer but don't mention he was shot."

Lewis nodded slowly.

"Mr. Henry Kershaw, the owner of the airship, remains in critical condition in a Le Havre hospital. Inspector Victor Colbert of Sûreté said, 'We hope that Mr. Kershaw will soon be able to talk with us and illuminate the circumstances of the accident.'"

"Oh boy," Lewis said.

"I have no idea what he'll say," Mitch said. "Except that he won't say 'I was possessed by a demon and crashed my own airship.'"

"Um, no," Lewis said. "I take it we're the four passengers who're missing?"

"I expect so," Mitch said, sitting down on the lower berth. "For now they probably assume we were killed and that our bodies are somewhere in the wreckage, or maybe pulled out to sea."

"For now," Lewis said. "And then what?"

"I don't know," Mitch said. "Show up at the American Embassy in Rome and profess utter amazement that anyone is looking for us? A lot depends on Henry."

"He could blame the whole thing on us," Lewis said. "It would get him off the hook."

"I'd like to think he wouldn't do that," Mitch said, the lines at the corners of his mouth tightening. "But it may not matter. Henry may die." He stretched out looking toward the window, his back to Lewis.

"Oh." Lewis remembered belatedly that they had been friends, back in the original lodge. He felt like he was going slow tonight.

He lay down on the upper bunk. After a moment Mitch turned the light out. Outside the window ghostly shapes of trees slid past under the moon. It was rising toward the full, gibbous and golden when the train flashed out of forests. Fields lay quiet. In the distance he could see the lights of a town. Trees again, a little river, the sounds of the wheels changing as they passed over the trestle. It was soothing. He should have fallen right to sleep, but he didn't.

Next door Alma was sharing the other compartment with Jerry. There wasn't anything in it. He believed her. Alma wouldn't lie to him about something like that, and if she did she wouldn't make up a story like this, like Jerry and Gil. She'd make up something more plausible, something less weird.

Mitch must have known, Lewis thought. Mitch had lived with them for years, close as the apartment over the garage. Surely he hadn't missed it if...if all this stuff was going on. And Mitch was a straight shooter.

"Did you know about Jerry?"

There was a sound below and a sigh, as though Mitch were turning over. "Alma told you, did she?"

"Yeah. And about Jerry and Gil." Lewis waited. He could feel his pulse pounding, the shadows of trees slicing through the compartment under the moon. He hesitated, looking for words. "Did it…bother you?"

"To each their own," Mitch said. His accent seemed more pronounced in the dark. "I don't reckon I get to go around telling other people how to live their lives. And Jerry's a good friend."

That last was a warning, Lewis thought. Jerry was his friend, and Mitch would tolerate questions but not insults. For a moment he wondered if Mitch…. But no. He'd seen the way Mitch looked at the pretty girl at the airfield in Los Angeles, like she was a forbidden treat. He always looked at women that way, at desk clerks and secretaries, even at the occasional pretty woman passenger, who he helped aboard with a special smile and a double dose of Southern courtliness.

"Was Alma happy?" Lewis blurted.

Mitch paused as though genuinely considering the question. "I think so. Leastways I never saw anything that made me think she was unhappy. She and Jerry have been like this, like brother and sister, or like two wives of the same man, just like Rachel and Leah. Or maybe it was more like Michal, David and Jonathan," Mitch added contemplatively. "I always wondered how she felt about that surpassing the love of women bit."

Lewis blinked. He hadn't thought of it quite that way before, like Michal and her brother Jonathan shared a husband, just like Leah and Rachel. Of course a lot of people did things in the Old Testament that you could pretty much count on a priest not approving of. All that begetting sons on handmaids, for one thing. That was definitely not ok. "You don't think it's wrong?"

Another sigh, as though Mitch wanted nothing more than to go to sleep, but he answered anyway, his voice quiet against the sound of the rails. "I'm Moravian," he said. "God is love. So how can love be evil? That would be like saying God is evil."

Lewis stared out the window. The train came out of a culvert, dashing suddenly across a railroad bridge over a river, the moon making a path of light across the water. He hadn't more than the vaguest idea what Moravians were, though he'd thought they were people from somewhere in Austria-Hungary, not a religion, but the stolen memory came back to him, if that's what it was.

The little church with its plain glass windows, beeswax candles wrapped in red paper ribbon, the scent of spiced buns on the altar, and the clear, high song of the old harpsichord. That was Mitch's memory. He was sure of it. Christmas Eve and family and peace, a child's sense of wonder that he could be loved by God.

"Way back long ago we were Hussites," Mitch said. "We lived in Moravia. But when the Church called a crusade against us, we had to go into hiding. The Moravian Brethren didn't give up, though. The Church never stamped us out. We kept on having our love feasts and our lay ministers just the same. And in the middle of the eighteenth century a bunch of us came to America. My mother's people are from Salem. We're Moravian. So I'm used to seeing the world a good deal different."

"You think it was love?"

A long pause, as though Mitch was assembling his thoughts. "Gil and Jerry were both wounded in October of '18, both of them in Vittorio Veneto. Jerry got a piece of shrapnel in his foot. They didn't take it right off. It got worse later, but right then he was ambulatory. Gil…Gil got gassed. He was real bad. Nobody thought he was going to make it. So there they both were in the hospital in Venice, and Alma half off her head with worry." A long quiet. The train plunged into darkness again, deep woodland. "Jerry was down there by Gil's bedside every day, not that Gil knew him or knew anything going on around him. Until they decided that Jerry had earned his ticket home. He was safe to move, you see, so they could ship him back to the states, back to a hospital there and his discharge. And Gil, they weren't moving him. I guess they figured they weren't taking him anywhere except in a coffin." He paused again. "I was there when Jerry said goodbye, not thinking he'd ever see Gil again. It was love."

There was a long silence. The train emerged from the wood again, banks and fields running swiftly past, the distant lights of a farm far over the fields. Cattle dozed in a pasture, heads down.

"Alma pulled him through. You know Alma. Nothing gets in her way, not even death. At least not for a while. They were married two days after the Armistice, when it looked like they were going to send Al off too. I found a chaplain that would marry them in the hospital. We propped Gil up on pillows and he said his vows good and strong. Iskinder (you don't know him) got the ring. It's the one you wouldn't let her pawn today."

Lewis nodded though he knew Mitch couldn't see him. Somewhere a dog barked, and Lewis blinked. He thought he'd seen it running beside the train, a lean white dog like a greyhound, legs stretched out in the sheer joy of the chase, but it couldn't have been anything but a stray moonbeam.

"Get some sleep, Lewis," Mitch said gently. "We've got enough to worry about. There's nothing here that won't keep till tomorrow."

"You're right," Lewis said, rolling over so that he faced the window. "Thanks, Mitch."

"Anytime, pal," Mitch said.

Lewis watched the shapes of trees under the moon, shadows flashing across the window, but it wasn't long before he slept.

Chapter Twenty-three

The train was due into Nice at noon, and to no one's surprise everyone slept very late. It had been a grueling two days. They had barely assembled and eaten breakfast before it was time to get off, Alma looking dowdy and respectable in the plain gray dress. Lewis had shaved and wore a clean second hand shirt, which at least made him look less like a prisoner fleeing arrest. Or an escaped slave, Jerry thought humorlessly. A desperate man seeking Aricia….

Something teased at his mind, pieces of a puzzle not quite fitting together, but there was no time. The train was pulling into the station at Nice, Lewis picking up the two cardboard suitcases.

Alma looked at him brightly. "Ok, Jerry. How about getting us some tickets for Rome?"

"Easily done," Jerry said. Nice was a major transfer point, and most Italy bound travelers changed trains there. To that end, there was a train for Rome scheduled to leave an hour after the train from Paris arrived, though there were no sleeping compartments left unreserved. "Leaving at 1 pm, arriving Rome at 9 am tomorrow. I'm sorry but there are no sleepers left."

Alma shrugged. "Just get us a regular compartment. We can sleep on the benches."

It was probably for the best, Jerry thought. The regular tickets were much cheaper, and the money they had needed to last who knew how long. He hadn't started thinking about how they were going to get back to the states. He supposed when push came to shove they could go to the American Embassy in Rome with a story about being robbed and ask the embassy to assist them in getting a wire transfer of funds for steamship tickets home. They couldn't exactly ask Henry to cover it. What with that and with the lost business from the time they'd spent doing this, it was turning out to be an expensive trip. Being a lodge was hard to manage if you didn't have a millionaire bankrolling it. Not that they ever had, but in the old days there had at least been more people....

The front page of one of the Italian newspapers on sale at a kiosk caught his eye, and he dropped behind the others to take a better look. The vendor gave him a fishy glance and he rummaged in his pockets for a franc or two, a cold feeling settling in his stomach. If this was what he thought it was....

Alma herded Jerry and Mitch aboard as soon as the train doors opened, waiting while Jerry managed the step. Mitch was moving badly too, Alma thought. Something wasn't right there. A couple of years ago he'd pulled some scar tissue badly, and she wondered if he hadn't done it again. She'd feel better if he'd see a doctor, but that was unlikely. So she'd just have to see if she could get him as much rest as possible.

As soon as they were well and truly underway, and the conductor had been by and checked their tickets, Lewis closed the door behind him. He sat beside Alma, who was at the window facing forwards, with Mitch and Jerry across.

"We need a council of war," Alma said. "Jerry, we'll be in Rome in fifteen hours. We've got to have a plan by then."

"We've got a problem," Jerry began, sinking into his seat.

"Only one?" Mitch said.

"You know that the excavation of the Nemi ships is an official dig, right?" Jerry asked rhetorically. "It's sponsored by the Italian government, with the government footing the bill and everything done right, all the artifacts reserved for Italian museums."

"Isn't that a good thing?" Alma asked. She was certain he'd had a lot to say about the desirability of government digs in the past, no fly by night operations with most of the treasures disappearing untraceably into private collections.

"Generally, yes," Jerry said. He pushed his gold-rimmed glasses up on his nose. "But in this case, not necessarily. This dig is a pet project of the Prime Minister. He got the funding for it and he takes a personal interest in it. He's going to make one of his frequent visits to the site day after tomorrow."

"And that's bad how?" Mitch asked.

It was Lewis who spoke up. "It wants power," he said. "The kind of power Henry doesn't have. Being a millionaire is great, but it doesn't give you the power of life and death. It doesn't give you the kind of power Caligula had."

"Neither does being Prime Minister of Italy," Mitch said. "Italy is a constitutional monarchy. There's a big difference between being a modern Prime Minister and being a Roman emperor." He shook his head. "I'm sure there are a lot of perks, but Italy isn't even a great power."

"But it could be, arguably," Alma said. "After all, isn't that one of the things that Mr. Mussolini keeps harping on? It's time to restore Italy to her former greatness?"

Jerry had a militant look in his eyes. "Don't underestimate the Fascists just because they're following the letter of the law. Mussolini's party is in control, and he's their Leader, Il Duce himself, with all that brings with it."

Mitch gave him a skeptical look, but Lewis interrupted.

"Besides, this thing has been trapped for hundreds of years. It probably overestimates the importance of Italy, because in its time Rome was so important. I mean, in terms of sheer power Stalin would be a much better choice, but would it think that way?"

Jerry grimaced. "A Scythian barbarian? Hardly worth its time. No, Rome has been the center of its world. I think it will return to Rome. And I think it will try to jump into the Prime Minister the day after tomorrow."

"If it does, we'll never get to it," Alma said. "The security around a head of state...."

"Ok," Mitch said. "That's bad news. He put his feet up on the seat opposite him, between Alma and Lewis. "How do we figure out who this thing is wearing now?"

"We don't," Jerry said with a glance at Alma. "We don't need to know who it is or where it is, because we know where it will be the day after tomorrow. It will be at the dig when the Prime Minister visits, and it will be someone who can get close enough to jump into him."

Lewis nodded gravely. "So we do something like the amulets?"

"I'm afraid not," Jerry said. "How would we get the Prime Minister to wear one? Not to mention his whole entourage, bodyguards, chauffeur, everybody.... We're going to have to do this the hard way."

"Ok," Alma took a deep breath. "Let's lay this out. We can get to Lake Nemi easily from Rome. It's only something like fifteen miles. I'm sure tourists hire cars all the time."

"Getting there isn't the problem," Jerry said, pushing his glasses back up on his nose. "But once we get there we have two problems. Number one is that we only have one of the tablets." He looked around the three of them. "This is the first tablet. But from the way it ends in the middle there is at least one more, and possibly two. We need the full set to make the binding work."

"Ok." Alma put her hands to her forehead, considering. "If the dig has already uncovered it, it's probably in one of the labs or storage rooms, right? It's not so intrinsically valuable that it would be taken to a bank vault, right?"

Jerry shook his head. "It's a nice piece, but I'm sure if this site is as rich as they say there are many finer artifacts with much greater market value. Statues and sculptures are worth a lot more than tablets, and this one isn't even pictorial. It's probably in one of the labs for cleaning, conservation and photography."

"So how do we get in?" Alma asked.

"I have no idea!" Jerry said. "Do you think breaking and entering is part of my skill set?"

Alma made her voice very calm. "Jerry, you're the archaeologist. You're the one who can best figure out where things are kept. Moreover, you're the only one with a legitimate reason to be there. Surely a visiting American archaeologist might come by the dig during normal working hours and show an interest?"

"With a stolen artifact in my pocket?" Jerry countered.

"Which we're trying to return," Mitch said mildly.

"Can't we do that thing with the map and the tablet and just find out where they are?" Lewis asked. "Like you did back in LA?" Everybody looked at him. "Just an idea," Lewis said.

"We don't have a map," Alma said, "But the principle works.

We could use the tablet to lead us to the others. I can do that."

"That would work," Jerry said. "Of course, if they're locked up in one of the workrooms...."

"We'll get to that when we get to it," Mitch said. "For all we know they've never been excavated. Isn't that more likely?"

Jerry nodded slowly. "In which case we have to do some after hours digging. But that ought to be manageable. If they have a security guard he's probably on the workrooms and storerooms where the artifacts are kept. The whole site is huge and heavily wooded. We ought to be able to move around the site after dark without too much trouble."

"And then what?" Alma asked.

"We need to rebury the tablets with the appropriate invocation to Diana," Jerry said.

Mitch sat up straighter. "That's all?"

"Well, no. Obviously we have to have the creature there and bound while we do it."

"Obviously," Alma said dryly. "Ok, can we summon it? And would that bring it out of whatever host it's jumped to?"

"I think so." Jerry nodded. "If we can summon it correctly, we can force it to abandon whoever it has, wherever they are, and return to the tablets."

Lewis looked spooked, and Alma didn't blame him. "But it can't jump into us because of the amulets," she said. "So if we summon it to a location where we're the only people, the only thing it can do is go into the tablets?"

"That's the theory," Jerry said. "It ought to work."

Alma nodded. "And we don't need to know who that person is or have them physically present?"

"I don't think so."

"That's the only break we've gotten so far," Mitch said.

"It shouldn't matter," Jerry said. "We're summoning the *animus infernus*, not its host. When we summon it, we should force it to leave the host. Then whoever that is can go on doing whatever they were doing with no harm to them except having spent a day or two in a fugue state."

"And then we put the tablets where?" Alma asked.

"That's something we need to talk about," Jerry said. "I think that when the Emperor Claudius did the same thing he put the tablets on the deck of the primary ship and then had the ship sunk in the lake. That effectively put the tablets out of reach to anyone, since they were beneath the surface of a lake on which boating was forbidden, and made an appropriate expiation to Diana at the same time. But the problem with us putting them back in the lake...."

"Is that the archaeological expedition is draining the lake," Mitch said. "So they'll just be found again in a few months."

"Exactly," Jerry said.

"Any ideas for an alternate site?" Alma asked.

Jerry nodded. "The most appropriate place would be the ruins of the Temple of Diana. The Sanctuary of Diana would be analogous to the lake, and should be as protective. The problem is that the archaeological expedition isn't just draining the lake. They're excavating the site of the temple complex as well."

"Which means they'll dig it up again," Lewis said.

"Unfortunately," Jerry said. "It may be possible that we could put it in an out of the way corner of the complex, but I have to tell you that if their professional archaeologists are worth their salt, they'll notice the fresh digging, assume it's treasure hunters, and be all over it in a matter of days."

"And then there we go again," Alma said. "Ok, how about a third option?"

Jerry shrugged. "The sanctuary of Diana isn't just the temple. The entire area, everything inside the cingulum, or temple grounds, was sacred to Diana, including the surrounding woods. We could bury it in the woods and technically we'd be inside the bounds of Diana's protection. There are acres and acres of woodland. There's no way anybody is going to excavate it all anytime soon."

"That sounds like it has more potential," Mitch said.

"And also more opportunity for privacy," Alma agreed. "If we're going to be summoning a demon I don't want to do it where we could be interrupted or some innocent person could wander up and break the circle or be the new host."

Lewis was looking strange, his eyes unfocused.

"Lewis?" Alma said gently. "Do you see something?"

He shook his head regretfully. "I wish I did," he said.

"Ok," Alma said. "I think we have a plan. Jerry, you work on the specifics of the summoning. When we get to Rome we'll hire a car and go out to Aricia. There should be somewhere we could stay around there, a penzione or something. We can do the dowsing there. Then we go over to the site with Jerry and see if we can find the tablets. Then tomorrow night we do the summoning and bury the tablets in the forest."

"You make it all sound easy," Mitch said wryly.

"It's perfectly doable," Alma said, and thought she sounded more confident than she felt. She half suspected that Gil hadn't known what he was doing most of the time, but his best try usually worked out. And it wasn't as though they could give up, not when it had shown such a propensity for carnage. "We can handle it." She looked at Jerry, willing him not to disagree.

Instead he nodded. "I think we can," he said.

From the moment they arrived in Rome, Alma took charge. Lewis was used to her, but he was still a bit surprised by how the Signora arranged all. Alma changed when she spoke Italian, he thought. She was more mobile, more animated. She put her head to the side and her hands on her hips, walked with a different swing in her step. Not a different woman, no. But a younger, more exciting one, one more confident of her charm. Alma was usually a little diffident, a little awkward, as though not certain where to put her feet. This Alma wasn't. Even in the dowdy gray dress, she sparkled.

Gil's bride, some part of him said. Ten years ago in Venice she had been Gil's bride, and if she had been honed by war she had also been changed by emerging passion. Having come to it late, the change was all the more profound. Twenty eight was old for a bride, old to transform into something else, as though delayed summer had come all at once, bursting into a riot of bloom and warmth. Alma was passionate, inventive, eager. He knew that. But now she knew what she wanted and how to ask for it. Then it must have been a voyage of discovery.

Mitch watched, unsurprised. He'd been there for all of that. Lewis envied him that for a moment. Not that he would trade what he had, summer full blown and rich, but that there were parts of their lives that would never touch, people they had each been the other would never know.

A car and driver for Lake Nemi. Alma bundled them into a hired car, talking a mile a minute with the driver. Everyone spoke Italian but him, so Lewis settled in the middle of the backseat between Mitch and Alma. Jerry took shotgun so that he would have more room for his leg, and Lewis put his arm around Alma as she leaned forward, telling the driver something.

She settled back against it and gave him an apologetic smile. "I'm sorry to go on like this. I lived in Italy for two years before."

"I know," Lewis said. He smiled to let her know he really didn't mind.

Clouds were rolling in, and before they left Rome the rain began. It was the end of May, everything green and growing, nothing burned by the heat of summer yet. The car jolted down the road, stopping and starting in heavy traffic in the city.

"This is the line of the old Via Appia," Jerry said, leaning over the seat in front. "Beneath the tar there's a Roman road, one of the finest in the world. It pierced the Servian Wall at Porta Capena back there. You can't see the line of the Aurelian Wall here, but we'll pass through it shortly, the one that was built to hold back barbarians like us." He gave Lewis a quick grin. "And then the road takes off straight as an arrow southward. We'll follow it about ten miles before we turn off for Lake Nemi."

"The same road," Lewis said. The same road they would have taken, Claudius and his people, on their way to Aricia to bind the demon that had consumed his nephew.

"The past is always right beneath our feet," Jerry said. "It never goes away. We may not notice it, but it's always there. It always matters."

Alma squeezed his hand.

Mitch looked out the window. "This rain will play hell with the ground," he muttered.

They made better time once they turned off what had been the Via Appia. The two lane road ran up into the hills, curving gently through woodland, the occasional pillared drive leading back to a house invisible from the road. The rain stopped, the sun breaking through streaming clouds. The long green leaves steamed in the sun.

Up a hill and then the driver stopped the car at the crest, gesturing. "Guarda, Signora!" he said.

Between pine trees a spectacular view opened out, a perfectly round lake reflecting the sky above. Green lawns surrounded it, hills gently rising on all sides to dense forest, the opposite side strangely terraced, only a few cypress trees marring its perfect symmetry.

"Diana's Mirror," Lewis said, feeling a cold touch at his back.

Jerry leaned over the seat again. "In Claudius' day there was a beautiful Hellenistic temple there with a gilded roof. You could see it perfectly from here, I expect. This would have been the first sight of Aricia for people on the pilgrim way – the lake like this and Diana's Temple across the lake reflected in the water. Right over there were the buildings. There were gardens and mazes that came down toward the lakeshore on that side."

"It's beautiful," Alma said.

"It truly is," Jerry agreed. "This whole valley is the caldera of an extinct volcano. It's a microclimate that's richer than the surrounding area. No doubt that's why the first people in this area marked it as a sacred place."

When they had looked their fill the driver went on, descending on the other side of the hill below the rim of the old crater. Lewis felt it. They passed under the shade of the trees, and he felt it like a distant echo. *Enter, and be changed.*

Alma's driver had recommended a penzione, one not too far from the dig, but too nice, he said for those scholars who didn't live in the houses rented for the expedition. Besides, his cousin had had bad experiences with archeologists—mud everywhere, and the drinking, and bones washed in the bathtub—and didn't think much of them. But tourists, visitors from America—that was entirely another matter. Mitch was grinning, translating sotto voce for Lewis, and Jerry hoped they still thought it was funny when he got them kicked out for being archeologists.

However, it wasn't so much archeologists that Signora Ruggieri minded as graduate students in archeology, and she was happy to rent them her two small second floor rooms with a shared bath and a view of the lake. From here, it was easier to see the mud, and to see that the water level had dropped considerably. It was also possible, if one craned one's neck, to see the tents and the dark fingers of timber sticking out of the mud. Caligula's pleasure barges: an extraordinary discovery, unique in the Ancient world, their true purpose a mystery.... Jerry shivered in spite of the revived sun, and made his way carefully down the stairs.

Signora Ruggieri was willing to send a note to the dig site, and to fix them lunch while they waited for an answer. They sat for an hour in the ochre-painted dining room, sun and shadow alternating outside the long windows, while Signora Ruggieri and her maid brought plates of pasta tossed with cream and new peas and slivers of prosciutto, and they drank most of a bottle of soft, sweet wine. The king of the grove lived like a king indeed, until his challenger bested him. Jerry pushed the thought away, and as he poured himself a second glass of wine, he saw that his hand was trembling. He stilled it with an effort, poured more wine for Alma and the others.

"So how'd they find out there were ships in the lake, anyway?" Lewis asked. He sounded as though he was trying to take his mind off something, and Jerry couldn't blame him.

"They were never really lost," he answered. "Supposedly on a calm day, you could see the shadow of the first wreck, and people tried to raise them throughout the Middle Ages and the Renaissance. In fact, there's a pretty good argument to be made that the first diving helmet was used in Lake Nemi, in an attempt to raise the larger of the two ships. One Francesco de Marchi tried to attach grappling hooks and pull the ship out of the mud, but all he did was rip off more pieces of the ship. Fishermen here had a thriving side business in artifacts through the seventeenth and eighteenth and even the nineteenth centuries—I can't even guess how many bits and pieces of the ships are scattered around Europe in private houses, antiquities picked up on the Grand Tour."

"Sounds like wholesale looting," Mitch said. He paused, choosing his words carefully even though he knew Signora Ruggieri spoke only minimal English. "I'm kind of surprised they didn't pull up more than they'd bargained for."

A tablet, he meant, or something else that would have released the creature. Jerry chose his words with equal care. "I don't think you could have gotten at—anything important—without modern equipment. They didn't bring in diving suits until 1895 and that group was more interested in the showy pieces, mosaics and bronzes and the like. Luckily, the Director General of Antiquities realized the damage that was being done to the site and called a halt to private explorations. He had a survey done of the lake bed back in, I think, 1905, and there was talk then of draining the lake, but between the war and politics, nothing got done until three years ago. Mussolini threw government resources behind the project, and—that's what's gotten things this far. What really interests me is that when they started to look at draining the lake, there was already a Roman tunnel in place, and all they had to do was to clear it—"

"Excuse me, signore," the maid said from the doorway. "Signor Averill is here. From the project?"

Jerry didn't recognize the name, but from the look on Signora Ruggieri's face, he had to be one of the graduate students. And so he proved to be, a fair, sun-burned English boy with a round clever face and unbecoming tortoiseshell glasses. He stood twisting his hat in his hands, but managed to convey apologies from both Professor Searce and Professor Ucelli: they were in the middle of preparing for the Prime Minister's visit, and Searce wasn't able to get away, but Averill would be happy to bring them down to the site and show them around a little. He was an epigrapher himself, Averill admitted shyly. His particular expertise wasn't currently in demand.

Jerry accepted gladly, and there was a moment's awkwardness as Alma started to suggest that Mitch stay behind and rest. He stared her down, and in the end they all piled into Averill's ratty car—it might have begun life as a Fiat, but had been rebuilt enough times to be unrecognizable—and drove bumping along the track that led to the lakeside.

They could hear the heavy rhythm of the pumps, filling the air, and Averill pulled to a stop well shy of the exposed lakebed. A gang of laborers was working a frame sieve, while others pushed wheelbarrows up the muddy path, and another pair worked a hand pump, playing lake water gently through the frame. Another group was laying a fresh set of duckboards, adding to the network of wooden paths that ran to the water's edge. Half out of the water, rising stark against the green hillside, the prow of a ship curved up from the mud, supported by a framework of new timber. The ribs of the bow rose behind it, shorter, stronger, also held up with props, and above it, higher than a man's head, the deck itself was partially intact. The photos didn't do it justice, Jerry thought. He had thought he'd pictured it properly, something like Cleopatra's legendary barge, but this was so much larger, so much more elaborate—no wonder the first treasure hunters had found marbles and mosaics and bronzes. This was a floating palace, impossible—and impossibly sacrilegious, when it first set sail. It would have dominated the lake, erased it, negated even the temple that had stood on the far bank. It would have drawn all eyes, its gilding and its paint and silk and sails capturing all the light, all worship. No wonder Claudius had sunk the ships: they were beautiful and bizarre and entirely, painfully wrong, here in this perfect lake.

"I had no idea it was this big," Alma said softly. Jerry glanced sideways, saw her shake her head. "I thought—I don't know what I thought."

Averill was nodding. "I know," he said. "It doesn't seem quite real, does it? And there were two of them." He shook away the unprofessional awe. "It's 67 meters long, that's just a hair under 220 feet, and we've exposed about a third of that. And the second ship is even bigger."

"How wide is it?" Mitch asked. He shaded his eyes, as though that could make it seem clearer.

"Nineteen meters," Averill answered. "62 feet, or a little less."

Lewis was silent, his face still and cold. He saw it, too, Jerry thought, saw the sacrilege, maybe more clearly than anyone.

"The second ship's 235 feet long and 80 feet wide," Averill said.

"How long will it take you to get that one out?" Mitch asked, and Averill gave an apologetic shrug.

"I'm not an excavator, I'm afraid. Very possibly another year or more. And there are funding issues, so there's been some talk of stopping the pumping until we have the first ship squared away. That's part of what the Prime Minister's visit is about, to make sure we can continue the project."

"It might make sense to secure the first ship," Jerry said, and Averill nodded.

"Except that, as I understand it, we'd have to keep pumping the whole time just to keep the water from coming back, so it's not as much of a saving?" He gave a shy smile. "But, as I said, I'm not an excavator."

Lewis was frowning slightly, his gaze wandering from the ships to the workmen and back again. There was something there, Jerry knew, something he felt or saw, and he was glad to see Alma take his arm. Lewis started, smiled, but looked away again. Not for the first time, Jerry wished his own talents lay in that direction. Or that Lewis was better trained. He saw Lewis lean close to Alma, and saw his lips shape words: *It's here.*

Not unexpected, Jerry told himself, but the cold crept over him anyway. Guessing and knowing were entirely different things. It was here, lying in wait for the Italian Prime Minister, here where it had been bound before. It would enjoy that irony. He glanced out at the mud, the sparkling water beyond. There were dozens of workers, and just as many archeologists. It could be any of them.

"I can take you out to the ship if you'd like," Averill said, and Jerry brought his attention back to the matter at hand.

"I'd like that," he said.

Alma declined, with a quick glance at Lewis, claiming her shoes wouldn't stand it, and Lewis offered to keep her company. Mitch seemed to have gotten the message, too, and in the end it was only Jerry who made his way awkwardly across the duckboards to the platform erected beside the ship. The noise of the pumps was much louder here, and the dead-fish stench of the mud was very much in evidence. The wood of the ship was dark and swollen, the grain soft and rotten-looking; there were dents where the supporting timbers pressed into the planks of the hull.

Averill was talking to another young man, his voice drowned by the thud of the pumps, and came back grinning. "Erich says we've just turned up another beam-end sculpture—a Medusa, this time. Perfect for the Prime Minister's visit!"

"Didn't I read the others were all animal heads?" Jerry asked.

"Yes, that's right. But now we've got Medusa."

Erich was short and dark and hairy, stripped to trousers and singlet in the damp heat. He exhibited his find with appropriate pride—a woman's face caught between a scream and a snarl, framed by writhing snakes that were nearly all intact—and Jerry leaned close to see the maker's mark scratched into the bronze inside the cuff that held it onto the beam

"It was toward the middle of the ship," Erich said, his voice only lightly accented. "Perhaps where the gangway was. Perhaps that's why it's different?"

"Jerry!"

Jerry turned, careful of his footing, smiled to see Harrison Searce clambered toward them across the boards. "Harris."

They clasped hands, Searce shaking his head. "I'm glad to see you taking an interest again. I thought you'd quit the business for good."

"Well, you know," Jerry said, and tapped his cane against the peg that finished his artificial leg. "But I was traveling with friends and I couldn't resist. Though I'm sorry my timing wasn't better."

"How long are you here?" Searce asked. "Once the Prime Minister's visit is over, I can give you a proper look at the whole site."

"I'm not sure yet," Jerry said. "It depends on what I can talk my friends into."

"You can talk anybody into anything," Searce said, with a smile. "And it's worth it, Jerry, I promise you. The things we're finding—there's been nothing like this in my lifetime."

"It's amazing," Jerry said honestly. "I'd seen the photos, of course, but they don't do it justice."

"Come on up," Searce began, and paused. "Can you make it?"

Jerry looked at the ladder that led up to the platform overlooking what was left of the ship's deck. This was the problem, the reason he wasn't here, wasn't still in the field. The words were bitter on his tongue. "I could probably get up, but I can't get down."

"Oh, down's no problem," Searce said. "We've got lots of rope."

There was no pity in his tone, just practicality, and Jerry smiled in spite of everything. "I'm not really dressed for it—"

"Scuse, Signor Dottore." It was one of the workers, a foreman by the look of him, slightly less muddy, with rubber boots that reached almost to his knees. "One of the men would like to speak with you."

"Has he found something?" Searce asked.

"He wouldn't say," the foreman answered. "He wanted to speak to you in person."

"I've offered a bonus for each significant artifact," Searce said, and Jerry nodded. It was a fairly common practice, though on a rich site like this, it was hard to pay the workers what a good piece was work. Although with government money to play with, and government sanctions behind them, maybe there was a chance. He remembered the tablet in his luggage, and wondered when Searce had established the policy.

"All right," Searce said, to the foreman. "Send him over."

"He says he's left it in the ground," the foreman said, and Searce gave a nod of approval.

"Well, he gets ten lire for that alone. Thanks, Marcello. Who is it?"

"That one there." The foreman pointed to a man standing toward the edge of the site, a few yards from a new-looking shed. Tools, Jerry guessed, and maybe shelter in bad weather. "Imperiale—Gianni Imperiale. One of the new men."

"I'm impressed," Jerry said. His mouth was dry. There was something wrong here, he could feel it. An old hand might have the sense to leave an object where it was found, but not a new man, not a new hire. The excitement always overcame them, made them pick whatever it was up out of the ground....

"So am I," Searce said. "Care to come along?"

The mud of the lakebed stretched toward the horizon, pocked with stones and still dotted with shallow puddles. It would be a painful walk, at best embarrassingly awkward, and at worst—at worst, he'd be stuck, someone would have to carry him out. Jerry took a breath, wanting to refuse, but the same sense of unease made him smile and nod. "Sure. Just—take it slow, if you don't mind."

"No worries," Searce said. There were planks lying around seemingly at random, and he caught up a few of them, tossed them out into the mud with a nonchalance that suggested this wasn't the first time they'd improvised a walkway. That bought them maybe ten yards, but after that it was mud all the way, and Jerry clung grimly to Searce's shoulder, the peg leg sinking inches deep with every step. Searce didn't seem to mind, just braced a hand under Jerry's elbow, and at last they reached a band of more solid ground near the little hut. The man who had been leaning on his shovel straightened, frowning slightly, and Jerry felt the hairs rise on the back of his neck. The man himself was a stranger, young, fair like a northern Italian, with a homely, pock-marked face, but the eyes, and the darkness behind them, were terribly familiar.

"So," Searce called. "Imperiale, is it? What have you found?"

"A tablet, Signor Dottore. At least, I think that's what it is."

The ground gave way under Jerry's leg, and he threw his weight onto his good foot just in time to keep himself from sinking knee deep. "Damn it."

Searce stopped, offered his hand, and Jerry hauled himself free again.

"Sorry."

"It's all right," Searce said. "This might be right up your alley."

Thank God for that. Jerry managed a smile and a nod. "I'm curious, I admit. What would a tablet be doing out here?"

"An excellent question," Searce answered. "Probably it was pulled free in one of the earlier attempts to raise the treasures? We'll see."

Imperiale said, "Signor Dottore, the ground is worse further on. It's not good for a one-legged man."

"Dr. Ballard is a colleague of mine who specializes in inscriptions," Searce answered. "He'll manage."

"I could bring the tablet," Imperiale offered. "After you've inspected it, of course."

Searce glanced over his shoulder, at Jerry struggling to keep up. "We could do that. I doubt there's any real significance in the location. This was all lakebed."

"No, no," Jerry said. "I'd like to see myself. Just in case." He couldn't let Searce be alone with the creature. That had to be what it wanted, he realized, a chance to take one of the senior archeologists. They would have plenty of time with Mussolini, showing him over the site—perhaps even time alone, or relatively alone, and that—that was what they had to stop.

"Suit yourself," Searce answered, and Jerry hauled himself through the mud. He couldn't see the others, couldn't risk looking for them to warn them, and he wasn't strong enough—didn't have the tools or the ritual prepared—to do anything except keep it from jumping.

Imperiale—the creature—gave him a single malevolent glance as he joined them, and pointed to a spot in the mud. "I was digging there, a sample to take to the sieves. And I saw that."

It was a rounded bit of metal, bronze rather than lead. Not a missing tablet, then, Jerry thought, though on second thought he doubted the creature could stand to get this close to one of them. Searce squatted in the mud, carefully feeling for the object's edges.

"Definitely a tablet," he said, and looked up with a smile. "Nice work."

"Thank you, sir," Imperiale answered.

Searce probed a little further, and then stood up, wiping his hands on his pants. "Let me have that," he said, and Imperiale handed him the shovel. Searce planted its edge carefully, brought up the tablet and the surrounding mud with a single deft movement. He held it out to Jerry, who took it automatically, reaching into his pocket for his handkerchief. His fingers brushed the sigil, and it took an effort not to palm it, keep it close against his skin. He concentrated instead on cleaning off the worst of the mud, revealing a square of bronze incised with Latin and inset with a stone seal.

"Interesting," he said, and felt the creature smile.

"It looks a little like a curse tablet," Searce said.

Jerry shook his head. "Votive—no, memorial," he amended, and adjusted his glasses. "See? That's a memorial inscription."

"Not a standard form, though." Searce leaned close. "And—is that Etruscan?"

"In gratitude to—no, *in honor of the Thracian Gaius Caesar offers this token to the gods below,"* Jerry said. "And, yes, then Etruscan. That's unusual."

"We've run into some other Etruscan inscriptions at the temple site," Searce said. "Very interesting." He straightened, wiped his hands on his pants again, and reached for his notebook. "Good job, Imperiale. Give this to your foreman, and he'll pay you your bonus."

The creature hesitated, but there was no excuse for it to stay. "Thank you, sir," it said, and backed away across the mud. Jerry put his head down, studying the inscription, but he could still feel it watching for what seemed like a very long time.

"We've run into some other Etruscan inscriptions at the temple site," Searce said. "But not associated with the ships."

Jerry fumbled in his pocket and came up with his small magnifying glass. With its help, he thought he could make out the design of the seal, worn though it was: a warrior, holding a net and spear. A gladiator. He shivered in spite of the sunlight. No, not part of the binding, not at all. This was Caligula thumbing his nose at the goddess, the thing that possessed him making an offering in pure mockery. The gladiator who had killed the king of the grove: that had to be what had released the creature in the first place, and from the gladiator, returning in triumph, it had seized an emperor. And feasted until finally the Praetorian Guard had risen against it.... And it had positioned itself to begin the terrible cycle all over again.

"The design, the seal, looks like a retiarius," he said. "So.... Caligula lost a gladiator here? The Etruscan formula looks like ones I've seen on burial stele, so I'd say it was a funerary marker. If the Thracian were a favorite, maybe Caligula wanted him commemorated? Perhaps there were even games aboard the ship?"

"Maybe," Searce agreed. "There's certainly room. And of course there's the story about Caligula and the Rex Nemorensis."

Jerry nodded. That definitely wasn't a subject he wanted to pursue. "Before I left the states, I was in touch with Bill Davenport, and he said he was particularly excited about tablet inscriptions from the ships. I was hoping there might be some more Etruscan evidence here on the ships, but you said not?"

Searce shook his head. "Bill had a bee in his bonnet about Etruscan material, I'm afraid. There's no reason we'd find anything Etruscan on the ships, they're much too late. We did find some nice stelae at the temple, though."

That was that, then. Good news and bad news: the good news was, the expedition hadn't yet found the remaining tablets. The bad news was the same—well, that and that the creature was here already. And that Mussolini was coming. The noise of the pumps beat in his ears, the smell of the mud and the rotting ship filled his lungs. Somehow, they had to stop it, and he still had no real idea how. He took a breath, and let Searce move them on, struggling back through the mud toward the solid shore.

Chapter Twenty-four

They returned to the penzione at mid-afternoon, collecting in Alma and Lewis's room. Alma sat down on the bed with crossed legs and looked at the three men.

"It's here," she said.

Lewis nodded, his face stiff. "Somewhere among the workers. It was watching—"

Jerry interrupted. "It's in a laborer called, or calling itself, Imperiale—ironic, but apparently it has something like a sense of humor. It tried to lure Harris—Dr. Searce—away from the dig, but I happened to be with him. And I stuck to him like a burr all the rest of the afternoon." He paused. "And they haven't found the other tablet, by the way."

"How the hell did it get here ahead of us?" Lewis asked.

"By air?" Mitch said. "A commercial flight from Paris to Rome while we were on the train?"

"They hired a bunch of new workers," Jerry said. "To get ready for the Prime Minister's visit. Which, of course, is exactly what it's waiting for. All it has to do it take one of the archeologists, someone who's going to be close to Mussolini, showing him something, and then, hey, presto! It jumps, Il Duce has a fainting spell, and we are all screwed."

"We could take out a laborer," Mitch said, thoughtfully.

"It could still jump," Jerry said. "May have already jumped, for that matter. It's got plans of its own, its own schedule to keep. We could easily go after Imperiale and find that the creature's long gone."

"So what do we do?" Mitch asked.

"What we planned," Alma said. "If we can bind it, tonight, before the Prime Minister gets here, then it doesn't matter whether it's jumped or not. We're calling the creature, not its host."

"But that means we need the other tablet, right?" Lewis said, after a moment, and Alma nodded.

"Which Jerry says they haven't found. So let's see what we can do. It must be somewhere on the site still."

Jerry sank down into the curved chair at the dressing table and produced a piece of stationary. "Give me a minute. I can sketch out a rough map of the site."

Alma unfastened the chain around her neck. Her wedding ring and the amulet hung together on it, glittering. She took a deep breath. She'd found Davenport this way when he'd fled Los Angeles. It ought to be easier to find the other tablet when they had its mate.

"Don't lose that," Mitch said, sliding the amulet off the chain and holding it out to her.

"I won't." Alma tucked it down her front to rest against her heart, loose inside her combinations. That would do for now. She'd put it back on the chain as soon as they were done.

Jerry was drawing on the paper with a fountain pen, swift sure strokes delineating the shape of lake and forest, of buildings and ruins. The boat dock, the pump house.... "Every archeologist can draw a site plan," Jerry said, glancing sideways at Lewis with a half smile. "It's one of those things."

Alma frowned at the map. "We may need a larger scale."

"We need to find the general area first," Jerry said. The ships were taking shape just as they'd seen them, half exposed in the middle of the lake. "There's no point in drawing a large scale map of the sanctuary area if we're looking somewhere else."

Alma shrugged. "Your call." She knew better than to tell Jerry his business.

This time when Jerry began the Hebrew invocations Lewis didn't flinch. He stood quietly beside Mitch as Jerry walked a circle around the room, truncated by the bed, speaking in a very low voice, presumably not to be heard by Signora Ruggieri. Alma bent her head over the map on the desk, the tablet unwrapped beside it, gleaming with a soft, oily sheen, her wedding ring held loosely in her hand.

There should be peace in this, or perhaps transcendent experience. She should feel something, some vast tide, some sense of presence. Instead there was nothing. If Diana spoke she did not hear her.

Alma closed her eyes, her fingers resting lightly on the tablet. But it didn't matter if she could hear the goddess or not. That was her limitation, not Diana's. And so instead she summoned memory.

The moon rising out of the clouds, or rather appearing to do so. It was they who rose out of the clouds, and there was nothing between Alma and the moon, not even the ghost of a pane of glass. The Jenny's open forward cockpit hid nothing. The clouds clung to her face like wisps of tears, and then they soared free of them, the low clouds streaming past like a blanket impossibly soft. Above, the countless stars paled before their lady, the full moon rising clear and untouchable in the heavens.

Behind her, in the aft cockpit, she heard Gil laugh with sheer delight. She could not speak. She could not find voice for this unimaginable beauty. They skimmed the surface of the clouds, the Jenny as graceful as a water bird just skimming the surface of a pond, mist rising beneath its wings. The mountains rose far above the clouds as well, standing like islands in a sea of glimmering white. Gil steered between them effortlessly. Even the familiar peaks of Colorado seemed new, transformed by moonlight, the entire world made into a white ocean beneath the moon.

"Do you want to take the wheel?" Gil called, and she nodded. She had no words yet, no words for this singing beauty in her heart, for this thankfulness that threatened to overwhelm her. From autumn rain and blood had come this, transformed in seven short months. Armistice and peace, home and Gil, and this—this transformation—to soar like a freed spirit. This he gave her, home and freedom both, and the magic of flight. To run, and to come home.

Diana, Alma whispered in her heart. All the contradictions made sense, huntress and protectress at once. The hound runs, and her coursing is a joy to behold. And then she comes home and sleeps by the fire she guards, safe beside those she loves.

Diana, Alma whispered. *Help us.*

Alma put her left hand on the tablet, and looped the chain

that held her wedding band twice around her finger, her elbow propped at ninety degrees so that the ring swung freely over the map Jerry had drawn. "All right," she said, clearing her throat. "Let's see where the other tablet is."

"Or others," Jerry said. "There might be more than one."

"Or others," Alma agreed. She closed her eyes again, letting the ring swing in wide loops, crossing and recrossing the page. "Where are you?" she said softly. "Show me."

The ring swung in tighter and tighter loops. She felt it tug against her hand, as though a magnet pulled it. Tighter and tighter, circling a single spot. Alma carefully let the chain out until it touched the page, and then opened her eyes. The band of the ring overlapped the smaller of the two ships midship, where they had found the Medusa earlier today. "I'm sure," she said.

"Damn," Mitch said.

Jerry shook his head. "It makes sense. They would have wanted the tablets aboard the ships. It makes sense if they hadn't been moved. Probably this one was the first excavated, but as we saw today the ships are only about half exposed. If the other tablet or tablets are still on the ship, they must be on the lower levels, either because they were put there or because they fell through the decking when it was waterlogged and rotting. They could be a couple of decks down, still underwater."

"I think they were aboard the ships to begin with," Lewis said. "That makes sense with what I saw."

"So we need to get aboard the ships," Mitch said. He shook his head. "That's going to be fun."

"Is this a good time to mention that I can't swim?" Lewis said.

Jerry laughed. "Neither can I. Not anymore."

"Well, you can row," Alma said. "Both of you. If there's any swimming to do I'll do it."

"Or I can," Mitch said.

Alma stared at him. "You're going to tell me you're up to diving on that wreck? I don't think so." Mitch couldn't fool her, much as he might like to think he did. He'd pulled something in the airship crash. She could see the way he moved. "Mitch, I know you'd give your all for this, but it's not necessary. I'm as good a swimmer as you, and I'm uninjured. This part's mine."

Slowly, Mitch nodded. "Ok. If we have to dive, you'll do it."

"We're going to have to wait until after dark," Jerry said. "There's no way we can get out on the lake without being in plain sight of everybody at the dig. We'll have to wait until everybody has gone home."

"Nine o'clock or better," Alma said. "It's the end of May. Full dark is late."

"Let's say ten," Mitch said.

Lewis cleared his throat. "The other question I have is this," he said. "What about it? The demon, I mean."

"It's bound to try to stop us," Jerry said. "It knows we're here, it saw me. It has to be able to guess what we're doing."

"That we're going to try to bind it, sure," Mitch said. "But not the details. It doesn't know where the other tablet is—does it?"

He looked at Lewis, who gave an embarrassed shrug. "I don't know."

"It doesn't matter," Alma said. She stood up briskly, opening the chain and reaching down to slide the amulet back on it. "We need to be prepared. It may be armed, and it's certainly willing to kill. We probably can't get guns, but we need knives and whatever else we can think of to defend ourselves. The advantage is that there are four of us and one of it, so if we stick together, we should be able to overpower it, even if it's gotten a strong host. But we have to stay alert and be careful when we do things like dive."

Mitch nodded. "We've got hours until nine o'clock. I'll go see what I can do about finding us knives."

"That's a plan," Alma said. "We'll do this tonight." And perhaps with Diana's help the price wouldn't be too high.

Alma had no idea where Mitch had gotten the boat, or how he'd managed to borrow a car from one of the Ruggieri cousins, but she was grateful he'd found a way. He'd gotten knives, too, and a heavy leather object that Alma had recognized after a moment as a blackjack. The Ruggieri cousin was definitely an interesting sort, she thought, but knew better than to say anything. Jerry was looking thoroughly unhappy already, and she didn't need to make things worse. At least there was a mist rising, tendrils curling off the still water like threads of smoke. That would help some, that and the clouds that seemed to be building. The moon was a waning quarter, but it hadn't risen yet, and wouldn't for some hours. By then the clouds should be thick enough to hide it, or, better still, they'd be safely off the lake.

They manhandled the boat out to the water, all of them with their pants rolled up and their shoes dangling from their laces around their necks. Jerry staggered and swore in the soft mud, but Alma couldn't spare a hand to help him. The mist coiled around them as they went, blurring the lights on the far shore.

They reached the edge of the water, and Mitch and Lewis walked it in far enough to float. Jerry stood for a moment with his head down, catching his breath, then dragged himself out and into the broad-beamed boat. Alma followed him, heard him say to Mitch, "You told them we were stealing artifacts?"

It was the tone another man would have used for "robbing churches." Alma fumbled for the oars, found them and readied herself to push off.

"I didn't tell them that," Mitch said. He stopped, wincing, and Lewis nodded for him to climb into the boat. "They may have assumed…."

"Do you have any idea what that will do to my reputation?" Jerry began, and Mitch shook his head.

"Look, Jer, there's no good reason for you to be out on the lake in the middle of the night. The point is not to get caught."

There was enough truth in that to silence Jerry, and Lewis walked the boat a little further into the chill water, Alma poling them along from the other side. He was up to his waist before he scrambled in, and settled himself on the thwart beside Jerry. "I'll start," he said softly. "Then you can take over."

Jerry nodded, though he didn't look very happy.

The lake wasn't very big, but in the dark and the rising mist it seemed larger. Lewis rowed steadily, strongly, pulling them toward the sound of the pumps. The mist parted reluctantly before the blunt bow, the boat rocking with every stroke.

"Those pumps," he said. "I'm a little worried about them. Won't they be a danger to Alma?"

"No," Jerry said. He twisted on the seat, trying to see how

far they had to go. "No, they're far enough away that they won't disturb the ships. She'll be fine."

"I hope so," Lewis muttered, and kept rowing.

"There," Jerry said. "Stop."

Lewis pulled the oars in, and the boat drifted, slowing, until suddenly a low platform loomed out of the dark. Jerry leaned out to grab a piling, pulled them in tight against it.

"No watchman?" Mitch asked.

"No," Jerry said again. "Harris said they're more worried about the artifacts in the workshops. It's too much of a long shot for most of the locals to risk diving out here."

"That's something," Alma said. Jerry unwrapped the hooded flashlight, flicked it on for a moment to study the wreck, and switched it off again.

"Back a little."

He pushed them away from the platform, and Lewis worked the oars again, bringing them close to where the first fingers of wood reached out of the water. "This is it," he said. "I think."

"Good enough for me," Alma said, and Jerry nodded.

This was the tricky part, and she wouldn't let herself think too much about it. She slipped off her blouse and slacks, tucking the necklace with the amulet and Gil's ring tighter into her underwear. The air seemed colder than before and made her feel more naked somehow. Not that it mattered, not that anyone could really see her, here in the dark, but she felt vulnerable, afraid.

And that was reasonable, she told herself. It was reasonable to be afraid of searching a wrecked ship in the dark: it was a dangerous thing to do. The main thing was to be careful, not to take unnecessary risks.

"Ok?" Lewis asked, and she smiled at him even though she doubted he would see even the gleam of her teeth. That was something he shared with Gil, something she hadn't known she could expect or ask for, that willingness to let her run her own risks.

"I'm ready," she said, and slipped over the side.

The water was cold, like any mountain lake. She suppressed a curse, clung to the side of the boat while she got her breath back, then stretched her feet down to feel for the ship's hull beneath the surface. She found it quickly enough, unpleasantly soft between her toes, let go of the boat to feel her way toward the space where the deck had been.

Abruptly the wood vanished, and she slipped under the water before she could stop herself and came up shaking wet hair out of her eyes.

"Alma?" That was Lewis again, voice soft but carrying, and she saw that Jerry had the oars now, moving slowly toward her, and Lewis was in the bow.

"I'm fine," she said, and caught the gunwale as Jerry backed oars again. "I'm going to have to dive, though."

"Hang on," Mitch said. "How are you going to find it?"

"It's there," she said. She was as certain of it as if she felt the tug of her chain, dowsing, as certain as if she saw it through the dark. When she had dowsed for it before, she had called on her memory of flight, of Gil and the Jenny skimming above the clouds. Now the mist swirled about her, as the clouds had done, and she could feel the metal beneath her, a little to her right.

Lewis caught her hand. "It fell," he said softly. "After the ship sank, a long time after, a fisherman came and hooked a piece of ivory, an ivory box covered with nymphs and satyrs. And when he came back for more, all he did was pull up a length of the deck, and the tablet fell. It's right there where it landed, just a little further…."

"How far down?" Alma asked, and he started and shook his head.

"Eight feet? Nine? Not far."

"Thank you," she said, and squeezed his hand. She pushed herself gently away, letting the current and the metal itself pull her, then took a last deep breath and let herself sink beneath the surface.

It was pitch dark, no more than she'd expected, but before she was even half out of breath, her feet touched more of the soft wood. There was debris as well, hard and painful; she doubled over, drawing her feet up, and let her hands sweep through the mud. Hard things, metal, a round thing that felt like stone—the head of a statue?—but still not the tablet. Her air was running out. She kicked off, broke the surface, and dove again.

It was closer this time, further to her right. The deck and the tangle of objects slanted away a little, and she touched them more lightly, not wanting to set anything moving. Closer—she could feel it, like a spot of sunlight in the water, and then her hand struck something hard and thick. Rope, she thought, rope caught on the wreck? No, more than just a piece of rope. It was a net, a fisherman's net, wrapped in a tangle around some post. And the tablet was beneath it.

She kicked off again, surfaced to wave the boat closer.

"Do you have it?" Mitch called, and she shook her head, scattering drops of water.

"It's right here. I need a knife."

Lewis handed it to her without question or hesitation. She clung for a moment to the side of the boat, breathing deep, and dove again.

She found the net quickly enough, traced the knotted length until she thought she'd found the place just above the tablet. She could feel its warmth, worked one hand into the strands of rope, trying to see if she could feel the metal. Yes, there it was, the same square shape, and something brushed across the back of her hand. She kicked back instinctively, and the net tightened, pulled tight by the movement, wrapping around her wrist. She jerked her arm back, the rope scraping along her skin, and could have screamed at the touch of bony fingers running across her hand. Fingers, definitely fingers, flesh long eaten—

She stilled herself with an effort and brought up the knife to saw at the ancient rope. The fingers tapped her knuckles, moved toward her wrist—No. There were no fingers, there was nothing there, nothing that could harm her. It was fish, or debris caught in the net; if it was more, she would know, she would feel it, and there was nothing there.

She put her knife to the rope again, her chest aching, let out a little more air to ease the pressure. Another strand parted, and then another, and then her wrist was free. She reached for the tablet, and in that moment, she felt a presence, a darkness, rising out of the net itself. She snatched the tablet, kicked away, and felt something wrap around her ankle. She kicked with all her strength, slashed blindly with the knife, and her head broke the surface long enough for her to catch a breath.

The net tightened around her foot and dragged her under again. She kicked again, hard, clutched the tablet tighter to her chest, close to the amulet. This wasn't the creature, it was something else, something slow and stupid and inexorable. She bent double, trying to find the strands of the net to cut them, but her knife passed through only water. Her chest was tightening again, and she reached for the strength of the earth, but she was cut loose, floating—drowning—and there was nothing there.

And then a light flashed, the vivid reflection of a word, and she shot to the surface, the tablet still clutched to her chest. She hung there for a moment, treading water, then swam slowly toward the side of the boat. Lewis was kneeling in the bow and reached out to gather her in, but she handed him the tablet instead.

Behind him, Mitch stood frozen, the gesture of unbinding just completed. He saw her hands on the side of the boat, and collapsed soundlessly onto a thwart. "God, Alma—"

"It wasn't the creature," she said. "Something else…."

Lewis handed the tablet carefully to Jerry, who stuck it in his pocket, and reached to help her over the side. She came over awkwardly, thrashing like a fish, sat up dripping in the bottom of the boat.

"There was a net," she began, and broke off, realizing that there was still a length of it around her ankle. Jerry flicked on the flashlight again, keeping it below the edge of the boat.

"Thrax," he said. "The Thracian."

He hadn't sounded so shaken since Gil's death. Alma reached out to pat his good knee, and Mitch said, "What are you talking about?"

"The thing's first host," Jerry said. "The gladiator, the Thracian retiarius—that's a net-thrower, Al, a gladiator's nightmare of a fisherman. That's the man who killed the Rex Nemorensis, that's what freed the creature. Harris showed me a tablet today, a funeral tablet for the man. That's why it was there, to bind his soul to the lake. Part of the profanation…."

"Are you all right?" Lewis said. He had brought a towel, wrapped it around her shoulders and held her through it. Alma leaned back, grateful for his touch.

"I'm Ok," she said. She leaned down and unwound the last piece of net from her foot. It looked ordinary, unremarkable, and she dropped it overboard with a shudder.

"He's gone now," Mitch said, grimly. "You sure you're Ok, Al?"

She nodded. "I'm fine. The main thing is, we have the tablet."

Jerry looked up, flicking off the flashlight. "And it's the only one." His voice was steady again. "This completes the binding."

"Good," Alma said, and reached for her trousers. "Then we can go on from here."

Chapter Twenty-five

It watched them from the grove. It felt when the woman touched the other tablet. It knew they were coming, certain as a hunted man hears the baying of hounds.

This one gave it no trouble. He was a strong young man with a whole body, but he was afraid. He believed in demons and their power to destroy. It could rule him.

Once it had waited thus, in the dark places beneath the Nemeton. Long years it had lain silent, held by a goddess's silver power, held by rites as old as men. It had waited. It knew patience. Sooner or later, one would come.

The Thracian had walked into the woods without fear. He was a big man, and strong, but that was not why he sought the grove's king. He did an emperor's bidding. He did not come as a fugitive but as an assassin. He came to the dividing paths with sword and knife, walking the forest pathways with his mind filled with an emperor's treasure, riches promised in return for death, and there he slew the king of the woods, spilled out his blood like a stag's on the thirsty ground.

It came.

And it tasted.

The Thracian came out of the woods in triumph, priest and king and something more besides. It held him. It ruled him. It savored power and blood.

But why settle for the sham of kingship when true dominion might be had? What could be better than to be ruler of the world?

It was easy, so easy, to take the young emperor. It was so easy to slake every thirst.

But now they came, her hounds. It saw them stop beside the lake, speaking together. The cripple and the woman bent their heads one to the other, the big one beside them. But the other....

His eyes sought it, raked the tree line, tension in every fiber of his frame. His eyes saw more than mere light illuminated, an oracle's eyes, the eyes of a priest. He knew it waited. And he watched.

The young man dodged back, a reflex born of its alarm, and it let him go, let him fade back behind the trees. It was going to have to get rid of them, now, or all its plans would come to naught. It paused in the deeper dark, the young man panting his fear. One man against three, and even if one was crippled there was still the woman. It had learned already not to underestimate her. Perhaps more mundane methods? There were men in plenty sleeping at the site, ready to defend what they had found. There was a pleasing irony in turning them against the hunters. It rose, enjoying the lithe play of the young man's muscles, and slipped further back into the trees.

"It's here," Lewis said.

Alma broke off. "What?"

"The thing. It's there in the edge of the wood, watching." Lewis scanned the trees, frowning.

"Is it the same host?" Jerry asked.

"I don't know," Lewis said, and Alma shook her head.

"It doesn't matter. It won't have picked on anyone weaker, that's for sure."

"Unless it's gotten to one of the archeologists," Jerry began, and Lewis thought he looked sick at the idea.

"It's young," he said, knowing that was only ambiguous reassurance. "And—it's moving away."

Mitch let out a long breath. "Ok," he said. "So what do we do now?"

"We have to get further into the woods," Jerry said. "We have to be far enough in that fresh digging won't be noticed. Then we do the binding. That's what we have to do."

"Wait," Alma said. "Lewis, where's it going?"

Lewis paused. He couldn't really see into the dark between the trees, but he could feel its movements, feel it fumbling through the brush—heading along the shore, back toward the ships, toward the dig site. "Damn. It's going back to the dig."

"To raise the alarm," Mitch said.

Lewis looked at Alma, who lifted her face to the sky as though she was trying to guess the time from the occluded stars. "Jerry, how long will it take—"

"Too long," Jerry answered, grimly. He reached into his pocket, brought out the first tablet in its wrappings.

"Jerry," Mitch said, warily, and Jerry peeled back the layers of burlap and silk, exposing the bronze.

"Creature of darkness!" Jerry's voice wasn't loud, but it had a peculiar resonance that sent a shiver down Lewis's spine. He heard Alma take a breath and hold it, her eyes wide. "By the virtue of the holy names that bound you, I defy you, you who are abhorred of mankind. You were bound, you are bound, you will be bound. As you were before, so shall you be."

The air was very still, echoless, but the words seemed to reverberate. Alma let out her breath with a sudden sigh. "Oh, Jerry."

"That—was not a good idea," Mitch said, tightly.

"Do you have a better one?" Jerry asked, winding the tablet back into its wrappings.

Lewis looked back at the woods. He could feel the creature hesitate, turn back, and then it was lost again, vanished into the trees where not even his Sight could follow it. "What was that all about?"

"Jerry challenged it," Mitch said. "Threatened it." He paused. "Lewis, do you think it has a gun?"

Lewis frowned. "No. If it had a gun it would already have shot us."

"Do you have a better plan?" Jerry asked again. "Look, we can't let it raise the alarm. Putting aside what could easily happen to us if it does, we'd lose our only chance to stop it. And then—then it takes Il Duce, and who knows what will happen?"

"But now it really knows we're coming," Mitch said. "And it knows what we're going to do."

"It knew that anyway," Alma said. She wrapped her arms around herself as a sudden breeze stirred the lake behind them. Lewis lifted his head at a sudden hint of sweetness, a breath of green herbs rising above the smell of the mud. "We go on."

"All right," Mitch said, and hefted the shovel. "Jerry, are you up to climbing around in the woods?"

The words were meant as a peace offering, Lewis thought, but Jerry glared. "I have to be, don't I?" he snapped. "There isn't anything else to do. Except split up, and you know that's a colossally bad idea."

"We'll stick together," Alma said, "and pick as level a path as possible."

"We can handle it," Lewis said, his eyes still on the woods. "It's afraid of us because it knows that."

Together they passed into the shadow of the trees.

The ground was worse on this side of the lake. Jerry knew he should have expected it, should have planned for it somehow—a better cane, more light, not standing exposed on the edge of the battery platform to make one last observation…. His leg slipped again, throwing him forward onto the slope. He caught himself on hands and knee, the mud and loam cold between his fingers, knew he made no more sound than the thud and the exhalation of his breath, but Lewis looked back at once, met his gaze, and looked away again. There was a calm there that frightened Jerry, the calm of a king, of a priest, and he wanted unreasonably to shatter it, to demand that Lewis keep the promise he'd made or half-made or anyway implied by sharing Alma's bed. But that wasn't how the story ran, wasn't the way the temple was built. He'd made his own promises, too.

He planted his cane again, digging into the soft ground, and hauled himself up by main force. *Take me*, he said silently, to the moon not yet risen. *Take me instead.*

The ground gave way again beneath the wooden peg, and he fell sideways, wrenching his knee. The pain shot up to his hip, down the missing ankle, so bright and hard that he almost expected to see a flash of light. His breath caught in his throat, and this time it was Mitch who looked back.

"Are you all right?"

"Give me a hand," Jerry said, softly. With Mitch's arm under his and the cane to brace him, he got himself upright, and carefully put his weight on the artificial leg. Pain flared, but not as strong, and he knew the knee would carry him at least a little further. "Ok. I'm Ok."

The ground eased a bit as they reached what must have once been the top of a terrace, and Jerry paused to catch his breath, looking back toward the lake. They hadn't come far, despite all his efforts; the mist still curled from the water like smoke, and the broken clouds hid the rising moon. In the distance, the pumps beat, the only reminder of the present.

A few yards ahead, Alma and Lewis conferred in low voices, Lewis with the hooded look that meant he was seeing more than was merely visible, and then they moved off again. Jerry followed, wincing as each step jarred the tendons beneath his knee. Mitch was making heavy going of it, too, his fist to his gut when he thought no one was looking. We're a fine lodge, Jerry thought. Gil would have made us plan—would have made us wait until we could get guns, made sure we had the advantage, not gone off into the woods armed with knives and a shovel, a cripple and a wounded man and a woman—and Lewis. That was how the dice fell every time. The ace of spades, the ten of swords, every time they cut the deck. Lewis.

I am willing, he said, to the night, to the grove. *Take me.*

Mitch hefted the borrowed knife, judging weight and length. His stomach throbbed with his heartbeat: clearly carrying the boat hadn't been a good idea after all. Not that there was anyone else who could have done it, that was the problem. And, that being the case, there was nothing to be done. Put it aside and move on.

He didn't like the way this was shaping up. The creature was ahead of them, Lewis said, up the slope and retreating into the thicker woods. Bad ground all the way, and plenty of chances to get them separated, pick them off one by one. He wished his charm had extended far enough to get them a gun—there had to be relics left over from the war—but the Ruggiero cousin had been worried enough when he'd asked for knives. A gun would have made him back out altogether.

He should have tried. Gil would have tried. Hell, Gil would have succeeded, told some crazy story that somehow sounded plausible, left them all laughing and with the gun and ammunition resting in their pockets. Gil was dead. Move on.

His gut spasmed again, and he dug his fist into the torn muscles, chasing pain with pain. He'd thought there'd been less blood this morning, had hoped it was healing again, but carrying the boat had nearly done him in. Thank God he hadn't had to row.

Something rustled in the thick creeper that grew beside what passed for a path. He turned, lifting the knife, and saw the leaves trembling at ankle height. Some ordinary animal, frightened by their presence: nothing to worry about. He took a breath, felt it hitch in his groin, and made himself move on.

They would find the spot, he told himself. They'd find the spot, and Jerry would set the circle, and they'd call the thing and bind it. If they could drive it out of its host, it would be trapped, would have no place to go but the tablets, and the tablets would call it, compel it. Then they would complete the binding, bury the tablets, and put an end to the creature. Or at least put it where it could harm no one else.

The path they'd been following took a sharp turn and came into a scrap of more open ground. To the left, the hillside dropped away toward the lake, a slope of earth and rock like the scar of an avalanche. The moon was up now, the third quarter lifting over the hills to the east, the clouds fading. A good night for flying, he thought, irrelevantly; good weather tomorrow, too.

"Well?" Alma said softly, and Lewis hunched his shoulders for a moment.

"Further up," he said. "Deeper in the woods. That way."

"Damn," Jerry said, under his breath.

Mitch glanced back, saw him take a step and stumble, the artificial leg catching somehow so that he fell forward and sideways, the cane clattering away from him down the slope. It wasn't the first time he'd fallen, but this time he was slow to get up, rolled to his knees and then sat back on the ground, reaching for the leg of his pants.

"No," he said. "Oh, not now."

The clouds cleared the moon, throwing sudden shadows, and Mitch caught his breath. The wooden peg was cracked through, bent at a thirty-degree angle a little above where the ankle would have been. There was no walking on that, not on this ground, and Mitch dug his fist into his stomach again.

"Are you all right?" Alma asked. "I mean, otherwise."

Jerry bit back something unpleasant, and nodded instead. "Yes. But I can't walk."

"I see that," Alma said, steadily. "All right. You'll—you and Mitch will stay here. It's as safe as any place we've passed, you'll be able to see anybody coming from the woods or from the lake."

"Al," Mitch began, and she fixed him with a stare.

"I told you before, I know you're hurt. And we can't leave anyone alone."

Lewis came back up the slope, carrying Jerry's cane. Jerry took it from him silently and handed him the wrapped tablets in exchange. "Al's right."

"I know she's right," Mitch said. He made himself smile, though he felt more like cursing. "She always is."

Lewis smiled back. "She's good like that." He looked at Alma, and she nodded. "That way."

Mitch watched them go, vanishing almost at once into the dark between the trees. The moon was behind a cloud again, and the air felt suddenly cold.

"Damn it," Jerry said again.

Right. Mitch took his fist away, and began looking around the slope for pieces of wood. He came back with a handful of sticks, the biggest as thick as three fingers, and sat down beside Jerry, who gave him a look.

"What the hell are you doing?"

"Trying to fix your leg," Mitch answered.

Jerry stared at him. "What's the point?"

"We're going to have to walk out of here sometime," Mitch said, and hoped it was true.

The trees arched overhead. Between their branches the stars shone, close and distant at once. Beneath his feet last years' leaves crackled unbearably loud on the forest floor. He held up his hand, and Alma stopped, silent in his shadow. Sight was useless, physical or otherwise; the creature had pulled the dark around itself like a cloak. Lewis listened.

There was no sound except for the wind in the branches, the

distant hooting of an owl. The woods were still.

And yet the wind told him something. A rank small, faint and real, a young man unwashed from a day of hard labor, his scent sharp with fear. He was there, just northwards, upwind. He was waiting.

Behind him Alma stood frozen, the shovel in her hands.

There was no sound.

And here was the problem. If they stopped where they were and started digging, it would be upon them. It had a knife. And it would have the jump on them. It could kill Alma before he could close, particularly if he were using the shovel, or it could attack him while she was digging. Certainly they'd never get a hole dug and some kind of ritual performed before it was on them, especially once it realized what they were doing. If Jerry and Mitch had been there—but they weren't. It was him and Alma, and they weren't enough. The creature had every reason to attack, and nothing to lose.

Which meant he was going to have to take it down first.

The knowledge settled over him, a cold certainty. This was what it came down to, just as it always had, hand to hand in the dark forest. He was going to have to kill its host.

And he was going to have to get rid of Alma. He couldn't guard and hunt at the same time. While she was here, she was his vulnerability. He would guard her with his life, and in so doing, gave up initiative. He had to be free to go after it.

Lewis beckoned to her, his voice dropped low, but not whispering. The sound would carry less that way. "We need to ambush it," he said. "This is going to take nerve."

"Ok." Her eyes met his squarely, light-filled beneath the stars, and it washed over him that this might be the last time he saw her. The last things he said to her would be lies.

Lies that kept her safe. "I want you to head back to the lake toward Mitch and Jerry. Don't try to be quiet. Make it follow you. I'll be right behind it, stalking it. That's the only way I see to get the jump on it. You decoy it, and I'll get it."

She stared at him, and he willed her to believe.

"No." Alma shook her head. "What are you really— Lewis, no."

"There's no other way," he said. "Tell me if there is, you're the Magister, but—there isn't one."

He saw her take a breath, saw her face crumple just for an instant, before she smoothed the fear and grief away. "No," she said again. "There isn't."

He took her by the shoulders, wanting to kiss her, one quick goodbye, just in case, and she lifted her thumb to mark a cross on his forehead.

"God go with you," she said. "You are the lodge, tonight."

He did kiss her then, a brush of lips that was almost chaste, and released her. "Go on."

With a nod she turned, walking straight-backed through the trees, her hair pale in the moonlight. Lewis turned his back on her, knowing it could see him, and lifted his knife. Challenge, a blade glinting in the dappled moonlight through spring branches. The oldest challenge of all.

Two men go into the wood and one returns.

There was a small, swift noise among the trees, a shadow of movement. It was angling off, uphill, deeper into the woods. It knew.

He was the hunter now. He would follow and avoid its traps, follow relentlessly. Every sense sang, and his sweat dried cold on his skin. Branches stirred in the wind, moonbeams making a track through the forest. He would do what had to be done.

Hunter and hunted, they passed into the eaves of the forest.

Alma walked straight-backed down the path that led back toward the lake, too proud to turn, too afraid of what she might already see. She was tempted to turn back, so tempted—she was the Magister, after all, she had more than a knife at her disposal, and Lewis, strong as he was physically, was metaphysically untried. But. She was Magister, and this was her task. The story had passed beyond her. She had given her blessing, and let him go.

Because now she could not mistake the story. Two men go into Diana's grove, and only one returns, but he returns a king. Two men go into the grove.... *He doesn't need to return a king, Diana, so long as he returns.*

She kept walking, careless of the noise she made. The creature was hunting elsewhere, neither she nor Mitch nor Jerry were at risk now, not unless.... She slew that thought. Her clothes were still damp, sticking to her body, and she pulled them free, scowling. Her wrist and ankle stung where the net had chafed them. Her heart leaped then, but Lewis had the tablets. Jerry had given him the other one after he had broken his leg. So he had all the tools, everything he would need except the training.

And that's why I should be there, she thought, rebelliously. That's why I should go back. I know what to do, I've been trained, and I'm strong. But I wasn't chosen. She lifted her head, looking for the moon among the leaves above her head. That was the heart of the matter, and the hardship: Lewis had been chosen, and she had not, and by all her oaths and training, she was bound to bless him and walk away. That was what it meant to command, to be Magister, to be able to send the right man and not go herself, even into the heart of danger, and she would pay that price. And if it required more.... She shook her head, refusing to allow the words to form. If it required more, well, she knew loss already. She would survive.

Lewis pushed his way through the undergrowth, leaves catching at his sleeves, slapping at his face. The creature had long since left the trail; he followed the noises it made, and it followed him, the two of them circling in the dark. He had no idea how to find the trail again, but that was a worry for later. Now there was just the dance, the hunt.

He could hear something moving off to his right, a sudden thrashing in the underbrush. He took a quick step back, and a deer leaped through the gap between two trees, disappeared again into the dark. Disturbed by the creature, he guessed, and braced himself for the attack. For an instant, he caught the smell of it, sweat and fear, and then it was backing away, the sounds receding, surprise lost.

Lewis took a deep breath, let heart slow, and touched the tablets in his pocket. Ok, he thought, still there. Jerry said if it was dragged out of its host and couldn't go anywhere else, it would go into the tablets, and, let's face it, I'm probably going to have to kill this guy to get anywhere. And then it will be in the tablets, and I can take them back to Al and Mitch and Jerry and they can do whatever they have to do to bind and bury it. Maybe, if I'm really, really lucky, I won't have to kill him. But somehow I'm going to have to force it back into the tablets. Somehow. If that was the story.

He looked up at the moon, just visible now between the leaves. Whatever else this was, it was her story, Diana's story, her grove and her injury and her ancient enemy, out there in the wood. He'd seen it when he sent Alma away, though he hadn't fully understood, and now that he did understand, he felt the chill of fear on his skin. Who was he to do this? Nobody, a washed up ex-Army pilot with a failed marriage, a weak sister who was happy to sponge off his friends, to let his girlfriend wear the pants, too cowardly to risk doing the right thing….

Alma's voice spoke in memory: *if we don't do this, who will?*

Who am I? A wry smile twisted his lips. I'm who there is.

I am yours, he said to the moon. *Merciless one, untouched and untouchable, I am yours.*

He passed between the trees where the deer had jumped, and found the path its herd had worn through the forest. The creature had moved off, out of earshot for now, but Lewis knew it was waiting, ready to strike. He followed the deer track anyway, figuring he'd trade mobility for exposure, and came abruptly to a fork in the path, the track dividing beneath the trees. The hairs at the back of his neck prickled. Crossroads.

He knelt down on the loam to taste the wind, to look for tracks and consider.

The procession came among the trees in bright sunlight, maidens in white leading it, their arms loaded with flowers. Youths followed, their tunics ungirdled, freshly leafing branches in their hands. And behind the ram walked, his horns wreathed with ivy, fresh to the sacrifice….

This way. This way was the grove, the original temple. It had not been a building of marble by the lake, not to begin with. It had been a grove in truth, a place in the wild wood where Diana laid Her hand long before Rome was built, before black ships plowed the seas.

The paths divided in the wood. Lewis took the left hand one.

⁂

Alma made her way out between the trees and found Mitch and Jerry waiting in the clearing where she had left them. Jerry had his cane ready to hand, a pitiful weapon, and Mitch bent over him as though he were bandaging Jerry's wooden leg. No, she realized, splinting it, mending it—so very Mitch, to ready himself for the future even at the worst of times. They both looked up at her approach, and Jerry closed his eyes, seeing her alone.

"Lewis?" Mitch sat back on his heels, frowning.

"Back in the woods," Alma said. Her voice threatened to break, and she controlled it ruthlessly.

"You didn't leave him," Mitch began, and she glared down at him.

"Yes, I did. It was necessary."

"But you're our Magister. It's your job to protect him."

"I did everything I could," Alma answered, stung, "and this is the way the cards fell."

"He's gone to the grove," Jerry said, and Mitch gave him a startled look.

"Damn it. It should have been me," Mitch said.

"Or me, or Jerry, or anyone, yes, I know." Alma made her voice hard so that no one could hear the tears. "But it's not our choice, it's moved beyond our choice. He's gone to the grove."

Jerry stretched out his arm and she came into its shelter, settling herself beside him on the cold ground. Mitch patted her knee, apology and proffered comfort, and went back to fixing Jerry's leg. The clouds were clearing, the quarter moon sailing free. The mist was fading from the lake, and the moon's reflection was visible, Diana's Mirror in truth. Jerry's arm tightened around her shoulder, and just for a moment longer she let herself lean against his warmth, and breathe in the smell of sweat and tobacco and the amber of his cologne. Then she pushed herself to her feet and went to stand on the edge of the slope, looking out onto the lake, her back to the grove.

Lewis slipped between the trees, the knife ready in his hand. He knew the creature was ahead of him in the dark, could guess that it was circling to his right, trying to drive him back onto the broken ground he had just crossed. The footing would be bad there for a fight. He edged left instead, between saplings springing from a shattered stump, feeling his way up the gentle slope.

The sudden movement had him turning even before his mind had fully registered what he'd seen, so that the rushing attack caught him on the flank and shoulder, not the back. The man it wore was young and strong, taller than Lewis by a finger's breadth, and heavier. Lewis went down under the onslaught, landed kicking and rolled free as his heel hit the other man's knee and his elbow caught him in the gut. He caught a quick glimpse of the stranger—young, fair, hair cut short over staring eyes—and then the creature was on him again, flourishing what looked like a gardener's pruning knife. Lewis dodged the first sweep, but the second touched him, the wicked hooked tip of the knife slicing across the point of his shoulder. He ignored the flaring pain, stepped into the younger man's guard, felt his own knife slice cloth and flesh, skipping along the other's ribs. The young man hissed with the shock and pulled away, vanishing into the dark.

One of the Marines, Lewis thought. One of the French Marines from the wreck. It must have jumped from Henry to him, and then dragged him south to the dig. Ok, he's younger than me, and it felt like he's faster, but I might be a little stronger. And I've killed, and I don't believe he has. He's too young to have fought in the War. I can take him.

He circled to his right, remembering the rocks behind him, remembering the pitch of the ground. It had been like this over France, time stretching between heartbeats, all the pieces of the dance sharp and clear in his mind. Here's the Fokker, there's the ack-ack, there's our line and theirs and the steeple with the sniper, and there's only one right move that brings you onto the enemy's tail, guns spitting fire, until the stranger crumples and falls from the sky, flames eating the wings.... He had loved the hunt then, that was his dirty secret, and a part of him reveled in it even now.

He moved deeper into the trees, ears cocked for the slightest hint of sound. It was darker here, the undergrowth ready to trip and tangle, but he moved with patience, the knife ready in his hand. The Marine was turning, trying to get on his tail; Lewis shifted his hand on the knife, shortening his grip, and moved left, edging into the greater darkness. He heard the Marine stumble, turned slowly. Yes, there he was, a black shape facing the path. Lewis gathered himself and sprang.

The Marine turned at the last moment, and the blow Lewis had meant for his heart sliced between ribs and arm. He ducked under the Marine's slashing counterstroke, and kicked out, trying to bring him down. The Marine dodged the blow, and brought the hooked knife around in another wild sweep. Lewis leaned out of the way, grabbed left-handed for the Marine's jacket, but the torn fabric ripped under his hand. The Marine yanked free, and disappeared into the shadows.

Lewis braced himself, and when no counterattack came, made himself stop and listen. He didn't think he'd touched him this time, but maybe he'd winded him. Yes, the other was moving away again, into the heart of the woods. He followed.

The underbrush opened up again, trees parting on a narrow clearing thick with grass. He could smell something sweet, some flower crushed by the Marine's passing, knew he was waiting in the dark between the trees. It was brighter now, the moon fully free of the clouds, caught in the branches of the trees that surrounded the clearing. Time to draw him out, he thought, and stepped into the open. He lifted his blade in salute, and the creature rushed him. Lewis swung to meet him, blocked the first wild sweep of the knife, but the second curled across his biceps, drawing a line of fire. He ducked, grabbed for the knife hand, and blocked the knee that rose for his groin. The Marine was off balance, and he drove his shoulder hard into the younger man's chest, flattening him as though they were playing football, playing for money and pride and without many rules. The Marine flailed, trying to throw him off, trying to free his knife hand; Lewis slammed his wrist against the ground, trying to get him to drop the knife, but the turf was too soft to do much good. He planted his knee in the younger man's gut, felt him try to double up, retching, and caught him by hair and arm, pulling him up to his knees so he could get his knife against the other's neck

The Marine froze, trembling. His fingers opened, the knife

falling to the turf. Lewis marked where it fell, but he had no chance to push it away. He could see the Marine's face clearly now, the moonlight at last falling full into the grove: a plain, slightly pock-marked kid, dirty and unshaven and terrified.

It's not his fault. The voice that whispered in his ears came from nowhere. *He's innocent, he had no choice. You cannot kill him for this. It's only me you want.*

Above them, the moon was silent.

Lewis hesitated, though he didn't loosen his grip. It wasn't the kid's fault—he hadn't asked the demon to possess him, had just been in the wrong place, trying to help the survivors of a terrible crash. But if he let him go—the creature controlled him, any weakness, any mercy would just be an invitation for another attack. Or it would flee, and they'd have to begin all over again, at the cost of God knew how many deaths. If the others were here, maybe they could have driven the creature out, but he'd passed beyond that point a long time ago. They had come to the heart of the grove, beyond mercy, and there was only one way out.

"No," Lewis said. Innocents died in war, he'd killed a few himself. The men he'd killed then were no more guilty than himself. And he had more to protect now, he had chosen his path. He drew the knife across the young Marine's throat.

Blood spurted, black in the moonlight. He jerked away from it, shivering, knew this was not the first time this grove had seen the sacrifice. This was where the kings were made, this was where they died—this was where the thing had first been imprisoned, the demon held at bay, bound by the bargain, the gamble of desperate men. He could see that now, the first priest, the first killer, squatting in the dark by an open grave, his life forfeit to any successful challenger, all to keep the creature bound beneath stone earth. The Thracian gladiator had never made that bargain, never looked up to the merciless sky and known his life was given, forfeit, win or lose. If he had, it could never have touched him.

He knelt on the turf, looked up at the quarter moon sailing free of the trees. This was supposed to be Jerry's job, Alma's, Mitch's.... If there were spells, prayers to be uttered, he didn't know them. *I'm yours*, he said silently. *I took your bargain gladly. Help me now.*

This was the grove. The oldest temple, older even than the procession he had glimpsed, old as the gods themselves. This was the oldest rite of all. Life for death. Two men enter the wood and one returns. He saw them then, king after king, young and old, scarred and whole, each one scraping a grave from the broken ground, burying either the challenger or the defeated king, digging the hole with knife and hands. The one who does not return is forgotten, unknown, unremarked, except by the man who killed him. The kings remember. That is also the bargain of Diana's grove.

He touched the Marine's face, feeling the skin already cool, and curled him into a fetal position so that he would be easier to move when the grave was ready. He took the tablets from his pockets, tucked them into the Marine's shirt, against the skin of his chest. Then, methodically, he began to carve the turf, marking out a grave.

The dawn was coming over the lake, stars paling though only at the far horizon was there the faintest flush of pink.

Jerry sat silent, waiting. He could only watch through the night, and so that was the thing he would do. Not for anything would he have ever watched through another night like this with her. Gil had passed at dawn, as the dying so often do. He and the doctor and Alma.... Mitch had made coffee. Because it was what he could do.

Now there was no coffee, only silence. Only the sound of the distant pumps, the first chirpings of birds in the eaves of the woods, singing aloud to their mates.

Alma sat with her knees drawn up, her arms around them, staring at the lake.

Mitch said nothing.

But sooner or later one of them would have to. One of them would have to say, "Let's go back to the dig." One of them would have to say, "Alma...."

It could damn well be Mitch this time. Jerry bent his head, his face against his arms.

Alma made a tiny sound, some strangled sort of cry, and Jerry's eyes popped open.

Lewis was coming through the edge of the woods. His hands and clothes were smeared with blood and dirt, a day's growth of beard on his face. He walked stiffly and he bore no weapon.

Alma started to her feet, a choked noise escaping from her throat, and Lewis came down the bank carefully. His eyes were dark.

She came to him but did not embrace him, just stood forearm to forearm, looking into his face.

"It's me," Lewis said. He took the amulet from his pocket and held it in his hand, unblemished steel shining with power. Beside it lay a red stone, carved carnelian. His voice was steady, almost dispassionate. "I buried him in the woods in the old grove, where the first altar was, the tablets with him. He was a French Marine. I don't know his real name." His eyes roved over Alma's face as Jerry and Mitch came up, Mitch's hand on his knife. "I buried him as king of the grove. That's what took so long. I dug the grave with my hands."

Jerry swallowed.

"Is that only Lewis?" Mitch asked.

Jerry nodded and put his hand on Lewis', the amulet and stone between them. "Yes," he said. Lewis, marked with blood, with fading marks of power. "You are Her priest," he said.

Lewis nodded. He looked at Alma, and his eyes were bright with pleading. "It was the only way," he said. "It was the only way for the story to work. Don't you see? The only way to fix it was to make it right."

"Two men go into the wood," Jerry said. "And one returns Rex Nemorensis, Diana's priest." He looked up at the paling sky. "But Her grove is the world, and Her dominion far greater than this valley."

Alma lifted one hand, put it against Lewis' cheek. He almost flinched, stilled himself with will. "You killed him."

"Yes."

Her eyes were on his. "And you are Hers for how long?"

Mitch made a slight movement. He knew the answer, but Jerry gave him a warning look.

"For the rest of my life," Lewis said gently. "And God willing that will be long."

Jerry felt his eyes prickle. "Until She takes back what she has given," Jerry said. "Until She calls for the sacrifice. Until it is needed."

Alma nodded, her gaze never moving from Lewis' face. "Ok," she said. She looked away, casting around at the valley. "Do you actually have to stay here? I mean, I like Italy, but…."

"I don't think so," Lewis replied. "It's like Jerry said. Her grove is the world, and we are all within it, hunters and hunted alike."

The rose flush of dawn crept higher, and a water bird took flight, long slow lazy strokes gliding over the lake. Jerry took the stone from Lewis' hand, held it up to the growing light. "Seal stone," he said. "Roman, probably second century." The carving was deep and sharp, clear as though it had been carved yesterday. A running hound.

"I found it when I dug the grave," Lewis said. "I thought…."

Jerry handed it back to him. "It's yours," he said. "Your office." His voice was oddly choked, and he cleared his throat. "We should get out of here before people start showing up for work."

"Right," Mitch said. "Let's go."

Jerry needed Alma's help to get down the bank, and she put her arm around his waist to do it. Mitch fell back beside Lewis, and Jerry heard what he said, though he spoke quietly. "I'll be here when the time comes," Mitch said.

"I know," Lewis said, and there was certainty there.

They came slowly down out of the hills in the swelling light, Jerry leaning heavily on his cane and whoever was closest to hand. Except Mitch, Alma saw with relief. Jerry managed himself so that it was always her or Lewis who took his weight, and that was a good thing. Mitch was looking gray, not bothering to hide the fist pressed into his belly, and she'd seen Lewis steady him when they thought she wasn't looking. One more thing to deal with now that they had survived.

The sun was not yet up beyond the rim of the hills, but the sky was bright, the last clouds fading to the west into the promise of a clear day. A beautiful day for flying, the air gentle, thermals on the hills and cooler air in the bowl of the lake. She'd seen the birds soaring yesterday, too high to be more than the flicked sketch of wings against the blue. They'd be up again today, riding the rising air, circling silent and uncaring over the bustle of the Prime Minister's visit. And no one would faint, there would be no political shocks, no spreading scandal. All the things that might have happened now would not. She closed her eyes for a moment in silent thanks, then concentrated on keeping them moving together toward the road.

The woods looked vastly different by daylight, but Lewis led them unerringly, down paths that at first were so faint that Alma barely recognized them as more than an occasional break in the undergrowth, and then by wider tracks that had been made by human feet, and finally at last onto the rutted track that led to where they had left the car. The sun was up at last, just breaching the ring of the hills, and Alma paused to take stock.

They looked better than they had after the airship crash, but that wasn't saying much. There was mud on the knees of Jerry's trousers, and on the elbows and cuffs of his well-cut jacket. Mitch was muddy, too, and disheveled, but Lewis.... She grimaced, and he met her eyes with a apologetic shrug. He was frankly filthy, and in the rising light, some of the stains showed rusty brown. She doubted she looked much better herself, crumpled and water-stained. At least the car would hide the worse of their disarray, and there was a back entrance to the penzione from the old stables where they'd been told to leave the car.

"We need to keep moving," she said, more for the sound of a human voice than because they didn't know it, and Jerry dredged a smile from somewhere.

"Thank God for modern transportation."

He made easier progress on the road, and now it was Mitch who lagged behind. Alma watched him out of the corner of her eye, saw him disappear into the woods for a moment and return wincing. It was the old trouble, then, and that meant they'd have to find a doctor sometime soon.

The car was where they had left it, pulled neatly off the pavement into the shadow of the pines. Alma rested her hand on the door, still chill with dew, and waited for the others to come up. Jerry couldn't drive, of course, and Lewis needed to be hidden—

"I'll drive," Mitch said.

She drew breath, ready to protest, and he smiled.

"Come on, Al, three guys, and you're driving? That's asking for the Carabinieri to take notice."

And Jerry couldn't drive, and Lewis needed to be hidden. Alma gave a reluctant nod. "You're right. But—take it easy, will you?"

"Trust me," Mitch said, and she almost believed him.

The back seat was narrow, a struggle for Jerry, but once they were in, it was hard to see past the round rear windows. Jerry had taken off his jacket, handed it to Lewis, who flung it over himself like a blanket. They might pass for travelers, Alma thought, living rough. She took her place at Mitch's side, and waited while he coaxed the engine to life. They waited, letting the car warm up, and Alma tipped her face to the sun, relaxing for what seemed like the first time since they'd left Los Angeles. She could almost sleep now, safe here, all of them safe for now....

"Al?" Mitch said, and she shook herself awake.

"I'm ready if you are."

"Ok," he said, and slid the car into gear.

There wasn't much traffic on the road at this hour. They were behind the milkman, Alma guessed, and ahead of even the first workmen, though as Mitch swung the car onto the main lake road, they passed a farm cart piled with hay. And then they were at the crossroads, where the pilgrim road came down from Rome, and a man in a dark uniform and a bicorn hat worn crossways held up a hand to stop them.

"Carabinieri," Jerry said quietly, to Lewis, and Alma saw Lewis slump down further beneath the concealing jacket.

Mitch downshifted, bringing the car to a smooth stop, and rolled down his window. "Is there a problem?"

The man looked down his nose and didn't deign to answer, but a second policeman moved back from the intersection. He was carrying a carbine in white-gloved hands. "The Prime Minister is coming," he said. "The road is temporarily closed."

"Oh," Mitch said. "All right, then. Thank you."

He left the window down, and Alma could hear already the sound of engines, coming rapidly closer. Across the road, a third policeman had stopped another cart and a pair of young women on bicycles; another bicycle stopped behind their car, and then a battered canvas-topped truck. The engines were louder now. She could make out motorcycles, the deeper note of several heavy cars. And then the first of the motorcycle escort flashed into view, more dark uniforms and polished boots and gauntlets. The Carabinieri snapped to attention, arms extended in the Roman salute, and the first of the three cars slid by. It was followed by an open car, and in it sat a man in uniform, jaw jutting proudly, the sunlight glinting from a chest spangled with medals.

"That's him," Jerry said, leaning forward.

We were in time, Alma thought. We did it—Lewis did it, at a cost I don't want to think about. But—we did what we came to do.

"He'll go to Nemi," Jerry said, softly, as though he'd read her thought, and the same tired wonder was in his voice. "He'll look at the finds, and he'll make a speech, and he'll go back to Rome none the wiser."

A third car roared past, and a fourth, smaller: a press car, Alma guessed, and shook her head. Dust hung in the air behind it, hazy in the morning light. The policeman checked the road, then motioned them impatiently across. Mitch put the car into gear, and eased forward.

"Let's go home," he said.

Chapter Twenty-six

The warm morning sunlight danced on the cobblestones of the terrace of the Hotel St. Charles in Paris. Alma sipped her café au lait, sweet and rich with cream, her forearms resting on the edge of the white clothed table. Hotel St. Charles had been built in the 18th century as a private house, and no doubt in that day this had been the stable yard, but now it had been converted into a lovely outdoor dining area surrounded on three sides by the hotel. An ancient elm tree made up the fourth side, spreading its limbs over the courtyard, while palms in pots created secluded seating areas. It was late morning, but she and Lewis were nearly the only patrons.

Lewis took his coffee black. Freshly shaved and washed, his hair combed like Valentino, he looked quite handsome. If there was a shadow in his eyes, it was less than it had been. The awesome weight seemed to sit on him less heavily every day. Perhaps he was just growing used to it, or perhaps Diana had nothing she demanded of him at present, and so her power and her favor rested lightly upon him, an ordinary seeming man of thirty nine, good looking and a little shy.

"It was nice of Henry to spring for the hotel," Lewis said. "I mean, under the circumstances."

"Under the circumstances that we saved his life, prevented the complete ruination of his business, and haven't gotten him indicted for murder?" Alma asked. "Yes, under the circumstances paying for the hotel was nice of him."

"It wasn't Henry's fault," Lewis said fairly. "It could have happened to anybody. It didn't seem right to rat him out when he couldn't prevent what was happening."

"I know." Alma took another sip of her coffee. "Henry's not

guilty of anything except the unwise decision to go after Davenport alone, and he feels responsible for everything that happened anyway." She put the cup down with a sigh. "Sûreté seems to have decided that it was an anarchist plot against capitalists. Which I suppose makes as much sense as anything else. Jerry and Mitch are having one more meeting with Inspector Colbert, and then perhaps they'll be satisfied."

Lewis shook his head, looking around the pretty dining area. "It seems so unreal."

"Everything that happened?"

"No, this." Lewis gave her a rueful smile. "That seems like the realest thing in the world." He reached across the table to take her hand, his eyes on her fingers as though he dreaded to look at her face. "Alma. I can't ask you to go through this again, through losing someone like that. I'm a marked man, and…."

"Let me be the judge of what I can take," Alma said tartly. She closed her eyes, closed her fingers in his, searching for the words. "I know you're hers. I know She can take you at any time, call for the sacrifice to be made. But it's no difference, do you see?" She opened her eyes. "You and Mitch are in the Reserves. You could be called out any time for mountain search and rescue or for a disaster. Or God help us if there's ever another war, though maybe we're done with that for our lifetimes! You're already on call, and I already accept that, just as you accept my oaths. I know Diana will take you, sooner or later when the time comes. But I can't think about that and worry about that, not anymore than I can about the other. There's plenty of time to mourn when the time comes."

Lewis closed his eyes, his fingers tightening around hers. "I love you so much. You know that."

"I was beginning to guess," Alma said. Unexpectedly, tears prickled at the corners of her eyes. "I love you too."

"Well," Lewis said. He swallowed. "I suppose the lodge isn't so hard to accept next to that." He looked up at her. "You make a great Magister."

Alma smiled. "Thank you," she said, oddly touched. "So you'll stick around then?"

Lewis squeezed her fingers. "I think I'll stick around."

Mitch made his way down the stone steps outside the Sûreté, pausing on the sidewalk to wait for Jerry and Henry. They were still arguing over something, Jerry with his cane in his hand, the mended leg braced against the marble, Henry with his hat pushed back on his head and both hands in his pockets. With his neatly trimmed beard and curling hair, he looked a bit like a bull at bay, and Mitch looked away to hide his grin. Henry'd been through hell, it wasn't fair to laugh at him. And his story of saboteurs, farfetched as it must have sounded, at least offered something like an explanation for the crash. It had also made the *aviateurs américains* who'd kept *Independence* from a worse wreck into heroes for a day, and incidentally offered an explanation for their disappearance from the crash scene. He wasn't sure Inspector Colbert really believed the story, but it was a better set of headlines for Sûreté than anything else that was likely to come out of that mess.

He arched his back slightly, feeling the scars pull: painful, but not nearly as bad as they had been. Alma'd been right, a few days of actual rest had stopped the bleeding entirely, and allowed new scars to form. And, all right, there had been a consultation with a first-class medical man, who'd examined him to be sure none of the fragments still in him were working their way toward anything life-threatening, and then shrugged and said that monsieur knew perfectly well what to do to take care of himself, and perhaps should try those things instead of racing about the countryside chasing anarchists. He wasn't in perfect shape yet, but by the time they got home, he'd be perfectly capable of flying. They'd collect the Terrier at Flushing, head back to Colorado Springs by easy stages....

Jerry was working his way cautiously down the stairs, and Mitch straightened. "Everything settled?"

"It seems to be," Jerry answered. "I'm not sure Inspector Colbert fully believed us, but there won't be any repercussions."

"I'm sure he didn't believe us," Henry said. "I don't believe it, and I—came up with it."

Mitch glanced over his shoulder, but there was no one in earshot, and Henry had spoken English anyway. "Well, I can't see the inspector going for the real story."

Jerry grinned. "No, 'possessed by a demon' isn't going to look good on his books. Anarchists are much better."

Out of the corner of his eye, Mitch saw a grimace cross Henry's face. It wasn't fair to make light of what he'd been through: half his crew dead at his own hand, his airship wrecked, his company damaged God only knew how badly, most of all the guilt of knowing it was all his fault, one bad choice.

"Will you be all right?" he asked, and Henry gave a flickering smile.

"I have reparations to make, that's for sure. And a lot of work to do—and undo, for that matter. But I'll be fine." He paused, and lifted his hand for a passing taxi. "And speaking of which, if you'll excuse me...."

"Of course," Mitch said, and watched him drive away.

Jerry shook his head. "I have no idea how he manages—"

"He's paid for what he did," Mitch said, shortly, and Jerry gave him a look.

"And he'll keep on paying, I know." He sighed. "Back to the hotel?"

It wasn't a long walk, the sun warming the air, releasing the fragrance of the flowers in every windowbox and front-door urn. Alma and Lewis were still in the courtyard, finishing a last cup of coffee, and Mitch was glad to see the look of peace on Lewis's face. And Alma—there was an ease there he hadn't seen since Gil died.

"How did it go?" she asked, and Lewis waved the waiter over.

They all ordered more coffee, and Mitch leaned back in his chair, feeling the new scars stretch and pull. "Well. The Sûreté has pretty much decided that it was anarchists, and will pursue that line if possible. And we are free to go home whenever we like."

"Yes, but how?" Lewis asked. "I mean, none of this is coming cheap—"

Jerry reached into his pocket and tossed a thick envelope onto the table. "We have tickets on the *Bremen*. Courtesy of Henry."

Alma opened the envelope and looked up sharply. "First class?"

"That's pushing it," Mitch said.

Jerry shoved his glasses up further onto his nose. "Henry tried to throw me out of the window of his airship," he said. "I think first class passage, and on a first class ship, is only fair."

"*Bremen*," Lewis said thoughtfully. "Isn't that the one with the mail plane on board?"

"Henry did suggest we might take a look at it for him," Jerry admitted.

"Oh, Jerry." Alma looked down at the tickets and slid them back into their envelope.

Something rustled in the branches above their head. Mitch squinted up into the sun-sparked leaves, but couldn't find the source. He looked at the others, Lewis watching Alma with the faintest of smiles on his face, Alma frowning at the envelope, obviously calculating the best way to meet the boat, Jerry lighting a cigarette, long face at last relaxed. "It'll be good to get home," he said.

About the Authors

Melissa Scott is from Little Rock, Arkansas, and studied history at Harvard College and Brandeis University, where she earned her PhD in the Comparative History program. She is the author of more than twenty science fiction and fantasy novels, and has won Lambda Literary Awards for *Trouble and Her Friends*, *Shadow Man*, and *Point of Dreams*, the last written with her late partner, Lisa A. Barnett. She has also won Spectrum Awards for *Shadow Man* and again in 2010 for the short story "The Rocky Side of the Sky" (*Periphery*, Lethe Press) as well as the John W. Campbell Award for Best New Writer. She can be found on LiveJournal at mescott.livejournal.com.

Jo Graham worked in politics for fifteen years before leaving to write full time. She is the author of the Locus Award nominated *Black Ships* and the Spectrum Award nominated *Stealing Fire*, as well as several other novels, including the *Stargate Atlantis* Legacy series. Her next book, *The General's Mistress*, is highly anticipated from Gallery Books. She lives in North Carolina with her partner and their daughter. She can be found online at jo_graham.livejournal.com.

About the O. C. L. T. Series

There are incidents and emergencies in the world that defy logical explanation, events that could be defined as supernatural, extra-terrestrial, or simply otherworldly. Standard laws do not allow for such instances, nor are most officials or authorities trained to handle them. In recognition of these facts, one organization has been created that can. Assembled by a loose international coalition, their mission is to deal with these situations using diplomacy, guile, force, and strategy as necessary. They shield the rest of the world from their own actions, and clean up the messes left in their wake. They are our protection, our guide, our sword, and our voice, all rolled into one.

They are O.C.L.T.

TALES OF THE O. C. L. T.

AVAILABLE NOW:

Brought to Light: An O.C.L.T. Novella by Aaron Rosenberg
The Temple of Camazotz: An O.C.L.T. Novella by David Niall Wilson
The Parting: An O.C.L.T. Novel by David Niall Wilson
Incursion: An O.C.L.T. Novel by Aaron Rosenberg

UPCOMING:

The Highjump: An O.C.L.T. Novel by David McIntee
Schrodinger's Tomb: An O.C.L.T. Novel by David Niall Wilson
Digging Deep: An O.C.L.T. Novel by Aaron Rosenberg

NOTE: *Lost Things* connects to the O.C.L.T. series but is not part of it, being the first book in a separate but affiliated series.

Want more O.C.L.T.?
Turn the page for a sneak peek at

Prologue

"Damn it!"

He ran, brushing limbs and branches from his face as he moved, the needles and leaves stabbing at his hands and wrists above his leather jacket and tugging at his long hair in its braid. In the dark they were mere shapes, fluttering shadows that blurred by as he moved, feet churning, his heavy boots stomping flat leaves and cones and bristles alike as he charged headlong through the night.

And behind him, the wind howled in the trees, and it sounded like screams of rage.

He'd tried to warn them, he reminded himself as he ran. He'd warned them not to do it, shown them the right way and urged them to follow it—but of course they wouldn't listen. They never did. Why had he thought this time would be any different?

But this time *was* different.

This time their arrogance might prove fatal.

And now he was caught in the middle.

"I'm sorry!" he shouted over his shoulder, the wind taking his words and whipping them away into the dark. "I tried to stop them!" That was a lie, though. He had warned them, yes, but had he really done anything to stand in their way? Had he really put forth his best effort to prevent them from moving forward with this insanity?

Or had he let them sway him from his own better judgment, and cow him into keeping silent?

Deep in his heart, he knew the answer to those questions, and the shame of it made him weak.

But was that enough reason for him to be facing this himself?

He didn't think so.

So he ran on, stumbling over sticks and roots, reeling as branches struck out at him, and crying as the wind continued to howl behind him and alongside him.

And then the tenor of the wind changed.

Its howls shifted, shortened, rose in pitch, became thin, reedy whistles.

And the whistles surged forward, circling him, ringing him in.

Surrounding him.

"I'm sorry!" he called out again, the words little more than a sob. "I'm so sorry! Please!"

He raised his hands high even as he dropped to his knees.

One of the flickering shadows detached itself from the darkness and raced forward, trailing his descent. Long and slender and lightning-swift, it took him just under the chin, and he felt his life leave him all in a rush, not gently tugged free but roughly shoved aside, slammed from his body by the same lethal impact that took his last breath and made his vision go dark.

He toppled to the ground, blood bubbling up in his throat and choking him, the rich scent of the earth filling his nostrils as his head hit the thin grass and the loose soil beneath, and he spasmed, unable to control his body's last urges—

—and all around him, the whistles continued through the trees, and they sounded like laughter.

1

"Remind me again what we're doing all the way up here?" R.C. muttered as he turned off Interstate 90 and onto the narrow two-lane. The sign by the road read "Flathead Indian Reservation" but there wasn't a gate or even a fence, and the land they were now driving through looked much like what they'd seen for the past hour since landing at Missoula International. Western Montana wasn't known for its variety. Or its densely populated areas.

"Just taking in the scenery," his partner Nick answered, waving one hand at the sights in question. "Which includes mountains, rivers, a lake or two, possibly some valleys—oh yeah, and a few dead bodies."

"Ah, now you make it sound interesting." R.C. grinned at her, one big hand wrapped loosely around the steering wheel and the other resting casually on the lip of the door just below the window, and she laughed and grinned back.

"You're a terrible vacation buddy, you know," she pointed out, still laughing as their rental barreled down the road, raising dust all around them in a thick cloud.

"Maybe, but I'm a good partner," he countered. That quieted them both for a second, and he cursed himself in his head for not thinking before he spoke. Would he ever learn?

Probably not.

"Where're we heading, exactly?" he asked instead, and Nick looked just as grateful as she pulled the map from her purse and checked where it had been marked.

"Pablo," she answered finally. "That's the home of the tribal headquarters, as well as the BIA local office, the Flathead Tribal Police Department, and the Salish Kootenai College. And it's only seven miles south of Polson, which is the largest community out here, at a whopping eighty-five hundred residents. Polson's also the county seat for Lake County, and home to the Kwataqnuk resort and casino."

"Thank you, Miss Tour Guide," he told her. "But no gambling while on duty, remember?" For a second he worried that he'd strayed too close to dangerous topics again, but she smiled and he relaxed a little.

"Look at that!" she said a few minutes later, as the road crested a small rise and they spotted a wave of dark shapes moving through a valley below. "Aren't they amazing?"

R.C. glanced over briefly, and had to agree. Even from this distance the massive, woolly-coated bison were impressive creatures, and the surge of their herd running full out across the plain shook the road beneath their wheels and filled the air with the pounding of their hooves. He'd never seen anything so majestic, or so powerful, at least not in person. It was truly awe-inspiring.

He wondered if the rest of this trip would prove to be as pleasant, or as easily spotted.

It took them another three hours to pull into Pablo. They'd passed five or six other communities along the way, none of them more than a few dozen homes and buildings clustered around the main road and perhaps one cross street, and the few people they'd seen had barely bothered to glance their way. But then R.C. supposed they were used to visitors. The reservation made a lot of its money off the casino, so there were always people heading too and from Polson, plus students going to the small community college in Pablo. And then there were the tourists here to see the Kerr Dam, or the Flathead Lake State Park, or seeking the St. Ignatius Mission, or looking to walk through the National Bison Range.

And then there were people like them.

"Special Agent Reed Hayes, FBI," R.C. announced after he'd

parked in front of the two-story adobe council building and he had Nick had climbed the front steps and stepped into the dark, cool inner lobby. "This is my partner, Danika Frome." He showed the woman behind the front desk his badge and ID, and beside him Nick did the same. "We'd like to speak to the tribal council."

"Just a minute," she told them, and then turned away, whispering into the mic at her throat. She was short, dark, and heavy-set, though not nearly as dark as R.C. himself—he was way beyond Native American in coloring, just as Nick was nowhere near. He knew they made a striking pair, him tall and broad-shouldered and still fit even with the gray starting to show in his short dark hair, and her average height and slender but still curvy, with her blonde-brown hair cropped close and her pale skin and big blue eyes. Even in the fitted suit, Nick didn't look like any FBI agent he'd ever imagined before joining the Bureau.

But the times, they'd certainly changed.

"Special Agent Hayes? Special Agent Frome?" The man who approached them was young, maybe thirty, with the typically glossy black hair pulled back in a ponytail, and his face was round and very friendly. He wore jeans and a denim shirt, though his leather belt had a hand-tooled silver buckle, a braided rope-tie with a carved turquoise eagle hung around his neck, and moccasins adorned his feet. Tribal casual, R.C. guessed. "I'm Detective Jonathan Couture, with the Flathead Tribal Police Department. I was assigned to the murders. Right this way."

R.C. shook hands with him, as did Nick, and then they followed him through the doors at the far end of the lobby, and up the broad staircase to the second floor. Along the way R.C. set his phone to "voice recorder" mode, and spotted Nick doing the same. It was the quickest and easiest way to take notes on the situation—they'd download those to their laptops later, run them through the dictation software to translate the audio files into text, and then clean them up to use as the basis for their status reports. He did carry a small notepad and a pen in his jacket, of course, but that was more for doodling or jotting down reminders to himself than for any real note-taking.

He was glad to see that the local cops were already on the case. The FBI took charge of any situation it was in, and some local authorities didn't appreciate being ordered around. He tried to keep things on as friendly a basis as possible—he'd always believed it was better to have willing partners than grudging assistants—and the detective's friendly attitude suggested that wouldn't be a problem here, plus obviously he would be the man to ask for details about the situation.

Detective Couture led them down the hall to a wide room that took up the entire middle of the floor, the sides of which were filled with tiered wooden seats facing a long table. It was like a courtroom—or a council room.

Ten men sat that table, most of them older if their gray-streaked hair was an indication, and all of then Native American. The reservation actually had many non-Native residents—in fact, only eight towns here were predominantly Flathead Indian, or Bitterroot Salish as the largest tribe was called—but the tribe still controlled the reservation as a whole, and non-Natives couldn't be members of the tribal council.

"Welcome, agents Hayes and Frome," one of the men announced. He didn't look like the oldest member present—that honor was reserved for the elderly gentleman to the far right, whose braids were almost snow-white and hung down his chest probably to his waist—but his face was deeply lined and his braids were adorned with feathers and beads. He was wearing jeans and a denim shirt as well, though his shirt had embroidery woven into it at the collars and cuffs and down the front panels, and his bolo tie had a silver and lapis image of a leaping trout. "I am Willy Silverstream, chairman of the tribal council. Your superiors notified us that you were coming. We appreciate the FBI's help in this matter." That was a good sign, as well—the federal government didn't have the best track record of treating Native Americans fairly, especially with regards to the reservations, and many Native Americans still resented them, but it sounded as if the council leader really was happy to have them here.

"Glad to be of service," R.C. answered, giving the old man a polite nod. He wasn't sure he could refer to him as "Willy" and still keep a straight face, and hoped it wouldn't come to that. "Why don't you tell us exactly what's been going on here, and we'll see what we can do to help?"

"Of course." Willy frowned and placed both hands flat on the table—they were lined and wrinkled, but still looked strong, the fingers thick and blunt and marked with tiny scars here and there that showed white against his weathered skin. "Men have been dying, out in the woods."

"What men?" Nick asked. "How long ago, and how often? And where in the woods?"

The old man's gaze flicked to her for half a second, and R.C. wondered if they were going to have a problem, but if the tribal elder didn't like speaking to a woman he didn't let it show in his face or his tone. "Three men so far," he answered instead, "starting a week ago. The first one, Elk in the Trees, was hunting. The second, Peter Colman, was a student at the community college, studying animal husbandry, and had been given an assignment to study the local wildlife—easy enough to do around here. The third, Roger Tanner, was a fisherman."

"All of them had lived here on the reservation their whole lives," another of the council members offered. "None of them had any enemies beyond the usual rivalries and minor arguments. Elk in the Trees was a widower with grown children, Peter Colman was engaged, and Roger Tanner was married with one small child and another on the way."

"Any connection between them, beyond being here on the reservation?" R.C. directed that question to Detective Couture, and wasn't surprised when the local cop shook his head. Of course they would have investigated that.

"How did they die?" R.C. didn't miss the pause after his question, or the way neither Willy nor this other council member would look him in the eye. He knew Nick hadn't missed it either.

It was the detective who finally answered. "They were each shot through the throat. With an arrow."

R.C. studied him, but the younger man wasn't smiling or laughing. "An arrow? Each of them? Through the throat?" He scratched at his jaw. "So we're looking for William Tell here?"

"That was a crossbow," the oldest elder corrected, though there was a trace of humor in his raspy voice that R.C. saw was mirrored in his sharp blue eyes. "Better to say you are looking for Robin Hood. But a Salish version."

"Fair enough." R.C. considered the matter seriously. "Do you have anybody who could make a shot like that, repeatedly? I'm assuming it wasn't at close range or these guys would have run, or fought back, or something?" He knew from his time on the firing range that hitting a target as small as the human throat wasn't easy, especially if you needed that first bullet—or arrow—to be a kill shot. That took real skill.

"That would make sense, yes," Willy agreed, finding his voice again. "But we don't know for certain. There were no witnesses with any of the deaths. Each time the man in question was alone in the woods, and his body was found the next day."

"So each of these attacks occurred at night?" Good of Nick to pick up on that.

"We think so, yes."

"Where did they happen?" was R.C.'s next question. He could tell from the muffled growl behind him that he'd beaten his partner to the punch on that one, and he hid the smirk that threatened to cross his lips. He could rub it in later.

"Along the edge of the Hog Heaven range," Detective Couture replied. There was a large map of the reservation tacked to the far wall above the massive stone fireplace that took up the space between two wide windows, and he stepped over to it and gestured toward an area near the northwest corner. Polson and Pablo itself were a bit south of the northeast corner, which was dominated by the lake.

"All three of them?" R.C. moved closer to study the map, Nick half a step behind him. "How big is the reservation, in all?"

"Almost two thousand square miles," Willy answered proudly. "We are one of the largest reservations in North America."

"And yet all three deaths occurred in one area," Nick pointed out. She caught R.C.'s eye. "I think we'd better take a closer look at this mountain range."

He nodded. "Can we get a guide to show us the way, and the original locations of the bodies?" He made a mental note to ask about autopsy reports as well. Assuming any had been performed.

Willy nodded, but before he could speak Detective Couture stepped forward. "I can show you," he offered, with a glance at the council members, who silently nodded permission after a second. "I know the area well, and I know where each of them were found."

"Perfect." Something else had been caught his attention, and R.C. figured he'd better mention it now before they really got into anything. "Where's the BIA in all this?" The FBI was tasked with investigating major crimes on Indian land, but the BIA, or Bureau of Indian Affairs, was responsible with maintaining law and order on the reservations otherwise, including police matters. He'd expected to find a BIA officer here waiting for them, and didn't want to step on any toes, especially if that could foul the investigation later.

A few of the elders made harrumphing noises, but they seemed as much amused as annoyed. "That would be Martin Proudfoot and Isaiah Fisher," Willy explained after a moment. "They're the only two manning the local BIA office—the rest are up at the regional office in Portland. But Martin broke his leg a few days back, bike accident, and he's stuck in traction for a bit. And Isaiah's wife's expecting—their first, and there's some complications, so he's sticking to her side over at St. Luke's." He removed a folded-up paper from a pocket in his vest, smoothed it out, and slid it across the table. "Isaiah dropped this off, though, says they were duly notified of your presence and cooperate fully, so you're in the clear." He was definitely holding back a grin, and though his lips only twitched his eyes crinkled and the lines around his mouth deepened so much they looked like furrows.

Nonetheless, the news was good. As long as the BIA knew they were here and didn't have a problem with it, R.C. wasn't too worried. He'd copy any reports to their regional office, of course, just to keep them in the loop, but honestly this way was probably better. Now he didn't have to worry about some paper-pusher dogging his steps along the way.

He turned back to Willy and the others. “We’ll let you know what we find, of course. Hopefully we can resolve this quickly, and before anyone else gets hurt.”

Willy nodded. “That is our hope as well. Thank you.”

There were nods all around, and then Detective Couture led them back out into the hall. “The council’s booked you into the Hawthorne House, a really nice bed-and-breakfast over in Polson,” he explained as they headed down the stairs and outside. “Did you want to rest for a bit, or head straight out?”

“We should probably check in and drop off our bags,” R.C. decided. “But I’d like to get going right after that. How long will it take to get over there?”

“A few hours,” the detective answered. “I’ll get my Jeep and meet you over at the hotel in a few minutes.”

“Sounds great.” R.C. shook hands with him and watched the young Native walk off, then turned to his partner. “What do you think?”

“He seems like a straight-up guy,” she answered as they unlocked their car and got in. “And this could be as simple as one crazy guy staking out an area and shooting any ‘trespassers.’” Her tone said she wasn’t convinced, however, as did the sigh she released right after that.

“But?” he urged as he backed out and drove to the bed-and-breakfast.

She gave him a tired smile in reply. “But when is it ever that easy?”

2

"I still don't see why they couldn't have booked us there instead," Nick groused for the tenth time as they walked. She'd been complaining about the accommodations off and on since they'd checked in, and R.C. knew she was only half-kidding. The Hawthorne House where they were staying at seemed decent enough—big airy rooms, clean whitewashed walls, hardwood floors, high ceiling beams, nice big beds.

But Nick was stuck on the fact that there was a resort only a few blocks away. And that they weren't staying there.

"We're just government grunts," he reminded her yet again. "We're lucky the council is putting us up at all." Most of the time they had to arrange their own accommodations, and pay for them, too. The Bureau would reimburse them, of course. Eventually. After a mountain of paperwork and what seemed like an eternity. This time, they didn't have to deal with any of that. The council was covering their room and board, which was a lot more generous than most local agencies that had asked for their help.

But that still wasn't swaying Nick any.

"In for a penny, in for a pound," she grumbled. "It's not like we're asking to gamble. But a massage sure would be nice."

R.C. almost offered to give her one, then stopped and cursed himself for that impulse. Then cursed again for stopping what would have been a completely reasonable and harmless remark, but now would seem either forced or salacious. Damn it! Would this ever get any easier?

"It's just up ahead," Detective Couture called back. He was obviously at home in the woods and had quickly moved in front of them, though perhaps that was just to get out of range of Nick's complaints. "Where we found Elk in the Trees."

"Did you find him?" R.C. asked, pushing away questions of his partner's comfort level and focusing on the investigation again.

"No, it was a young family, the Singing Doves," their guide replied. He slowed to let them catch up a little so he didn't have to shout. R.C. had already learned that Detective Couture was very helpful but also very soft-spoken—nice when sharing a car ride but not good when trying to be heard while climbing a mountain.

Not that they were really climbing a mountain, of course. The Hog Heaven Range might contain some genuine mountains, but they were only in the foothills here. There were some decent peaks and valleys, to be sure, but R.C. had gotten used to Denver these past two years. Compared to the heights around that city, these were barely speed bumps.

The land did have a rugged beauty, however. They were well beyond any towns or villages out here, and as far as the eye could see there was nothing but thick grass and tall trees, broken here and there by a jumble of rocks or a narrow, swiftly flowing stream or a small, dark lake.

There were birds aplenty, their calls and cries and wingbeats echoing all around. R.C. had spotted a few deer as well, and Nick swore she'd seen wolves peering at her from behind a fallen tree. Detective Couture had assured her that wolves would never attack three armed men—he'd brought a hunting rifle along, grabbing it from the Jeep's back window probably out of reflex, and R.C. had decided not to raise a fuss about it. They were the guests here, after all.

"They were out on a nature walk," the detective was explaining, and it took R.C. a second to rein in his thoughts and return to the subject. "Their little girl, Sophie, ran ahead to pick some wildflowers, and then screamed. Her parents came running, and that's when they found him." The three of them topped a low crest, and Couture surveyed the area from beneath one hand, then pointed. "Right over there."

R.C. followed him across the small valley, scanning the area for signs of trouble or ambush. Old habits died hard. He'd been in the Army a long time, mostly Military Intelligence but you still had to serve a stint of active duty and he'd never forgotten those skills, or lost those reflexes. Which was a good thing—he was fairly sure he would have died on the job several times otherwise.

But the area seemed clear, aside from a lone falcon and a few small deer, plus the ubiquitous birds. The spot in question was right at the edge of a small clearing, the first trees of the renewed forest springing up just beyond, and R.C. crouched down to study the area better.

Much of the ground had been trampled here, unfortunately. Probably one of the local officers and whoever had collected the body, plus anyone out to help and whoever took the Singing Dove family home, and then anyone who'd heard about the incident and wanted to see for themselves.

Christ.

"Yo, check this out." Nick hadn't stopped with them, and now she was calling from just inside the treeline, some fifty feet beyond. R.C. joined her, and found her kneeling in the loose underbrush.

"What've you got?" he asked.

"This." She indicated a spot just to her side. "I figured the space right around the body would get too much foot traffic but if we were lucky the killer might have struck from back in the trees, where nobody thought to look and thus destroy the evidence." Her smug expression finally gave way to a grin. "Guess I was right."

R.C. studied the spot she'd gestured down at, and stiffened when he realized he was looking at a shape depressed into the leaves and moss and pine needles that coated the forest floor.

A shape that looked an awful lot like a footprint.

Fishing out his phone, R.C. snapped a photo of the print. Then he ran the image through a special FBI app, one that stripped out everything but the outline and a few pertinent physical characteristics.

A few second later his "Message Waiting" icon blinked on. He checked the phone's logs and found the image there, waiting.

But when he'd called it up, all he could do was stare.

"That can't be right," he muttered. He glanced down at the actual print, then back at the display, which did appear to match.

But it didn't make any sense.

"What's up? Let me see!" Nick demanded, practically ripping the phone from his hand.

"Here." R.C. showed her the image. After a second she shook her head as well.

"What the hell did that?" she wondered aloud. R.C. didn't answer. He was still trying to process what he'd seen. Even if it didn't make sense.

Just like a certain incident many years ago.

But he tried very hard not think of that anymore.

Especially at times like this.

The print was a footprint, all right. The program had rendered it out, clear as day. It was a left foot, and bare, with long, thin toes spread wide—

—and a total width of no more than two inches, but a total length of close to eighteen. Which made it half again as long as one of his own feet—and only half as wide. No way a man had a foot like that. A monkey, maybe, or some kind of lizard, though whatever had cast that print had five toes and a heel, and the general shape was a lot more like a man's than it was any sort of animal R.C. had ever seen.

Printed in Dunstable, United Kingdom

66468394R10198